Kyu, The Unknown
Book 1

~*~

The Coming of Dis

By

Paul Magnan

WA MM Writers AMuse Me Publishing

To Alex —
I hope you enjoy the book!
Paul Magnan

The Coming of Dis
by Paul Magnan

The Coming of Dis is a work of fiction. Names, characters, places, and incidents are either the product of the author's imagination or are used fictitiously. Any resemblance to actual persons, living or dead, business establishments, events or locales is entirely coincidental.

Published by Writers AMuse Me Publishing, August 2016

ISBN: 978-1-927975-57-2
ISBN-10: 1927975573

Acknowledgements

Kyu has traveled a long road and gone through a lot of changes. Many people have known him throughout the years, too many to mention here. Still, there are people who have helped in his development that need to be thanked.

First, I need to thank my wife, Donna, for her patience and perseverance in putting up with a sometimes cranky husband (usually during the times said husband was revising). The same is true for my two sons, Nicholas and Jeremy. A husband and father couldn't ask for a better family. I love you.

A big thank you also goes out to my parents, who have always supported my dreams. My gratitude also goes to my sister and her family, and to the wonderful Gousie clan, who cheer me on while making sure I don't spend too much time at my keyboard. Beer and laughter are the usual ways they lure me away. I have great relatives.

Lee Pearce was the first person to read my rough manuscript, and he pointed out many glaring mistakes. My friend, you are a trouper for volunteering to read over 100,000 words of unfinished draft! My second reader was the fantastic Emma Lindhagen, who showed me many unraveled knots to tighten, character- and story-wise. And my hat is off to my Tuesday writing group (Laura, Jan, Stephen, Carole, Randy, Christa, Mary, Mike, and David), who never hesitate to show me the errors of my writerly ways. Thank you, one and all!

Finally, I give a most grateful bow to Mary, Paula, DeeJay, and everyone else at Writers AMuse Me for their editorial and publishing powers in taking Kyu, making him look presentable, and giving him a chance to shine, and Greg for the great cover art. They have supported and guided me throughout the entire publishing process, and I couldn't ask for a better group of people to bring my debut novel into the world.

Dear reader, I hope you enjoy *Kyu, The Unknown*!

Dedication

This book is dedicated to my wife, Donna, and my sons, Nicholas and Jeremy. My family is my support system. I love you all so much.

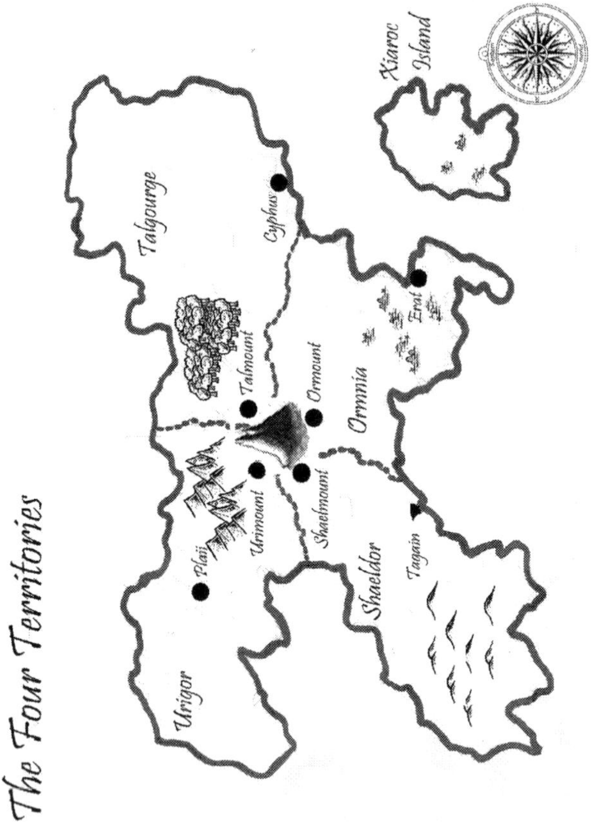
The Four Territories
Talgourge
Cyphus
Xiaroc Island
Talmount
Ormount
Erat
Ormnia
Urimount
Shaelmount
Plaij
Urigor
Tagain
Shaeldor

CHAPTER 1

Kyu had always known the shadow that hid his face; as far as he could tell, it had been conceived along with the rest of him.

The face was there, even though the mirror could not show it. Kyu ran his hand over his eyes, nose, and mouth, careful not to slice the skin open with his claws. The shadow did not extend beyond his face. The rest of his head was visible. Lanky black strands of hair fell to his muscled shoulders. He could see his ears underneath the hair, and his neck was visible. His body, hard and slim, flexed with ease beneath the gray cotton shirt and black shorts. His legs were balanced and moved with grace.

His face, though, from chin to forehead, was cast in shadow.

Kyu flexed his clawed hands and felt the power beneath the thick skin. The claws could shear through flesh, and had.

He looked away from the mirror, tamping down the urge to send a hard fist through it. The inner maelstrom had to be coiled and restrained. It would be released in due time.

The door opened, breaking Kyu's self-reflection. The man who walked in was huge, six feet five inches in height with a solid three hundred and fifty pound body. Kyu marveled that gravity had yet to win its battle with this man, who was dressed in a vulgar bright yellow suit, crafted to order by a high-end tailor in the upmarket section of Cyphus.

The man ran a hand across his bald head. Each chubby finger shone with diamonds and gold. "Syrra's balls, Kyu, this is a dressing room, yet here you are; undressed, with your match coming up soon."

"My match isn't for another half hour, Yuv. It takes about five minutes to put my stupid outfit on."

"Stupid outfit?" M.C. Yuv picked up a black leather cuirass; the torso-protecting armor had been boiled to give it a hard veneer without taking away from its flexibility. A number of slashes crisscrossed the material. What was left of a gaudy design in red thread hung in tatters. "How many times has this 'stupid' outfit saved you?"

Never, Kyu thought, but he said nothing and turned away.

Yuv chuckled and put the cuirass down. "Lucky for you that you're as good as you are. Lucky for me, too, I admit. We have a wonderful thing going here. You're the best fighter in the business, but don't go thinking you're immortal."

A muted roar rumbled through the room.

"That match ended quickly." Yuv's head turned toward the arena. "Get dressed, Kyu. You may be going out there earlier than scheduled."

"It'll take the crew some time to clean everything up."

The dressing room door opened. "Kyu, The Unknown in ten," a voice said, and the door closed.

Yuv arched an eyebrow. "You were saying?"

Kyu shook his head. He slipped on his greaves and vambraces, made of the same hard leather as the cuirass, which he pulled over his head. Yuv helped him buckle it tight at his side. Finally, Kyu put on a plain leather helmet and buckled it under his chin.

"When are you going to get a new helmet? That one looks so… blah."

"It meets the requirements of the Arena Commission." Kyu double-checked each strap and buckle. "It's good enough."

"You're famous throughout the Territories, Kyu.You need to push your brand. Corporations fall all over themselves to sponsor you. You make a ton of money."

"And so do you."

Yuv spread his arms in a *well, of course* gesture.

"I don't want to use my 'brand', as you call it, to advertise someone else's product," Kyu said.

Yuv frowned and looked at his watch. "We'll talk about this later. We have to get to your match."

"What if I'm not around to talk to later? You seem to take an awful lot for granted."

Yuv gave him an incredulous look. "Don't say shit like that."

Kyu chuckled and pulled his sword from its scabbard. The tempered steel shone in the overhead lights. The grip, wrapped with wire to prevent slippage, protruded from a pewter-colored guard and ended in a round bronze pommel.

With the sword came a calmness that settled over Kyu, along with a heightened awareness of everything around him. His senses attained a clarity that picked up individual dust motes drifting through the air and the sound of oxygen being heaved into Yuv's laboring lungs. Beneath that, a thick, dark pool of fury waited.

He looked to Yuv. "Let's go."

Yuv led the way through corridors strewn with cables and technical gear for the televised broadcast. Arena workers greeted Kyu with shouts: "You've got this one, Kyu!" "Kick his ass, Kyu!" "I got twenty marks on you, Kyu!"

They came to a pair of thick double doors. Behind them, Kyu heard the low growl of thousands of people. The muffled voice of the match announcer introduced his opponent for the night. Kyu heard scattered applause and quite a few boos.

Yuv pulled out a massive cigar and lit it. Pungent blue smoke drifted Kyu's way.

"Must you, Yuv?"

"It's my trademark. The public expects it of me."

Kyu coughed. "Those fucking things will kill me faster than anyone I face out there."

Yuv smiled and turned to the doors.

The announcer's voice rose in pitch. The reverberation increased as the crowd's excitement grew.

With a hiss of pneumatics, the doors swung open. The mob's roar buffeted Kyu and Yuv. Bright lights and television cameras swung toward them, and they entered the maw of Cyphus Arena.

The announcer had to scream to be heard. "And here he is: Kyu, The Unknown!"

The sudden acclaim was deafening. Yuv led the way down the inclined ramp. His teeth held his burning cigar as he waved his bejeweled hand to the cheering crowd. Arms reached out from between the steel rails, trying for a quick touch. The smell of fried food and beer was thick. Higher up were the luxury suites, where those who were willing to pay five thousand marks or more were treated to an unimpeded view of the arena, gourmet food, top-notch liquor, and, upon request and an additional one thousand mark charge, a professional 'escort', either female or male, with whom to cap off the evening.

Twenty feet above the arena floor, an enclosed control booth hung from the ceiling. A man, the arena's master controller, gave his monitors and control board a quick check before the match. Beneath the control booth long, mantis-like metal rods were folded up against a revolving base. Some of the tubes were capped with blades. Others were capped with more interesting items. The master controller tested the base and jointed rods for ease of movement, and he made sure what was waiting under the arena floor would have no deployment issues. Once he was done, he informed the arena director, in a back room with broadcasting technicians, that everything was a go.

Kyu ignored all of this. He held his sword loosely at his side as he approached the door to the arena proper, held open by an employee. The door was acrylic glass, an inch thick, part of the ten-foot wall that surrounded the oval arena, for protection of fans and fighters both. The floor was ribbed so the combatants could retain traction without slipping, white to show the blood to good effect, and plastic for ease of cleaning after each match. Grated grooves ran excessive blood spillage to hidden drains.

Kyu's opponent for the night stood in the middle of the arena. He was Talgourgese, like Kyu, with the almond-shaped eyes and honey-tinged skin common to those of the Territory. He looked thin, but Kyu saw the wiry muscles coiled in his arms and legs. His leather armor was a bright yellow. Like Kyu, he had no shield; very few fighters used them anymore. He wore leather gauntlets on his hands, with metal-spiked knuckles. He held a sword, with a blade fractionally longer and thinner than Kyu's own.

"See you after the match," Yuv said.

Kyu briefly wondered what his opponent's name was. Then he entered through the open door, which was closed and locked behind him. The roar of the crowd increased. Kyu pushed all distraction aside as he opened his mind and allowed his consciousness to expand and flood through his body. Time slowed down. Kyu looked into his opponent's brown eyes; he saw the discomfort there as the man searched for his face. Would fear cripple this opponent, as it had others?

The man's eyes cleared and focused. He spaced his feet apart for balance. This wouldn't be an easy kill. The crowd would get their money's worth.

Giant screens, hung from the ceiling, allowed those in the upper-level seats a close view of the match. Right now they flashed numbers, counting down from ten.

5…4…3…2…1!

A klaxon sounded. The match was on.

Immediately a long, curved blade, attached to one of the jointed rods, swooped down and sliced through the air between Kyu and his opponent moments before they closed in. Kyu had expected it. His opponent appeared momentarily startled, but recovered quickly then advanced.

The fighter danced on the balls of his feet, jabbing quickly with his sword to test Kyu's defenses. Kyu ignored these attempts to provoke him into action and circled along with his opponent.

The man feinted with a backhanded slash and threw a punch at Kyu's face. Kyu turned his head just before the metal spikes tore open his cheek. He tried to grab the man's wrist but the fighter danced out of reach.

The crowd screamed for blood. The black pool of fury within Kyu rose, but he forced himself to remain patient.

The fighter, now with more confidence, closed in again. His sword swung up and came down in a flashing arc. Kyu caught the blade on his cross guard and lashed out with the claws on his left hand, tearing open three long, red gouges in the soft skin of the fighter's sword arm.

Blood splattered on the white floor. The crowd roared. The fighter hissed and backed away, holding his arm to his side.

Kyu pressed his advantage. The fighter stood ready, his face contorted. Kyu raised his sword. As the man prepared to defend the strike. Kyu kicked him in the torso. The fighter hit the acrylic glass with his back, splashing it with blood. Faces on the other side screamed with delight.

Kyu moved in, poised to strike the final blow. A deep vibration rattled his feet. He jumped back. A spinning circular saw cut through where, seconds ago, he had been standing. Rising up to five feet, the saw whined with seeming frustration at having missed its target then settled back beneath the floor.

A flicker of motion caught Kyu's eye. He raised his sword in time to block a blow from his opponent, but the motion caused Kyu to lose his balance. He staggered back, trying to regain solid footing. The fighter advanced and rained down blows on Kyu, preventing him from finding his center of gravity. It was all he could do to keep from falling over.

Something fast and metallic flashed through the arena lights above them. Kyu fell on his back and hoped he wasn't on another slot. The fighter above him adjusted his sword grip for a downward thrust.

A gleaming war hammer, its head blunt on one end and spiked on the other, whistled through the air. The fighter leaned back as the bludgeoning end swished by where his upper torso had been. The hammer lifted up back to the control base.

The fighter smiled and moved in for the kill. Kyu made no attempt to get away. Taking careful aim at Kyu's exposed throat, the fighter plunged down with his sword. He did not notice as the hammer, on a pendulum rod, made its return trip, this time with the spiked end out front.

The metal spike punched through the fighter's upper arm, tearing through flesh and propelling him across the arena floor. His sword went skittering over the white plastic. He howled as blood pumped from the ragged hole. The crowd roared; those in the front rows banged their fists against the acrylic glass.

Kyu got to his feet then advanced on his fallen opponent. The fighter's dark red blood stood out against his yellow armor. He held his hand over the hole in his arm, but the blood gushed between his fingers and collected in the channels that led to the drains.

The fighter looked in desperation for his sword. Kyu kicked it out of reach. He looked at Kyu with eyes alight with hatred and resignation.

"Fucking do it," he hissed at Kyu. "Make it quick."

Kyu saluted the fighter to show his respect. The crowd applauded in appreciation. Kyu tapped into his fury, absorbing just enough to do what was needed, and raised his sword for the killing stroke.

He hesitated, just for an instant.

The blade came down and severed the fighter's head from his body. Blood spurted across the white floor until the heart stopped beating.

Fifteen thousand voices chanted one word: *Kyu! Kyu! Kyu!*

The acclaim rang hollow in his ears.

#

Kyu stepped out of the shower and dried himself. He made sure the underneath of his claws were free of blood, then he stepped back into the dressing room and got himself dressed.

The sword, which Kyu had cleaned before he had taken the shower, hung within its scabbard on a wall peg. Arena weapons maintenance would inspect it afterward, checking for nicks to be buffed out and making sure there were no hidden faults within the steel.

He was buttoning up his shirt when Yuv entered. His manager was flush with triumph.

"Great match, Kyu! I knew that slacker didn't have a chance."

Kyu ignored the praise. Yuv was always free with praise when his wallet got fatter.

"It was a good purse tonight, Kyu. You got two hundred and fifty thousand marks; not bad for less than five minutes work."

"And how much of that went into your bank account?" Kyu asked as he finished with the last button.

"My usual twenty percent, just like our contract says."

Right, Kyu thought, twenty percent from the official purse… plus whatever Yuv was able to skim from television rights and sponsors – money Kyu never saw.

Yuv made no move to leave. Kyu was instantly on his guard.

"What is it, Yuv?"

Yuv smiled. "Can't you count, Kyu?"

"Get to the point." Kyu was in no mood to play games. All he wanted was some beer, and maybe a groupie for dessert.

"Tonight was your one hundredth win in the arena. You are now alone in second place in total wins, second only to your buddy Eulos Baak. If we knew your age, we could claim you are the youngest to reach this mark."

"So bake me a cake. Is that all?"

"Kyu, Kyu, Kyu." Yuv shook his head in mock frustration. "No one handles themselves better inside the arena than you, but outside? Well, you're pretty fucking clueless. You make no effort to promote yourself, but that's fine, because this is where I earn my twenty percent. This is why you signed on with me."

Kyu groaned. He knew the beer and groupie were going to have to wait. "What do I have to do?"

"We're going to the press room, where Naid Iodyne will interview you for TNC."

"An interview? Syrra's balls, Yuv, what am I going to say? 'He tried to kill me, I killed him instead, the end'? Why don't you give it? You enjoy that sort of thing, anyway."

"Don't worry. I'll be there." Yuv patted Kyu's shoulder with a sweaty hand. "I'll handle the tough questions, but it's you they want. Are you done dressing? Comb your hair and let's go."

#

"Good evening, everybody! This is Naid Iodyne from the Territories News Center, here in Cyphus Arena. With me are Kyu, The Unknown and his manager, M.C. Yuv. Tonight saw the one hundredth win in Kyu, The Unknown's phenomenal career. How do you feel about this impressive milestone, Kyu?"

Kyu sat in an uncomfortable chair as a bright camera light burned into his gritty eyes. Naid Iodyne was an Ormnian, with long black hair, olive skin, and wide, dark eyes. She had a beauty that was both natural and carefully prepared for television work, yet as professional as she was, Kyu noted unease in her eyes as she tried, and failed, to discern features behind the darkness that covered his face.

Yuv, standing behind him, gave him a none-too-subtle nudge to answer the question.

"Ah, okay, I guess." Kyu immediately felt like an idiot. For the thousandth time, he silently cursed Yuv for arranging this interview.

Naid Iodyne smiled mechanically and continued. "How would you describe your fight tonight?"

"Ah, my opponent," Kyu turned to Yuv. "What was his name?"

Yuv quickly broke into the interview. "This has been a strenuous night for my man. He means no disrespect to the family and friends of Tonti Jeran. Tonti was a worthy adversary for Kyu, The Unknown. Everyone who knew him should be proud."

Worthy adversary? Kyu thought. *Ten minutes ago you were calling him a slacker.*

"I'm sure no disrespect was intended," Naid replied smoothly. "So, Kyu, how does it feel to be one of only two people in all of arena fighting history to amass one hundred wins?"

"It feels okay," Kyu said. "I wasn't really counting, though."

Yuv broke in again. "What he means is that he's honored to be placed in the same category as the legendary Eulos Baak, and as Baak trained my man, and is his friend, is it any surprise Kyu has risen to this pinnacle so quickly? I have no doubt that Kyu, The Unknown will not only tie Baak's record of one hundred and twenty-six wins, but surpass it."

Naid directed her next question to Yuv. "There aren't many fighters who come close to Kyu, The Unknown's win record. Any ideas as to who his next opponent might be?"

Kyu sat back and remained quiet. The interview had swung from him to Yuv. They all did.

"Well, Naid," Yuv said, warming up. "A few names do come to mind. Havla Cort has over fifty wins, as does Pier Shoolo. Of course, it would be up to the Arena Commission to get everything together moneywise..."

Kyu tuned out the rest of the interview. He had heard it all before. He wondered if there was still time to squeeze in some beers and a groupie after Yuv finally let him go.

CHAPTER 2

The Bloodbath Pub was aptly named. Less than a mile from Cyphus Arena, it was patronized by arena fighters and their legions of groupies, along with wannabes, hangers-on, and students from the Talgourge Combat Academy a few miles away.

As usual, business was heavy. Music blared but was often drowned out by shouts and laughter. The air was humid with the heat from so many bodies. Alcohol-laced sweat dripped and evaporated, collecting as steam above the mob. Ceiling fans spun lazily, with an apparent lack of purpose.

In the midst of this congestion and clamor was an island of calm, two seats at the bar that pub patrons swirled around but dared not intrude upon.

Kyu finished his beer and laid the empty mug on the bar. He turned to the man sitting next to him, shorter than Kyu by four inches, but outweighing him with sheer muscle. Despite his bulk, the man could move with lethal swiftness. His head was shorn of hair, and a vivid, purplish scar ran the length of his scalp, put there by a battle axe years before. His gray eyes were heavy with middle years, and reddened due to continuous nights of heavy drinking.

The man let out a thunderous belch and refilled Kyu's mug with the new pitcher of beer that was set before them by the bartender. He swallowed what was left in his own and refilled that as well then smiled and clasped Kyu's shoulder.

"Syrra's balls, Kyu, one hundred wins! I'm so fucking proud of you."

Though he knew his friend couldn't see it, Kyu smiled back. Eulos Baak was the only person Kyu had ever met who was not uneasy with the darkness that hid his face.

"This fight had me concerned for a second," Kyu said. "I've never been knocked on my back before."

Eulos laughed. "You mean you actually broke a sweat this time? Don't tell me you're slowing down. You still have my record to reach and break."

"Does that mean that after I get my one hundred and twenty-seventh win I can retire, drink beer all day, and have a holiday declared every time I fart, like you?"

"Go ahead, be a smartass. You've earned it tonight." Eulos turned serious. "You'll break my record; I have no doubt of that, but you won't retire. You're the only true natural arena fighting has ever seen. No one will stop you, Kyu."

Kyu took another pull from his mug and tried to put in order the conflicting emotions he felt. "I don't know, Eulos. I never had any doubts before, but lately… look, when I first walk out and hear the thousands of fans cheering for me, it's great. When I face my opponent and hear that door close behind me, and I know that only one of us, or maybe neither of us, is going to walk out of there… I don't have to tell you what that feels like. You already know." Kyu hesitated, not sure how to continue.

Eulos kept silent, patiently waiting for Kyu to sort out his thoughts.

"During the fight itself, I'm fine; I know exactly what needs to be done, but at the end, just before the final strike with my sword, I feel… not doubt, but a twinge, somewhere deep within me. That doesn't stop me, of course, but once it's over, it's almost like I feel a bit of my opponent's death within myself. I don't know what the fuck's going on, Eulos. I'm afraid it's going to compromise me during a crucial moment in a future match."

Eulos chuckled. "I'd say you are feeling empathy or a crisis of conscience, but you've never exhibited signs of those dread diseases before. Maybe some Syssera witch is fucking with your mind."

"I'm serious, Eulos. I'm… concerned."

"Ah, you'll get over it, Kyu. If a fighter starts to develop a conscience, his career, and most likely his life, is over, but you're not like other fighters. You'll break my record and keep going. This is what you are."

Kyu looked at his friend. He loved Eulos like an older brother, but he regretted mentioning his concerns to him. Kyu was not surprised Eulos steamrolled over them. Self-doubt was not known in Eulos' universe.

Eulos refilled his mug. "Besides, you don't have anyone in your life to mess things up for you. Keep it that way. In this business, loved ones are a liability."

Kyu did not have to ask to whom Eulos was referring. He was all too familiar with the story, but when Eulos got drunk, he liked to repeat it. Kyu, as his friend, always listened.

"I can't count the number of groupies I've slept with," Eulos said. "But Erenia was always my favorite. We became a couple. She left the groupie world behind, and I stayed true to her as well. Sometimes I wonder what she saw in me, but I don't think we will ever understand how these things work. After a while, we got married."

Eulos sighed. "I continued to fight. It was what I did. I enjoyed it, and it made me a lot of money, more than enough to support us, but I could see the toll it took on Erenia. She never knew if I was going to survive each match I had, and she had a point. I was getting older. I was slowing down."

Eulos paused. Kyu did not break the silence.

"If only she had been able to get pregnant," Eulos continued. "That was the crux of the matter. Erenia couldn't get pregnant, no matter how hard we tried. We sought medical help. Tests were run. Neither of us was infertile, yet even with fertility drugs, Erenia couldn't conceive. She was devastated."

Eulos' features darkened with anger. "That's what drove her to that fucking Sysseran temple. She went there each night to light a candle, hoping the goddess of fertility would take pity on her. Then the fucking priestess told her that she couldn't get pregnant because she was married to an arena fighter, who was in the domain of Syrra. What utter bullshit, but Erenia believed every fucking word! The priestess got her to join the temple as an acolyte, and now Erenia is actually helping her run for a council seat in the coming elections. Can you believe that shit?"

The anger collapsed into sadness. "The day Erenia became an acolyte, she came home and gave me an ultimatum: I either give up arena fighting or she would file for divorce. I wanted to go to the temple and strangle that fucking priestess but, of course, killing is only legal inside the arena. So I retired. So few of us ever retire, but I did it… because I loved Erenia." Eulos stopped to take a bracing swig from his mug. "I still love her, even though I don't think she loves me anymore, even though she and all her new friends are looking to tear down everything that gives my life meaning, and now… we don't even share the same bed anymore."

Kyu knew the rest. Eulos, unable to stay away from arena fighting completely, accepted a post as a trainer for up-and-coming fighters, including, a few years ago, Kyu, The Unknown. Eulos had never been intimidated by Kyu's hidden face or his clawed hands. He never asked Kyu why he was that way, a question to which Kyu had no answer. He treated Kyu as he treated all the other students at the Combat Academy. Once Kyu left the Academy and began his career, he stayed in touch with his former trainer and the two became friends.

Kyu had met Erenia once. She had hated him on sight. She hated that he was a friend of her husband. She hated that the two of them frequented the Bloodbath Pub on a regular basis. Kyu wanted to like Erenia, but she wouldn't allow it to happen.

As usual, Eulos seemed to read Kyu's thoughts. "Yes, she hates you. I wish it could be otherwise. I wish she would return to being the woman I first fell in love with, but I don't see that happening."

Kyu laid a clawed hand on his friend's muscular shoulder. "That's what's so good about you, Eulos. You never give up on those you care about, even if one of them hates the other. You support us both. It's a rare man who can do that."

Eulos smiled. "Thanks, buddy. I appreciate that."

A hulking fighter with a tremendous blonde beard stumbled drunkenly into Eulos' back. "Look where the fuck you're going, old man," he said with a thick, guttural Urigish accent.

The Bloodbath Pub grew very quiet.

The drunken Urigish fighter didn't notice. He gave Eulos' back a shove. "I said, old man…"

The heavy glass mug, half-full with beer, moved with sudden, unleashed fury as Eulos spun on his stool and bashed it against the Urigish fighter's face. The blonde man's nose flattened into pulp and his two front teeth snapped off and flew down his throat. The mug remained unbroken.

The drunk staggered back and clutched his face. He screamed and blood spurted from between his fingers. His hip hit a table and he fell to the floor.

Eulos' eyes glittered with rage. Kyu knew he wasn't done with the Urigish man yet.

Eulos got off the stool and advanced on the bearded man. He held the blood-smeared mug that still, incredibly, contained beer. The drunk saw him coming and tried to crawl away. Eulos stomped down on his hand with a heavy-booted foot, breaking several bones. The Urigish screamed as Eulos grabbed him by the back of his shirt collar and, with amazing strength, lifted the large man to his feet. The Urigish, like most of his race, was tall. He stood at least a foot taller than Eulos, but he looked down at the shorter man with fear-stricken eyes.

Eulos brought the mug down on a heavy wooden table. The glass shattered, leaving only a jagged shard in Eulos' fist. He pushed the man against a wall and held the shard beneath his left eye.

"You want to fuck with me, tough guy? You think I'm just an old man? I'll show you what fucking tough is." Eulos jammed the glass shard into the fighter's eye. The man shrieked and struggled as Eulos twisted it in. The gooey remains of the ruined eye dripped down the man's face and mixed in with his beard.

Eulos released him and the man collapsed to the floor. Eulos kicked the man in the jaw, shattering it and mercifully driving him into unconsciousness.

The bartender broke the silence. "Eulos, you know that no one here is going to turn you in, but you have to get out of here now, before the police show up."

Eulos, his temper still up, looked hard at the bartender. "Who the fuck are you to…?"

"He's right, Eulos," Kyu said, intercepting his friend. "We've got to get out of here."

The bartender gave Kyu a gratified look of relief.

With Kyu by his side, Eulos calmed down. "Ah, Kyu, what the fuck." He shook his head. "Why are there so many assholes in this world? Why can't they just let an old man have a quiet drink?"

Although Eulos couldn't see it, Kyu smiled. "You're not so old, Eulos. You'll never get old. Now, let's get out of here before the cops come and really fuck up our night."

They left, leaving the pub's namesake in their wake.

#

Chief Detective Norn Sanna had one thought: *Here we go again – The Bloodbath Pub…* a broken body needing immediate medical attention, again; everybody claiming it was a 'stranger' who did it, again. Even the victim would say the same, again.

Of course, there was no sign of Eulos Baak and Kyu, The Unknown, again.

The ambulance pulled away. Sanna rubbed a meaty hand across his close-cropped, graying hair then ran his fingers down his monstrous moustache. Other detectives were finishing up their questioning of the few patrons who remained in the pub.

Sanna approached the bartender. "Okay, Borrie. What happened?"

The bartender kept his face neutral. "I don't know. Some guy I've never seen before came in and fucked up that guy. I have no idea why."

"Of course," Sanna said with disgust. "Another stranger, right, Borrie?"

Borrie didn't flinch. "That's right, Detective Sanna; another stranger, from another Territory, no doubt. The guy who got worked over looked Urigish. I think the guy who did it may have been Urigish as well. There're an awful lot of strangers around here now."

"And an awful lot of trouble in here. Maybe there would be less trouble if your license was revoked."

Borrie smirked. "Good luck getting that done, Sanna. Better men than you have tried and failed."

Sanna grabbed the bartender by the front of his booze-stained shirt and slammed him against the wall.

"What the fuck are you doing, Sanna?"

Sanna clamped his hand across Borrie's mouth. "Just shut up and listen. I want you to pass a message along to your two best customers, Eulos and Kyu. Tell them this shit is going to end." Sanna removed his hand.

"I keep telling you, Sanna, they weren't here tonight. Get that through your thick skull. Now, is there anything else? I gotta clean this place up."

"Just this." Sanna drove a hard fist into Borrie's midsection. The air was forced from the bartender's lungs. He fell to the floor, gasping.

"You'll pay for that, Sanna! I'll have your fucking job for this!"

Sanna gave him an innocent look and turned to the other detectives. "Did anyone see who did this terrible thing to Borrie?"

"It was someone short and dark, probably from Shaeldor," said one detective with a grin.

"No, it was someone blonde and thin from Urigor," said another.

"No, it was definitely someone from Ormnia," chimed in a third with a laugh. "There're an awful lot of strangers around here now."

"I think it was the Empress herself!" said a uniformed officer, and they all laughed.

Sanna turned back to Borrie, who was fuming. "See, Borrie? We can play your fucking game as well. Just pass along my message, like a good little bartender."

It was a hollow and petty victory, but a victory nonetheless. Chief Detective Norn Sanna walked out of the Bloodbath Pub.

#

Eulos' house was only three miles from the pub, easy walking distance for the two men, even in their inebriated state. Streetlights shone on roadways that were mostly empty; only a few cars passed by as they walked.

Kyu chuckled as he saw a few darkened shadows approach them on one dimly lighted street, only to melt away as soon as they saw who it was they were stalking, but his thoughts soon became serious.

"I'm a bit worried, Eulos."

Eulos laughed. "You? Worried? About what?"

"The upcoming elections for the Territory Councils. It looks like the Reformers will make some big gains. They want to outlaw arena fighting."

"They don't have a chance. Arena fighting is too popular and lucrative."

"I don't know. Reformers from Ormnia have been influencing a lot of people here in Talgourge. Even Traditionalists in the West have been losing power, especially in Shaeldor. Sysseran temple leaders have become more involved in politics, more so than those of Syrra.

"Then there's the Korl. They're gaining power again. They control all the gambling that stems from arena fighting. They pretty much are the Arena Commission. They have several Councilors in their pockets. You know as well as I do what happened the last time they gained this much power."

Eulos looked at Kyu in amazement. "How long have you been following all of this? I never knew you were interested in politics."

"When it comes to my livelihood, it interests me," Kyu said. "The Elder Regent is Parmen Warsas of Talgourge, and he's definitely a Reformer. He's described arena fighting more than once as 'barbaric'. That doesn't sound like job security for either of us."

Eulos was silent a moment. "Ah, Kyu," he finally said. "Now you've gone and gotten me depressed. None of this is anything we can control. We can't waste energy worrying about it."

Kyu and Eulos walked in silence for a few more minutes.

"I guess you're right, Eulos."

"Of course I'm right." Eulos paused. "Any word as to who your next opponent will be?"

"Not yet. Yuv will contact me once he strikes a deal."

Eulos' mood darkened. "Yuv. That guy's a slimeball, Kyu. He's asshole-deep in the Korl. Why do you keep him around?"

"Because I don't know the first thing about arranging and promoting matches. He's the reason I'm famous in all the Territories. He's the reason I make the money I do."

Eulos shook his head. "I don't trust him."

Kyu kept silent. In truth, his trust of Yuv had definitive boundaries. He knew that Eulos was right about Yuv's involvement with the Korl. On a personal level, he loathed Yuv, yet on a professional level, Yuv made Kyu lucrative matches. For now, Kyu would stick with him.

After walking the next half-mile in silence, Eulos turned to Kyu. "You need your own sword."

"What are you talking about? I already have a sword."

"What you have is a mass-market sword, one any weapons smith can make. You're too good for that, Kyu. It's time you got a one-of-a-kind sword, made exclusively for you by a master smith. I know just the guy."

"What's wrong with the one I have? It's gotten me this far. Why do I need a new one?"

Eulos smiled. "Trust me on this. Meet me tomorrow morning around nine at the Combat Academy. We're doing this."

Kyu shrugged. "All right, Eulos."

They turned a corner and Eulos' house came into view. It stood apart from the others, surrounded by a tall, wrought-iron fence. All the lights were on inside.

Eulos groaned. "Aw, shit, she's still up."

Kyu couldn't resist. "You're in trooooouble."

"Shut up, Kyu. It's nothing I can't handle. I've been handling it this long. Another night won't make any difference."

Eulos punched in a code on the security box at the gate. It swung open noiselessly. A neat gravel path led up to the front door.

"I'd invite you inside for a nightcap, Kyu, but…"

"Don't worry, I understand."

The front door flew open, bathing both men in light. A slight woman in her early thirties with short dark hair streaked with blonde strands, stood in the doorway. Her deep violet eyes blazed with anger.

So much for a clean getaway, Kyu thought.

"Drunk again, Eulos?" the woman asked. "Of course you are. What a foolish question. What else would you be doing with that faceless freak?"

"That's uncalled for, Erenia. Kyu is a friend."

"*Your* friend, Eulos. He's certainly not mine."

Kyu felt guilty about abandoning his friend, but he knew there was no use in hanging around. He turned back to the street. "See you tomorrow, Eulos."

"That's right, Kyu. Go," Erenia called out behind him. "Do us all a favor and keep going until you reach the Disian Curtain."

"That's enough, Erenia," Eulos growled.

Kyu kept walking. There was no need to listen to anymore.

Thank Syrra I'm not married.

CHAPTER 3

Two hours later, Kyu arrived at his home outside of Cyphus. It was still an hour or so before dawn; overhead the stars hurried for the western horizon before the sun rose and obliterated them.

Kyu's home was unlike any other. It was, in fact, a series of natural caves set within a large, rock-strewn hill, previously owned by a wine merchant who had stored his wares there. But the merchant had died, and Kyu had bought the property two years before for a cheap price because the merchant's children had no interest in continuing the business. He had seen potential in it that no one else had. He had then transformed the cold, dark caves into a marvel.

A heavy wooden door, weather-darkened, was recessed in the eastern side of the hill. Above it was a security camera. Next to the door was a keypad, where Kyu entered his access code. Locks inside audibly disengaged and the door cracked open.

Kyu entered and the door closed behind him, the locks snapping shut. He flicked a switch and an overhead light illuminated a hallway that led to the main living quarters. The natural hall had been lined with polished wood, and the floor was covered with blue carpeting. A small room had been excavated on one side and fashioned into a closet that held Kyu's jackets and winter gear.

Kyu breathed in air that was clean and dry. An air recirculation system, using a series of hidden vents and fans, kept the air fresh and moisture-free. The entire electrical system and all of the plumbing had been updated. A furnace in a lower room, connected to a gas pipeline, provided heat during the colder months. The heat of summer was kept at bay by the natural coolness of the hill interior.

At the end of the hall was an arched entryway. Kyu flicked another switch. The cavern had been transformed into a comfortable sitting room, with carpeting, a large, plump couch, and a reclining chair. A wide-screen television was mounted on the wall. Overhead lights cast a soft lambency over everything.

Short hallways branched from this room to others: a kitchen/dining room, with a gas stove and refrigerator, a well-lit, tiled bathroom and shower, a den lined with bookshelves and a monitor connected to hidden security cameras positioned at various points throughout the hill, an exercise room with free-lift weights, elliptical equipment, and an open space where Kyu did weapon drills. The bedroom was near the back. The walls had been evened out and painted with warm colors that reflected light. None of these rooms had doors; Kyu lived alone and, except for Eulos, never had any visitors.

There was only one door at the back of the bedroom. At first glance, it appeared to be an ordinary closet door, but it was reinforced with hidden steel bands and always locked. Kyu opened it with the only key and turned on the light.

Weapons lined the walls. One side of the room was devoted to arena weapons: swords, maces, flails, axes, morning stars, spears, daggers, hammers… all the edged and blunt weapons that were legal for arena fighting. The other side of the room held firearms. Various pistols, revolvers, semi- and fully-automatic rifles, and shotguns hung from wall mounts. Shelves were crammed with ammunition.

One spot on the arena weapons wall was blank. Kyu had left the sword he had used for this night's match back in the arena dressing room to be serviced. He would retrieve it later. Then he remembered Eulos' promise to take him to a master smith to get a new sword. Kyu shook his head and smiled. Fucking Eulos.

A door at the far side of the room led to an emergency exit. Kyu had two other bolt-holes in his home, hidden in his bathroom and den.

Everything seemed to be in order. Kyu shut off the light and relocked the door.

Tired but still too wound up to sleep, he grabbed a beer from the fridge and sat on the recliner. He pointed the remote at the television and turned it on. Maybe an arena fight was being broadcast from one of the Western Territories, who were several hours behind Cyphus time.

A red light on top of the television blinked on and an alarm buzzed. Kyu had lights like this in every room. When they lit up, it meant that the cameras had picked up movement outside.

Kyu was up instantly and strode to the den. He turned on the monitor. The cameras were on night-vision mode; greenish light glowed from the monitor from the various camera feeds.

Kyu searched for an intruder and found none. Then he saw movement where he kept his garbage cans.

The cameras were programmed to ignore small animals, such as raccoons. The animal Kyu saw now was the size and general shape of a large dog, but this was no dog Kyu had ever seen before. It had a sleek, muscular body, and the testicle sack identified it as a male. Its mottled pink and black skin had no fur. The hairless tail was whiplash thin. It had claws that looked longer and sharper than those of any other canine.

The feature that stood out was the creature's head. Powerful jaws, filled with teeth designed to tear into flesh, jutted from a large, square-shaped head. At the back of the skull, a round, skin-covered knob jutted out. Two small holes on either side of the cranium took the place of ears, and, Kyu noticed with amazement, unbroken skin filled the spaces where eyes should have been.

As Kyu watched, the animal stiffened and swung its massive head toward the camera above it. Even though it had no eyes, the creature seemed to somehow see him through the camera lens, as if it knew it was being watched. It bared its formidable teeth and growled.

Kyu pondered his options. He could ignore the animal, turn off the monitor, go to bed and hope the thing was gone in the morning. He could grab a gun, go out, and try to scare it off, or kill it if it attacked. Or he could…

Kyu turned on the outside lights before he carefully opened his front door. Once he was out, he crept as silently as he could around the rocks at the base of the hill. One clawed hand gripped an automatic pistol. The other hand held a paper-wrapped package.

This is stupid, this is stupid, this is stupid…

Yet Kyu felt a compulsion to do exactly this. The same, all-encompassing calm and sense of omniscience he always felt just before a match flowed through him. This was undoubtedly stupid, but, somehow, it was also right.

Kyu stepped out where his garbage cans were. The beast slammed into Kyu's chest and knocked him flat on his back. Its claws dug into his shoulders and its mouth opened wide, giving Kyu a close-up view of those killer teeth. The creature had to weigh close to a hundred pounds. A hot, deep growl rolled from its throat.

Kyu put the barrel of the pistol against the animal's eyeless head.

"I don't want to kill you," Kyu said slowly. "I hope you don't force me to. I have something for you, if you get off me." Kyu didn't know why he was talking to a creature that couldn't possibly understand a word he was saying. Still, he refrained from pulling the trigger and blowing the thing's brains out.

The beast sniffed Kyu with its wide nostrils. The knob on the back of its head vibrated. It got off Kyu and slowly backed away, keeping its teeth at the ready.

Kyu stood. "That's good. Now..." Kyu held out the paper-wrapped item in his other hand. "This is for you."

Kyu put the item down and backed away. He pointed his gun away from the animal in a sign of good faith.

The creature advanced slowly. It sniffed tentatively at the package and then, with considerable gusto, tore into it. Kyu watched as two pounds of expensive steak, along with the paper it was wrapped in, disappeared down the animal's throat.

"That tastes a little bit better than garbage, doesn't it?"

The animal looked up. The knob on the back of its head vibrated again. Kyu relaxed and he allowed his consciousness to expand as it did during a match. It flowed out and examined the creature.

There was intelligence there, much more than in any other animal Kyu had encountered. The knob at the back of its head housed a complex network of nerves and receptors. It allowed the creature to 'see' with more clarity than mere eyes could.

Kyu thought of the shadow that hid his face. If anything could see beyond it, this creature could.

Kyu sensed a deep solitude within the animal, an aloneness it had endured for its entire life. Food was not the only thing it craved. An overwhelming sense of rightness clicked in Kyu's mind. "Are you housebroken?"

The creature huffed and looked away as if insulted.

"Sorry," Kyu said. "Do you have a name?"

The animal looked back to Kyu. Its knob vibrated.

Kyu opened himself mentally to the creature and invited it to answer.

The animal was incredibly intelligent, but had thought processes not like those of a human. The use of vocabulary was foreign to it. Still, one word made itself known to Kyu: *Aest* – a simple, one-syllable sound that, for the creature, encompassed survival… and loneliness.

Kyu nodded. "Hello, Aest. My name is Kyu. Would you like to come inside?"

In a flash, the creature was by him and standing at the door.

Kyu stood in wonder. He couldn't believe he had just invited an unknown, potentially dangerous animal into his home… and the animal accepted! Kyu had always preferred to live alone. He had never wanted a housemate, never mind a pet, but the connection he had made with this creature didn't feel like a master-pet relationship. It felt like a budding friendship.

Kyu opened the door and welcomed Aest inside.

CHAPTER 4

The alarm clock went off five hours later. Kyu was attacked by a hot, dripping tongue. "Okay, enough! Get off me."

Aest backed away and looked at him expectantly.

"I suppose you'll want breakfast?"

Aest barked. It was the first time Kyu had heard him do so. The bark was definitely in the affirmative.

"I'd better put aside a little more money each week for groceries."

Kyu cooked a dozen eggs and two pounds of bacon. Aest devoured most of this in the time it took Kyu to get a fork.

"I have to meet my friend Eulos today, Aest," Kyu said. "I see no reason why you can't come along. Just don't bite him, because he'll bite you back. Plus, you'll get to see me part with good money to buy a sword I don't need. Won't that be fun?"

Aest barked.

"Right back at ya, big guy. I just need to shave and shower first. I'll let you outside so you can do your business. Then we can go."

After he put Aest out, Kyu got ready to shave. He considered the darkness facing him in the bathroom mirror, the only mirror he allowed in the house. He wondered why he kept it. It wasn't as if he needed it, or wanted it.

Kyu knew he could let his beard grow without anyone noticing, at least until it grew long enough to pop out of the shadow, but he liked the feel of a clean-shaven face. There was also the issue of a beard being a hazard during an arena match. Any opponent could grab it and twist his head around.

Kyu lathered up some shaving cream and smeared it on a face he couldn't see. *Who are you?* Kyu asked the apparition in the mirror, the same question he had asked many times before. Silence and frustration were his only answers.

As Kyu dragged the razor down the sharp planes of a face he tactually if not visually knew, with a hand that ended in vicious claws, he could not help but plunge into memories he'd just as soon forget:

He was an orphan, with no idea who his biological parents were, or even if they were alive or dead. It didn't matter. They had left him with nothing, not even a name. He was given the name 'Kyu' by someone unknown, with no last name for family identification.

The shadow over his face had always been a part of his life. It hid him from everyone, including himself. From the start, Kyu was bereft of a sense of self-identity. Was his face hidden because it was hideous? The claws he had would seem to indicate that this was so.

Before he reached his teenaged years, Kyu was sent to a foster home. His foster father was a prominent defense attorney with a strong, domineering personality. His foster mother was kindhearted, but always gave way to her husband.

Kyu's low self-esteem was fueled by his foster father. He had brought Kyu, a child no one else wanted, into his home purely as a public relations move, to soften his image as a cold, hard-nosed lawyer. In the privacy of his home, he considered Kyu a pariah, a misshapen freak to be treated with dismissal and contempt. Kyu was never allowed to eat at the same table as the lawyer and his wife, and his bedroom door was always locked from the outside at night. Kyu's mother would look at him with sympathy, but never tried to intervene.

His memories took him to school. He was reclusive. The other children ridiculed him, and he was a constant target for bullies. For the first time, Kyu became aware of the churning darkness within him, a well of fury that seemed bottomless and always at a constant boil. It built in pressure, demanding release. It scared Kyu, and he kept a cap on it.

One of the worst bullies, a huge lout named Sholer, with a wild mane of dark hair, backed Kyu into a corner and punched him in the stomach. The surrounding kids laughed. The cap that Kyu kept on the black rage shattered. His claws lashed out like a striking viper and carved four ragged gashes in Sholer's face. The bully screamed and backed away as blood spattered on his shirt. The other children ran, their eyes wide with shock.

Kyu ran as well. The black fury quickly settled back, leaving a corrosive residue behind. He searched for any trace of remorse within himself but found none. He was suspended from school. His foster father cut a quick and costly check for the parents of Sholer, who would carry the scars on his face for the rest of his life.

It was suggested that Kyu's claws be cut, but a medical examination showed that, far from being keratin, like fingernails, the claws were living tissues, with blood vessels and nerves. Any attempt to cut them would result in excessive bleeding and pain.

Nobody knew what to do about Kyu. Then a school counselor who had taken an interest in his case stepped in. Despite his reclusive nature, Kyu was a very intelligent student. His knowledge and abilities were beyond his peers. The counselor recommended he be placed in a school that specialized in talented yet troubled youngsters, one that enforced strict behavioral guidelines.

At first it seemed to work. Kyu easily kept up with the advanced learning material. The other students, aware of what he had done, left him alone, which meant Kyu was still the loner the counselor had hoped he would no longer be. She tried to get him interested in sports, as his physical abilities matched his intellectual ones. She talked to him about the Cyphus Junior Roball League. Kyu's quick reflexes and keen eyes, she said, would make him a natural in this team sport, where the object was to pass a round, rubber ball until one was close enough to challenge the opposing team's goalie and get the ball into either a cone-shaped net (four points) or hit a small, round lever behind the goalie that rang a bell (seven points). Kyu wanted no part of it. The only sport that interested him was arena fighting. The counselor, who loathed arena fighting, refused to help Kyu go in this direction.

He finished school two years before his classmates. Despite pleas from the counselor, he refused to enter Cyphus University. Nothing there interested him. The counselor admitted defeat and gave up.

Kyu's foster father tried to push him into higher education. Having come to grudgingly admire his foster son's intellect, he felt that the boy could overcome the unfortunate adversities of his hidden face and claws, and make a good living for himself, maybe even in law. Kyu flatly refused. His foster father's frustration built.

Then came the day that Kyu's foster father did something uncharacteristic: Brooding over the underachieving boy, he got drunk. He came home and started a loud, violent argument with Kyu. Kyu stood his ground. The lawyer's temper snapped. He struck Kyu across the face.

Dark fury consumed Kyu, claiming his entire body and mind. He struck back quickly, powerfully, lethally. Within seconds, his foster father's throat was laid open. The lawyer fell. Blood sprayed on the walls and floor. A ragged gurgle was the only sound he could make. His eyes, wide with shock, begged Kyu to stop.

With one massive blow Kyu cracked open his foster father's skull. Brain matter oozed onto the carpet. The lawyer's eyes glazed over. Kyu looked down on this torn and shattered figure and felt – elated... no sorrow, no guilt, no remorse. He was the victor, and he always intended to be.

Kyu heard a gasp and spun around. His foster mother stared in disbelief at her husband's ravaged body. Within five seconds, she joined him in bloody death.

The rage drained from him. Kyu looked around and knew it was all over. He would be sent to the Xiaroc Isle penal colony. The police came and Kyu surrendered without a struggle. He prepared himself for exile.

Then the truth about his foster family's double life emerged. It was no secret that Kyu's foster father made most of his money defending upper-echelon clients, notably those in the Korl criminal organization. What was not known was that he was also very active in the Korl's drug trade, often acting as a 'mule' for Korl kingpin Padanor Syche. His wife was also made to help.

The dirtiest secret of all then came out. Kyu's foster father had a self-created collection of child pornography. His nice, pleasant wife would lure the children to their home. Once the pictures, and liberties, were taken, he would pay them and their families off. It was automatically assumed that Kyu had been a victim of these depredations. He had not been. He honestly had no idea something like that had been happening in the house, but he knew better than to admit that. He played the role of the victim, and everyone believed him. Murder charges were dropped.

However, due to his obviously violent nature, Kyu could not just be released. A compromise was reached. Kyu realized his dream. He was sent to the Cyphus Combat Academy.

Kyu cursed as he realized he had cut his face with the razor. He pushed his finger beyond the shadow and it came away bloody. He quickly finished and doused his face with cold water. The bleeding stopped. It served him right for dredging up the past while shaving. At least no one would notice the mark.

Kyu got dressed and strapped on a shoulder holster. He checked the magazine of the pistol, slammed it in and chambered a round. He covered it with a light jacket and went outside.

Aest waited at the side of the road that led into Cyphus. Kyu punched in the security code and locked the door behind him. He turned to Aest. "I hope you don't mind walking. I've never bothered to get a car."

Aest turned and started trotting down the road.

"Well, okay."

#

Two hours later, they rounded a corner in downtown Cyphus. The Combat Academy came into view. It was housed in a renovated factory building, with a brick exterior and neat, painted metal frames around the doors and windows.

Eulos stood outside the main entrance. He caught sight of Kyu and glared at him. “Syrra’s balls, Kyu, why don’t you get a car? Maybe then you wouldn’t always run late.”

Kyu looked around. “You could have picked me up with your car. Where is it?”

“Yeah, well, Erenia’s car is broken down, so she took mine to her fucking temple this morning. After last night, I felt it was best not to push the issue. Where we’re going is only a few blocks away, anyway, and… what the fuck is that?”

Aest had stepped out from behind Kyu.

“Eulos, this is Aest,” Kyu said. “Aest, this is Eulos.”

Eulos looked at Kyu as if he had just sprouted wings. “Kyu, what the fuck is going on here? Is that a dog?”

“I don’t think so. I’m not quite sure what he is. All I know is that he’s quick, strong, and always hungry.”

Aest approached Eulos, who stiffened and reached for a weapon.

“Easy, Eulos,” Kyu said. “I think Aest just wants to get to know you.”

Eulos kept still. Aest sniffed his hand. The knob on the back of his head vibrated. Aest barked with satisfaction and returned to Kyu.

“I guess you pass Aest’s examination, Eulos.”

Eulos let out his breath. “That’s just great. Would he have bitten my balls off if I hadn’t?”

“Possibly.”

Eulos shook his head in bemusement. “Okay, let’s get going.”

#

Within half an hour they were in one of the nastier neighborhoods in Cyphus. Boarded-up houses and failed businesses, smeared with graffiti, lined a street that was littered with broken glass and piles of ancient garbage.

"Syrra's balls, Eulos, you sure know how to find these people. I thought you said this place was only a couple blocks away?"

"The distance is much shorter by car. No matter. We're almost there."

Two men, slouched in a faded, paint-chipped doorway, stood and approached them. Guns appeared in their hands.

"Your money, assholes. Now!"

Eulos' face reddened. "Get the fuck out of here, you punks. Do you know who we are?"

"I don't give a fuck who you are," said the taller of the two, whose thin face was covered with a mossy beard. "And I don't care if you're dead or alive when we take your money."

He raised his gun and squeezed the trigger. Kyu went for his gun, knowing he was already too late.

A thing of snarling fury slammed into the tall gunman. The gun went off and the bullet flew over Eulos' head. The thief fell to the pavement. Aest's teeth sank into the man's wrist. Bones snapped like twigs. The would-be robber screamed and dropped the gun.

The second robber, frozen during this unexpected attack, found his wits and aimed his gun at Aest. Kyu shot him in the stomach. The second robber clutched his abdomen and fell.

Aest's teeth sank all the way through the wrist. He jerked his head and the thief's hand was torn away. Blood drenched the animal, who swallowed the hand whole. The robber held his stump and screamed. Aest fastened his teeth around his throat. The robber was silenced for good.

Kyu could only watch with amazement. *If I had tried to kill Aest last night, that very well may have been me.*

Eulos, meanwhile, was busy with the second robber. With a dagger, Eulos carved the skin off the screaming man's face.

"Fuck with us, asshole? You tried to take our money. I think I'll take your fucking face instead."

Once the skin had been torn from the red, raw meat, Eulos plunged his dagger in the robber's heart.

Kyu looked around. He was the only one not covered with blood. He put his gun back in the holster. “Let’s get the fuck out of here before the cops arrive.”

“Nah.” Eulos straightened. He cleaned his dagger on the dead man’s clothes and wiped away as much of the blood from himself as he could. “The cops never come down here. This sort of thing happens all the time. They don’t care, as long as it happens to lowlifes like these two. They’ll send a meat wagon down here to clean up the mess.”

Kyu turned to Aest, who was busy digging into the taller man’s entrails. *Just how much can he eat? Hopefully now I won’t have to buy him lunch.* “Aest, I gotta hand it to you. You saved our asses. Thanks. We owe you one.”

Aest, his muzzle dripping blood, turned to him and barked. Kyu could swear the creature was smiling at him… and acknowledging the debt.

“Let’s find a gas station with a rest room,” Eulos said. “I need to clean off this mess.”

#

Eulos pushed a button under a callbox. The building was a two-story structure with fading paint, much like most of the other buildings in the area. The windows had thick iron bars over the frames. There was nothing on the outside to indicate that this was a business of any kind.

“May I help you?” A tinny voice came from the callbox speaker.

Aest’s knob vibrated and he growled. Kyu looked up. Above the door a small, opaque square of glass looked down on them. Kyu knew they were being watched on a security camera. Like last night, Aest’s specialized senses detected it immediately.

“It’s Eulos, Hirn. Open up, will ya?”

There was a pause. “I’ll let the two of you in, but that… thing has to stay behind.”

Aest bared his teeth and growled louder.

"There's nothing wrong with him, Hirn," Eulos said. "In fact, he helped us out of a bad situation."

"I allow no animals in here, Eulos. That's a firm rule."

Eulos looked at Kyu and shrugged.

Kyu bent down to Aest. "Look, Aest, I don't want to leave you behind, but I suppose we have to play this his way. Please stay out here, as a favor to me. We shouldn't be too long. I'll make it up to you later with a big, juicy steak."

Aest wasn't happy, but he stayed put.

They heard a click, and the door cracked open. Kyu followed Eulos inside. They entered a small foyer. The door closed and locked behind them. A red light from above passed over them. It came back and remained on Kyu. A small bin opened up in the wall next to him.

The tinny voice returned. "Please place your handgun in the storage area provided. It will be returned to you when you leave."

Kyu looked at Eulos. "How come he isn't saying the same thing to you about your dagger?"

"Because Hirn knows me. He doesn't know you yet. Just put your gun in the bin. It'll be fine."

"Shit." Kyu hated being disarmed, but he put his gun in the bin, which closed tight.

They heard another click. A door in front of them opened. They walked into the smithy. The smell of molten metal permeated everything. It was hot, but not uncomfortably so. Fans roared in hidden ventilation shafts.

Kyu looked around. Swords, maces, axes, spears, tridents, flails, morning stars, and other weapons of the arena were on display. Everything was clean and polished. Kyu knew he was looking at top quality work. The smithy itself was clean and well-kept, with the large, gas-fired forge free of soot and dust. Grinders, hammers, tongs, and other metal-working tools were well-maintained and stored in their proper places. Nowhere was there any disorder or carelessness. This was, as Eulos had said, a professional establishment… and, undoubtedly, expensive.

"Eulos! How wonderful to see you again!"

Kyu turned toward the voice. The man before him was short, almost scrawny. His arms, however, were corded muscle. He had an open, friendly face, with thinning gray hair and thick eyeglasses that gave him the appearance of an owl.

"Hirn, you old devil, how are you?" Eulos grasped the man's hand.

"As well as can be expected." Hirn turned to Kyu. "Now, won't you introduce me to your friend here?"

Kyu felt disconcerted that Hirn Gaxtos didn't recognize him.

"Certainly. Hirn, this is Kyu, The Unknown. Kyu, this is Hirn Gaxtos, the only man capable of making the sword you deserve."

Hirn ignored the compliment. He also seemed unfazed by the shadow that covered Kyu's face. "So, Mr. Kyu, it's a sword you'll be wanting?"

"Yeah, I suppose. But please, call me Kyu, not 'Mr.' Kyu."

"Certainly," Hirn said. "I use only the best steel for my weapons, Kyu. What good is a weapon if it's made out of some base metal that breaks during combat?"

Hirn brought Kyu to a glass display case that contained some truly fabulous swords. The blades, illuminated with soft light, shone with beauty and restrained strength. Intricate patterns were engraved on the steel in flowing, circular designs. The handles were wrapped with gold wire.

"These swords are made of ten ninety-five carbon steel, which has a very high carbon content that makes the sword extremely hard and sharp. However, they are prone to brittleness and can shatter upon contact. They look nice, but they are primarily decorative swords. My high-end clients like them."

Kyu had to ask. "How much do they cost?"

"The least expensive is two thousand marks. My highest-priced one, which I recently sold to a collector in Shaeldor, went for twenty thousand marks."

"For a sword that's going to do nothing but hang on a wall?"

"Indeed. Needless to say, none of these are for arena combat. I just wanted to show them to you to demonstrate my handiwork."

Kyu shook his head. "Okay, so what kind of a sword would you make for me?"

"It depends on what you're willing to spend," Hirn Gaxtos said. "The cheapest swords I make are made of ten forty-five carbon steel, which are your basic, machine-milled swords. They're fine, but they lose their edge quickly. They can be made better with proper tempering, but they're not the best. Those can go anywhere from one hundred to five hundred marks."

"That's not too bad—"

"Oh no you don't, Kyu," Eulos interrupted. "If you're going to do that, you may as well just keep the one you have. I didn't bring you down here for a cheap sword. You're going to get one of Hirn's best."

"I agree," Hirn said. "I think a ten sixty carbon steel sword would be best. Double-edged, I assume? If I remember right, the arena regulation length is no more than twenty-six inches for most forms of single combat. In melees, of course, they can use anything, but you're not a melee fighter, are you, Kyu?"

A melee match was when groups of five to twenty fighters hacked at each other until only one was still standing. If one was still standing. Non-discerning audiences loved it, but it was, in Kyu's opinion, where talentless fighters went to literally stab other talentless fighters in the back.

"Nope. I'm strictly a singles fighter."

"I thought as much. So, a regulation-length blade, with a tang that runs into a peened pommel. I will measure your...

rather unique hand for a proper grip on the hilt. I prefer to wrap my hilts with good leather, with risers to prevent slippage. Copper-braided hilts may look nice, but it doesn't take long for them to oxidize, especially with the sweat from combat. Do you agree, Kyu?"

"Um… yeah, sure."

"Splendid!"

"So how much is all this going to cost?"

Hirn closed his eyes and did some quick calculating in his head. "As a friend of Eulos, I think I can squeeze in a discount for you. Fifteen hundred marks."

"Fifteen hundred? And that's with a discount?"

"Stop being so fucking tight-fisted, Kyu," Eulos grinned. "You can easily afford this, especially after your last payday. I guarantee you, once you see the finished product, you'll see it's worth the price and more."

Kyu acknowledged, grudgingly, that Eulos was right. "Yeah, okay, let's do it."

"Excellent!" Gaxtos stuck out his hand. Kyu admired that he was not hesitant about the claws. They shook hands.

Gaxtos went to a shelf that contained several small glass containers. He grabbed one, brought it to Kyu and gave him an expectant look.

Kyu, at a loss, looked to Eulos, who chuckled in a way Kyu did not like.

"Give me your hand, Kyu," Eulos said.

Despite his growing apprehension, Kyu held out his left hand.

Eulos pulled out the dagger he had used to slice off the thief's face and cut into Kyu's palm at the base of his thumb. Thick red blood oozed out.

"Hey! What the fuck!" Kyu tried to pull his hand back.

Eulos tightened his grip and squeezed. Blood spattered on the floor. "Keep still." Eulos took the glass container from Gaxtos and held it under the wound. Within seconds it was filled with blood.

Gaxtos took the container and screwed a lid on it. He went to a medicine cabinet and gave Eulos some antibacterial cream and bandages.

The cut was shallow and did not take long to clean and wrap. To Kyu's consternation, Eulos beamed with good humor the entire time.

"Would someone mind explaining to me what the fuck just happened?" Kyu asked once Eulos was finished.

"This is a specialty of mine," Hirn Gaxtos said. "To make this sword truly, uniquely yours, I will pour your blood into the molten steel, fusing them as one. No one will be able to claim this sword but you, and your descendants if you have any."

Kyu looked at Eulos. "Are you kidding me?"

Eulos couldn't control his laughter any longer. "I really wish I could have seen your face when I cut your hand. It must have been priceless."

"Don't be angry with your friend, Kyu," Hirn said. "Having one's blood mixed with his weapon is an ancient tradition which has, sadly, all but died out throughout the Territories over the last few centuries. I am one of only a handful of weapons smiths left who still do it."

"Did you have your blood mixed with your weapons?" Kyu asked Eulos.

"Of course. This is one of the reasons I come here for my weapons."

Now that the shock of the event was over, Kyu felt himself warming to the idea. "All right, I admit it's a pretty neat thing, but you could have warned me first."

"And ruin my fun? Come on now."

"You know what, Eulos? You really are an asshole."

"Compared to what Erenia calls me, that's a compliment."

Kyu chuckled and turned to Gaxtos. "Do you take credit cards?"

"Yes, but I'll accept no payment now. Your sword will be ready in one week. After you've inspected it and are satisfied with it, then you can pay me."

"Sounds good to me." Kyu looked out one of the barred windows to the blighted street beyond. "Just out of curiosity, why do you do business out of this crappy neighborhood?"

Hirn sighed. "I've been here for over forty years, Kyu. It wasn't always like this. This neighborhood has never been wealthy, but it was always clean and safe, until the drugs came in, and the Korl along with them. People starting selling their souls for a few minutes of being high. Nobody cared about anything anymore. And now…" Hirn waved to the window. "I could move, and probably make more money in a better neighborhood, but I don't want to. I've set roots here. Everyone knows me. This is home."

#

"I'm all right," Kyu told Aest, who sniffed dubiously at the bandaged hand.

"You won't be disappointed in this sword, Kyu," Eulos said. "Hirn is the best weapons smith in the Four Territories."

They walked back the way they had come. They passed the spot of their encounter with the muggers. The bodies were gone. Pools of congealed blood were the only testimony of the violence that had happened. As Eulos had predicted, there were no police anywhere in sight.

Kyu looked around. "I understand why Hirn said what he said."

Eulos looked at him in puzzlement. "Which was?"

"This is home. No matter how much it changes, home is home. I grew up an orphan. The concept of home to an orphan is an important one, and elusive. Once you find it, you never want to let it go, no matter how shitty things get." Kyu wondered where all this sudden empathy was coming from. It scared him.

CHAPTER 5

The temple of Syssera in Cyphus was a large building, constructed with white limestone quarried from Shaeldor, and surrounded by several acres of expertly-landscaped grounds of grass and sylvan groves of trees. The interior was cavernous, with the vaulted ceiling supported by two rows of glassine pillars of light-blue marble. Polished wooden pews, split in half by a smooth stone aisle, faced an apse that was decorated with a fresco of the brown-skinned goddess holding a sheaf of wheat in one hand and a newborn infant in the other, in predominant hues of blue and green.

The gilded altar at the center of the apse was covered with a light blue linen cloth that flowed over the top. Syssera's symbol, a wheat stalk, was embossed on the front.

Acolytes moved around. Some lit incense; others swept the floor between the pews. All wore hooded robes of dark blue.

A woman dressed in a white robe, with sleeves, hem, and collar trimmed in the same dark blue as the robes of the acolytes, emerged from a chamber behind the apse. The acolytes bowed their heads and continued working. The priestess walked to one of the acolytes and touched her shoulder. The acolyte followed the high priestess into the chamber.

Once the door closed, the formality stopped. The two women pushed the hoods back off their heads.

The priestess, a handsome woman with graying hair close-cropped to her skull, smiled. "Thank you for coming on short notice, Erenia."

Erenia smiled back. Her dark hair was short, though not as short as the priestess'. Thin lines etched the skin at the corners of her eyes and mouth. "You know it's never a problem, Enna."

The priestess dropped her smile. She gestured for Erenia to sit in a chair in front of her desk, where she settled down.

Enna folded her hands together on the desk and leaned forward. "We've been compromised."

"Compromised? How?"

"There's a certain reporter, one of those investigative ones, who works for the Territories News Network. His name is Corl Navha."

Erenia nodded. "I've heard of him."

Enna sighed. "Well, Mr. Navha discovered something I had hoped would be overlooked."

"Enna, what are you talking about?"

"My grandfather."

"Your grandfather? I don't understand."

Tears gathered in Enna's eyes. "My maternal grandfather was a member of the Korl, a high-ranking one. Sixty years ago, he was convicted on several counts of murder and sent to Xiaroc Isle."

Erenia shook her head. "But that's your grandfather, Enna, not you. You have no connection to the Korl at all."

"It doesn't matter." The tears in Enna's eyes broke free and ran down her face. "Anyone with a familial connection to the Korl is forbidden to run for public office. It means my bid for a Talgourge Council seat is over."

"No." Erenia forced back her own tears. "We've worked so hard for this! You're ahead in the polls. There's a real chance of the Reformers getting the majority in the Council if you're elected, and with your leadership skills any number of reform bills will get passed into law. All of that is lost because of a distant relative you never even knew?"

Enna remained silent.

Erenia tried a desperate tact. "Is there any way the reporter can be convinced to quash this?"

Enna laughed bitterly. "Are you kidding? The story is going out on tonight's news. I've already written my press statement withdrawing my nomination for the Council."

Despair ate through Erenia. "Is there nothing we can do?"

Enna's tears dried. She fixed Erenia with a fierce gaze. "There is only one way. You must take my place, Erenia."

The shock of Enna's words froze her. "Me? How...? I couldn't possibly run for the Council."

"You can, and you must." Enna's gray eyes held Erenia in place. "You've organized and managed my campaign. You're a sharp thinker and quick on your feet. You're more politically astute than you give yourself credit for. Most importantly of all, you have no connection to the Korl."

"But the Arena Commission is infested with Korl corruption. Won't the fact that my husband is a former arena fighter and a current trainer at the Combat Academy compromise my own situation?"

"I've already looked into that. Legally, this does not stop you from running. Even though everyone knows otherwise, there is no concrete proof that the Korl is involved with arena fighting. Plus, I've approached our biggest sponsors and contributors, and they have agreed to back you. As soon as you agree, I will add to my withdrawal speech the fact you are taking my place. Our sponsors will brand your image all over the media. There is still enough time for voters to get to know you. You can win in my place, Erenia."

Enna paused, and then added, "I know your husband can get a bit wild sometimes. It will be up to you to handle that situation. Take whatever measures are necessary."

Erenia knew that what Enna actually meant was, 'if you divorce your violence-prone husband with his arena fighting connections, you will have more support and a better chance of winning.' Erenia looked away from her friend and took a moment to tamp down a flare of anger.

Erenia's marriage to Eulos was rocky. Any number of times she had thought about leaving him. She had grown up and moved past her shameful groupie days. Unfortunately, Eulos had not.

Erenia had hoped that a child would settle Eulos down, but she never conceived. Now that he was a friend of that nightmare, Kyu, The Unknown, there was little chance he ever would.

However, each time Erenia was on the verge of leaving, she stayed. Eulos, despite all his faults, had never been anything but kind to Erenia. As violent as he was to others, he had never raised a hand to her, even during their more heated arguments. He always treated her with respect. Erenia had never wanted for anything during their marriage, which was much more than she could say for many others. Eulos was collecting a decent pension from the Arena Commission, making steady money as a trainer at the Combat Academy, and he was no longer in danger of losing his life in the arena. Unfortunately, since the appearance of Kyu, Erenia feared for Eulos whenever he went out.

If only they could have had a child. Erenia winced as she remembered her own childhood. Her parents were negligent to the point of abandonment. Erenia had turned to those she thought were friends, who introduced her to drugs, alcohol, and the lure of arena fighting. By her early teens, Erenia was an official groupie, carelessly sleeping with one arena fighter after another, taking money they offered her to buy more drugs. She was beautiful, with long, dark, blonde-streaked hair and sparkling violet eyes, but on the inside there was only hollowness, a dead, empty space. By the time she was eighteen, Erenia had undergone three abortions and had been treated several times for sexually transmitted diseases.

Then Erenia had met Eulos, who treated her with kindness and took her in. Something stirred in the dark caverns of her soul, something that brought light, and grew. With Eulos, Erenia finally knew security. With Eulos' help, she kicked her drug habit. Erenia joyfully put her groupie days behind her and married Eulos.

She hungered for what she never had. She wanted love and stability. She wanted a family. Having a child was very important to her, but after a year of trying, it didn't happen. They saw a physician who, after tests, declared them both fertile. They tried timing her cycles and, in desperation, turned to fertility drugs.

Nothing happened. Erenia's sense of security ebbed away, leaving her with dry-mouthed panic attacks. She looked at Eulos in a new, unpleasant light when he announced that he would be fine without a child.

Erenia had never been religious, but in desperation she turned to the Sysseran temple in Cyphus. She went to the temple each morning, lit a candle, and prayed to the goddess of fertility for a miracle.

The priestess at the time was an elderly woman named Pien Horrle. The priestess brought Erenia to a black brazier set on a tripod in front of the altar and told her she needed to make an offering to the goddess. Erenia had no idea what was required. The priestess smiled and produced a pair of silver scissors. She snipped a lock of Erenia's long hair and threw it upon the hot, fragrant charcoal in the brazier. The lock of hair burned away, leaving a brief, acrid stench. The priestess told Erenia to kneel as she studied the smoking residue for signs from Syssera. After a few minutes, the priestess gestured at Erenia to rise to her feet.

"The goddess has spoken to me," the priestess said. "She is displeased that you are wed to a follower of Syrra. As long as you are with him, you will remain barren."

Dismay flooded through Erenia. She turned from the priestess and, dazed with sudden, crushing hopelessness, walked down the aisle. A gentle hand fell upon her shoulder. Erenia turned to a figure dressed in the blue robes of an acolyte.

"Come outside with me," the acolyte said.

Erenia meekly followed. Once outside, the acolyte led Erenia to a bench that overlooked a small, placid pond.

"Whatever priestess Horrle told you weighs terribly upon you," the acolyte said after they sat.

Erenia looked at the acolyte. She had graying, close-cropped hair. Her eyes were gray and gentle with understanding.

A year of despair, brought to a head by the devastating words of the priestess, came out in a torrent of tears. The acolyte held Erenia as she cried.

"Do not be overly concerned about what the priestess said to you," the acolyte said. "She's getting on in years, and senses her mortality. She has become very conservative in her views. Whatever she said, the temple of Syssera is all about family and love. We support any who seek our aid."

Erenia looked up with hope behind her tears.

The acolyte smiled. "My name is Enna Racyne. What's yours?"

Erenia grasped the offer of friendship like a lifeline. Within four months of Erenia's meeting with Pien Horrle, the priestess passed away in her sleep. Enna Racyne, as senior acolyte, was sent to a seminary in Talmount for three weeks of training to become the next priestess of the Cyphus temple.

Despite Enna's reassurances, Erenia took Pien Horrle's words to heart. She put emotional distance between herself and Eulos. She became a steady communicant of the temple, and within two months had shorn off most of her hair and taken a vow to become an acolyte. Erenia's new duties, along with cleaning and lighting of incense, included helping the priestess administer to the congregation and organize activities.

Two years passed. Erenia's marriage to Eulos became increasingly remote. Eulos was a child of the violent warrior god Syrra, the antithesis of Syssera, yet she remained with him. Despite her new, fervent philosophy, she could not shake the love she felt for him. Eulos was not happy with her newfound faith, and he hated the fact that she had cut her long, beautiful hair, but he remained a loving husband who did not try to force her back to what she was before. The situation was making them both miserable, but they persevered.

When Enna had announced she was running for a Council seat as a Reformer, Erenia had been elated. She took on the role of campaign manager, organizing donations, ads, media coverage, and appearances. Enna excelled at public speaking, and her compassionate yet firm personality garnered a lot of support.

Now, due to a situation beyond her control, it was all for naught. Erenia was being asked to pick up the fallen torch, which, Enna insinuated, would be much easier to carry if Erenia left her husband.

We haven't shared a bed in months, Erenia thought. *We argue incessantly, I hate his drinking and his friends, but he is always there for me. He has never cheated on me despite the fact we no longer have sex. I still see the hope in his eyes for reconciliation. I still feel the love he has for me. Despite everything that has happened... I still love him.*

This was something that Enna would never understand. Not to mention... Erenia shook her head. That was one thought she could not deal with right now. She was about to take on a whole host of other worries. "I'll do it," Erenia told Enna. "Don't concern yourself about Eulos. I'll ensure he's not a liability."

Enna's eyes sparked with disagreement, but she bowed her head in acquiescence. "As you feel you can do, Erenia. Thank you for agreeing. May Syssera bless our cause."

"As the goddess wills," Erenia said. They closed their eyes in silent prayer.

"When do I announce my candidacy?" Erenia asked when they finished.

"I've called for a press conference tonight, to announce my withdrawal. Then we hit them with your succession of my candidacy. Can you prepare a speech in time?"

Erenia's mind swirled as she comprehended the totality of what she was doing. "If I leave now, I'll have something. We need to plan, and we don't have much time to do it. I'll be back in a few hours."

Enna smiled. "I know we'll succeed."

Erenia smiled back and left. She wished she felt half as confident as Enna.

Countless thoughts filled Erenia's head as she walked down the central aisle of the temple. She did not notice the large acolyte standing in front of her, and nearly plowed into the robed figure.

"Did you accept?" It was strange to hear a masculine voice from an acolyte of Syssera.

Erenia looked up in anger. "Am I the last to know about this?"

"No," the figure said. "I'm the only other one who knows. Being the Chief Detective in the Cyphus Police Department does make me privy to a lot of information." The robed figure pulled back his hood. The sharp eyes of Norn Sanna looked down on Erenia.

She glared at him. "As Enna's campaign manager, I should have been the first to know, especially about being asked to take her place!" Erenia took a breath and calmed herself. She lowered her voice. "Now, if you'll excuse me, I've got a speech to write, or do you already have one written for me?"

Sanna smiled. "I'm good, but not that good." The smile disappeared. "What are you going to do about that husband of yours?"

Erenia looked away. "Not now, Norn, all right?"

"Why not now? I can't believe you're still with that maniac. Now that you're running for a council seat, he's nothing but a liability to your cause... Our cause."

Erenia knew the real reason why Sanna wanted her to break up with Eulos, and it had nothing to do with a Council seat. Despite herself, Erenia was tempted to give in. "I have to go."

Sanna backed off. "Fine. I'll remain here and hope you come to your senses."

Erenia stalked toward the exit. First the whole Council business, and now this…

The door to the temple swung open just as Erenia reached for it, causing her to jump back in surprise. A slim, blue-robed acolyte walked in and noticed her.

"Oh! Pardon me!"

Erenia's frazzled emotions snapped. "Watch where you're going!"

The girl, who could not have been any older than nineteen or twenty, jumped at Erenia's tone. "I apologize. I didn't mean to startle you."

Erenia felt a pang of guilt. There had been no need to bark at this young lady. "No, I apologize. I shouldn't have snapped at you like that. It's just… well, never mind."

Erenia looked at the girl. She must have just taken her vows as an acolyte, as she was unfamiliar to her. The girl was quite pretty, with dark hair cut acolyte-short, smooth, honey-tinged skin, soft brown eyes, and a smattering of freckles across the bridge of her nose. Her mouth was wide and expressive. "Are you new to the temple?"

"Yes. This is my first day. I'm afraid I already made a dreadful first impression."

Erenia smiled, warming to the girl. "No, no, it wasn't your fault; it's mine for not paying attention. My name is Erenia. What's your name?"

"Ocelot."

Erenia was struck with the peculiarity of the name. "Ocelot? Is that your family name?"

"It's my entire name. If I have a family name, I don't know what it is. I'm an orphan. I reached my age of majority a year ago and had to leave the orphanage. I bounced around a bit before I decided to become an acolyte of Syssera. I can't speak for the future, but for now I'm happy."

"Well, welcome to the temple, Ocelot. I have to leave, but I look forward to talking with you again."

"So do I, Erenia." Ocelot smiled. Erenia was struck with the beauty of it.

Erenia walked out of the temple and took a deep breath of fresh air. The reality of what had just happened settled on her like a weight. She was going to run for a council seat. Erenia was woefully unprepared. She had never taken an active interest in politics, a field that was every bit as ruthless as arena fighting. She was nowhere near adequate enough for this challenge.

A surge of fear rose within her. Erenia choked it down. She was intelligent and driven. She would not shy away from what needed to be done, no matter what opposition she faced. She had the backing of the temple and, with Enna, the best advisor anyone could ask for. Most important of all, Erenia had the desire to do this. Victory wasn't guaranteed, but Erenia would sail beyond the Disian Curtain before she surrendered without trying her best to win.

Wait until Eulos finds out. Erenia didn't know whether to laugh or cry at the thought.

CHAPTER 6

Back home, Kyu took off the bandage that covered his hand. The cut Eulos had made was now nothing but a thin, pink line that would disappear before the day was over.

He had always healed quickly; never had any of the numerous wounds he had suffered in the arena gotten infected. It was not uncommon for a fighter to win a match, only to lose an arm or leg due to a wound that festered. Weapons were cleaned, but never sterilized. Bacteria thrived on them. Yet

Kyu knew that Eulos' blade, dirty from slicing off a man's face, would do him no lasting harm.

As far as he could remember, he had never gotten sick. He had never contracted any of the common childhood diseases while he was growing up. He had never even had a cold. Not once had he caught a sexually-transmitted disease from any of the many groupies he had slept with, something no other fighter could claim.

Aest curled up in a corner and napped. Kyu felt a surge of warmth toward the creature. He was glad Aest was here, even if his grocery bill would soon reach new heights.

He grabbed a bottle of beer from the refrigerator, sat on the couch, picked up the remote and clicked on the television. Sipping his beer, Kyu perused the channels. It was mostly shit. Then on one of the news channels he saw Tagain Arena, in Shaeldor. He had fought there a few times. The Shaeldoris loved a good arena fight and Kyu, despite being from Talgourge, was always made to feel welcome.

There was a sizable crowd outside the main gate of the arena. Was there a big-ticket match he hadn't heard about?

Then Kyu noticed that many in the crowd were holding signs. One said 'Stop the Butchery. Outlaw the Arena.' Another read 'End the Madness. Reform Now!' He also noticed what appeared to be a very nervous police contingent in the area.

Reformers? In Shaeldor, a Territory that was proudly Traditionalist?

As Kyu watched, a pro-arena group confronted the protestors with shouts and taunts. The news reporter became animated as she realized the story was about to get bigger.

It was unclear which side threw the first punch, but a melee broke out with astonishing speed and force. Signs and clubs were used as weapons. The Shaeldori police stepped in and were caught up in it. Batons swung, mostly at the heads of the Reformers. More than one body lay motionless on the ground. The reporter screamed in excitement and the camera caught it all.

He shook his head in bemusement. Un-fucking-believable. If things were getting this bad, in Shaeldor, what must things be like in Ormnia, the heartland of the Reformist Movement, or even here, in Talgourge? Would Kyu have to fight his way into the arena for his next match? With his shadowed face and claws, it was not as if he could sneak by incognito. Hopefully Yuv would insist on extra security wherever his next fight may be.

Kyu clicked off the television. The phone rang. It was Yuv.

"Did you watch the news just now?" Yuv asked.

"Yes."

"Did you see that fucking disgrace at Tagain Arena? Who the fuck do those Reformist assholes think they are?"

"I don't know, Yuv, but I know that I want a secure ride back and forth from any venue I appear at next."

"Do you know how much that's going to cost? Why can't you buy your own car?"

"Because it's your job to take care of your meal ticket. Just squeeze some extra money out of the sponsors. You're good at that."

"Yeah, right," Yuv said. "With all of this shit going on and the Reformers gaining in power, sponsors are disappearing faster than virtue in a whorehouse."

"I don't care. Make it happen."

"All right, all right."

There was silence for a bit, and then Kyu asked, "Any idea as to who my next match is going to be with?"

"It hasn't been finalized yet, but it's shaping up to be with Havla Cort."

"He's the axe man from Ormnia, right?"

"Axe and mace. He fights with one in either hand. From what I've seen of him, he's strong and quick. You know,

Kyu, it wouldn't hurt to watch some film of his matches. You'd better believe he's watching film of yours."

Yuv had a valid point, but Kyu knew he wasn't going to watch any film. It wasn't laziness or arrogance so much as it was impatience with the whole process.

"I do have some bad news, though," Yuv continued. "The match will be at Erat Arena."

Aw, shit. "I'm really going to need security in that case."

"I know, I know. Ormnia is seriously considering outlawing arena fighting. The Arena Commission is desperate to keep it there. Since you are the biggest name in the business, they want you down there to drum up some excitement, and hopefully change a few minds."

"By fighting and defeating their local favorite? The riot they just had in Tagain will be nothing compared to what will happen in Erat."

"Don't worry. The Commission will take all of that in hand. There will be security and police task forces up the ass. Just worry about Havla Cort, and let everything else take care of itself."

"Listen to me, Yuv. I don't want whatever hotel I stay at made public knowledge. I want plenty of security at said hotel. I also want an armored car to transport me to and from the arena, as well as back and forth from the airport. I don't care how much it costs. If the Arena Commission wants this bad enough, they'll pay for it."

Yuv sighed. "I'll talk with the Commission."

"I mean it, Yuv. I'm not going down there unless this is done."

"All right, all right, it'll happen, you pain in the ass."

"Yeah, a pain in the ass who's made you a lot of money."

"I know," Yuv said. "Is there anything else you wanted?"

"I don't know. You're the one who called me."

"Pain in the ass. I'll let you know when things become finalized. Until then, train and please watch some film."

#

Two days later Kyu watched a news story out of Ormnia. A reporter was interviewing a very attractive woman, mid- to late-forties, with olive skin and dark eyes common to natives of that Territory. Her hair had a touch of gray at the temples and was cut short, which told Kyu she was a devotee of Syssera. The overlay at the bottom of the screen read 'Ormnian Regent Fey Gherren.'

With several microphones shoved in her face, Fey Gherren was not shy. "What happened in the city of Tagain two days ago is an outrage," The Regent's eyes blazed, her Ormnian accent coming out in smooth, elongated vowels. "Peaceful Shaeldori protestors were trying to make their voices heard. The mob that attacked them without the slightest provocation was organized by top Traditionalists within the Shaeldor government, as were the police forces that, instead of protecting the protestors, joined in on the assault. Seven people were killed!"

Fey Gherren drew in a breath and looked around with eyes that flashed with conviction. "This madness has to stop. I, along with my Council, have determined that this barbarity will no longer continue in Ormnia. I have submitted a bill, which the Ormnian Councilors have voted into law, that outlaws arena fighting within the borders of Ormnia, effective one month from today.

"I have also taken steps to allow Ormnia autonomous action in other areas of government. We will no longer be bound by Magisterial Court decisions that limit Ormnia's self-determination. We will observe Ormnian laws, with executive, legislative, and judicial actions answerable only to the Ormnian people, and no one else."

The reporters were stunned into several seconds of silence. Then they exploded with questions. Kyu could not believe what he had just heard. The Ormnian Regent was taking a very provocative and unprecedented step. She was, in essence, announcing Ormnia's secession from the Unification.

And Kyu's next match was going to be in Erat, the heart of Ormnia. *Oh, fuck.*

"That is all I have to say for now," Fey Gherren told the incredulous mob of reporters. "Rest assured I will have more to say at a later date."

As the cameras followed, Fey Gherren left the podium. A huge Ormnian held open the door to a shining white limousine. Once the Regent was inside, the bodyguard closed the door and got in on the driver's side. The vehicle sped off.

Kyu's telephone rang. He shut off the television just as 'Breaking News!' appeared on the screen.

"Hello, Yuv,"

"Did you catch that press conference?"

"Yes."

"Who the fuck does that Ormnian bitch think she is? Does she know what she's fucking with here? She'd better have an army of bodyguards around her, that's all I've got to say."

"I'd better have an army of bodyguards as well. This is going to get ugly in a fucking hurry. Is there any way to have this match outside of Ormnia?"

"Not a chance. The Arena Commission is desperate for it to happen in Erat. They feel that a good contest between you and Havla Cort will help bring back demand for arena fighting in that Territory. There is some good news; you're going to earn two million marks for this match, more than any other fighter has ever gotten."

The Arena Commission really is desperate, Kyu thought. *Of course, to collect that money, I have to survive not only the match, but my exit out of Ormnia.*

"And don't worry about security," Yuv continued. "The sponsor for this match is Urigor Oil. They'll provide a professional security company for you."

Kyu wasn't happy, but he knew it was a done deal. "When is the match?"

"A week from today."

Shit, that was quick! "That won't leave any time for promotion."

"We have to get this in now, before their law banning arena fighting goes into effect."

"Are the travel arrangements made?"

"Yeah, you'll be flying into Erat on Unified Airways five nights from tonight – first-class, even. The plane will arrive in the early morning hours, with no fanfare. An armored limo will transport you to your hotel, the Erat Ultra. The oil company's security team has it staked out. On the day of the match, the limo will take you to the arena three hours before it opens to the public. Once you win, which, after all of this, you damned well better, the limo will take you immediately to the airport for the flight out. A team of doctors will be on hand in case you need medical attention. Any post-match statements will be made here, in Cyphus."

"You're going to have to make arrangements for another traveler. Aest is coming with me."

"Aest? Who the fuck is Aest?"

"A friend. Tell airport security to allow him on. If the Commission wants me down there that much, they'll accommodate him. He's to be given a private, secure booth to watch my match. Maybe he can share yours, Yuv." Kyu almost laughed at Yuv's silent frustration.

"You fucking pain in the ass," Yuv finally said. "Okay, just make sure you get down here. You and your… friend." Yuv hung up.

Kyu chuckled. Despite the fight being in Ormnia, he found himself looking forward to it. He was going to pick up his new sword tomorrow from Gaxtos' smithy. This would be its first action. Gaxtos had better live up to his reputation.

CHAPTER 7

Hirn Gaxtos called the next morning.

"The sword is completed, Kyu, but…" Gaxtos did not finish the sentence. Kyu was immediately alarmed.

"But what? If there's something wrong with the sword, I'm not paying for it."

"Oh, no, there's nothing wrong with the sword. In fact, it's the strongest and best-crafted sword I have ever made. It's just… you need to see for yourself."

Kyu left Aest at home and walked to the smithy.

"Okay, Hirn," Kyu said once the weapons smith buzzed him in. "Let's see the sword."

Hirn was silent as he led Kyu to a table where a long, cloth-wrapped bundle lay. He undid the cloth and the sword was revealed.

Kyu stood in shock, trying to comprehend what he was seeing. He couldn't speak or look away.

The handle was wrapped in the finest black leather, with corded risers to prevent slippage. The crossguard and pommel shone with gold plating. *Kyu, The Unknown* was etched with flowing calligraphy on both sides of the guard, and a spectacular *K* was set within a crystal at the base of the pommel, but it was the blade that caught the eye: Twenty-six inches of gleaming, sharpened steel – steel the color of blood.

As Kyu watched in amazement, a subtle flow coursed through the steel, a rhythmic cycle of back-and-forth, as if the crimson color was real blood being pumped by a heart within the blade.

Kyu found it hard to catch his breath. His fingers slowly wrapped around the handle and lifted the weapon free from the cloth covering. The molecules of the sword merged with those of his body. The crimson beat within the blade matched that of Kyu's own heart. There was no separation of flesh and steel. They were one.

Furious, ecstatic pressure built within Kyu, and with a gasp he allowed it release. A bright, silent explosion blew wide his senses. Atoms of air swirled in intricate dances before him. Molecules beneath his feet shifted in a rhythm of solidity. Kyu attained a wholeness with the reality in which he existed; he caught glimpses of innumerable realities beyond, flickers of worlds and concepts that passed too quickly for his mind to process as more than alien images.

The maelstrom of sensory input receded as fast as it had come, settling into a low-burn presence within his psyche.

Kyu put the sword down and, with something close to sorrow, released it. He closed his eyes and focused, like he did before a match. The awareness, as Kyu now thought of it, was quiescent, waiting for a command. Kyu looked at the sword. The red pulsations within the blade continued.

"Did my blood do this?" Kyu whispered.

"I don't know!" Distress and awe clawed at Gaxtos' words. "I've mixed blood with molten metal countless times, and nothing like this has ever happened. The blood is purely symbolic. It burns away as soon as it contacts the molten metal." He shook his head. "I ran any number of tests on this blade as soon as it was forged. The color does not affect its integrity in any way. If anything, this blade is stronger than any I have ever made. It will never break on you. But what that is, running through the blade, I have no idea. For the first time in forty years, I don't know what I have wrought."

Kyu took the sword again. The awareness once more bubbled to the surface, but he took control of it. Whatever it was that flowed through the blade circulated through Kyu's body. The beat of his heart was perfectly timed to the pulses within the steel.

He turned to Gaxtos. “We agreed on fifteen hundred marks, right? Let’s make it an even two thousand.”

#

Kyu stepped into the main training room of the Combat Academy. Shouts echoed off the walls as trainers yelled at their charges. The loudest shouts came from Eulos.

Two young students flailed at each other with wooden swords, displaying no form or skill whatsoever. One of them tried a fancy but utterly unnecessary sidestep, got tangled in his own feet, and fell to the floor.

Eulos bellowed for them to stop. He went to the fallen student and delivered a vicious punch to the back of the head. The student collapsed to the padded floor. Everyone else in the vast room, students and trainers, froze in silence. The other student looked at Eulos in horror.

Even Kyu was surprised. Eulos had a nasty temper, but Kyu had never seen him get physical with a student. Something was upsetting him, and it wasn’t the unconscious student’s poor practice.

Eulos caught sight of Kyu and dismissed the other student, who wasted no time getting to the showers. He ordered two other trainers to pick up the inert form and take him to the infirmary.

Eulos shook his head and put a meaty hand on Kyu’s shoulder. “I could really go for a beer right now. Or ten.”

“I guess so. What’s the matter?”

“My fucking wife, that’s what.” Eulos looked away in disgust. “You’re never going to believe what she’s going to do.”

“Is she filing for divorce?”

“No.” Eulos chuckled mirthlessly. “That’s something you would believe. This is something you’d never guess.”

“Well, tell me, already.”

“She’s running for a seat on the Talgourge Council.”

Eulos was right. Kyu couldn't believe it. "I thought the priestess at her temple was running for the Council seat."

"She was, but she had to withdraw because it came to light she's the granddaughter of a Korl chieftain from the bad old days, so she asked Erenia to take her place. Erenia accepted. It was all over the news last night. I'm surprised you didn't see it."

Kyu remembered the 'Breaking News!' that had appeared on the screen just as Yuv had called. That had to be it.

"Did you have any idea she would do that?"

"Not until two hours before she went on television to announce it to the rest of Talgourge. Fucking great, huh?"

Kyu tried to comprehend what his friend was telling him. "What did you say to her when she told you?"

"What could I say? Erenia's her own woman. If she wants to run, I can't stop her."

"I take it she's running as a Reformer."

"Of course."

"How will the fact that you're her husband go over with those whose support she'll be looking for?"

"That's her problem, isn't it? I asked her that; she didn't seem overly concerned."

Both men fell silent. Eulos noticed that Kyu was holding something. Kyu lifted the sword, the blade hidden within a black leather scabbard.

Eulos' eyes widened. "Is that the sword from Gaxtos?"

Kyu nodded, glad his friend couldn't see the ridiculous smile on his face.

"Well, don't keep it hidden from me. Let's see it!"

Kyu unbuckled the strap that held the blade in the scabbard and drew it out. The red steel pulsed with pride.

Eulos' mouth dropped open. "That's fucking beautiful! I've never seen anything like it. How did Hirn get the steel that color?"

"He doesn't know. He thinks it may have been my blood."

"That's impossible. Blood doesn't do that to steel."

"That's what Hirn said, but he swears there were no contaminants within the steel, and I believe him. He can't think of any other explanation. Neither can I."

Eulos looked at Kyu with eyes the size of dinner plates. "What kind of fucked-up blood do you have?"

"The kind that makes swords like this."

"I should bleed you dry and get rich selling a bunch of swords like that."

"Don't get any fucking ideas." Kyu slid the blade back into the scabbard. Eulos couldn't hide his disappointment as the blade disappeared.

"I bet you can't wait to use that in the arena. Do you know when your next match is yet?"

"In five more days, at Erat Arena."

"Erat Arena? In fucking Ormnia? Are you kidding?"

"Unfortunately, no. The Arena Commission is trying one last-gasp effort to promote arena fighting there before it becomes illegal."

Eulos shook his head and frowned. "I hope that manager of yours is providing security for you."

"He is."

Eulos looked like he wanted to say something more, but all he said was, "Be careful down there, Kyu."

"I'll be fine."

"I'll watch your match on television. It'll get plenty of hype. I wish I could go with you, but I have to stay here and train future corpses."

"Great attitude you have. I suppose you felt the same way about me when I was training?"

Eulos lapsed into silence for a few seconds. "No," he finally said. "You're the only one born to this sport. No one will beat you."

#

Kyu felt the tension as soon as the jet landed in Erat. The flight attendants had told him he and Aest would be the first to disembark; they seemed anxious to get it over with.

Dressed in a charcoal gray suit with a blue tie, Kyu felt the reassuring weight of the gun in its shoulder holster hidden underneath the suit jacket. That had been one of his conditions to flying there.

His clawed hand clutched the new sword, something far too precious to banish to a cargo hold. Even sheathed, he felt the warm comfort of the blade.

The aerobridge was attached to the door. The attendants looked nervously at Aest, as they had throughout the five-hour flight. The jet door opened and they were ushered through. Waiting there was a knot of security personnel, large men in dark suits. The bodyguards silently surrounded them and they walked toward the terminal.

Barricades were set up along the way to the arrivals area. The crowd behind them held signs that read 'End the Barbarism' and 'Go Home Kyu, The Unknown.' They started shouting as soon as Kyu and his bodyguards came into view. Dozens of police were on hand to ensure no one tried to charge him.

The blade tapped into Kyu's new awareness and begged to be released. It took considerable willpower to keep from doing just that. Aest growled, his teeth bared, his head swiveling in all directions.

"I know. I don't like it either," Kyu told him. "The sooner we're out of Ormnia, the better."

The heavy tropical heat hit Kyu like a wet, suffocating blanket as they were whisked outside, where more protesters screamed at him. The crowd was held back by more police as Kyu and Aest were hurried to an armored limousine with bullet-proof, tinted glass. The driver, another bodyguard, opened the door and practically pushed Kyu inside. The other bodyguards climbed into cars in front of and behind the limo.

The vehicle was air-conditioned but that did little to protect Kyu from a lungful of pungent cigar smoke.

"Syrra's balls, Yuv, do you have to smoke those fucking things in here? That mob outside won't have to worry about killing me. Your cigar is doing the job for them."

"This is the gratitude I get for your safe conduct." Yuv griped but bowed to Kyu's wishes and snuffed out the cigar.

The limo pulled away from the curb. Even though the police tried to hold them back, several protestors hit the limo with their fists and signs. Kyu and Yuv sat in nervous silence amid the constant thumps that echoed within the car. A few pressed their faces against the glass and screamed at the occupants they couldn't see. Finally the limo pulled away and into Erat.

"I booked us two rooms at the Erat Ultra," Yuv said as they drove toward the skyscrapers of downtown. "I've been assured by Urigor Oil reps that the security is airtight. It fucking well better be. This limo will take you to Erat Arena tomorrow night and, let's all hope, take you directly to the airport immediately after the match."

For the first time, Yuv noticed Aest, who was sitting on Kyu's other side.

"Syrra's balls, Kyu, what the fuck is that?" Yuv shifted his considerable bulk to the far side of the seat. Aest turned toward him and growled.

"This is Aest. I told you about him."

Aest continued to growl at Yuv, whose sweat had nothing to do with the heat.

"You've got to be kidding me. That thing looks dangerous."

"Oh, he is," Kyu said with a grin Yuv couldn't see. "Especially if you piss him off. I don't advise you piss him off."

Yuv wiped his face with a wet palm.

Kyu chuckled. "I don't think he likes you, Yuv."

Sweat stained Yuv's suit. "Just keep that thing under control, all right? There's no way it's going to share my luxury box tomorrow."

"Yes, he is. Don't worry, Yuv. Aest will leave you alone, unless I lose the match. Then I don't know what he'll do."

Yuv glared balefully at Kyu. "You really enjoy complicating my life, don't you?"

"Someone's got to keep you honest." Kyu sat back in his seat and put a clawed hand on Aest. The creature stopped growling. His knob continued to vibrate but he never took his attention away from a very uncomfortable Yuv.

#

The room was quite nice, with a massive bed and a fully-stocked mini-fridge. The luggage containing Kyu's armor and spare clothes had already been delivered and was sitting by a chair that faced the television. The room was ten stories up, with a fantastic view of the buildings and sea port of Erat.

There had been protestors outside the Ultra, but Kyu, Aest, and Yuv had once more been swallowed by professional security personnel and brought without incident into the hotel. More bodyguards were stationed at various points throughout the hotel, including at the doors to Kyu's and Yuv's rooms.

Aest made himself comfortable on the bed, his belly distended from the five pounds of raw meat served to him upon arrival. His limbs and tail were sprawled out, taking up the center of the bed. He breathed deeply in contentment.

"Don't go thinking you'll have that whole bed to yourself tonight," Kyu said. "I'm claiming half of it."

Aest grunted and let out a noxious fart.

"You keep that up and you're going to be on the fucking floor." Kyu futilely waved his hand in the air to clear the stench.

Someone knocked at the door. Yuv was doing a promotional conference with the media – it had been agreed, much to Kyu's relief, that the situation in Ormnia was too volatile for Kyu to do any open press statements – so it wasn't Yuv knocking. He hadn't ordered any room service. Was it the guard?

Not taking chances, Kyu pulled the gun from its holster. Aest sensed Kyu's tension and leapt to his side.

They stood to one side of the door. "What is it?" he called out.

"It's Jurl Henna, sir." He was the guard assigned to watch Kyu's room.

"What do you want?"

"There's a visitor here for you, downstairs."

Kyu liked this even less. "Who is it?"

"A lady, sir. I assure you all is well. Your safety is not compromised."

Was this some sort of elaborate set-up? If so, it didn't make sense. If the security was part of some plot to kill him, they could have done so as soon as he had landed at the airport. What 'lady' would be here to see him? Obviously not a groupie. Security would not insist on his presence just for a groupie.

He turned to Aest. "Be prepared for anything."

Aest growled acknowledgement.

Kyu whipped the door open and stuck his gun in Jurl Henna's face. Aest was out in a flash, looking for other threats.

The guard threw his hands in the air. "Please, Mr. Kyu, nothing is amiss, I assure you. There's no need for that gun."

Kyu kept the gun trained on him. "Anyone else around, Aest?"

Aest barked, and Kyu knew it meant no. Communication between them had grown almost to the point of speech. Kyu knew it had something to do with his awareness, but he didn't have time to marvel about that now.

Kyu pushed Jurl Henna around, grabbed him by the back of the collar and stuck his gun in the small of the guard's back. "All right, let's go. If anything happens, my first bullet goes in your spine."

"Sir, please, there's no need for this. Please put the gun away."

"Just move. Not the elevator, the stairs. I'm not going to get trapped in a box."

They went down ten flights, Kyu pushing the guard forward while Aest watched their rear. As they entered the hotel lobby, the other security guards spun around. When they saw Kyu's gun, they went for their own.

"Stop! Stand down!" Jurl Henna shouted. "Put your guns away!"

Kyu kept his gun on Henna. "All right, where's this lady?"

"She's outside, in her car. You have to surrender your gun before you see her. That is nonnegotiable."

Kyu looked out the window and saw a white armored limousine – one he had seen before.

No fucking way. It couldn't be.

"Now do you believe me?" Henna asked. "Can we now dispose of your gun?"

Kyu made his decision. He hoped it was the right one. He released Jurl Henna and handed him the gun. "Make sure this gets back to my room."

The guard took it with relief. "Of course, sir. You will be frisked before you enter the vehicle, and I'm afraid your… friend… must remain behind."

Aest growled.

"Easy, Aest," Kyu said. "I'm pretty sure I'll be safe. If anything does happen to me, though, feel free to have this guy's face for dinner."

Jurl Henna backed away several nervous steps.

Kyu was led outside, which was remarkably free of protestors. The heat embraced him in a damp fist. Shadows stretched as night fell on the Ormnian city. The same chauffeur he had seen on television a few days ago walked to him and expertly patted him down. Satisfied, the driver opened the rear door of the limo and ushered Kyu into the dark interior, which was cool and dry. The leather seats were spacious and soft.

The driver stuck his head in the door. "I don't like this, ma'am. Those claws are like knives. I wish you'd allow a guard to sit with you."

"Thank you for your concern, Rheid." A woman's voice, deep and smoky, came from the seat across from Kyu. "I am perfectly safe. Let's go."

The driver's face spoke miles of dissatisfaction, but he obeyed and closed the door, which shut almost soundlessly. Through the opaque partition, Kyu saw him climb behind the wheel and pull the limo into the street.

The Ormnian Regent Fey Gherren smiled. "I must admit, seeing you in person is rather intimidating." She had an easy, relaxed tone. "I'm amazed I cannot see your face. Is it true that it's been hidden since birth?"

Kyu didn't answer right away. Fey Gherren was even more attractive in person than she was on television. There were a few age lines on the olive skin of her face, but they did not distract from her beauty. Her short hair was only slightly touched with gray, which, more than anything else, gave her a regal bearing. Her dark eyes shone with sharp intelligence. She looked great, and she knew it. Kyu realized this was one of her weapons.

Fey Gherren leaned forward, her blouse open just enough to reveal cleavage. Her breasts were large and firm, but natural. The faintest outline of her nipples protruded from the thin fabric. Her moist, full lips parted ever so slightly, and she ran her hands down her short skirt and her slim, bared legs.

Despite himself, Kyu felt his penis harden. He forced himself to ignore it and set his mind to work. He had to be very careful. Fey Gherren was every bit as dangerous as any foe he had faced in the arena.

"Don't be nervous, Kyu," Gherren cooed softly. "You have my assurance that nothing will happen to you while you're with me."

Kyu finally found his voice. "What's this about?"

The Regent sat back, a slight smile still on her lips. "How much do you know about the history of the Territories?"

What kind of a question was that? "Just what I've read."

"Tell me, Kyu, are you a follower of Syrra?"

Talking to this woman was like trying to juggle. "Not particularly. I'm not the religious type."

"Would you say that the followers of Syrra and the followers of Syssera are at odds with one another?"

"Of course. They have completely different doctrines."

Gherren looked out the tinted window as the dark streets flashed by. "It wasn't always that way, Kyu. The temples of Syrra and Syssera used to work very closely together at one time."

Kyu had never heard this before.

"It's true." Gherren looked back at him. "A man and a woman are totally different, but if they are put together under optimal circumstances, they are two halves that make a whole. They are stronger together than they are apart. The same is true for the temples of Syrra and Syssera. Syrra is the warrior, the hunter. Syssera is the child-bearer, the nurturer, the grower of crops. Syrra is the Husband and Father, and Syssera is the Wife and Mother." She sighed. "They are stronger together, but their differences sometimes pull them apart. This is such a time."

Kyu shook his head in confusion. "Why are you telling me this?"

Gherren laughed, a lusty sound that got Kyu's groin going again. "Oh, Kyu, don't you see? We, each and every one of us, are the children of Syssera and Syrra. When parents argue, the children are made miserable, and act accordingly. Look how truculent and divided everyone is. It's because our parents are bickering."

Kyu wondered how gods could bicker. "What does any of this have to do with me?"

"More than you realize. Now, more than ever, the peoples of the Territories need to be unified. A thousand years ago, Harra Ardrassis tried to do just that with force of arms. The history books say he succeeded, but it wasn't quite that simple. Ardrassis was a bloody tyrant, and he wanted complete control over the Territories, spiritually as well as physically.

"As you are undoubtedly aware," Gherren continued. "Syrra's color is red, and Syssera's color is blue. Ardrassis, in his insurmountable arrogance, adopted the color purple as his own, purple of course being the blending of red and blue. Harra Ardrassis named himself the head of both temples."

Kyu had not known this.

The Regent leaned forward again. Her brown eyes found Kyu's as if they were visible to her. "Many people think Harra Ardrassis' actions were noble and done for a common good. They ignore the atrocities he perpetrated. Nobody remembers the bloody snow fields in Urigor, when entire villages were put to the sword. Nobody remembers the downfall of the mighty city of Tagain, where blood flowed like rainwater through the streets, where women were raped and then thrown off the city walls. He's remembered as the Unifier, the magnificent man who united the Territories and eliminated warfare between them. Since Ardrassis hailed from Talgourge, the Talgourgese to this day feel that Ardrassis is a hero, and that his vision and philosophy is embraced by all.

"But when you forcibly unite people by the sword, they will never feel united here." Gherren made a fist over her heart. "Though they may outwardly obey the new laws being enforced, inwardly they are separate. They embrace even more their own culture and traditions, and resent any intrusions that conflict with them. One set of people will always feel animosity toward another. The Eastern and Western Territories in particular have never liked one another. This is something that Harra Ardrassis, and his sister Haena, the Sorceress, could never understand.

"If we truly are a unified people, how is it that firearms were invented and are now so pervasive throughout the Territories? One reason was supposedly the creation of the Isle Accords, the agreement between the four Territories to create the Isle Patrol to guard against escape attempts and depredations from Xiaroc Isle. Ships were built, and, once they were invented, so were aircraft, all armed with guns to keep an eye on the criminals off the Ormnian coast, but don't believe for an instant that the heavy weaponry stopped there. Each Territory has its own secret armada of guns and artillery, tanks, fighter aircraft and bombers, and a flotilla of naval craft with some very heavy guns. There are hundreds of missile bases along each border. The officers of the militias who control these weapons only await the word from their respective Councils and Regents to launch attacks against their neighbors. It's not a question of if this will happen, Kyu. It's a question of when."

Kyu was aware that each Territory had 'defensive' militias that were supposedly more ceremonial than anything else. To hear the extent of the weapons they controlled and their obvious expectation of conflict with their neighboring Territories sobered him.

The limousine continued to glide through Erat. A misty rain pelted the windows. Outside, street lights and neon signs flashed garish colors across the Regent's face.

Kyu returned to the subject of ancient times. "I've read that the Unifier killed his sister, who later came back as the Empress."

The Regent smiled. "That is correct, but do you know why Ardrassis killed his sister?"

"I think it had something to do with his wife, but I don't know why."

"It was because the Unifier's wife was a woman of uncommon wisdom who was steering her husband to a less violent path. She was usurping the influence the Sorceress had on her brother, who had always looked to his sister for guidance.

"As formidable as he was on the battlefield, as charismatic as he was with his army, Harra Ardrassis had absolutely no mind for governance. Once peace had been gained with untold gallons of blood, he was clueless as to what to do, so he turned to the women in his life, who were smarter and stronger than he. His sister Haena manipulated him with her dark arts, arcane magicks she had learned from creatures summoned from beyond the Disian Curtain. She wanted total subjugation of Ormnia, Urigor, and Shaeldor, with Talgourge the ascendant Territory. She had every intention of eliminating her brother once all was conquered, and making herself the lone ruler over all.

"Ardrassis' wife, Tana, knew what Haena was about and tried to get her husband to open his eyes to see his sister for what she was. Ardrassis was conflicted. The two women he loved were pulling him in different directions, but then something happened that made Ardrassis side with his wife. She became pregnant."

Kyu had never heard of the Unifier having any heirs.

"There's a reason for that." Fey Gherren seemed to read his mind. "Once Tana became pregnant, the Sorceress knew her plans for domination were over unless she took drastic action. She confronted Tana, along with her brother, in their tent. She denounced Tana as an Infernal from the Disian

Curtain, which was of course ludicrous. Harra was having none of it. In desperation, the Sorceress brought her dark arts to bear and attacked Tana. Tana screamed for Harra to help save her and their unborn child.

"Madness, brought about by his sister's magick, seized him at that moment. He grabbed his sword and plunged it through Haena's black heart. The Sorceress' body died, but not before her vile spirit put a spell within her brother's mind – a worm that ate away his rationality. The Sorceress' spirit, kept within this world by her powers, slipped away to await its time.

"It did not take long. The spell overcame Ardrassis with a false sense of guilt that overwhelmed his every waking moment. Tana tried to assure him that what he had done was necessary to save her life and that of their child, but the worm within him grew and emptied his soul, leaving nothing but desolation. In the end, he banished his faithful wife, still pregnant with their child. Darkness overcame him. He refused to eat or move from his bed. A few weeks later he died, alone and unloved."

"According to what I've read, this was when the Empress appeared and established the system of government that exists to this day, keeping the Territories unified. If she was as bad as you say, why didn't she just let everything collapse into chaos?"

Gherren nodded. "Yes, why didn't she? She understood that allowing her brother's work to slip into anarchy would strip her of power, so she pushed the new political system into place. She knew there would always be divisions between the disparate Territories, which would work in her favor as the final arbiter of any disputes. To exacerbate this, she manipulated the temples of Syssera and Syrra, convincing each that one was working at opposing ends to the other. A schism was created between the temples, and through them the gods they represented. This is the paradox that the Sorceress understood all too well. Syssera and Syrra, even with their power and transcendence over humans, are at the mercy of their worshipers, for it is the worshipers who give them power. Without worshipers, they are impotent. They are as much, actually more so, at the mercy of the doctrines they have given their worshipers as the worshipers are themselves. If the temples of the Father and Mother see themselves as adversaries then the deities themselves must adhere to these convictions. In the end, the final say – both secular and ecclesiastical – is centered on the so-called Empress."

Kyu looked away, trying to digest everything he was being told, not just what, but why. What possible reason could there be for someone like the Ormnian Regent to explain all of this to him, an arena fighter?

Fey Gherren put her hand on his knee. Surprised, Kyu spun to face her. The Regent's brown eyes were so intense that Kyu felt not only was she seeing his eyes, but his soul as well.

"The Territories are meant to be unified, but not by the methods Harra Ardrassis used." She spoke with conviction. "Each Territory, and their people, must have equal say. They must want to be part of a whole, not forced to be. The first step must be the reconciliation of the temples of Syssera and Syrra."

Fey Gherren came off her seat and sat next to Kyu. She kept her hand on his knee; their hips met. The contact points blazed with carnality. Kyu found it increasingly hard to breathe.

"There are several points of contention between the temples," Gherren said softly, her mouth mere inches from his ear. "All are minor except for one – that one is the horrible blood sport you excel in."

Kyu pulled away as far as he could from the Regent. He should have known this was where everything was leading. "I don't know what your game is, Madam Regent, but I've heard enough. Please have your driver return me to my hotel."

A bemused smile twisted Gherren's lips. "I fear my choice of words has alienated you. That was not my intention.

In fact, I have a proposal in mind that I think you will find very interesting."

For the first time, Kyu became aware of the Regent's scent, a clean yet musky natural aroma that immediately gave him another erection. Her soft, dry hand grasped the side of his face and turned it toward her. Her glistening, red lips nearly touched his own. Her breath washed over him, sweet and intoxicating.

"Join with me, Kyu." Her bare leg rubbed against him. "We can reunify the temples of Syssera and Syrra. Everybody knows who you are. Everybody knows who I am. Together, we can be the catalyst of something truly revolutionary. We can heal the schism the Empress created and start the changes the Territories so desperately need. Change is coming, Kyu. There is no stopping it. As it is proceeding now, it will be violent and painful, but if the Territories see you, an adherent of Syrra, and me, an adherent of Syssera, working together, the transition will be peaceful."

Her lips came forward and found his. Their softness sent waves of electric pleasure through Kyu's body. Her tongue pushed through and caressed his like a bold, confidant lover.

Kyu's arms went around Gherren's slim body and pulled her closer. Her breasts pressed against him. The hand that had been on his knee ran down his thigh and cupped his hardness. Her fingers traced the lines of his straining penis.

Her lips broke from his. "I know you've had your share of groupies, but I can show you things in the bedroom that will put all of them to shame." The Regent's lips again melded with Kyu's. Her hand gained momentum on his crotch.

All conscious thought, except regarding Fey Gherren's pliant, willing body, were blanked out by hot red lust that surged through Kyu. Her legs parted as he leaned into her. Her fingers grasped his zipper and pulled.

STOPSTOPSTOPSTOPSTOPSTOPSTOPSTOPSTOPSTOP!

Sudden clarity filled Kyu's mind. He pulled away from the Regent. His breath came hard as he backed from a precipice he had been blinded to until the last second. What was over the precipice he did not know, but it was something wrong and irreversible.

Fey Gherren's eyes widened in disbelief then flared with rage. For a brief moment, they flickered and became something empty, a terrible void that housed nothing but hate and hunger. Gherren lowered her gaze for a second then looked back up, her brown eyes seemingly solid and belying what Kyu could have sworn he saw.

Kyu felt fear, which surprised and rattled him. There was more to Fey Gherren than he could discern; something terrible and dangerous… and Kyu had just made her an enemy.

The Regent's face settled into blank indifference. "It is unfortunate that you have refused me, Kyu. We could have changed the course of everything, and had a lot of fun in the process. You have chosen to throw it all away." She returned to her seat across from Kyu and rapped her knuckles against the glass partition that separated them from the driver.

The return to the hotel was done in silence. When they pulled in front of the Ultra, the driver opened the door for Kyu. Gherren ignored him as he got out and the door was closed.

The limo sped from the curb. Kyu entered the hotel and ignored the curious looks he got from the security guards. He climbed the ten flights of stairs back to his room, where he found his gun on his bed and a very anxious Aest waiting for him.

Kyu sat on the bed. Aest jumped up beside him. Kyu put his arm around him. "I've faced death countless times, but nothing has scared me as much as what happened tonight. I can't wait until we get out of this fucking Territory."

CHAPTER 8

Erenia entered Enna Racyne's chambers. The priestess wasted no time on pleasantries. "You're slipping in the polls. You have to travel and make more speeches. You need to be seen. Time is running out."

"I already make three speeches a week. I've been to every major city in Talgourge. There just hasn't been enough time to make my name a familiar one, even with all the ads our sponsors have been pushing. What more can I do?"

"There's always more you can do. We can't afford to wait another five years for the next election. You have to win now!"

"I'm trying! I think we've made remarkable progress over the last few weeks."

"It's not enough! All that progress means nothing if you don't get elected."

Erenia was taken aback at Enna's vehemence. Since handing over the reins to Erenia, Enna Racyne had become obsessed with the election.

"The Reform Movement will proceed, with or without me on the Council. I can help push it along, true, but it will move forward whether I'm there or not."

"No!" Enna's pale eyes widened in outrage. "We cannot afford to lose even one seat on the Council. You must win!"

Erenia was stunned by her friend's anger. "Enna, take it easy. It isn't the end of the world."

"Why can't you understand how important this is? How come you're not taking this seriously?"

Erenia felt heat rise in her face. "I am taking this seriously. You're taking it to extremes."

"It's your husband, isn't it? That damned Syrra-worshipping brute! He's dragging you down. Get rid of him, Erenia!"

Erenia was speechless for several seconds. Then her anger rose quick and sure, breaking the surface. "How dare you tell me how to run my personal life? Being the priestess of this temple does not give you that right. Do not tell me how to run my life again, Enna Racyne! As Syssera is my witness, I'll drop my candidacy if you do."

The two women glared at each other. Finally, Enna Racyne dropped her gaze. "I only want what's best for all. With you on the Council, everyone has a chance for a better life. You know how strongly I feel about this. I'm sorry if I upset you, but I do ask that you think about what I've said."

Erenia's anger didn't cool. This wasn't exactly an apology from Enna, but Erenia knew she would get no better. She forced herself to calm down. "I will do everything I can to win this, Enna. I feel just as strongly about this as you do, but I will not, will not, be told how to run my personal life. Understood?"

Enna Racyne's head bowed ever so slightly. This was as much a concession as Erenia would get. She stood and walked out of the priestess' chambers without another word.

CHAPTER 9

Kyu, already in his black leather armor, sat in his dressing room at Erat Arena, watching a monitor as he waited for his match to begin. Unable to stay seated, he paced around the room for the fifth time.

Unlike Cyphus Arena, Erat Arena was an open-air facility with a sand floor. No surprises dropped from the ceiling; they came from other directions. The twenty-five thousand seat arena was filled to capacity, belying Fey

Gherren's televised assertions that the Ormnians were on the verge of voting out arena fighting. Yet there had been thousands of protesters outside the arena when Kyu, Yuv, and Aest had arrived in the armored limo. The mob had surrounded the vehicle, rocking it back and forth, striking it with signs before the Erat police had pushed them back.

The match before his was a teams match: two fighters squaring off against two other fighters. The local team was armed with long pikes. The visiting team, dark-skinned fighters from Shaeldor, was armed with traditional Shaeldori curved swords. To make the match more challenging, the combatants were surrounded by large, heavy booths, each with a 'murder hole' facing the fighters. Within each booth was a crossbowman, who fired into the arena every few seconds. They fired blind, so as to not target the visiting fighters. Everyone within the arena had an equal chance of being hit. Some bolts were embedded in other booths, and a few littered the floor of the arena, but as yet no fighters had been struck. Strong acrylic glass surrounded the first few rows of fans to prevent them from being hit with stray shots.

As Kyu watched on the monitor, one of the Shaeldori fighters raised his sword for a strike only to have his forearm punctured by a crossbow bolt. He screamed and dropped his sword. One of the Ormnian fighters drove a pike into his neck. Blood gushed over the Shaeldori's cuirass and he fell to the sand. The fans roared with approval.

Now it was two on one. The Ormnians circled the remaining Shaeldori, who to his credit fought well for several more minutes. He even opened a shallow gash in the inner thigh of one of his opponents, but eventually he tired and the Ormnian fighters moved in for the kill.

When it was over, the twenty-five thousand fans stood and applauded, honoring both their own fighters and the Shaeldoris who had fought so well. The Ormnian fighters saluted them with their pikes and walked off.

The television coverage aired a commercial break while arena attendants rushed in to clean up the bodies and collect the crossbow bolts. The crowd rose from their seats to stretch, go to the bathroom, and get food and drink for the next match, which was Kyu's.

Kyu pulled his new sword from the scabbard. The blood-red steel sucked in the light of the room and reflected it with eldritch brilliance. It pulsed in time with his heart.

The door to his dressing room burst open to the stench of cigar smoke. Kyu thrust the sword back in its scabbard.

"Well," Yuv said. "I'm glad to see you're ready for once."

Kyu did not look at his manager. "Is Aest taken care of?"

"Yes, that beast of yours has been taken care of. He has his own private booth."

"With an escort to my limo once the match is over?"

Yuv sighed. "Yes, yes, it's all set."

"Good, because I'm not leaving without him and neither are you."

Someone knocked on the door. "Kyu, The Unknown to the gate!"

"Don't kill this one too quickly," Yuv said. "Put on a show. Let the excitement build before the payoff."

"Are those orders from the Arena Commission?"

Yuv ignored the question. "See you after the match, Kyu." He left for his own secure seat.

Kyu was not surprised that Yuv wasn't walking out with him for this match. Between the protests and the fact he was fighting the local favorite, the crowd was bound to be a step or two beyond hostile. Syrra forbid that Yuv's suit becomes stained from a thrown beer or sausage kebob.

The Erat Arena staff looked at Kyu sullenly as he neared the entrance to the sand floor. Once there, he waited, listening to the announcer build up to the introduction.

Pneumatics within the gates hissed and they opened. Bright lights bathed him, and the announcer cried out, "Kyu, The Unknown!"

The crowd growled as many of them rushed the acrylic glass that separated the seats from the arena floor. Beer bottles and trash were thrown onto the sand before Kyu had a chance to step out. He waited where he was until, several minutes later, security had the crowd under control and attendants had cleaned the garbage from the arena floor.

As Kyu was the visiting fighter, he had been announced first. He strode to the center of the sand floor and pulled the blade from the scabbard.

A connection, alive and sentient, flowed from the sword to Kyu and back again. Red light pulsed, in time to his accelerated heartbeat. The crowd grew quiet, the silence heavy as all eyes feasted on the magnificence before them. Kyu's blood powered through his veins, filling him with a sense of omnipotence he had never experienced before. For a timeless moment, he and the crowd were one until they remembered who he was: the enemy. With the spell broken, Kyu turned to the doors opposite the ones from which he had emerged and waited for the announcer to introduce his foe.

Kyu's awareness expanded to encompass the arena. Virulent hatred and grudging respect heated his skin in waves, like an intermittent summer sun. For the first time, he felt the mob to be what they actually were: a collective that made a single entity. Like birds who turned wing at the same time, or an ant colony that worked together without error, the mob was one, and acted as one, despite perceived considerations of free will amongst individuals; the entirety of this collective was against him. Arena security had supposedly checked everyone for firearms. Kyu hoped none had made it through.

He also sensed the crossbowmen behind their barricades, waiting for their signal to start firing bolts.

Kyu looked at his sword. It was his flesh, his consciousness, made steel. He breathed easily and awaited his opponent.

The announcer's voice rose, inciting the crowd to rise and cheer. The doors at the other side of the arena opened. "And here he is, Havla Cort!"

The noise level rocked the arena. Havla Cort stepped out and acknowledged the adoration with a winning smile. He was a handsome man, clean-shaven with a strong, angular jaw. He had a mace with a ridged head in one hand and a hand axe in the other. Both were carried with intimate ease, confirming Yuv's report that Cort was ambidextrous, a deadly advantage for an arena fighter.

Havla Cort was without any armor, or even a shirt. His slim torso, with well-defined musculature, was bare. He wore only black leather pants, which were tight enough to reveal a conspicuous bulge in front.

Kyu marveled at the audacity of this vanity, yet Cort was considered one of the top fighters in the Territories. Kyu would have to be careful not to underestimate him just because he liked to show off.

Havla Cort raised his arms in the air and spun so everyone could see his face, which was magnified several thousand times on the big-screen monitors at either end of the arena. His movements were smooth and easy, deceptively quick. Cort's dark hair was long and braided down his back, with the hair at the end styled in a peculiar ball shape.

The Ormnian, finished with his self-exhibition, faced Kyu with a fierce grin, showing no intimidation for Kyu's unseen face. A klaxon went off, signaling the start of the match. The crowd roared for Kyu's blood.

Calmness settled over Kyu and he brought the red sword up to a guard position. Havla Cort closed in quickly and, with his left hand, swung the axe. Kyu jumped back from the strike and thrust with his sword. The blade was knocked away by the mace before it could bite into flesh and the axe came back in an uppercut swing. Kyu pulled back his exposed arm just in time and backed up a few steps.

The first crossbow bolt shot out. Kyu sensed it and stopped. The missile flew past where he would have been if he had continued to retreat.

The crowd roared with approval. Havla Cort smiled and advanced.

Kyu brought the sword up in a two-handed grip and swung down. Cort crossed his weapons over his head to block the blow. Steel rang loudly with the impact. Cort held his position with ease. Kyu was impressed with the Ormnian's strength.

Keeping his blade pressing down on the upraised weapons, Kyu kicked Cort in the stomach with a booted foot, knocking him back.

A warning blazed through Kyu's mind and he ducked. As he did, another bolt, coming from a different direction, cut through the hair that peeked from under his helmet, missing his scalp by less than an inch. He rolled through the sand as a third bolt zipped past his body. He regained his feet just as Cort charged him. Unable to bring up his sword in time, Kyu hit him in the stomach with his shoulder, knocking the Ormnian aside.

As Havla Cort fought for balance, Kyu slashed his sword at the man's exposed abdomen. Cort, even unbalanced, displayed his agility and deflected the sword with his axe. Kyu did not let up. He swung down with another overhand blow, which was knocked aside by the mace. Havla Cort took a step back.

Kyu turned and knocked another bolt out of the air with a flick of his sword. The power of the fired projectile sent a jolt up his arm, but the sword was not damaged. The bolt, its metal tip bent from the impact, embedded itself in the sand. The crowd gasped in disbelief.

All of these bolts are being aimed at me. I thought the bowmen were supposed to be firing blind.

Havla Cort took another step back and spun around. The ball of hair at the end of the braid flew at Kyu's face. Kyu couldn't understand why this skilled and experienced fighter was making such a foolish move. Kyu reached up to grab the hair.

His clawed hand closed around the ball and he felt immediate pain. Kyu released the hair and looked at his hand. A small drop of blood ran from a puncture wound. He looked at Havla Cort, who grinned in triumph. A small metal barb stuck out of his hair.

Kyu brought his sword up. His arm was heavy and lethargic. The deafening noise of the crowd dimmed, and his vision darkened. Kyu's lungs struggled to inhale, and he fell to his knees.

Poison.

Arena fighting did not have many rules, but the use of poison or drugs to incapacitate an opponent was absolutely forbidden. Fighters who violated that rule were either sent to Xiaroc Isle or killed outright, yet here was Havla Cort, not only using poison, but using it openly.

The Ormnian walked up to Kyu. With an easy movement, he knocked the red sword from Kyu's hand then brought his axe up for the final blow. Knowing his opponent was helpless, he couldn't resist taunting him. "Say goodbye, Kyu, The Unknown. Ormnian soil will feast on your flesh and blood tonight."

Kyu struggled to get air into his lungs. His extremities tingled. He looked in desperation for his sword. It lay in the sand, out of reach.

It wasn't right. If Kyu had been bested by a superior opponent, he could have accepted his death, but not like this – not through foul treachery. *It wasn't fucking right!*

Rage built within Kyu, a black spiral that tore through his body and mind. Kyu grasped it and screamed; the deepest part of his consciousness blew open and expanded. It was just like what had happened in Gaxtos' smithy, when he had first picked up the red sword, but this time he saw the flip side of existence, the negativity, the darkness inexorably intertwined with the light. Desolation filled Kyu, but it was fulfilling, it was right, it was the completion of the half that he had seen before.

The red sword is not out of reach. It will never be out of reach. It is part of the whole that is Kyu, The Unknown.

The sword was in Kyu's hand. The blade glowed, a deep, greedy crimson that demanded immersion in flesh and blood. Havla Cort, his axe raised, looked at Kyu with wide, shocked eyes and stepped back. Kyu thrust the blade deep into Havla Cort's bowels. The Ormnian's dark eyes flashed with agony and his weapons dropped from his hands. Kyu twisted the sword savagely through Cort's abdomen and yanked it free. Entrails, along with a great effusion of blood, spilled onto the sand floor of Erat Arena. The Ormnian collapsed to his knees then keeled over on his side, his hands futilely covering the mortal wound.

Kyu looked at the sword. The red blade absorbed the blood and chunks of viscera stuck to it. Within seconds it was clean of gore.

Kyu's vision was nearly gone. He fell next to Havla Cort. "Why?" he asked the dying man.

Havla Cort chuckled. Blood sprayed from his bluish lips. "You're so fucking stupid. You were never meant to leave Ormnia alive." Cort's eyes closed as he released his last breath.

Kyu could not stop his own slide into blackness. He felt bad for Aest, and hoped his friend took out a few of these treacherous Ormnians before they killed him.

The crowd, which had been shocked into silence at the turn of events, growled with intensifying ugliness. There would be a riot. Kyu didn't care. Havla Cort's final words followed him into oblivion.

You were never meant to leave Ormnia alive.

#

Yuv had never seen so many police in one location. Doctors and nurses couldn't walk through the hospital corridors without nudging them aside, especially in front of the door to the room that contained the barely-alive Kyu.

Outside the hospital, a throng of news vehicles and reporters from all four Territories, were being held back by more police as they awaited word of Kyu's condition. Joining them were protestors, with more than a few willing to end Kyu's life if it didn't end on its own.

The scene at Erat Arena at the close of the battle had been a horrific nightmare. Arena attendants had gotten Kyu's body out of there just before the enraged crowd had overcome the security and police presence and stormed the floor. All doors leading to the interior of the arena had been locked and braced. Yuv and Kyu had been placed in the back of an inconspicuous vehicle, hidden under blankets, and driven out through a subterranean exit and to the hospital.

Aest, thinking Kyu had been murdered, went into an uncontrollable fury in his box. No one had dared enter until someone had shown up with a tranquilizer gun and shot the beast with it. Aest was now in a sturdy cage in a veterinarian's office somewhere in the city. Yuv thought they should have just killed the vicious creature and been done with it.

Thousands of crazed fans had gone on a rampage, causing millions of marks worth of damage to the arena, and had then turned on the thousands of outside protestors. In the end, the police, along with militia from the Isle Patrol, had restored order, but not before over two hundred people had been killed. Of that number, thirty-six had been police and militia.

What a complete and total fuck-up, Yuv thought. The Arena Commission had been so desperate to reinstate the fan base of arena fighting in Ormnia. The idea had backfired in the worst possible way. The Regent, Fey Gherren, was screaming at any camera pointed her way that this was the last straw, that arena fighting had to be outlawed in Ormnia right now. The Ormnian Council backed her unanimously.

How had Kyu retrieved his sword? It had been kicked well out of his reach, yet it had just... appeared in his hand. Then Kyu had summoned enough strength to disembowel Havla Cort.

This was it. Yuv knew that arena fighting was over in Ormnia. A quarter of the market was going to disappear, and along with it a quarter of the income for everybody involved. *What a fucking disaster.*

The bustle around Kyu's room grew in intensity. Looks of alarm, followed by resignation, filled the faces of the medical personnel.

Kyu, The Unknown was finally dead.

Now Yuv had to make plans to get out of Ormnia in one piece.

CHAPTER 10

Kyu found himself floating above his body. He was light, insubstantial. Beneath him, Ormnian doctors desperately tried cardiopulmonary resuscitation to get his heart beating again. They injected anti-cholinergic drugs into his bloodstream and forced air into his lungs. As incredible as his body had been in healing itself, it appeared that the poison had been too much. The physicians admitted defeat and started to disconnect Kyu's body from the medical equipment.

Now that his mortal life was over, Kyu wondered what was next.

"You're not through with mortal life yet, Kyu."

Kyu's incorporeal form spun to the speaker. Standing among the doctors, apparently unseen and unheard by them, stood a short, slightly heavy woman, somewhere in her thirties, with dark hair, honey-colored skin, and almond-shaped eyes. She wore a long, white dress with purple trim that looked several hundred years out of style. She smiled benignly at Kyu's spirit floating in the air.

Kyu found he still had a voice. "Who are you?"

"I am Haena Ardrassis, or at least I was at one time. Most people call me the Empress now."

Kyu did not know if what was happening was real, or some weird death experience. "What do you want with me?"

"I want you to reenter your body. Then I want you to come to Empress Mountain as soon as you can. We have much to discuss."

"Does this mean I'm not dead?"

The Empress laughed; a clear and joyous sound. "Not if you don't want to be. Do you want to be dead, Kyu?"

"No."

"Then return to your body. You will find it quite easy to slip back in. As for the poison, just will it away. Once you recover, come to the mountain."

Kyu floated toward his body. He looked once more at the Empress before everything went dark.

Kyu's eyes snapped open. He felt his physicality in the hospital bed. Awareness flooded through him, burning away the last of the poison. He looked to the place where the Empress had stood, but no one was there. With some effort, he pulled himself into a sitting position.

All activity around him came to a sudden stop. Doctors and nurses looked at him in shock. Finally someone shouted. "He's alive! He's alive!"

Kyu got to his feet. His legs were wobbly, but they held his weight. He noticed that his armor had been stripped away, leaving him in his shorts and undershirt. Immediately doctors tried to push him down on the bed. Kyu shoved them away. He was getting out of there.

He walked from the room as the physicians yelled and chased after him. The police who had been guarding his room were no less shocked at Kyu's sudden revival, but they did not try to stop him as he walked down the corridor. Kyu pulled away from the last of the doctors and saw a huge, unmistakable shape ahead of him, walking away.

"Yuv! Hold up, you fat fuck."

Yuv spun around with a speed that amazed Kyu. His eyes were wide with disbelief. "Those fucking doctors told me you were dead!"

"Those fucking doctors don't know what they're talking about. Where's Aest?"

Pale and unnerved, Yuv stuttered. "I'm not sure. I know they had to subdue him. I think they brought him to some vet's office somewhere."

"Find out where he is. We're going to get him and get out of this fucking Territory. What happened to my sword?"

"It's… it's in my limo."

Kyu's claws dug into Yuv's soft arm. "You were going to sell it for big money, weren't you, you fuck? And you were going to leave Aest to die in this fucking stinkhole of a city."

Sweat ran down Yuv's white face. "What matters is that you're alive, Kyu. Let's find your friend and get the fuck out of here."

After some phone calls, Aest was located at a veterinarian's office a few blocks away. Outside the hospital, the amassed media exploded to see Kyu alive. They dashed past, ignoring the shouted questions, and dove into the limo. Kyu was relieved to see his sword on one of the seats. They knew they didn't have much time before the media made Kyu's status known to all. The limousine raced to the veterinarian's office.

Kyu walked to the row of cages that housed various animals. *Bang!* Kyu turned to a cage on the floor. The bars were bent. The creature within charged the cage door again;

the lock broke off. Aest leapt out and drove Kyu to the floor. His knob vibrated with joy and his thick, wet tongue bathed Kyu's hidden face.

"Okay," Kyu laughed between licks. "Get off me before you drown me in spit."

The veterinarian was cowering against the far wall. Yuv was standing next to him.

"What kind of animal is that?" the vet asked Kyu. "That's no dog or wolf that I've ever seen."

"I don't know," Kyu said once he got up. "I really don't care. He's my friend. That's all that matters."

They made it to the airport and boarded the plane. Kyu looked out the window and saw a mob of Ormnians charge the security fence between them and the runway. The jet taxied and picked up speed. The weight of outraged humanity tore the fence down and thousands of screaming people raced toward the runway in an attempt to block it off. It looked like they might succeed.

"Fuck," Yuv swore from his own window. "Go, man, go!" he yelled at the pilot.

The aircraft's wheels lifted off just as the first of the mob hit the runway. Hands grabbed the wheels and tried to hang on as the plane lifted. They let go and fell away as the wheels retracted into the body of the plane.

Kyu settled into his seat. He put his arm around Aest. "What happened back there, Yuv?"

Yuv, sitting in front of him, turned. "What do you mean, what happened?"

"Havla Cort used poison on me. Firearms, drugs, and poison are forbidden in arena matches, under penalty of death or banishment to the Isle. Yet Cort used poison openly. Everybody saw it. He didn't care. Why?"

Yuv shook his head. "Who the fuck knows? Everyone knows that almost all illegal drugs come from Ormnia. They use too much of their own shit and get crazy."

"Havla Cort wasn't crazy. He wasn't high on drugs. He was a skilled fighter who could very well have won that match on his own. No, he was given permission to use that poison. He may have been ordered to. His last words to me were how stupid I was for not understanding what was going on."

Kyu did not tell Yuv about what had happened with Fey Gherren. Was it possible Gherren had ordered the use of poison after her failed seduction attempt? That would indicate she had a connection with arena fighting, which, publicly, she was adamantly opposed to.

Why would the Regent have tried to seduce Kyu in the first place? Kyu did not buy for a second that the two of them together could bring about unification and harmony to the Territories. That was beyond absurd. There had to be another reason… Kyu closed his eyes. Maybe Havla Cort was right and he was too fucking stupid to understand, but understand what? He was too tired to guess.

Then there was that whole surreal conversation with the Empress, where she had summoned him to Empress Mountain. Had that been just a near-death hallucination? If so, it had been incredibly vivid.

Kyu's overwhelmed mind succumbed to fatigue. The sky outside darkened as they crossed into Talgourgese airspace. He rested his head against the window and fell asleep.

You were never meant to leave Ormnia alive.

CHAPTER 11

Erenia grabbed her coat with a gloved hand and tightened it around her throat. The northern Talgourgese city of Gener Pass was much colder than Cyphus this time of year.

Still, she mused as she looked around, the turnout had been great.

Below where she had stood on a platform in the city common area lingered a crowd of several thousand people. Many held signs with Erenia's name on them. All were cheering the words she had just spoken about improved economic development and infrastructure repairs in this depressed city, whose best days as a coal mining capital were long gone. Erenia promised Gener Pass that she would not forget them if she were elected, a promise she had every intention of keeping. She had already started talks with a major lumber company, a progressive one that was committed to the conservation of trees as well as the harvesting of them, to start operations here. There were millions of acres of untouched forest, and the business would provide plenty of needed jobs. This was her second day here, and she had seen a shocking amount of poverty and destitution in what was once an important city.

Erenia was flanked by the leader of the city's Board and the priestess of the local Sysseran temple. Both had pledged their support of her candidacy and had treated her visit here wonderfully. *More wonderfully than my own priestess has been treating me...* Erenia shook away the pointless thought. This was not the time for it.

As television cameras broadcast her speech throughout Talgourge, Erenia concluded it by thanking Gener Pass for its hospitality and praising the perseverance of its people. She raised her arms; the crowd cheered and chanted her name. It was a heady moment. Erenia now understood the lure and thrill of running for office.

At her hotel that night, sitting at a table in her room, she stayed up late with her campaign manager, Nia Kalla.

The next stop on Erenia's campaign swing was Luxior, in the far east of Talgourge. After that were two more cities along the southern coast before they came back to Cyphus. Travel and hotel expenses alone cost tens of thousands of marks, paid for through the Sysseran temple treasury and the donations of supporters. Erenia was well aware of what was being invested in her, and what was expected of her in return. If allowed to wander, this could become a very intimidating thought.

She rubbed her eyes and leaned back in her chair. "How do you do it, Nia? How do you always manage to look so indefatigable and refreshed, even after a fifteen-hour day?"

Nia smiled and raised the cup that was at her elbow. "Coffee. Lots of coffee."

Erenia marveled at Nia's stupendous capacity for caffeine consumption. "If I drank as much coffee as you did, I'd be a shaking, jabbering mess. More so."

Nia laughed. "You're not that bad yet, Erenia."

Erenia grimaced. "I'm not that far away from it, either." Fifteen days into a twenty-day campaign swing throughout the Territory, she was surprised and dismayed that she was feeling this level of exhaustion already.

"It's not the travel; it's the stress," Nia said. "You constantly have to maintain a high-level of energy and optimism. You have to be out there at all times. This is the reality of campaigning, but it's worth it. Trust me."

Erenia smiled. "I do trust you. In that regard, you belong to a very small group of people."

Later, despite her fatigue, Erenia found sleep elusive. She had been given a double-sized bed and kept looking at the empty side. She wondered what Eulos was doing while she was gone. Chances were good he was at the Bloodbath Pub, getting drunk with Kyu, The Unknown. Erenia shuddered at the thought of Kyu. What kind of creature was he? Who had no visible face and claws for hands, and who was nothing but an amoral killing machine? Well, if Erenia got elected, a top priority would be to push legislation to outlaw arena fighting, like Ormnia was about to do. That would leave only Urigor and Shaeldor with that horrible blood sport. Hopefully it would force Kyu, The Unknown to move west, out of Talgourge and away from Eulos.

Yet Erenia had to admit that, even if this did happen, Eulos would keep in contact with Kyu. They had an inexplicable friendship that drove her to despair, but it was real. She knew Eulos would not end it just because Kyu was forced to move across the continent.

Erenia stared at the empty space beside her.

Just like at home, the only difference being the presence of a physical body.

Erenia squeezed her eyes shut to prevent the tears from falling. Why did she stay with Eulos? Was there really any love left? They were so different now. She had grown and moved on. He had stayed in the dirty morass of arena fighting, even though he was now too old to participate. He couldn't – indeed, he had no desire to – let it go, but Eulos still loved her. He still tried to be a good husband, despite their opposing ideologies.

But now… someone else was pushing to get involved. Norn Sanna had made no secret of his interest in Erenia. The tears finally came as Erenia admitted to herself that the interest was mutual.

CHAPTER 12

It was fifteen hundred miles from Cyphus to Talmount. Since Kyu had every intention of bringing Aest with him, public transportation was out of the question. He would have to rent a car.

Empress Mountain straddled the nexus point of all four Territories and rose more than forty thousand feet over the surrounding lands. It was visible for several miles in all directions, yet its glacial peak was hidden in clouds most days. Eastern Talgourge was relatively flat. As Kyu and Aest drove westward, the flatlands gave way to hills, which soon gave way to mountains. It took three days to reach Talmount, with Empress Mountain visible the last day of their journey.

On this day, Empress Mountain was free of clouds. The icy peak rose above its rocky shoulders and stabbed the sky, its walls sheer and unforgiving. The trees at the base, many more than a hundred feet tall, looked like twigs, their leaves turning color early in the high, chilly altitude.

Nobody had ever successfully climbed to the top, though several hundred had died trying. A century ago all four Territories passed a law forbidding anyone from climbing the mountain higher than twenty thousand feet, but every year at least two or three groups of climbers tried to attain the summit. Every effort ended in surrender, rescue, or death.

The biggest building in the city was the Government Complex, a monstrous structure four stories in height that sprawled over five hundred thousand square feet in the center of Talmount.

They reached their hotel just before nightfall, tired, irritable, and very hungry. All Kyu wanted was juicy steaks for himself and Aest, several mugs of cold beer, and a nice, comfortable bed, in that order. Empress Mountain could wait until the next day.

The service was good and the food even better. Kyu had made sure ahead of time that Aest would be allowed in. The hotel staff, all fans of Kyu, The Unknown, treated Aest as well as they treated Kyu. The mattress on the bed was firm, as Kyu liked it. Aest, well fed, stretched out on the soft carpet beside the bed and fell asleep. A few seconds later, Kyu lay on the bed and followed suit.

#

The road ended a few miles short of Empress Mountain. Well, Kyu reasoned, it was a good thing he and Aest were used to walking. He pulled the car over, locked it, and they set off on a foot trail. The ground got steeper as they went on. Individual trees became woodland, and the overhead canopy sometimes blocked out the sun.

After hours of walking the trail petered out. They found a small stream and drank their fill. Kyu refilled a canteen he had purchased at a local camping supplies store.

Doubt gnawed at him. The sun was sinking behind the mountain and darkness was building quicker than he had anticipated. They had nothing to eat except for a few strips of dried meat he had brought along. He hadn't been sure what to expect, but if the Empress was real and not just a phantasm he had imagined in a hospital, he expected something. Now they were far from the road, possibly lost, and would never find their way back to the car before nightfall. Who knew what might come out at night on this mountain? Kyu had brought his handgun, but he doubted it would stop a two thousand pound bear.

He sat on a fallen tree in front of a rock wall. Aest joined him. The creature ate first, some dried meat and water from the canteen. Kyu took a swig, looking at the darkening sky. Some stars were already visible. His light jacket would not be enough against the plummeting temperatures. *We're fucked. How could I have been so stupid?*

"I'm sorry about this, Aest. We're stuck here tonight." Aest rubbed against Kyu. He opened his jacket and wrapped it around the animal. "I don't know how to build a fire; I didn't think to bring matches. Hopefully we don't freeze to death or get eaten by something." A gust of wind seemed to shred Kyu's jacket. He pulled Aest closer. "If we get through this night we'll go back to the hotel, eat and warm up, then get the fuck back to Cyphus. I can't believe I took a hallucination on faith."

As the deep violet sky succumbed to night, Aest turned his head and growled at the rock wall behind them. His knob vibrated. Kyu pulled out his gun and spun around, hoping not to find a massive carnivore rearing up behind them.

There was a round opening in the face of the rock wall, one that hadn't been there before. As Kyu watched, a soft, incandescent light grew from within. Aest's knob continued to vibrate, but he was no longer growling. He seemed at a loss for what he was facing.

Kyu looked at him. "What is it?"

Aest faced the opening for a few more seconds then grunted in the negative.

Kyu shook his head. Now that the sun was gone, the temperature was dropping fast and the wind was picking up. At the very least, the opening would give them shelter. Kyu decided that the risk of whatever was within was not as great as that of exposure and hypothermia.

"Let's go."

The opening led to a tunnel that bored through the rock. The path was flat and even, the sides curving to the top, the rock unnaturally smooth. Bits of mica reflected light, the source of which Kyu had not yet discerned. The temperature was at least twenty degrees warmer than it had been outside.

Fifty feet in, the tunnel ended at a wooden door with a round knob. Light came from behind the door, shining through the seams.

Kyu turned to Aest. "What do we do now?"

Aest barked.

"My thoughts exactly." Gun ready, Kyu grasped the knob and opened the door.

A clear stream ran nearby, gushing over smooth stones and sand. Trees, tall and green, grew from soil that smelled clean and rich with nutrients. Birdsong filtered down from the canopied branches. Here and there roots pushed from the ground, squirrels darting amongst them. They scampered up the trunks when they saw Aest.

A trail of fresh grass, lined on either side with rows of exotic flowers of red, yellow, and violet, twisted through idyllic fields. The sky was a deep blue, with a few fair-weather clouds drifting about. The crisp, clean air was untainted and pure. The temperature was perfect for physical comfort. All was relaxed and contented.

"Welcome to my home."

Kyu and Aest spun around. The doorway and the rock tunnel were gone. Instead, sun-washed meadows stretched into the distance. The Empress was sitting on a bench that appeared to be made of living wood. She was exactly as Kyu remembered her from the hospital.

Kyu looked at Aest. His knob vibrated in a way Kyu had not seen before. The beast seemed completely lost.

"He has trouble sensing me," the Empress said. "It's understandable, since I'm not physical. I'll make myself visible to his senses."

The Empress held out a hand. Aest approached and sniffed it with his large nostrils. The knob stopped vibrating and Aest froze in place. A second later, Aest's body relaxed. His long, wet tongue came out and licked the Empress' hand. He looked back at Kyu and yapped with satisfaction.

The Empress smiled and leaned back. She made a gesture and another living bench appeared across from her. "Please, have a seat. Put away that gun; you have no use for it here."

Kyu slowly holstered the weapon and, without taking his eyes off the Empress, sat down. Aest sat on the grass next to him. "So you are real. I didn't just imagine you... unless I'm imagining you right now, while I'm freezing to death on the side of the mountain. I distinctly remember that night was falling, yet now it's bright and sunny."

"This is my home, Kyu. I control all reality here. The weather and time of day is whatever I wish it to be. I have always been partial to mountain mornings, so that is what it is."

Kyu did not understand. He laid his clawed hand on Aest's smooth head and remained silent.

The Empress leaned forward. Her smile disappeared. "Do you know who you are, Kyu, the Unknown?"

It was a simple question, yet one Kyu had never had the answer to. He looked at his claws. He shook his head slowly, unable to bring himself to reply.

"What do you remember about your past?"

He looked up at the Empress, who smiled gently. He hated thinking about those unhappy times, but he found himself telling the Empress about his miserable school years, his life in a foster home that ended in blood and rage, and his introduction into the world of arena fighting, the only place that seemed to accept who and what he was.

Kyu felt lightheaded once he was done talking. This was the first time he had ever told anyone his story, and he felt equal amounts of relief and fear at having gotten it out.

"That past was engineered for you, Kyu, at least to a certain degree. All of the outside elements were placed before you. Your decisions on how to deal with those elements, however, were solely your own. Your life, as it is now, is entirely of your own making."

Kyu felt his stomach drop away, as if he were teetering on the edge of a sheer cliff. "What do you mean my past was 'engineered'?"

The Empress looked away. "What do you know about Harra Ardrassis?"

Kyu disliked this change of subject, but went along with it. "Only what I've read in history books, which not everyone agrees with."

The Empress looked back at him. "I am Haena Ardrassis, Kyu, or, to be more accurate, I am her essence, able to keep a presence in this world by altering the molecules around me to take the shape of this body. My actual, physical body died on the end of my brother's blade a thousand years ago."

The Empress' dark eyes lowered with grief. "Despite the tragic way we parted, I loved my brother dearly, and I still cherish his memory. Yes, he had flaws as everyone does, but he was a great man. He united four diverse, feudal Territories under one banner, and the four were made stronger because of it. Many people, then and now, consider him a tyrant. Maybe he was, but the Territories would have torn themselves apart with incessant warfare if he hadn't united them. It is true that the Territories, even after a thousand years of Unification, still have many cultural and political differences, especially between the East and the West. Such is the contrarian nature of people, which even my brother couldn't change."

The Empress sighed. "As I said, my brother had his share of flaws. While he was the military tactician and strategist genius of his age, he completely lacked political acumen. He preferred total honesty over guile, which, while it is a virtue few men attain, is a fatal liability for a world leader. This was especially true in his relations with those of the opposite sex, and herein laid the seeds of his destruction."

The Empress stood and indicated Kyu to do the same. She reached out and took his hand. Hers felt warm, soft, and very physical. He looked at Aest, who lay sprawled on the grass, snoring in perfect contentment.

"He'll be fine, but he cannot accompany us where we now need to go."

Kyu was airborne, shooting into the sky at an incredible speed. Below he saw his body, standing on the grassy path, his arm out and holding the hand of someone who was no longer there. He looked to the side. His hand was still being held by the Empress. Everything looked physical, though Kyu could not feel anything as they flew up past the mountain, the atmosphere, and into the outer darkness of space.

Kyu had the sensation of constant free-fall and panicked. Reassurance radiated through the Empress' hand. *Do not fear, Kyu. You are in no danger.*

Kyu's equilibrium returned and his fear sloughed away, to be replaced with awe. Stars and distant planets shone around him. Multi-colored galaxies, unfathomable distances away, spun in their timeless cycles. Behind him, the sun blazed with fiery red and yellow plumes shooting into the void.

Look down.

Kyu's feet hung over a vast, spinning globe that he knew was his world. The massive continent of the four Territories was directly beneath him. The peak of Empress Mountain at the center of the continent, tiny from this distance, poked up at him. Kyu marveled at the multi-colored terrain that sprawled beyond the mountain, the green fields and darker green mountains and forests of Talgourge, the misty, greenish brown jungles and swamps of Ormnia, the beige sands in the deserts of Shaeldor, and the towering, white peaks of the mountains in Urigor. Lakes and glacial melt gave birth to rivers which twisted and curled their way to the sea. Off the coast of the Ormnian peninsula was Xiaroc Isle, covered with an impenetrable thick, green wilderness except for a thin strip on the western and northern coasts, which had been cleared for the penal colony. He saw a decent-sized storm forming in the Ormnian Sea, and a strong cold front bringing blizzard conditions to northern Urigor.

All around the continent and surrounding ocean waters covering the rest of the world was a thick, pulsating cloud cover, black with shifting shades of gray. Massive bolts of blood-red lightning flickered within it as it roiled and churned from pole to pole. There were no breaks to show what was within this mass, which seemed alive and sentient, aware of the spirits watching it from above.

It was the Disian Curtain, from which no one who had crossed into, whether by plane or boat, ever returned.

From Kyu's vantage, it looked as if the Disian Curtain was poised to swallow the Territories and claim the entire planet as its own. His fear returned. This time there was no reassurance from the Empress.

It grows in power. It feeds off hatred, distrust, disunity. It has sent forth agents to foster this. Everyone below has chosen to ignore it, but they will not be able to for long. It's already at the outer island.

Kyu looked closer at Xiaroc Isle. The Disian Curtain had closed in and was now touching the eastern coast.

Horrors are being introduced there that the jungles will not long contain.

Kyu looked at the Empress. "I've always thought the Disian Curtain was stable and unmoving." Kyu's thoughts flowed to the Empess with ease. "How is it now encroaching upon the Territories? What will happen if it does sweep over all?"

Faith in the gods has been pulled apart. It is divided and weak. Spiritual unity is the key to holding back the Curtain, but now there is none. The rest has fallen on me to try to hold it back, but I've never had the power to do it alone. My strength is nearly gone. I do not know how much longer I can hold on to this world.

It shook Kyu to see how close the Disian Curtain was and be told it was getting closer. "What exactly is within it?"

Life as you know it but altered beyond recognition. Humans, animals, plants, even microscopic organisms... the few that have survived have been forcibly transformed into terrible creatures. They know no sunlight, nor starlight. Time matters not to them. All they know is insatiable hunger, which overrides anything resembling free will – that, and fear: Fear of the Diaboli Domini, the Dark Gods who rule within the Curtain. That is who made them what they are and can destroy them with no effort. Ruling the Diaboli Domini is the one called the Son of the Morning, whose reach extends beyond the Curtain, even beyond this world.

Something about the name sent a shiver through Kyu. "How much time do we have before the Curtain covers all?"

It's taken several millennia for it to get as far as it has, but the more it covers, the quicker it moves. Now that it touches Xiaroc Isle, it has a fresh supply of life to feed on. I fear this will give it momentum. If it is not stopped, the Disian Curtain will cover all within one hundred years.

"How can it be stopped?"

The Empress gave Kyu a look of sadness. *We must return.*

They fell back to the earth, shooting down at a speed Kyu's rationality could not comprehend. Within seconds, they were in the garden on Empress Mountain. Kyu sat on the bench before his legs gave out. Aest continued to snore on the grass.

The Empress gave Kyu a few minutes to regain his composure. "There is one more thing I need to show you."

"No," His voice quivered. "I've seen enough."

"I'm sorry, but time is against us. You need to see this now."

Kyu found his hand back in the Empress'. Reality lurched around him, changing shape and focus. Kyu closed his eyes and willed his stomach not to empty.

"Open your eyes, Kyu."

He desperately did not want to, but he complied.

Together they flew above a dry, sandy plain. Sparse clumps of grass dotted the area. A multitude of tents surrounded a massive walled city that looked to have recently fallen to invaders. Platoons of soldiers walked through burnt and shattered gates, carrying loot. Thousands of dark-skinned Shaeldoris, their faces drawn with defeat, were herded in work details. Smoke rose from countless fires within the city, filtering the fierce sun that scorched the land.

This is Tagain, the last major city to fall to my brother. He took it several weeks previous to where we now are.

They landed near the center of the city. In front of them was a massive sandstone building, topped with purple banners that snapped in the wind, surrounded by guards wearing archaic metal armor with teal badges on their breastplates. Each held a spear and had short swords strapped to their sides. They ignored the sudden appearance of Kyu and the Empress.

We do not exist to them nor they to us. What you are seeing are images from the past, a motion picture if you will, but one that happened exactly as we are seeing it.

A horse and rider approached. The guards immediately stood straighter as the horse pulled up. One of the guards came forward and grasped the bridle to keep the animal still. The rider dismounted.

It was the Empress, but instead of a white dress, she wore dark riding clothes. Her hair was blown back and tangled from the wind, and her brow was wrinkled with determination.

Of course, I wasn't known as the Empress back then. Most people had another name for me, one they dared call me only behind my back – The Sorceress.

The Sorceress approached the tall double doors to the building. The guards saluted her then opened them. She entered, with Kyu and the Empress right behind.

The interior was constant motion. Officers and messengers swarmed to and fro like an insect colony, coming in with reports, leaving with orders. The noise level was low but continuous.

The Empress pointed to a man who sat at a desk in the center of the room. He had long black hair tied back in a ponytail. His face featured a strong jawline, and his dark eyes shone with energy and vitality. Despite the seeming chaos that swirled around him, the man was calm and focused as he poured over reports and issued instructions to the generals who stood around him.

Kyu knew without having to be told that he was looking at none other than the Unifier, Harra Ardrassis. Though he knew this wasn't real, he was nonetheless awed at being in the presence of this legendary man.

The Sorceress approached the desk. She sent out a command to everyone in the building, amplified by her powers. "Leave us!"

Everyone, including Harra, looked up in surprise. The generals turned to the Unifier, who nodded. They left, leaving

Haena and Harra, along with their two unseen onlookers, alone.

Harra looked at his sister with bemusement and more than a little irritation. Kyu saw the familial resemblances between brother and sister. While Harra was taller, they both had solid, muscular physiques. The shapes of their faces were the same, and while Haena's hair and eyes were slightly lighter than Harra's, their noses, mouths, and chins were perfect compliments of each other.

Harra Ardrassis spread his arms. "What is it, Haena? What's so damned important you have to chase everyone out?" The hard, clipped words were spoken in Old Talgourgese, but Kyu had no trouble understanding them.

Haena took a deep breath. It was clear that what she wanted to say was not going to be easy. "It's time, Harra. You know to what I refer."

Harra's face darkened. "I cannot believe that what you say about her is true. Damn your powers! They're not always right."

Haena kept her gaze steady under her brother's anger. "Others may lie to you, brother, but I never have. You must believe me when I tell you that Tana is using you and will end up destroying you. You are the only one who can banish her back from where she came, and you must do so now, before it's too late."

"Damn your words!" Harra exploded from his desk, knocking it over and scattering papers. "She is human, damn you. For once, you are wrong. I have proof that she is as human as you and I."

Haena's face froze in dread. "What proof?"

Harra smiled vindictively. "Proof even you cannot gainsay. How does the title 'Aunt Haena' strike you?"

Haena stood in shock, unable to speak. Her eyes welled with tears. "Oh, Harra," she finally whispered. "What have you done? Why didn't I have the courage to act before now?"

"What is this nonsense?" Harra stood before his sister. "You should be happy for us! I love you, Haena, but I warn you, if you keep on with this, you'll be the one banished."

"Why wait? Banish her now, Harra."

All spun toward the sound of the voice, including Kyu and the Empress. A woman entered the building and approached Harra and Haena, the latter stiffening with surprise. Kyu's first impression was that this newcomer was, simply, the most beautiful woman he had ever seen. Long black hair tumbled over bared, slim shoulders and spilled down her back in a glistening ebony waterfall. Her face was soft yet had firm lines, with a straight nose, full, moist lips, and large, stunning emerald eyes.

I should have been able to detect she was there, but I couldn't. This is part of how I failed my brother.

"Tana." Harra smiled for the first time.

Standing at Harra's side, Tana threw Haena a look of pure hostility. "Face it, Harra. Haena will never accept me. She has grown jealous of the special bond we have. She feels usurped, and will stop at nothing to remove me from your presence. I know she's your sister, but you have to choose between her and me, and our unborn child."

Harra wavered. Despair and uncertainty clawed at his features. Kyu looked at the Empress and was surprised to see tears running down her face.

"Asrath!" Haena shouted. Tana's eyes blazed with hatred, the green irises consumed by a dark, terrible hunger.

Kyu's heart froze. He had seen that before.

Haena's and Tana's essences flew from their bodies. Two amorphous blobs, one fuchsia, the other obsidian, swirled and struck at one another in a rapid, frenzied dance that accelerated into a pulsating maelstrom of things torn and ravaged, a fight to oblivion.

It was clear that Harra did not know what was happening. He stood in despair between the stilled physical bodies of the two women he loved, knowing something terrible was happening but helpless to do a thing about it.

The black essence was weakening. It broke contact and fled.

Though we fought in a spiritual realm, we were still connected to our physical bodies. I had hoped that Asrath's pregnancy would drain her quickly, and it did.

Harra's desperation made him grasp Tana's body and shake it. He yelled at her to come back to him.

Asrath's essence shot back into the physical form she had named Tana. Her green eyes reanimated and she grabbed Harra. "Help me! Haena is trying to kill me and our baby. You must stop her!"

Haena's essence reentered her body. Her eyes focused. She opened her mouth to speak. Harra's sword plunged into her heart. Haena's physical body died quickly. Her essence flew off in defeat. Harra's face paled in horror at what he had done. He collapsed over his sister's bloody body and howled in grief, which brought his guards running. Behind him, the woman he knew as Tana smiled in victory.

I have one more thing to show you, the Empress said, her voice thick with emotion.

The scene shifted. They were in another room of the same building. A woman, the one known as Tana, lay on a bed, her bared legs spread wide. Attending her was a nurse.

Harra Ardrassis stood at her side. Kyu was shocked at how much the Unifier had changed. His face was gaunt, carved with long lines. His hair was falling out; what was left was more gray than black. In his hand was his bared sword.

Tana screamed and arched her back. The nurse bent to her, hands ready. Tana grunted then laid her head back against the pillow as the nurse took the baby and expertly cut the umbilical cord.

The nurse, whose back was to Kyu, went stiff. She looked at Harra Ardrassis, her mouth open in disbelief and horror. She held out the baby.

It was a boy, glistening with the viscera of birth. His face was hidden in shadow. No matter in what direction the newborn moved his head, no features could be discerned. His tiny hands ended in curved, sharp claws.

"What is this?" Kyu felt sucker-punched. The Empress gave him a look of sorrow and regret. "How can this be?"

Harra's eyes blazed with hatred and fury. He spun toward Tana, who regarded him with a contemptuous smile.

"Haena was right! Damn you for twisting my mind and heart, woman. Are you even a woman? I think not!"

"Too late, Harra Ardrassis," hissed the creature on the bed. "My child is born, and your time is done."

"No!" Harra Ardrassis pointed his sword at Tana. "I banish you! Return to the far side of the Disian Curtain, and never return."

Tana screeched and rose from the bed. Her human eyes fell away, replaced with twin holes of awful, ravenous nihility. Her body bloated, and her skin stretched and paled to a maggoty white. Her hands became claws, much like the infant's. Her mouth widened, revealing long, black teeth.

The nurse stood still, frozen in terror. The baby squirmed in her arms.

Asrath laughed. "All this does is delay what is to come." Her voice was a grotesque parody of human speech. "The banishment lasts only as long as the one who decrees it, and you, my love, have very little time left in this world." Asrath looked at the baby. "He and I will unlock your gates, made corrupt with faithlessness, and Dis will be released to claim all."

She snarled and swiped at Harra with her claws. The Unifier brought up his sword. Upon contact, Asrath vanished, leaving behind a stench so noxious that even Kyu could smell it.

The nurse, eyes wide, quivered in shock. With his free hand, Harra took the baby from her arms and laid him on the bed. He then drove his sword through the nurse's body. The nurse gasped and fell to the floor. She looked at Harra in shock.

"Please forgive me," Harra whispered as she bled away. "There must be no witnesses to the abominations that have occurred here this day."

Harra took his bloodied sword and held it above the infant. He looked at the claws and the hidden face and shook with revulsion. "I do not know if you are an innocent or a diabolic, but it does not matter. You are a child of Dis, not a child of mine. I will not allow you to become a weapon for the Infernals."

Harra placed the tip of the blade against the newborn's chest then braced himself to push.

Another presence entered the room, unseen by Harra. Just as he pushed down on the sword, the baby was taken from beneath the blade and whisked away. The sword plunged through sheets and mattress to embed itself in the wooden floor.

Harra Ardrassis stared at the empty space where the baby had been. He stared at the sword, stabbing through nothing but fabric and down. His body shook, and tears fell from his eyes. The Unifier fell to his knees and screamed, expunging the remnants of his decaying soul. He fell to his side and shivered. No one came running to his aid.

My brother lasted for five more months before he succumbed to guilt and desolation. When he died, his generals were ready to go to war with each other over who would succeed him. This would have caused untold destruction, with millions of lives lost. Though I was still inexperienced in my new state, I knew I had to intervene, so I came down from the mountain, known then only as the Crux, and dazzled everyone with lights and illusions to give the impression of power I did not have. I made myself recognizable and intimidated them enough with my reputation as The Sorceress to enforce my brother's vision of a true Unification. I kept returning for over two centuries, until the system of government you know today had been, if not fully accepted by all, at least enforceable enough to stay in place.

The Empress sighed. *Even now, a thousand years later, each Territory has strong nationalistic desires. They want to be sovereign countries again, not part of a whole. I fear that, sooner rather than later, they will get what they wish. The wars will start again as the Disian Curtain closes over all.*

Kyu and the Empress once again stood in the pastoral meadow the Empress called home. Next to the bench, Aest stirred from his slumber.

Kyu found the bench and sat down, struggling to arrange all he had been shown into a cohesive whole in his mind. The Empress looked at him with pity.

"That baby looked just like me. What happened to him?"

The Empress shook her head. "That baby did not look like you. It was you."

Kyu's mind blanked out. He had to be hallucinating. There was no way any of this could be real. "That was a thousand years ago. I'm not a thousand years old."

"No, you are not," the Empress agreed. "You're not even thirty years old yet."

"Then how...?" Kyu shook his head. "I don't understand what's going on."

The Empress laid a hand on his shoulder. "I'm so sorry for all of this, Kyu. I will explain as best as I can and hope that it is enough.

"It was me who took you away from your father's sword. Despite your hybrid blood, I knew a time was coming when this world would need you, so I took you and placed you in a plane of existence that has no time, where nothing ages or changes. This is where you have been for all these centuries, until I saw it was time to bring you back."

Kyu was the son of Harra Ardrassis? How could that be? And his mother… "That woman, Tana or Asrath or whoever she is…"

"Asrath is not a woman, at least not in the human sense. She is a creature from beyond the Disian Curtain, a minor-level Diaboli Domini. She calls herself the Queen of the Succubi, and perhaps she is. Succubi are among the few Infernals who can penetrate the Disian barrier into this world, under the right circumstances. There are two ways they can do this. She initially gained entry into this world by appearing to my brother in a dream. In that state she seduced him. Once he ejaculated, his semen provided the means for her to exist here. However, the one from whom a succubus accepts semen also has the power to banish her back to Dis, which is what my brother did once he realized Asrath's true nature."

Kyu's heart lurched. He held up his clawed hands. Everything now made sense, and it was horrible. "So I'm half human and half… whatever? Just what am I?"

"You are Kyu Ardrassis, son of Harra Ardrassis… and my nephew." The Empress smiled.

"But I'm also the son of whatever this Asrath is." Kyu looked away. "Does that mean I don't belong here? Is my real home beyond the Curtain?"

"No, it means you are incredibly unique, for you share many of the abilities of those from Dis, without the limitations imposed on them. The Diaboli Domini and their denizens, for all their power, cannot help but be what they are. Many would refer to them as evil, but true evilness means choice. The Diaboli Domini did not choose to be evil; they were created that way by their master. Therefore they must remain that way if they are to survive. The only one who chose this path is the Son of the Morning.

"You are not one of them, Kyu, despite your shared heritage through your mother… not unless you choose to be. You have human blood, therefore you have free will."

Kyu looked again at his claws. "I will never be seen as human, not with these. Then there's my face. It's hidden for a reason. It feels normal to me when I touch it, but if my hands are like this, I can only imagine how horrible my face is."

The Empress smiled. "Yes, there is a reason your face is hidden, but we will address that shortly. First, you must understand the other half of your bloodline, the human half. You now know you are the son of Harra Ardrassis. You are also my nephew; some of me is in you, including a latent ability to control your reality."

Kyu tried to understand. "Are you saying I have magic, like you?"

The Empress shook her head. "There is no such thing as magic, at least not as people perceive it. There is nothing mystical about my abilities, or those of the Diaboli Domini. It is all quite natural, and accessable to anyone. It is, essentially, a higher extension of our consciousness. People create their own reality all the time without realizing it, but almost no one is born with an instinctive knowledge of how to tap into it and use it willfully, with conscious purpose. I was and, through me, so are you."

Kyu thought of how his mind expanded during moments of high stress, of how his awareness perceived everything around him during those moments. He mentioned this to the Empress.

"Yes, Kyu, that is exactly what I mean. Awareness is a good word for it, but you have only skimmed the surface of your abilities. There is so much more for you to discover. I will teach you how to get started."

A full-length mirror, set in a living wood base, appeared before them. Kyu immediately turned away.

"Face the mirror, Kyu," the Empress commanded. "The first step on your new journey through life has to begin with you facing and accepting yourself."

Panic flared through Kyu. "Please, no, I can't. I can't do it."

"Kyu, turn around." Her tone made it clear this wasn't a request. "If you do not, you will forever be a prisoner of your life. It will be as if you were still in that timeless place, unable to grow and develop… unable to *be*. You will suffer, and you will not be the only one who does so."

Kyu, his heart galloping, clenched his fists and spun to the mirror. He saw what he always saw, the body of a fit, well-muscled man with claws for hands and an impenetrable shadow where his face should be. He hated it. He wanted to punch the mirror and shatter it into a thousand impotent pieces.

"Listen to me." Her tone was softer. "Concentrate on the sound of my voice. Do not look away from the mirror. Do not hate what you see. It has no power over you. Now, take a deep breath and clear your mind. Release your emotions. Make yourself a blank slate."

Kyu was frightened, but he did as the Empress told him. It took several minutes for him to find a measure of calmness and stillness of mind. Beside him, Aest watched the proceedings quietly.

"Good. Now imagine you are a bud pushing its way through the earth, catching the rays of the morning sun."

Kyu did so and immediately felt the internal buzz of his awareness flowing through his veins, dancing on every nerve ending.

"Feel the warmth of the sunlight. Feel it coax your petals to open. Allow it to do so, but open up slowly. Drink in the sunshine a bit at a time, and use the energy to blossom."

Kyu's entire psyche opened and emanated outward, encompassing everything. He looked around in awe, seeing everything for what it was, seeing the building blocks of molecules everywhere, ready to be shaped to his desires. There was no deception, nothing hidden. He looked at Aest and his awareness asked to bond with the neurons within the animal's brain and nerve center in the knob. Aest shivered, but gave him permission to do so. Kyu saw the world as Aest did, as concepts realized and dealt with that did not rely on the ordinary visual senses of other creatures.

"Return your attention to the mirror, Kyu."

I still can't get beyond that. Despite his newer, powerful awareness, the reflection remained out of reach.

"Raise your hands."

Kyu did so, the claws hard and ugly.

"Concentrate on them. See how they are made."

Kyu saw the cells that made up his claws, alien flesh that did not belong to this world, melded unevenly with the natural, human cells of his wrists.

"Change them. Make your hands human."

Kyu concentrated on the makeup of the human and non-human cells, saw the difference, and began to alter the non-human cells. The process got easier as he went along, but there were millions of individual cells, and doing them one at a time would take forever.

"Do not focus on limitations," the Empress said. "Use your awareness to will what you wish into being. Everything will take care of itself."

Kyu blanked his mind and started over. He released his awareness into his hands, infused with his desire that they become human. The claws and thick skin disappeared. He looked down on two large, powerful, but decidedly human hands. He looked at the Empress in amazement.

She smiled brilliantly. "Excellent, Kyu. Now, let's remove that shadow."

Kyu looked at the mirror. Apprehension chilled his blood. He was not sure he wanted to do this.

The Empress did not give him time to think about it. "Focus your awareness on the shadow and let it know you no longer require it."

Let it know? Kyu looked away from the mirror and concentrated. He sent his awareness into the shadow to remove it and was shocked when he felt resistance. He eased back and studied the shadow. It pulsed with life and had a measure of sentience.

"It is a low-level life form from Dis that is able to exist here," the Empress said. "Your mother put it in place. You have command over it, but even with that, if you try to force it away, it will resist. You need to inform it of your desire, and it will go of its own accord."

Kyu tried again. He approached the shadow carefully and asked it to leave. Nothing happened. Kyu felt no change.

"The mirror, Kyu."

Kyu looked. The shadow was gone. In its place was the face of Harra Ardrassis.

Kyu was lightheaded as he looked at the strong, sharp planes of the face, the honey skin and almond-shaped eyes, in the reflection. It had to be some sort of trick. The image looking back at him did not resemble the Unifier; it was the Unifier, down to the last detail.

Kyu looked at the Empress, unable to speak. This was too cruel. If the face had been hideous, like he had long thought, at least it would have been his own, but this? This was someone else's face. With the shadow gone, and wearing his father's face, Kyu had no identity to call his own. For the first time Kyu could remember, tears ran down his face. "Why?"

The Empress held Kyu's face with both hands. "It is the inherent nature of those born to succubi to bear the faces of their fathers – one of the countless twisted effects of Dis. Your mother put the shadow in place because she didn't want to reveal your nature too quickly. Her plan was to hide you away while she slowly drove your father to madness and death. She believed she had enough control over him that he would acquiesce to her schemes. She thought she had broken him when she had coerced him into killing me. In time, she was going to replace him with you, and use you to serve up the rest of this world to the Diaboli Domini, but there was still a small reservoir of strength in Harra, which he used to banish her after you were born. Once he did that, and I had taken you away, the strength was gone; he perished."

The Empress looked away as tears ran down her face. "Watching my beloved brother deteriorate and die in misery was awful, but I saw what was to come and knew it was necessary. If he had lived, he would have become a true tyrant. Despite his honorable intentions, the amount of power centered in his hands was already shutting him off from others. The system of government he envisioned would have become distorted, with him and his heirs the monarchy ruling over all. I had to let him go."

The Empress fell silent. Kyu kept looking at the mirror, seeing a man that, as far as he was concerned, was not him.

Finally he looked away and turned to Aest. "Do I seem any different to you?" Kyu held out his new human hands for Aest to sniff. He bent so Aest could sniff his face.

Aest shook his head and barked softly. *I perceive no difference. To me, you are as you have always been.*

Kyu felt no surprise at the direct communication he now shared with Aest. He turned to the Empress, who stared into the distance.

"So, if I understand correctly, you put me away in a timeless reality for a thousand years. Now I am here, no longer an infant. Why now?"

"Because the time has come for you to be here." The Empress didn't look at him. "This world is speeding exponentially toward a crux that will determine how it exists, and you have a major part to play."

Haena faced Kyu. "When I brought you back, I knew I couldn't raise you. Your character would have been compromised. You had to learn hard lessons and make hard decisions on your own, based on nothing except your own concepts of right and wrong. I had to see just how much the certain alienation and solitude your features forced upon you affected both your Disian and human attributes. I had to see which half would become the dominant one. I must admit, after you killed your foster parents and became a natural at arena fighting, I thought your mother's influence would win out, but as you got older, you seemed to embrace the killing less. You hungered for more human interactions, like companionship. Though you were friends with Eulos Baak, you felt the need for a deeper emotional connection, and you found one." The Empess gestured toward Aest.

"As I said earlier, Aest is a very special creature. In fact, he is the last of his kind. In my brother's time, his species were known as raveners, a more intelligent, and vicious, cousin of dogs and wolves. They ran in packs and were excellent hunters. They had always been the bane of humans, especially after herd animals were domesticated. This provided the raveners with an easy food supply. Over centuries, humans hunted them down to what was thought to be extinction two hundred years ago, but small packs hid themselves away. Unfortunately, that was not enough, and over time they died out. The last mating pair was Aest's parents."

Kyu looked at his friend, the only one of his kind in the world, just like himself. He turned back to the Empress. "So what is it you expect me to do? What is this major part you say I am to play? Maybe I do have abilities that others don't, but I don't see them countering the Disian Curtain, if that's what you had in mind. I wouldn't know where to begin. As you said, I'm an arena fighter. I don't know much else."

"But you do, Kyu. You've discovered a lot tonight. For now, it is enough. You need to think about what you've seen and learned. You need to practice your awareness. Change your face and hands back and forth until you learn to do it with barely a thought. Practice spirit traveling, but make sure you stay in this reality for now. There are an infinite number of realities, many of them dangerous, some impossible to leave once you enter, unless you are very experienced. You are not. Most important of all, do some internal traveling. Discover all you can about yourself, and feel what your true bond is to this world. Find out what you really want and hold on to that inner truth."

Kyu shook his head. He fought off a moment of panic, nearly overwhelmed with the life-changing knowledge he now had. It was too much. He couldn't comprehend it.

He looked into the mirror at Harra Ardrassis. Kyu willed it, and the shadow returned, obliterating the Unifier's features. He lifted his hands and claws sprouted from his fingers. Kyu felt better, but knew this changed nothing. He had to come to grips with who and what he was, or the newfound knowledge would weaken and ultimately destroy him. He had fought for his place in this world. Now, even though his place was not quite what he had thought, he would continue to fight. That was the common denominator, and nobody fought better than him.

The Empress, seeing the nascent acceptance, nodded her head. "Our time here for tonight is almost through, but there is one last thing you need to know. Asrath has returned to this world, and if she hasn't done so already, she will seek you out."

"I thought you said my fa—, Harra Ardrassis banished her to Dis." Kyu was shocked, not altogether pleasantly, that he was already refering to the Unifier as his father.

"He did. As I told you, Asrath was able to steal into this world by invading one of Harra's dreams as he slept and manipulating it into an erotic one. However, I also said there was a second way for a succubus to return to this world. For Asrath, that way is you."

Kyu was confused. He hadn't had any erotic dreams lately, at least none that he remembered. "How do I provide her a way back?"

"You are of her, half of you a physical manifestation of her essence. Once I brought you back into this world, I opened the door wide for her, as well. She wasted no time; she quickly adopted a new physical identity and blocked every effort I made to track her. Asrath is here, there is no doubt. I don't know in what physical form, but her vanity will ensure it is an extremely attractive one, exuding sexuality that few will be able to resist. Her top priority is you."

Kyu felt a chill as dreadful comprehension filled him. "Why am I her top priority?"

"She needs to mate with you. Your seed in her will create the Apollyon, a creature of immense power and malevolence – one that will unlock the Disian Curtain, open the way for the Diaboli Domini to rule this world, and provide them a base to invade other worlds. The Apollyon will be under her control. She intends to rise in the ranks of the Diaboli Domini. It would not surprise me if she vied for total control with the Son of the Morning, such is her ambition and hunger."

Kyu flew into panic. All the groupies that he'd had sex with over the last few years; could one of them have been Asrath? His mother?

"It would be fatal to think of Asrath as your mother, at least in human terms. True, she gave birth to you, but anything maternal ends there. This is an infernal creature that has no moral values; indeed, she is incapable of it. To her, you are merely a tool, to be used and discarded, just like your father. This is why I don't think you've had sexual relations with her yet, because if you had, her next step would be your death."

Kyu thought back on the image of Asrath, as Tana, that the Empress had shown him, how her eyes had emptied into a horrible nothingness when Haena had called out the creature by her true name. Kyu had seen this happen before. Nauseous and dizzy, Kyu had to sit on the bench.

"Syrra's balls, I know who she is." He was unaware of the coarse language he used in front of the Empress. "She's the Ormnian Regent, Fey Gherren." Kyu told the Empress about his unexpected encounter with the Regent, and the shocking sexual moves she had made on him. He told her how his awareness had given him the power to resist.

"Once I backed away, I felt a rage within her, something so powerful it scared me. At the time, I thought it was her wounded pride."

"Part of it was. You are the first to reject her. That must have shocked her. Plus, she sensed your awareness; she knows you inherited that from me. She now knows that you are more powerful than she thought. This cannot sit well with her. From now on, you must proceed with extreme caution. I assure you, this is not the last you've seen of Asrath."

"Now that you know who she is, can you banish her back?"

"No, I am powerless against her. The only threat to her in this world is you, Kyu. Like your father, you have a physical connection with her. As you were the portal that allowed her to return, you are the only one who can banish her back to Dis."

"Then all I have to do is return to Ormnia, walk up to her, and banish her?"

The Empress shook her head. "It won't be anywhere near that easy. Asrath is undoubtedly working on another plan to keep her power here. She knew I would reach out to you and reveal everything. Physically, she won't let you near her, unless she has something solid in place to defy her banishment."

"Will she try to kill me, even though we didn't have sex? I was poisoned in my last arena match. Was Fey Gherren behind it?"

"No, for a number of reasons. Asrath is a complex creature; I think she feels she can still twist this, and you, to her advantage. She is not done with you. If she had wanted you dead, she would have made sure of it. She knows that, with your Disian heritage and awareness, poison is a poor weapon against you. Your body is too strong to succumb to it. No, whoever decided to poison you had more, shall we say, secular motives in mind."

Just fucking great. Kyu was used to people trying to kill him within the arena; you saw them coming and knew exactly what they intended to do, but outside the arena, between a creature of Dis and unscrupulous humans, no rules applied.

Something warm and wet slobbered against Kyu's hand. *You have me. Don't forget that.*

Kyu smiled at his friend. "I can't thank you enough for that."

Two pounds of rare steak might be a good start.

Kyu laughed. The weight of overwhelming emotions sloughed off him in the catharsis of the moment. "You've got it, buddy."

"One last thing before you go: Your sword – the one with the red blade… you already know how different it is from other weapons. With your blood in it, it is a physical manifest-tation of you. In a very real way, it is a part of you. It is a staca, a 'familiar', if you will. It exists as you do, and will always be within your reach. No one can ever take it away from you or destroy it, unless you are destroyed first. As long as you draw breath, the sword will be there when you need it, no matter the physical distance between you."

"Are you saying my sword is alive?"

"In a sense, but its life is dependent upon your own. It will never shatter or break while you live, and it can never be lost. All you need do is call for it, and it will be there."

Kyu remembered his last match in Ormnia, when it seemed his sword was out of reach. His need called for it. The next thing he knew, the blade was buried deep within Havla Cort.

"Call for it now, Kyu. Allow your awareness to bloom; call your staca to you."

With just a wish for it to happen, awareness washed through Kyu. He held out his hand and imagined the sword in his grip.

The sudden weight took him by surprise, but he held on and raised the red blade to his face. Within the steel, the blood pumped in rhythm to his heart. Warmth from the staca ran through his body. Kyu relaxed as a needed burst of assurance and confidence enveloped his troubled soul.

He looked to the Empress. "What happens now?"

"Now you go back. Your life has changed this night, and even if you decide to remain an arena fighter named Kyu, The Unknown, you know that will not be the direction your life will take forever. We will talk again, nephew. For now, you need time to think and make some decisions. You need to accept."

The Empress was right. Time to think was the most important thing.

"You are an Ardrassis. You come from strength. All I've done is illuminate the road you've already traveled, and a bit of what's in front of you. You need to remember that all your choices are your own to make. No one, not me, not Asrath, not anybody, can force you to make a choice you do not wish to make. This is both a freedom and a burden. I have faith in you, Kyu, but more importantly, you must have faith in yourself."

Kyu looked into the mirror and the shadow disappeared. Harra Ardrassis looked at him with a mixture of foreboding and determination. *No, not Harra Ardrassis. Kyu. Kyu Ardrassis.*

"Close your eyes."

Kyu obeyed. A subtle shifting happened just beyond the range of his senses.

Whenever you have need of me, just call.

Kyu opened his eyes. He was sitting in his rental car at the end of the road. The sun peeked over the eastern horizon, bathing Empress' Mountain in shades of ochre and pink. Aest sat on the seat next to him.

In Kyu's lap was the red sword.

CHAPTER 13

Once they returned to their hotel, Kyu had a notion. He would go out and explore Talmount, not as Kyu, The Unknown, but as a man no one would recognize.

He looked at his reflection in the bathroom mirror. The fact of actually seeing his face was still unreal to him, although he found himself beginning to accept it. Intellectually, he knew this had been his face all along. As time went on, he would see less of Harra Ardrassis and more of himself.

He looked at his human hands. Kyu was used to the razor-sharp claws and the unconscious, instinctive care he exercised in their everyday use. Now that his fingers could be 'normal', he had to exercise a different kind of care. The human hands looked more prone to injury. No matter.

After a shave and shower Kyu put on a decent suit and combed his hair.

"Ready, Aest?"

Aest barked. *I'm ready for that two-pound steak you promised me.*

"You're not a cheap date, are you? All right, let's go."

Kyu and Aest walked out of the hotel, and for the first time in his life Kyu was totally anonymous. Although Aest got a lot of curious looks, no one gave Kyu a second glance.

He found a promising restaurant two blocks from the hotel, but was rebuffed when the staff wouldn't allow Aest in with him. Kyu had no doubt Aest would have been allowed inside if he had come as Kyu, The Unknown.

They wandered until they found an outdoor café where Kyu could sit with Aest under a canopied table. Unfortunately they served no two-pound slices of steak, but they did serve smaller sizes, along with bacon. Aest settled for that and chewed happily as Kyu had some eggs and coffee.

Aest finished his breakfast in half the time it took for Kyu to finish his. He ordered another coffee then settled in his chair as Aest relaxed at his side. Kyu closed his eyes and enjoyed the cool mountain breeze blowing across his brow.

"What is this fabulous creature? It's so fascinating!"

Kyu's eyes opened. He turned to the voice. A young woman with short dark hair squatted by Aest, petting him as if he were an ordinary dog. To Kyu's immense surprise, Aest loved every minute of it, licking the stranger's hands with his long, wet tongue. His knob vibrated with satisfaction. This wasn't like Aest. He had a habit of tearing off and eating hands, not licking them like a happy puppy.

The girl looked at Kyu. She was very pretty, with soft brown eyes and a smattering of freckles across the bridge of her nose. Kyu guessed her age to be twenty, twenty-one tops. Her smile was infectious, and Kyu couldn't help but smile back.

Her dark hair was thick, but cut very short. Kyu wondered if she was an acolyte at a local Sysseran temple.

"Is this animal yours, sir?"

"I wouldn't say he belongs to me," Kyu answered. "We're more like friends."

"That's wonderful! What's his name?"

"Aest. I'm told he's a ravener, an animal that's… very rare."

The girl smiled and petted Aest's furless body. "That's fascinating! How did you meet him?"

"Honestly, he just showed up at my home one day. We've been together ever since."

The girl looked up with a beaming smile, and Kyu's heart beat a little faster. "I think it's great you treat him like a friend instead of a pet."

"You do?" Kyu's capacity for speech seemed to have been reduced to monosyllables.

"Absolutely! It shows what kind of a person you are. Oh, please excuse my manners! I just keep babbling along like a nut. My name is Ocelot." She stuck out a slim, fine-boned hand.

Kyu took the hand in his own, normal one. "It's nice to meet you. I…" Now what? A lie? Kyu didn't want to lie. However… "I am Kyu Ardrassis."

Ocelot looked at Kyu in wonder. "Your family name is Ardrassis? I didn't think there were any left."

Kyu kept quiet. Silence wasn't a lie, was it?

"And you have the same first name of someone famous," Ocelot continued. "You know, Kyu, The Unknown, the arena fighter from Cyphus, where I live. I'm sure you've heard of him. I always thought 'Kyu' was a unique name. Apparently I was wrong."

Kyu shifted the topic. "You're from Cyphus? So am I." He indicated an empty chair at the table. "Would you like to join us for coffee? It's quite good."

"Of course. Thank you!" Ocelot pulled the chair next to Aest so she could continue petting him. Aest soaked in the attention with pleasure. Kyu was amused and a bit jealous. He signaled for the waiter, who took Ocelot's order.

She looked at him with those eyes he was finding so attractive. "So you're from Cyphus as well? Imagine that! Have you been there all your life?"

"As far as I know. I'd have to check the records at the orphanage to be sure."

Ocelot's eyes widened and her hand flew to cover Kyu's own. The contact was unexpected, but very agreeable. Kyu flushed with warmth.

"You're an orphan? So am I! You must have been adopted by a family named Ardrassis. Lucky you!"

Her eyes fell. "I was never adopted. I have no family name. After I reached my majority age two years ago, I had to leave the orphanage. I had nowhere to go. After bouncing around for a bit, doing pay-nothing jobs and staying in absolutely horrible places, I became an acolyte at the Sysseran temple in Cyphus. I don't get paid to be an acolyte. They feed me and give me a clean place to stay, but I don't want to be there forever…" Ocelot trailed off, her face a mask of resignation.

Kyu cleared his throat. "Are you happy at the temple?"

Ocelot remained silent as the waiter brought her coffee. Once he had left she took a sip. "Don't get me wrong, I'm not complaining. I have my duties to perform, but they're not that bad. I even get to travel. The reason I'm in Talmount is because the priestess at the temple here asked Enna Racyne, the Cyphus priestess, to send a temporary replacement for an acolyte who needed to take some time off. However, that person has come back, and I'm returning to Cyphus tomorrow. It's just… when you take the vows to become an acolyte, the expectation is that you'll dedicate your life to the goddess."

Ocelot looked at Kyu. Behind the soft eyes Kyu saw a hint of steel. "I don't want to stay there my whole life. I like to think I can do something more."

She still had her hand over Kyu's. It was an innocent, unconscious gesture, but unfamiliar feelings stirred within him. Kyu tried to tell himself he was being ridiculous. How long had he known this girl? All of ten minutes? So why was his mouth so dry?

Ocelot shook off her gloom and smiled. "Now you know my story. What do you do for a living, Mr. Ardrassis?"

Kyu had known the question was coming. Now that it was here, dread clenched his heart. What would he say? If he told the truth, Ocelot would probably walk away in horror. He had a pretty good idea that Ocelot was no fan of arena fighting.

No matter. Kyu loathed lying, and he would not do so now.

"You mentioned that famous arena fighter who shares my name. There's a reason for that. It's because that's who I am. I know my face isn't in shadow, and my hands aren't claws, but I am Kyu, The Unknown."

Ocelot stared blankly at him and removed her hand. Her smile faded. "No, you're not."

He felt awful. "It's the truth. I'm Kyu, The Unknown."

Ocelot's face tightened with bemusement. "Why would you say such a thing? Why would you lie like that?" She shook her head and stood from the chair. "I'm sorry. I made a mistake bothering you. I'll go."

"Wait!" Kyu felt awful at what he was about to do. "I can prove I am who I say." Kyu willed it, and his human hands morphed into claws. His face disappeared behind the shadow.

Ocelot gasped and stumbled away from the table, nearly knocking over her chair. Her mouth worked, but no words came. She turned and fled.

Kyu quickly restored his features. Crushed by self-loathing and despair, his throat tightened and tears he could not stop flowed from his eyes. He wanted to scream at the gods and demand to know why he had been placed in this body. Why would he never be able to enjoy simple human interaction? Would he forever be considered a dangerous freak whose sole purpose was to kill for the amusement of others?

Aest looked up at him. *What happened? Why is she gone?*

"Because I'm what I am," Kyu said. "A creature who has no business being here."

Kyu wiped his tears away and cauterized the gaping wound within. He shut away his self-pity and sought to find some semblance of emotional equilibrium. He didn't have time for these ridiculous feelings over a chance encounter with a pretty girl.

"Let's go, Aest. I've had enough of Talmount."

CHAPTER 14

Erenia stalked down the central aisle of the temple and tore off her robe. She was gaining in the polls, peaking as the election drew closer, but of course this wasn't enough for Enna.

I'm doing everything I can, Enna. I've stumped in every major city and town in Talgourge. I'm doing interviews on television. Our campaign workers have plastered my image everywhere. What more can I do?

You cannot stop, Erenia! You cannot rest. Relaxing at home is not an option for you. In fact, the more you distance yourself from your home, the better off you'll be.

I don't want to hear another word about that! Leave it alone! I am going home to rest. I need my own bed for a couple of days.

Have you no idea of the importance of this, of being seen and heard every day? You better believe your rivals do. You're going to give them the upper hand just because you want your own bed? Toughen up, Erenia! You'll never survive in the political world if you remain this soft.

Erenia had finally stormed out of Enna's office. She briefly considered going back and telling the priestess that she was dropping out of the race, but they both would see the lie of that. Erenia was now too vested in the race to quit. She didn't want to quit. She wanted to win that Council seat. Enna, however, was obsessed with it. Ever since Erenia had taken up Enna's candidacy, the priestess had changed. Gone was the dear friend Erenia once knew. In her place was a demanding, insatiable woman who felt she had not just the right, but the sacred duty to control Erenia's life.

Erenia was having none of it. She knew she needed the temple's support if she wanted to win, but she would not make herself a puppet to it. She would follow her own conscience.

The other acolytes studiously ignored her as she stormed to the exit. Erenia was relieved Norn was on police duty and not here; he would insist on his say, leading to an argument that Erenia did not need.

One acolyte sat alone in the rearmost pew, her cowl hanging over her face. Erenia paused and stared at her, wondering why she wasn't working. The acolyte lifted her head. It was the new girl, Ocelot. Normally bright and vivacious, Ocelot stared at the image of Syssera behind the altar, as if hoping for answers.

Erenia's anger bled away and she sat next to Ocelot. She liked the girl and hoped she could help with whatever was troubling her.

Ocelot, breathing silently, continued to stare straight ahead.

Erenia took her hand. "What's wrong, dear?"

Ocelot stiffened but then relaxed. She didn't take her eyes off Syssera's image. "It's nothing. Just something that happened in Talmount."

Erenia knew that Ocelot had been sent to Talmount for a short time. "What is it? Did someone mistreat you at the temple?"

"No, the temple was fine. It was afterward, during my last day. I… met someone."

Ah. Erenia should have guessed. This pretty young girl had met a boy, and apparently things had not turned out so well.

"And this person, whom you liked, said or did something that displeased you."

Ocelot shifted in the pew. "Well, kind of. Actually, he was only being honest with me. He told me something about himself I didn't believe, but then he proved he was telling the truth. When he did, I ran."

"What did he say?"

"He told me he was an arena fighter."

Erenia sat back and put an arm around the girl. "It sounds to me like you got out of a bad situation. An arena fighter is no one you want to be involved with. My husband used to be one. They kill for a living, and you never know if their next match will be their last. It's a terrible burden for someone who cares about them. Trust me, Ocelot, you were better off running. Try to put it out of your mind, dear."

Ocelot looked at Erenia. "But he went out of his way to tell me the truth about himself. He did so knowing I would probably react badly, which I did. He could have lied, and I never would have known, at least until much later. Erenia, so many other people have lied to me all my life. The administrators at the orphanage lied to me all the time, first about potential parents looking to adopt me, and then, at the end, they lied about helping me find employment and an inexpensive place to live once I aged out of the orphanage. For as long as I remember, I have been lied to. Now I finally meet someone who tells me the truth, and what do I do? I run away." Tears ran down Ocelot's cheeks.

Erenia hugged her. "It doesn't matter. You still made the right decision. You don't want to get involved in that world. There are plenty of other sincere men out there, with practical, decent jobs."

Ocelot said nothing.

Erenia stood. "I have to get going, but I'm always here to talk with whenever you need it, okay?"

Ocelot wiped her eyes. "Thank you."

#

After Erenia left, Ocelot stared at the tapestry hanging behind the altar. Syssera's brown arms rose above thick stalks of wheat and corn, as if to welcome anyone who sought her solace.

Mother, why am I so conflicted?

The image had no reply, but then, it didn't need to. Ocelot knew why.

Her reaction to Kyu's transformation at that café in Talmount had taken her by surprise. She hadn't meant to run away, but the emotions had been sudden, uncontrollable. Afterward, it took some time for Ocelot to admit this was her new norm. It was going to be harder than she thought, but it had to be seen through. Too much was at stake.

CHAPTER 15

"We need to talk."

Kyu was not used to Yuv sounding nervous. "Well, I'm talking to you now on the phone. So talk."

"Not on the phone – in my office. How soon can you get here?"

Kyu and Aest had arrived back in Cyphus two days ago. With his mind whirling over everything the Empress had told him, and still bitter over his encounter with Ocelot, Kyu had put the shadow and claws back in place. He wanted only to be Kyu, The Unknown. It was foolish to pretend otherwise.

"What's going on, Yuv?"

"Just get down here, all right? Don't waste time walking. Call for a taxi."

"A taxi? Are you going to reimburse me for the fare?"

"Yeah, fine. Just get down here." Yuv hung up.

For Yuv to agree to reimburse Kyu without an argument meant something serious was happening. He wondered if it had to do with the mess in Ormnia.

Kyu decided to leave Aest at home because of the creature's hostility toward Yuv. He could summon his red sword if there was any trouble. Plus, he would be wearing his gun underneath his jacket.

He called for the taxi. Fifteen minutes later he arrived at Yuv's office.

Yuv's receptionist, Shanna, looked up as Kyu walked in. Her eyes were wide with fear. Two men were in the reception room. They were big and well-dressed, and they watched Kyu with steady, fearless gazes. Kyu now regretted leaving Aest at home. There was no doubt in his mind that these men were Korl underlings.

"Go right in, Kyu," Shanna stammered.

Kyu opened the door to Yuv's office. One of the men in the reception area got up and followed him. He gently but firmly pushed Kyu against the wall and searched him, finding the gun. Kyu's newfound ability to call his sword to him was now very important.

Yuv had his bulk squeezed into one of the visitor's chairs. Behind his desk, in the opulent, leather chair he usually occupied, sat a man with a smaller than average build. He had blonde, almost white, hair and eyes the color of ice, which contrasted sharply with his dark olive skin.

Kyu recognized him immediately. He had seen the man's face on the news often enough, leaving a courthouse, surrounded by a battery of expensive lawyers. He usually had a big smile on his face for the media after defeating yet another murder or racketeering charge. Born of an Ormnian father and an Urigish mother, at thirty-six years of age he was the youngest undisputed head of the Korl in that organization's history. He was Padanor Syche.

Yuv's profuse sweating made him appear to be melting. He was in very deep shit; now he had gotten Kyu involved.

"Kyu, The Unknown." Padanor Syche's voice was deep and sonorous. He hadn't gotten to the top of the Korl just through murders. He was charismatic and intelligent, with a compelling voice that begged to be listened to. "I am very glad to finally meet you. Please, have a seat." The Korl leader gestured to the other visitor's chair.

Kyu's pride told him to remain standing, but he took the seat. Now was not the time to see who had the bigger dick.

Syche smiled. "Doubtless you are aware of what is going on in Ormnia. This is a very bad situation, for all of us. If they ban arena fighting, we will lose significant revenue, and your very livelihood will be threatened."

Syche paused. Kyu said nothing to fill the silence.

Syche continued. "On the night before your match in Erat, you were summoned to a meeting with the comely Regent of Ormnia, Fey Gherren."

Yuv looked at Kyu in surprise. Kyu realized just how much of a presence the Korl had, not just in the world of arena fighting but in government as well. More than a century after the bloody war had driven them out of these posts of power, they had done much to infiltrate back in.

"She wanted you to join her cause, didn't she? I bet she offered you some interesting… benefits, but you turned her down. Good for you, Kyu. I applaud you. The following night was your match with Havla Cort. How did that match end?"

Syche waited, and Kyu finally answered. "I killed Havla Cort."

Padanor Syche chuckled. "Yes, you did. You'll have to tell me sometime how you accomplished that trick with a sword that was out of reach – quite impressive.

"Of course, that's not the answer I'm looking for, and you know it. Before you killed him, he poisoned you. Havla Cort flagrantly broke one of the few rules of the arena. He knew he would not be punished for this act. He had the patronage of someone in a very high place, and I, for one, cannot think of a higher station in Ormnia than the Regent. Can you?"

The hypnotic voice was persuasive, but after his visit with the Empress, Kyu knew this theory was incorrect.

"What if I told you that you can right this act of cowardice?" Syche leaned forward, bringing the full power of his personality to bear. "What if I gave you the means, and what if, after I helped you to this satisfaction, I made you a million marks richer? Your livelihood would be secured, and you would have plenty of money for the finer things in life."

Kyu was never happier for the shadow that hid his face. Padanor Syche could not see his contempt. "And how would all of this be done?"

Syche sat back, a feral grin on his face. "Contact her office. Request another meeting, and hint that you have had a change of heart because of Havla Cort's treachery. I'm certain she will agree to meet with you. You are too much of a prize for her not to." The Korl chieftain produced a small, velvet box. He opened it to reveal a jewel-encrusted brooch. "When you meet her, give her this, as a token of your newfound affection. Whatever you do, don't touch the brooch yourself. It's coated with a powerful poison. I know you survived your last brush with poison, but why take chances? As soon as Gherren touches the brooch, the poison will seep through her skin. It will not kill her right away. The poison works slowly, taking a full day to overpower its victim. It also dissolves quickly, leaving no trace for a medical examiner to find. By then, you will be long gone. People will be suspicious at first, but nothing will ever be proven. Eventually everyone will forget. Life will go on, with us continuing to make money, and you doing what you do best, all the while sitting on a neat bundle of money. Plus, you get payback." Padanor Syche closed the box and slid it across the desk toward Kyu.

Kyu glanced at Yuv, who begged him with his eyes to take the box. What was his stake in all of this? Syche obviously held something over Yuv, something that would be settled if Kyu took the box.

Kyu had to keep from shaking his head at the folly of what Padanor Syche wanted from him. The Korl leader had no idea Fey Gherren was an Infernal named Asrath, a creature from beyond the Disian Curtain, and Kyu was not about to clue him in.

But that wasn't why Kyu knew he would have no part of this. He looked at Syche, who smiled expectantly. The killing rage built within him. He wanted his red sword so he could take this self-assured fucker's head off, but that would bring trouble he was not sure he could handle.

He pushed himself from the chair and stood. "I'm an arena fighter, not an assassin. Find someone else to do it."

"Kyu, please!" Yuv spoke for the first time. "This is not the time to decide you have morals. You have to do this!"

Kyu continued to stare at Padanor Syche, an iciness settling over him. The Korl leader's smile was gone, and his pale gaze held no pity.

"No, Yuv, I don't have to do anything. I don't know what trouble you're in, but I'm not becoming a puppet of the Korl just to get you out of your own shit. Mr. Syche, you have my answer."

Padanor Syche sneered. "Such lofty principles from one such as yourself; what makes you so different from me? We are both killers. We have both taken the lives of innocent people. Don't deny this. You slaughtered your own foster family without threat or provocation, so don't take the high road with me, Kyu, The Unknown, not when your belly is dragging through the slime. You have refused me. That is your choice. There is nothing more to discuss. Leave now."

The pool of fury churned and bubbled upward at the abrupt dismissal. Kyu turned to the Korl guard who had disarmed him and held out his claw for the gun.

The guard glared at Kyu, making no move to return the gun to him. Kyu's arm tensed for the strike that would open the man's throat.

"Give him his gun," Syche ordered. "He'll not use it here. That would be the action of an assassin, and we all know that the upright Kyu, The Unknown is not an assassin."

The Korl guard was unhappy, but he gave Kyu his gun.

Without looking back, Kyu left the office and the building. He walked home, the exercise needed to settle the fury within. Aest barked in relief when Kyu returned.

"I made a powerful enemy today," Kyu told him. "I seem to be doing that a lot lately. We're going to have to be very careful."

Aest barked: *Fuck 'em. We'll take them as they come.*

For the first time since Yuv's call, Kyu smiled. "Thanks for being here, Aest. You don't know how much I appreciate it."

Another bark: *Stop getting mushy on me. I'm hungry. Let's eat!*

CHAPTER 16

It sucked getting old. Eulos was nearing fifty, and his body knew it. After a day of training young, clueless idiots at the Combat Academy, his muscles, back, and knees were letting him know why he had retired in the first place. He would have a pounding headache before long.

Eulos was also worried about Kyu. The open attempt to poison his friend during the match in Erat had shocked and infuriated him. To make it worse, it appeared the Arena Commission was uninterested in investigating the matter. In their eyes, it was the doing of Havla Cort. Since Kyu, The Unknown had killed Cort and recovered from the poisoning, they were burying the matter. He didn't buy that for a second. The Reformists were trying to discredit arena fighting, and Eulos knew they wouldn't hesitate to stoop to this level of treachery if they thought it would achieve their end.

He had called Kyu when his friend returned home. Kyu had assured Eulos that he was all right, but he also sounded distracted and politely cut Eulos' call short. Kyu was in some sort of trouble. It bothered Eulos that his friend would not confide in him what was going on, but he didn't know what to do about it.

He really needed a beer – several beers, actually, but he was trying to be good… for Erenia's sake.

The house was empty. Erenia had come home for two days then had taken off again on her campaign tour. Despite posting some decent numbers in the recent polls, Eulos knew that just the fact he was Erenia's husband was holding her back. Eulos could not change what he had been or done, but he could try to change how he conducted himself now. This meant no more visits to the Bloodbath Pub, no more drunken brawls, no more embarrassing the woman he loved, despite her fervent association with a political party he loathed.

Eulos looked at the empty bed and wondered if Erenia still felt any love for him. True, she hadn't left him, or filed for divorce, but when was the last time she told him she loved him? When was the last time they made love on that bed? His throat tightened. Eulos growled in anger at his own self-pity. It was not so easily vanquished.

What would happen if Erenia actually won, and became a Councilor? The impact on their lives would be tremendous. Would their marriage survive? Syrra's balls, he *really* needed a beer. Instead, Eulos poured himself a hot bath and soaked his aching muscles. Afterward he popped a handful of painkillers and went to bed.

He had nearly drifted off when the bedroom door opened. Instantly awake, Eulos went for the gun he kept in his nightstand.

"Relax, Eulos, it's just me."

Erenia? It couldn't be. She was off in central Talgourge somewhere. Wasn't she?

Still holding the gun, Eulos turned on the light. Erenia stood there, looking down at him. Eulos exhaled and put the gun back in the nightstand.

"Syrra's balls, Erenia, I nearly shot you. What are you doing home? You told me you wouldn't be back for several more days."

"I missed you, Eulos. I didn't realize until tonight just how much." She sat on the edge of the bed, her short skirt riding above her knees.

Damn, she looked great. Eulos looked at her face. Even with her hair cut short, she was still beautiful. Erenia looked at him with softness, for once.

She laid her hand on his, which surprised him. "I've been so busy running for Council that I've forgotten what's really important. We're important, Eulos. I don't want to gain that seat just to lose you." She leaned forward and kissed him on the lips. "I want it just to be us tonight. I want us to love one another again."

Eulos reached out and embraced his wife. Could this really be happening? He was shocked to find himself near tears. Could they really be a couple again, as madly in love as they had been when they first got married?

"Oh, Erenia…" How could he explain these feelings?

"Shh," she hushed softly. "No words. Let's just make love like we used to do."

She removed her clothes. Eulos had to remind himself to breathe as he gazed at her nakedness. She lifted the sheet that covered his hard, nude body. Her legs, silky and soft, straddled his midsection. Her hand ran down his muscled body and cupped his swollen genitals. Eulos thought he would explode.

Erenia guided his penis deep within the velvety warmth of her vagina. She rocked back and forth, her eyes closed in ecstasy. Every nerve in Eulos' body flared with white-hot pleasure which built and raced to his groin.

His climax was tumultuous. Wave after wave of release flooded from him and into Erenia. His back arched and his body sang in rapture as Erenia expertly adjusted her position on top of him to keep the connection unbroken.

The sexual crest finally, regrettably, ended. Eulos felt as if his very existence had been taken away. A deep lethargy settled over him. He looked up at his wife, who still straddled him.

Erenia's eyes became pits of annhiliation. Her short hair grew out dark and long, and her skin turned an unnatural white.

Eulos struggled to fight but his limbs wouldn't respond. Nor did he feel any shock at what was happening.

Fatigue numbed everything, including his mind. He couldn't stop his eyes from closing.

Erenia, or whatever this thing was, laughed with glee.

"That's right, Eulos." The voice came from a distance. "Go to sleep. Your seed will be my retribution against the one you call friend."

The creature on top of Eulos dissolved into nothingness, leaving behind the rancid odor of an old grave. Eulos could no longer resist the sleep that pulled at him and he tumbled into darkness.

CHAPTER 17

There was someone knocking at Kyu's door. The image on the security monitor showed a slight figure, robed and wearing a cowl that hid the face. This was not good. Kyu could see no weapons, but he knew better than to take that at face value.

"We've got a visitor, Aest."

Aest followed him to his arsenal. Kyu put on an armored vest and grabbed a shotgun, loading it with heavy, deadly slugs. He led Aest to one of the hidden exits then opened the door quickly and moved out, his head swiveling for threats. Aest was out immediately afterward, his knob vibrating and his long teeth bared.

They worked their way around to the main entrance. Kyu peered around a rock. The stranger was still standing there. If there was any backup, they were well hidden.

Aest's knob cleared the rock and vibrated, gauging the stranger. The beast lost all control. Yapping wildly, Aest bolted from the cover and ran full-bore toward the figure, who spun in surprise. Kyu was flabbergasted. This was a potentially lethal situation, and his companion was acting like a maniac. Knowing he had no choice, Kyu left the safety of the rock to cover his friend's advance, his shotgun pointed at the target while his eyes scanned the surrounding area. *What a fuck-up.*

The stranger bent down, arms extended. Aest jumped into the offered embrace, and his fat, wet tongue pushed through the cowl to the figure's face, which proceeded to get a good saliva bath. The stranger laughed. It was a woman. The cowl fell away. Kyu found himself pointing the shotgun straight at Ocelot's face.

Stunned, Kyu quickly lowered the weapon. His hands shook. His trigger finger had been a few pounds of pressure away from decapitating her. Ocelot laughed and played with Aest. She had no idea the shotgun had been trained on her.

"Yes, Aest, I missed you, too!" Ocelot's face glistened with saliva. She looked up as Kyu walked over and noticed the weapon. "Why the gun? Are you expecting an army?"

Kyu looked away and shook his head, trying to decide whether to laugh or curse. "Honestly, I was expecting an army."

Ocelot looked at him in confusion.

Kyu ignored the unspoken question. "Please excuse my bluntness, but what are you doing here?"

Aest backed away from Ocelot. His tail wagged furiously. Kyu had never seen him so happy around someone, not even him. Ocelot stood to face Kyu. Once again he was struck with the beauty of her soft, brown eyes.

"It was you in Talmount, wasn't it? You may not understand. I'm not sure I understand, but I had to come to see you as… this."

Kyu understood 'this' to mean as he usually was: Kyu, The Unknown, with the face-concealing shadow and claws for hands. He couldn't understand why.

Ocelot studied his tell-tale features. "When your hand changed at that café, I ran. I panicked, I admit it, but when I got back to Cyphus, I found I couldn't stop thinking about you. You knew that revealing who you really are would drive me away, but you did it anyway. You didn't lie or try to hide anything. I don't think you even considered lying."

She looked away. "I have no idea who my parents are, so it seems my very existence is something of a lie. The only life I know is the Sysseran temple.The only truths I know are work, food, a place to sleep, and this nifty robe." Ocelot held out her arms, her lips tight in a self-deprecating smile. "I don't have many of my own clothes, but I get to wear as many of these as I want. I shouldn't complain. The temple has treated me well, but I'd still like something different to wear." Ocelot paused, waiting for Kyu to respond.

"So…" He was at a loss for words. "So," he repeated, feeling increasingly foolish, especially while trying to have this conversation while holding a shotgun and wearing body armor. "Now that you're here and you've seen me, what now? You know who I am. You know I'm an arena fighter. You should also know that there are quite a few people, not just my opponents in the arena, who would like to see me dead, and you are a follower of Syssera, who supposedly abhors everything I do."

Ocelot stepped forward. Kyu saw something harden behind her eyes. "I may currently be an acolyte at the temple, but I follow nothing and nobody blindly. I am my own person, Kyu, the Unknown."

Kyu realized this woman had a deep well of fortitude and determination behind her slight, bubbly exterior. He had to admit it appealed to him.

"I know your reputation," Ocelot continued. "I know you are one of the best at a blood sport that I can't say I agree with, but I sense a lot of good in you. I don't think Aest would be by your side otherwise. You are skilled at what you do, but tell me: how much joy do you derive from taking another's life?"

Kyu opened his mouth, then closed it and looked away. How much joy did he feel from killing in the arena? Most of his kills were fueled by the rage that burned within;

rage he now suspected came from his mother's side. In the grip of that fury, he was exalted, he was unstoppable, and every victory was relished. When the match was over and the rage settled to a slow churn that was easily controlled, he felt…

Empty… alone… void of humanity in a cold, dark isolation, masked with booze and quick sex with anonymous groupies. Joy? When had he ever felt joy? Kyu looked at Aest. Yes, establishing their friendship had been joyous, but that was it. *That was it.*

Ocelot was silent, waiting for an answer. She did not flinch, nor would she allow him any denial.

Why? Why this? Why now? The shotgun dropped from Kyu's hand. Dark, smothering tendrils of despair wrapped around his soul.

Ocelot's hand reached up and pushed past the shadow that hid Kyu's face. Her palm cupped his cheek. To his astonishment, a single tear fell from his eye and onto her hand.

"No." Kyu felt beyond himself, watching events unfold. He couldn't possibly be standing there with this wondrous girl, having this impossible conversation.

Ocelot nodded. Her hand did not move away. "I don't know why we entered each other's lives, but I feel a need, in both you and me. Do you feel the need, Kyu Ardrassis?"

Kyu stood, not knowing what to say. A fissure opened within him. It hurt, and it scared him. It left him vulnerable. Ocelot's unrelenting presence demanded an answer. More than that, it demanded a decision.

"Yes." The fissure widened. What was he doing? His life was much too dangerous for one such as Ocelot. How could he be so selfish as to share any of it with this beautiful innocent? Yet, he needed her. Kyu felt this as keenly as hunger, as naturally as breathing.

He hated himself. With him, Ocelot's life would always be at risk, but he made no move to separate himself from her. The fissure, raw and molten, bled. It burned through him and made him shake.

Ocelot's voice came to him. "I feel your fear. Release it. Dispel the darkness that hides your wonderful soul."

Who are you? Kyu wanted to scream. *How can you know so much of what is within me?* He did not trust himself to speak. His throat was too constricted for words.

Kyu wept. He was so pathetic, so alone.

Ocelot took his face and forced him to look at her. Tears ran down her cheeks, yet she smiled. "You are the man I met," she whispered. "You are Kyu Ardrassis. Let him live." She embraced him.

The fissure burst open, releasing a scalding flood that Kyu had no power to stop. The shadow and claws disappeared. His arms wrapped around Ocelot and held her tight. They cried together, sharing and releasing the burdens they had carried for so long. Aest wisely kept his distance and waited them out. When it was over, Kyu knew he was still Kyu, but he felt lighter, free, as he had never felt free before.

Beneath this brief euphoria a stubborn weight clung to him, for the outside world was a malignancy perched to invade his life at any moment. Ocelot needed to know. She still might choose to walk away… *which would be better for her*, Kyu acknowledged with a rationality that tore his heart in half. "We need to talk. I have a lot to tell you. Please, come inside my home."

He made sure Ocelot heard the gravity in his voice, yet she still gave him a dazzling smile. At that moment, something clicked inside Kyu, a strange, scary, yet wonderful feeling.

"Why, yes, Mr. Ardrassis. I would be delighted to enter your home." She skipped to Aest who, sensing that everything was all right, jumped up and licked her face again. She laughed. Kyu watched as the two of them walked to his door. He wondered why his cheeks felt so tight then realized it was because he was grinning like an idiot.

#

Once inside, Kyu sat Ocelot down on the couch in the living room and settled himself at the other end. With a deep breath he began to speak.

Kyu left nothing out. He described the killings of his foster parents. He told Ocelot about the reservoir of rage within him that led to those killings and to his career in the arena. He shared how he had lived his life, his friendship with Eulos, the drinking and the groupies. She heard about his trip to Ormnia, and his attempted seduction by the Ormnian Regent, followed by his poisoning, his summons by the Empress, and his subsequent visit to Empress Mountain at the same time Ocelot was also in Talmount. Kyu told her everything about his newfound powers and his incredible family history, including who and what his mother really was and the fact that she was disguised as the Ormnian Regent. Finally he told her about his confrontation with Padanor Syche, and how he knew the Korl would make a move against him at some point in the future.

Ocelot did not interrupt.

"So there you have it," Kyu concluded. "This is who I am… an arena fighter. I cannot promise I'll quit; it would be empty. It's how I make my living. I can't think of anything else I would be good at, or that would bring in nearly the same money." Kyu swallowed hard. "I cannot ask you to stay with me, Ocelot. Your life would be in danger. You are undoubtedly better off leaving and forgetting about me." Kyu bowed his head, waiting for the affirmation of his words.

"Look at me, Kyu."

He looked up, his dark eyes meeting Ocelot's.

"If you can tell me, truthfully, that you want me to go, then I'll go. Do you want me to go, Kyu?"

"But what about the Korl and the—"

"I don't care about any of that!" Ocelot snapped. Kyu again saw a strength that rivaled the steel of his red sword. "I care about what you want. Do you want me to go, Kyu?"

Kyu wanted to tell her to go. Her life could very well depend on it. He opened his mouth. Nothing came out. Shame wracked him, and he tried again. He couldn't do it.

Ocelot was strangely satisfied. "That settles it. I'm staying. I'll hear no more talk about me leaving. Do you understand?"

Kyu was being nagged, just as Erenia always nagged Eulos, yet in this case, it felt good. He allowed himself a sly smile.

Once again, Ocelot showed an amazing ability to read his mind. "This Eulos that you are friends with – he is married to Erenia Baak, isn't he?"

"Yes. You should be aware that Erenia hates my guts."

"I know. I have heard her speak ill of you."

"Yet you, a Sysseran acolyte along with her, are now here with me. When Erenia finds out, you'll end up on her shit list as well."

Ocelot's anger rose once more. "Have you learned nothing about me? If the Korl and a creature from beyond the Curtain aren't enough to drive me off, what chance does Erenia's disapproval have? Honestly! Men!" Ocelot huffed then turned away.

Kyu couldn't help himself. He started to laugh.

Ocelot's eyes blazed. "And just what is so funny?"

Kyu laughed harder. He tried to answer, but couldn't catch a breath.

Ocelot stood, hands on hips. "Well?"

"Stop! Stop!" Kyu begged between gasps. "I can't take any more of this. I can't believe how beautiful you are."

The sentence stopped her cold. "What did you say?"

It stopped Kyu cold, as well. "I, uh, well…"

It was Ocelot's turn to smile. "I distinctly heard the word 'beautiful'. Why would you say such a thing?"

"Uh, well…" Kyu wanted to return his face to shadow. He knew it was turning red from embarrassment.

"Because," Ocelot answered for him, playfully slapping his muscular shoulder. "Not only are you decent, you're also nice. What a charming rogue you are."

Kyu's face felt like a beacon in the night. It was time to change the subject.

"How about I get out of this body armor and take you to eat somewhere? It'll be nice stepping out as someone other than Kyu, The Unknown."

"I like seafood."

"Seafood it is."

From around the corner, Aest heard the mention of food and barked. *What about me?*

"Sorry buddy. You're staying home for this one, but don't worry; I have a huge, horribly expensive cut of meat in the refrigerator. Try to make it last for more than three seconds."

He replied with a bark of resignation. *All right, I'll give you this one, but no promises on that meat.*

#

Kye paid for a cab to take Ocelot to the temple to change. Before she returned, he changed into a nice suit, with tan pants and jacket, white shirt, and a brown and tan striped tie. Ocelot returned wearing a dark blue dress and short heels. Her hair was brushed to one side, and she had on just enough makeup to accentuate each feature of her face.

"My, don't you look handsome. I can only hope this old dress of mine passes muster."

Kyu's open-mouth gawk was his only answer.

Ocelot smiled. "So, where are we going?"

Cyphus was a coastal city, so there were plenty of seafood restaurants to choose from. Kyu and Ocelot returned to the waiting taxi, where Kyu gave instructions to go to the Ocean View, one of the more upscale restaurants. He knew the chance of running into anyone associated with arena fighting would be slim. He also doubted anyone would recognize him with a visible face and no claws. Still, he hoped his time with Ocelot would be free of distractions.

Being midweek, no reservations were required. Once seated, they both ordered baked redfish smothered in a lemon butter sauce.

The time spent together was surreal. Sparkling banter floated between Ocelot and himself. Her smile, her laugh, her shining eyes opened Kyu's consciousness, bathing it for the first time with a bright, cleansing light. His mind could not retain anything spoken between them, but the words nestled comfortably within the warmth of his heart. The meal was over all too soon. They walked outside. Night had fallen.

Kyu hailed another taxi and gave instructions to drive to the temple. The back seat was cozy. Ocelot threaded her arm through Kyu's and grasped his hand, as she rested her head on his shoulder. No words were spoken. None were needed.

At the temple, Kyu had the driver wait while he and Ocelot walked to a shadowed side entrance.

"Well, Kyu,thank you for a delicious meal."

"Thank you for the pleasure of your company." *And for so much else*. "When can we get together again?"

"Whenever you want. I hope soon," Ocelot replied softly.

Kyu's experience with women had been quick sex with groupies. The formal dance of courtship was as unfamiliar to him as the inside of the temple. Not sure what else to do, he leaned forward to give Ocelot a kiss goodnight.

As their lips met, her arms wrapped around his neck to pull him closer. Her kiss was hungry. Kyu's arms went around her slender waist as he returned the hunger. Their tongues probed and touched. Their bodies melded as one.

Kyu had no idea how much time went by. Nor did he care. This feeling of joy surpassed any inkling of happiness he may have felt before.

The kiss ended, the embrace loosened. Kyu's hands remained on Ocelot's waist. Her breasts were tantalizingly close. Kyu wished nothing more than to cup them in his hands.

Lust surged through him, but it was not animal or indifferent. This was imbued with something more. It was fulfilling, where something wonderful would remain after the physical part had reached its climax.

Not yet. Kyu's hands fell to his sides.Ocelot's smile lifted his spirits higher than they had been. "Until next time," she whispered in his ear. She turned then disappeared inside the temple.

Looking out the cab's window, Kyu was euphoric. Before Ocelot, his world was nothing more than a dark, twisted dream. He now was waking up to a sunlit day.

Kyu was not religious, but as he stared out the cab window, he prayed to both Syrra and Syssera. Could this wonderful chance become more? It seemed so fragile. Kyu's nightmare was that he would do something to shatter it.

CHAPTER 18

The Regent for Shaeldor was in his mid-fifties, but still had the virility of a man thirty years younger. Mabb Youri kept up with the woman, thrusting, licking, scratching. The bed sheets were twisted and damp. After two hours, things were speeding up, racing for the orgiastic conclusion.

With a final cry, Youri spent himself inside his partner. She scoured her long nails down the dark skin of his back, drawing blood.

Exhausted, Mabb Youri laid back. His broad chest rose and fell with exertion.

"By Syrra, you'll be the death of me yet."

"We all must die sometime," the woman answered. "Can you think of a better way to go?"

The Shaeldori Regent loosed a deep chuckle. "You have a point."

They lapsed into silence. Youri knew it wouldn't last.

The woman looked at him. "The general elections are nearly upon us. Once the Councilors are voted upon and sworn in, the Seat will convene in Talmount. I trust you are ready?"

"Of course I'm ready. I said I would be"

"You won't surprise me with a last-minute change of heart, will you?"

"Syrra's balls, woman, I gave my word, didn't I? Are you saying you don't trust me?"

"You'll have considerable opposition from your own Council. They may try to remove you from office. This does not concern you?"

"I can handle them."

The woman ran her fingers through the hair on Mabb Youri's chest. "You stand to lose everything if we fail, your career being the least of it."

"I'm not stupid. Of course I know what's at stake. Are *you* prepared for the firestorm that will come of this?"

The woman sat up. "I've been in the flames this long, haven't I? How can you even question me on that?"

"Calm down. I was just making a point; I won't question your commitment if you don't question mine."

The woman got off the tangled bed. Mabb Youri admired her sweat-slicked body.

"When can we get together for our next… meeting?" he asked.

Fey Gherren gave him a lascivious smile. "As soon as you can think of another excuse to get away from your wife."

CHAPTER 19

Bawm's Tap was mostly empty. Its one saving grace was the close proximity to Kyu's home. The air outside was chilly so Kyu wore his fleece-lined jacket. The holstered gun underneath the jacket was a comforting weight. He sat at the bar, Eulos on the stool beside him.

"Just soda for me." Eulos held a hand up to the barkeep, preventing him from drawing a beer. He turned to Kyu. "You know what that shit does to me… the fighting, Erenia? Now it's causing bizarre dreams."

Kyu requested the same.

"Don't you be denying yourself because I can't handle it. Go on."

Kyu accepted the soda anyway. As Eulos didn't want to elaborate on the dreams, Kyu took a sip. "I had a date… an acolyte of Syssera. She knows Erenia."

Eulos shook his bald head in amazement. "I can't believe it. Kyu with a girlfriend! She knows my wife from the temple? Are you sure about this? I have no doubt she's nice, but you know what it means to be with her. One of you is going to have to change if you want it to work. I know you too well, Kyu. You may give in a little, but for the most part you'll remain the same. Can you make this work?"

"I hope so. Besides, I don't think she'll be at the temple much longer."

"That doesn't matter. She believes in the Sysseran doctrine. You're an arena fighter, and a very well-known and successful one. How are the two of you going to reconcile this?"

This was the question that had plagued Kyu since the morning after his date with Ocelot. The euphoria he had felt, though not completely gone, had been tampered down by the reality of the situation.

When Kyu didn't answer, Eulos smiled sadly. "Ah, Kyu, you're in love with her, aren't you?"

Kyu drank some of his soda. "I don't know. I think I might be. All I know is that I can't get her out of my head."

Eulos chuckled. "Sounds like love to me, my friend."

"Did you feel this way about Erenia when you first met?"

"Yup."

Kyu fell silent, not wanting to ask the obvious. Eulos answered it anyway.

"And yes, I still do. Kyu, don't make the mistake of comparing my marriage to your current relationship. When we got married, Erenia was an avid follower of arena fighting. It wasn't until we were unable to conceive a child that she turned to the teachings of Syssera. Her entire belief system changed in a very short period of time. I went from being her hero to being her shameful embarrassment.

"I tried to change," Eulos sighed. "Even retiring and becoming an instructor wasn't enough. It didn't sit right with Erenia. It still doesn't, especially with her running for a Council seat as a Reformer, but I can't do any more than this. I am who I am."

Eulos looked hard at Kyu. "So are you. I can see how you feel about this girl. The world looks a lot brighter, doesn't it? I know; I remember. Love is funny like that. When it first hits you, it has an immediacy and intensity that seems to outshine the sun. Over time, these feelings become deeper, less flashy and more secure."

Eulos took a sip from his soda. "I wish you the best, Kyu. Just be careful, all right? Keep some emotions in reserve, just in case things don't work out."

Kyu was quiet. Not all of Eulos' advice sat well with him, but it was spoken from the heart, and honest.

Eulos turned to him. "Don't take this personally, but what exactly does she see in you?"

"'Don't take this personally'? Gee, thanks, Eulos."

"I'm serious. You know as well as I do that your appearance is conspicuous and… unusual. You are well-known and instantly recognizable. You always have fans and groupies tailing you. Will Ocelot be able to handle this?"

Kyu made a decision. "Come with me to the bathroom."

Eulos chuckled. "You know I don't swing that way."

"Shut up, you asshole. Just come along."

The men's bathroom, empty but for Kyu and Eulos, was small: two stalls, a urinal, and a chipped sink. The floor was white tile, and everything was surprisingly clean. A mirror hung above the sink. Kyu looked at his reflection, at the shadow that hid his face.

Eulos, bemused, did likewise. "All right, here we are. What is it?"

In answer, Kyu held up his claws. They transformed into normal hands. The shadow that hid his face disappeared. Kyu's now-visible eyes locked onto Eulos'.

Eulos registered no response at first. Then his eyes widened, his jaw dropped, and he backed away from the mirror, going as far as the urinal. "What…? Wait… What the fuck is this? What the fuck is going on?"

Kyu turned his face toward his friend. "This is who I am, Eulos. This is Kyu, Unknown to you no longer."

Eulos shook his head, his face a mixture of amazement and denial. "You always told me you didn't know how to remove the shadow. And your hands! How did you do that?"

"I couldn't, until very recently."

Eulos recovered his composure and walked to Kyu. His face was bare inches from Kyu's, studying every detail, as if looking for the secret behind the illusion, the punch line to the joke Kyu was playing on him.

"Would you care to explain to me how you can do it now?"

"I'm still coming to grips with the answer to that question. I had to show you. This is how I go out with Ocelot without drawing attention." Kyu got an idea. "Let's go to my place! I know Aest would like to see you again. And Ocelot! I really want you to meet her, Eulos. We'll go to the temple and pick her up."

The shadow reformed over Kyu's face, and his fingers sprouted their familiar claws.

"Quit it, will you? You're starting to fucking spook me."

"Sorry. Shall we go?"

"Yeah, sure, but I might get a real drink first. I need one after this." Eulos swung open the restroom door.

The automatic gunfire was deafening. Eulos' body slammed back into the small space of the restroom, nearly knocking Kyu off his feet. Eulos' arms flailed as bullets punched into him. He hit the wooden door of one of the stalls, cracking it, and slid down, leaving long crimson smears.

The sudden silence was as deafening as the gunfire had been. Kyu's gun was in his hand. He didn't remember pulling it out. He glanced quickly at his friend. Eulos was sprawled on the white tile floor, a deep pool of blood spreading from his body.

Kyu couldn't tell if Eulos was alive or dead. Before he could do anything, he had to deal with the threat outside.

Sounds returned to the bar. Glass broke and patrons screamed in panic as they bolted for the door. The burnt odor of spent rounds wafted through the air. Kyu knew there was at least one automatic weapon out there – judging from the size of the holes in Eulos' body, it was a heavy caliber one.

Kyu crouched down and risked a glance through the open doorway. The gun outside opened up. The doorframe burst into thousands of flying splinters. Thankfully the gunman's aim was high. Kyu jerked his head back then stood. He pointed his gun around the mangled doorway and fired three blind rounds.

A voice spoke from inside the bar. "Is that all you have? This is going to be easy."

Kyu's mind raced. It had to be one of Padanor Syche's goons, but was he alone, or did he have backup?

Kyu dropped to his hands and knees then crawled to the other side of the sink, wedging himself between it and the wall. It wasn't nearly enough cover, but he was trapped. He had no other options. He aimed his gun down the wall to the doorway, hoping to get a lucky shot.

Gunfire erupted again. Bullets drilled through the wall above Kyu, ripping through the old drywall with ease. Dust and chunks of plaster showered Kyu.The mirror above the sink shattered, raining slivers of glass upon his back.

Silence returned. Then Kyu heard something that told him he had a slim chance: the sound of a spent clip being ejected and a new one fumbled for. Kyu stood and peered through one of the impromptu peepholes created by the gunman.

Smoke and dust hung heavy in the barroom. Through the haze, Kyu saw the shape of a large man, holding what appeared to be a large assault rifle. The gunman slapped a fresh clip into the weapon.

Kyu stepped back, stuck his gun through the hole, and emptied it in the direction of the gunman. He was rewarded with a shout of pain. The gun dropped to the floor, and the heavy body crashed down.

Kyu quickly replaced his clip then crouched by the doorway, listening for any sounds. It was likely the man was alone, but he didn't want to take chances. A peek around the door showed him the slumped figure on the floor. He fired two more bullets into the body for good measure then dashed out of the doorway and crouched behind one of the bar's tables, gun leveled, looking for targets. There were none to be seen.

He approached the huge form lying on the floor, gun ready. The man had long hair bunched together in greasy locks. Blood poured from several holes but the gunman, incredibly, was still breathing. Kyu kicked the automatic rifle away and gave him a quick search. He had no other weapons.

Kyu ran to the bar and found a phone. He called for an ambulance for Eulos. He then ran back to the restroom. His shoes splashed in blood. Eulos' face was ghastly white. His chest fluttered up and down. Kyu put a hand behind his friend's head. Eulos' eyes were glazed, unable to focus. Kyu called to Eulos, knowing it was useless. Bloodless lips moved. Kyu bent over.

He managed four words, barely audible but unmistakable. "I love you, Erenia."

Eulos' chest stopped moving. His body settled into itself.

Fury bubbled to the surface then exploded. Kyu was out the door. He bent over Eulos' killer then grabbed the puffy face with his claws.

"Who sent you? Was it Syche? Was it fucking Padanor Syche?"

Though he was riddled with bullets, the killer smiled. "She said you would blame him. She pays a lot better than Syche."

Erenia? The thought was ridiculous. The killer spat a huge glob of blood into Kyu's face.

Kyu's world turned red. His gun rose then fell on the man's face, knocking out teeth, shattering bone. Blood splashed on Kyu's clothes. His claws tightened. He tore away chunks of flesh. With a clawful of the gunman's dirty hair he slammed the head onto the floor, opening the skull with a liquid crack and spraying brain matter several feet.

"Freeze! Drop the gun!"

Kyu spun around. Hordes of police swarmed the barroom. All had their guns trained on him. Fury burned through Kyu. He wanted nothing more than to blast his way out, taking as many with him as he could. One thought froze the rage within.

Ocelot.

The gun, dripping blood, fell from Kyu's hand.

"Arms in the air! Face the wall! Hands on the wall!"

Kyu complied. Someone picked up his gun and the killer's automatic weapon. Rough hands frisked him. Police examined the gunman's body. One called out when he found Eulos in the restroom. The ambulance Kyu had called wailed in the distance.

Kyu's arms were yanked behind him and cuffed.

#

Erenia was exhausted. Endless travel, endless speeches, and a different bed, not all of them comfortable, to sleep in every night, was leading to the boundaries of burnout.

The crowds cheered wherever she spoke, but the numbers didn't lie: her standing in the polls was falling. If it continued, she would lose the election.

Behind the safety of the hotel room door, she allowed her tears to fall. She'd put everything into this election, body, mind, and soul. She had balanced the demands of Enna Racyne and the top supporters of her campaign with the expectations of potential constituents. She had done everything she possibly could. Still she was losing.

A knock came to her door.

"What?" Erenia yelled, not caring how haggard she sounded.

"It's Nia, Erenia,"

Erenia was in no mood to talk. "Please, Nia, no more today. We'll talk tomorrow."

"Erenia, it's important. Please open up."

Erenia's frustration spiked. She grabbed the door and flung it open. "What?"

Nia's eyes were red. Her lips trembled.

Dread clutched Erenia's heart. Her trivial self-pity vanished. Whatever news Nia had, Erenia knew she did not want to hear it, but was powerless to silence what her heart already knew.

Fresh tears spilled down Nia's cheeks. "Erenia, I'm so sorry… it's Eulos…"

CHAPTER 20

The small room had one door and an obvious two-way mirror. Kyu, claws shackled, sat at an old, scarred table. He had been there for two hours. He could have freed himself with his new abilities but decided it would be better to stay; he would get more answers that way.

The door opened. A large man with angry eyes and short hair that was dark and gray walked in. He wore a moustache that was monstrous, with thick, salt-and-pepper hairs that covered his upper lip and curled back along his cheeks. Silent and glaring, he took the chair opposite Kyu.

They stared at each other for several seconds. The man didn't wear a uniform, which meant he was a detective. He showed no intimidation at the shadow covering Kyu's face.

The detective leaned forward. "I'm Chief Detective Norn Sanna. I knew this day would come. You're in a lot of trouble, Kyu, The Unknown."

"How am I in trouble?"

Sanna smirked. "Well, let's see. Two bullet-ridden bodies, and one man left standing, holding a gun. I think that qualifies."

"One of those bodies was my best friend. I didn't shoot him. I did shoot the other guy, in self-defense."

"So you say. Every murderer on Xiaroc Isle says the same thing. You can add your voice to theirs."

"Eulos and I were walking out of the restroom when that asshole opened up on us. Maybe you should be trying to figure out why he did that."

"Yeah, why would anyone want to hurt men of fine standing like you and Eulos Baak, who have a habit of leaving torn and broken bodies whenever they go out on the town to have a good time? It seems to me that you and your friend have more than your share of enemies."

Kyu ignored the sarcastic tone. "This wasn't personal. This was a hit. The gunman was hired by a third party."

"And who would this mysterious 'third party' be?"

Kyu remained silent. He was tired of the detective and this interrogation. For some reason, the detective was taking this personally. Kyu couldn't figure out why.

Sanna leaned back and smiled. "Well, it doesn't matter. I've waited for this moment for a long time. You're going to Xiaroc Isle. There isn't a judge…"

The door opened. Sanna spun, irritated at the interruption. A well-dressed man with a briefcase, followed by a uniformed police officer, strode into the room. He was about thirty, with thick glasses and a wiry energy.

"Do not answer another question, Mr. Kyu." The man turned to the detective. "Chief Detective Sanna, I am Kelvin Varai, Mr. Kyu's attorney. This interrogation without my presence is illegal. In fact, this interrogation, and the unlawful holding of my client, is over. Mr. Kyu is to be released to me immediately."

Sanna's florid face bloomed several shades redder. "What is this? Get out of here!"

"I don't think so. In fact, Detective Sanna, don't be surprised if my client files a lawsuit against you and the city of Cyphus for infringement of his rights."

"This man is the only suspect in two homicides!"

"Not anymore. A witness has stepped forward."

"A witness? What witness?"

"The bartender. He had dived behind the bar and watched around the edge when the shooting started. He verifies that the man with the automatic weapon opened fire upon my client and his friend when they were exiting the restroom, killing Eulos Baak and trapping Mr. Kyu with no means of escape. My client – with a legally registered handgun that he is licensed to carry – had no choice but to return fire to save his own life. Mr. Kyu is not guilty of murder."

Kyu did not see any necessity of adding that it was his bludgeoning of the killer's head on the floor that had ultimately killed him.

The lawyer produced a paper from his briefcase and handed it to Sanna. "Here is the order authorizing his release to me. May I recommend, Detective Sanna, that you canvas more carefully for witnesses in the future?"

Sanna read the paper. His face flushed even further. He turned to the uniformed man. "Release him!"

The shackles were removed from Kyu's wrists. He stood along with Sanna. The big detective looked ready to say something, but instead stormed out of the room.

Kyu and Kelvin Varai were escorted out of the police station. Once outside, Kyu turned to the lawyer. "Thanks for getting me out of there."

"My pleasure, Mr. Kyu."

"So, would you mind telling me just who you are?"

Varai laughed. "I am exactly who I said I am. I'm your attorney."

"I don't remember hiring an attorney."

"You didn't. Mr. Yuv hired me."

"Yuv?" Kyu was alarmed. After the meeting in Yuv's office with Padanor Syche, there had been no more contact with his manager. Kyu wasn't sure if Yuv considered himself his manager anymore. "Why? What does he want?"

"I'm sure I don't know. Regardless, he paid me a retainer, and I am here to represent you if you need me. Here," Varai handed Kyu a business card. "Call me if the police decide to detain you again."

Kyu took the card. "That guy who killed Eulos, was he connected to the Korl?"

"I can't say, Mr. Kyu. Rest assured, I have no connection to the Korl in any way, if that is what you are worried about." Varai was silent for a moment. "I will tell you what I do know. The man who attacked you and Mr. Baak was named Borl Joros. Though he'd never been convicted, he was a hired killer, one of the better ones. Whoever contracted him for this hit paid him a lot of money. Of course, trying to trace that money will be impossible."

Kyu thought that over.

The lawyer stepped off the curb and opened the door to a large car with metallic blue paint. "Call me if you need legal help, Mr. Kyu. For all other inquiries, contact Mr. Yuv." Kelvin Varai did not offer Kyu a ride as he drove away.

Kyu hailed a taxi. He didn't bother trying to retrieve his gun. Undoubtedly that would be more trouble than it was worth. Besides, there were plenty more where that came from.

The Korl was still the obvious choice as the party behind the hit. They certainly had enough money to pay the contract killer. But Borl Joros had indicated otherwise. *"She said you would blame him. She pays a lot better than Syche."* That could only mean one person: Fey Gherren, or Asrath, as she was also known. Good ol' Mom.

Kyu understood why Gherren would want him dead, but why kill Eulos? It didn't make sense. Was Eulos just at the wrong place at the wrong time? Guilt gnawed at Kyu, followed by a return of the rage. Something had to be done, but what?

Why had Yuv hired a lawyer for him, after Kyu had thrown him to the Korl wolves? Events were playing behind the scenes of Kyu's life. That was unacceptable. It was time for some answers.

At his home, Kyu told the taxi driver to wait. He punched in his access code and entered. Aest yapped and jumped on him. Kyu petted his friend. In the living room, Ocelot sat on the sofa. Kyu was surprised, until he remembered that he had given Ocelot his access code. He was now glad he did.

Ocelot ran to him and wrapped her arms around him. Kyu gratefully returned the hug. "Kyu! Praise Syssera you're all right."

Kyu released the embrace. "I'm glad you're here, but I have to go back out." Kyu walked to the arsenal room.

Ocelot followed. "Why? What's going on? I only caught bits on the news of what happened, and when I called the police, they wouldn't tell me anything. Is your friend Eulos really dead?"

"Yes," Kyu said through a tight throat. He selected another handgun and, for good measure, a small automatic rifle with a folding stock and a shoulder strap.

Ocelot's eyes widened. "What are you doing? Please don't go back out like this."

"I have to. Actually, I'm hoping to avoid trouble, but I have to be prepared."

"Kyu, no! Please, stay here. We can think this through."

Kyu banished the shadow from his face and gave Ocelot a gentle kiss on the lips. "I *am* going to think things through, but I need some information first."

Ocelot stepped back, anger and anguish in her eyes. Finally, she said, "Please be careful."

"I will." The shadow reappeared. "Let's go, Aest."

Aest barked. *Right behind you.*

#

The taxi driver, to his credit, made no mention of the weaponry or of Aest when Kyu returned. Directions were given; Kyu dismissed the taxi once they arrived at Yuv's office.

"Be ready for anything, Aest, but don't tear anyone apart unless it's necessary."

Aest barked. *Thanks for taking the fun out of this trip.*

Despite his heartache and anger, Kyu had to chuckle. He gave thanks to Syrra for bringing Aest into his life.

His hand on the automatic rifle hanging from his shoulder, Kyu and Aest entered the reception area of Yuv's office. No Korl goons stood around.

Shanna looked up in shock. "Mr. Kyu! Was Mr. Yuv expecting you?"

"I sincerely hope not."

"Let me see if he's available." She picked up the inter-office phone.

Kyu pulled the phone out of her hand. "He's available, trust me." He opened the door to Yuv's office, Aest close behind.

Yuv was talking on his phone when they entered. Aest immediately growled. Yuv's eyes widened in shock. Not pausing for niceties, Kyu ripped the phone jack out of the wall, disconnecting Yuv from whomever he had been talking to.

Yuv's protests died as Kyu spun the rifle's barrel toward him, his claw on the trigger.

"What's this all about, Kyu?" Yuv asked as calmly as he could.

"That's what I want to know. What's the deal with the attorney?"

"I hire a lawyer to get your ass out of jail, and this is the thanks I get?"

"Stuff the injured innocence. That fits you about as well as last year's clothes. I'm sure that lawyer wasn't cheap, and you don't spend money like that for no reason. The last time I was here, I left you on the hook because I wouldn't play nice with Padanor Syche, so why are you helping me now?"

Yuv sat back and regained his composure. "You refused the business proposition Mr. Syche offered you. That's in the past. I am still your manager, unless we agree otherwise. Am I still your manager, Kyu?"

Kyu decided to play it through. "Keep going."

"Gladly, but please point that weapon away from me."

Kyu lowered the barrel. Aest continued to growl and Yuv looked at the animal nervously.

"Was it really necessary to bring that thing here?"

"I find he's a very good judge of character, which doesn't bode well for you. Keep talking."

"All right. As your manager, it is in my best interest, as well as yours, to have this allegation of murder dismissed. By the way, I was sorry to hear about Eulos Baak. I knew he was a friend of yours."

Kyu ignored the disingenuous statement. Aest growled louder.

"Can't you put that beast in the office with Shanna?"

"Shut up. I find it very hard to believe that everything is back to normal after that meeting with Syche. You were scared to death, especially when I refused to assassinate Fey Gherren. Now you're acting as if everything is fine. For once in your life, cut the shit and tell me what's going on."

Yuv leaned forward. "You are losing sight of the fact that Padanor Syche is, above all, a businessman. My business with him is just that: *my* business. You refused his proposition; therefore, your business with him is over. Mr. Syche has moved on. So should you. This paranoia does not suit you, Kyu."

"Paranoia suits me just fine. Somehow I don't believe it's as simple as that. Padanor Syche didn't strike me as the type who would dismiss business so easily."

"You think the attack on you and Eulos Baak was done by the Korl? Believe me, Kyu, if Padanor Syche wanted you dead, you wouldn't be standing here right now."

Kyu's doubts returned. Was Yuv telling the truth? There were so many pieces missing, and this confrontation with Yuv was not going as Kyu had hoped.

Yuv's voice grew more certain. "Whoever this guy was who tried to kill you, he was not doing so on the orders of the Korl. I'm telling you the truth, Kyu. I don't know why he wanted to kill you and Eulos, but it had nothing to do with what happened here."

Kyu opened his mind to discern the accuracy of what he was being told. Yuv was telling him the truth, at least as far as he knew it.

"Go back home, Kyu. Let me do my job and find you another opponent. Mourn your friend. I'll call you in a couple weeks."

Something remained hidden, but Kyu knew he would not get any more answers today. His frustration threatened to release his rage, but filling Yuv full of holes would not give him any more information.

Kyu and Aest left Yuv's office. Once home, Ocelot embraced him as if she would never let him go.

CHAPTER 21

A surprising amount of people had shown up for Eulos' funeral. Kyu, wearing one of his best suits, stood in the background of the cemetery. He didn't want to be recognized, so the shadow and claws were gone.

Erenia ignored everybody. Dressed in black, with a dark veil covering her face, her shoulders shook from crying. Nobody comforted her. She wouldn't allow it.

A priest from the small Syrran temple in Cyphus gave the eulogy. Kyu was surprised Erenia didn't have the priestess of her temple doing it.

There were cameras everywhere. This was a big news story. The media stood behind a cordon of police, who attempted to keep things respectful.

Kyu watched Erenia, his feelings indecipherable. When Eulos was alive, it had been so easy to dislike her; yet, here she was, grief-stricken and inconsolable at her husband's funeral. Kyu found that in his own pain, he wanted to reach out to her, and knew he would never dare do so. She undoubtedly blamed him for Eulos' death… just as he blamed himself.

A large man broke from the crowd and approached her. Erenia did not drive him away. He took her arm and drew her away from the gravesite. To Kyu's surprise, she went meekly. They got in the back of a car that was chauffeured by a uniformed police official. The cameras followed their every move. As the car pulled away, Kyu noticed Erenia lean against the man for emotional support.

Kyu didn't know what to make of it. He had recognized the man immediately. It was Chief Detective Norn Sanna.

The crowd, along with the news crews, dispersed. Kyu waited them out. Before the cemetery workers came to lower it into the grave, he approached the casket that contained his best friend's body. He laid a normal hand on the polished lid. With nobody looking, he willed it into a claw.

"I guess those like us are not meant to die peacefully of old age in our beds, my friend." Kyu's throat was tight. "I know you would slap me in the head for saying this, but I feel your death is my fault. Life isn't going to be the same without you, Eulos. A part of my heart is in that box with you." Kyu paused and allowed himself to cry. "Goodbye, Eulos. Syrra willing, we'll meet again and down some beers in the afterlife."

Kyu turned to go. He stopped and turned back one final time. "I know she won't welcome it, but I'll try to keep an eye on Erenia for you. I owe you that much."

#

Ocelot was waiting for him at home. They held each other on the couch, neither of them saying a word. Aest was on the other side of Kyu, nestled close to him. Aest understood that Eulos was gone and was doing his best to offer comfort. Kyu felt boundless gratitude for both of them.

After a few minutes, Kyu felt Aest move. Ocelot looked at Aest and gave him a slight nod. Aest scampered off, leaving the two of them alone. Kyu marveled at the level of communication that existed between Ocelot and Aest after such a short period of time.

Ocelot put her hand on the side of Kyu's head, burying her fingers into his hair. She kissed him gently on the brow. Kyu clung to her, bathing in her comfort, her presence a balm to the open wound of his grief.

Ocelot stood and took Kyu's hand. Confused, he stood as well. She led him to the bedroom. He gave Ocelot a questioning look. Ocelot smiled. "It's time."

Kyu was still confused. "Time for what?"

Ocelot was patient. "It's time to affirm our lives." Then, more softly, "It's time to affirm our love. I love you, Kyu Ardrassis."

Kyu finally understood. He and Ocelot had gotten close over the past two weeks, but they hadn't made love yet. However, he had just returned from his best friend's funeral. Eulos was still very much on his mind.

As usual, Ocelot read his mind. She embraced his head with both hands. "I know you grieve. I know your heart hurts. I also know you feel alone now, more than ever." She pulled his head down until it was almost touching hers. "But you're not alone, and you never have to be again. You have Aest, and you have me."

Ocelot kissed him, first soothingly, then with need and hunger. To his surprise, Kyu found himself responding. Somehow, this was right. In fact, this was what he needed the most.

She drew back and pulled Kyu into the bedroom. Like all the other rooms in his inner-hill home, it didn't have a door. Aest would respect their privacy.

Ocelot stood Kyu by the bed. She removed his suit jacket, then the shirt. She ran her fingers down the fine hairs of his muscular torso. Kyu shivered. She drew back. "Are you cold?"

Kyu shook his head. He tried to speak, but had to pause and swallow. "No. I can't believe I'm saying this, but I'm a bit… scared."

Ocelot's beautiful soft brown eyes misted over. "That's all right. I'm scared, too. This is my first time."

Ocelot had told him that she hadn't had much in the way of relationships with other men, but Kyu hadn't guessed she was still a virgin. Suddenly, he felt shamed, thinking on his own promiscuous past with countless groupies.

Yet, with Ocelot, it felt like the first time for him, as well. Kyu realized why. All those other women had meant nothing to him, forgotten about as soon as they walked out the motel door. Ocelot meant everything to him. This wasn't about sex; it was about love, and the consummation of that love.

The shaking stopped. He looked at Ocelot. "It's my first time, too." He meant every word of it.

"I know." Ocelot unbuckled Kyu's pants, letting them fall to the floor. She sat him on the bed and removed them, along with the shoes and socks. She grasped the elastic band of his underwear and slid them off his torso.

Ocelot straightened and, never losing eye contact with Kyu, undressed herself. After removing her shirt, she unhooked her bra. The dark pink of her nipples stood out against the pale skin of her breasts. Her pants came off, one slender, beautiful leg at a time. Wearing only her panties, Ocelot approached Kyu.

Without speaking, he pulled her panties down, reverently running his fingers through the dark hairs before him. Ocelot pushed him down on the bed and climbed on top. Her lips fed on his. A clean, joyful lust surged through Kyu, a feeling no other woman had come close to bringing out in him.

Her legs straddled his hips, and the tip of his penis encountered warm moistness. Kyu hesitated, afraid of hurting her. Ocelot's lips mashed his. Her tongue thrust into his mouth, demanding satisfaction. She tightened her legs around his torso and pushed down.

Kyu entered her. He hesitated when he felt the hymen. Ocelot continued the pressure and he pushed through the barrier. She moaned then relaxed, their hips working together in a rhythm of life.

Her lips broke from his and found his ear. "I love you."

"I love you, too. I love you so much," Kyu told her.

Their souls, as well as their bodies, bonded. Kyu had never felt so alive, or so happy to be alive. Later, they lay naked and intertwined, neither one letting go of the other.

#

The next day, Ocelot told the priestess she was leaving the temple. She gathered her few belongings and, an hour later, was a permanent part of Kyu's home. They made love many times, sometimes two or three times a day. They pared it down only after they felt guilty about leaving Aest alone for so long.

Ocelot allowed her hair to grow. In Kyu's eyes, she got more beautiful with each passing day.

A call from Yuv grounded things in a hurry.

CHAPTER 22

A week after Eulos' death, Erenia sat in Enna Racyne's chamber at the temple as the priestess pleaded with her to continue with the campaign.

"You must continue, Erenia! You can't throw it all away now. Too much is at stake."

"Not for me, there isn't. I'm out of it, Enna. Find someone else."

"There is nobody else! The elections are a month away. You can't drop out now."

"I think I just did."

"No!" Enna Racyne shook with fury, her pale eyes wide and animalistic. Erenia sat, unmoved. With a tremendous effort, Enna composed herself. "You're not thinking right." The priestess' tone was much calmer. "And it's understandable. You just lost your husband to an appalling act of violence. I won't be a hypocrite and say that I'm shocked and saddened by this, but I know you cared about him. I respect your sorrow, but your life can't end because his did. The whole political landscape is shifting. The Reformers will be in a position to bring about major change to the Territories, and you have a chance to be in the vanguard of those changes. This is about the future, Erenia. If we lose heart now, Traditionalists will stay in power and things will revert back to the bad old days. How can you turn your back on this?"

Erenia closed her eyes and sighed. "Haven't you been paying attention to the polls, Enna? I've lost too much ground. I'm already out of the running."

Enna Racyne's smile froze Erenia's blood. "You are in a much better position than you realize. You have a new, powerful ally pushing for you."

"Who?"

"The Talgourgese Regent, Parmen Warsas. I contacted him and told him about you. He's quite enthusiastic about your stance on any number of issues and your work ethic. As the Elder Regent, he exerts a lot of influence and has a huge support base among the citizens of Talgourge. You're being given a second chance, Erenia. Don't throw it away."

Erenia looked away. Damn this bitch. Damn her own convictions. "All right. I'm still in."

Enna Racyne sighed in relief. "That's settled. You need to get to Talmount as soon as possible."

"Why?"

"Because you're going to meet with Elder Regent Warsas. There is very little time left, and your strategy for election has to be intensified." Enna handed Erenia a thick envelope. "Here are your plane tickets and a temple credit card for expenses. Make sure you save your receipts. There is also a personal letter to the Regent from myself. Go home and pack. Your flight leaves in six hours."

Erenia took the envelope, numbed. Enna Racyne's arrogance was stunning. Outrage kindled and burned within her. "You were so sure I'd acquiesce?"

Enna Racyne smiled, fanning the flames within Erenia. "I knew once we got beyond your grief we would reach your common sense."

Erenia felt light-headed. She had been manipulated, and very easily at that. Her anger found its center and she grasped it tight. *No more.* She stood. "Yes, I'm still in the running. I know what I need to do, but Enna, your agenda is not part of it. I see it now. You intend to use my husband's death to bolster my chances of winning."

"What's wrong with that?" Enna spat out, her measured calm gone. "You just don't get it, do you? This is how the game is played. Welcome to the real world, Erenia. You use what you have, including loss, to achieve what's important… and there's nothing more important than you winning this fucking election!"

Erenia didn't know what shocked her more: Enna's wholly uncharacteristic use of profanity, or the bright gleam of madness in her eyes. She realized what this was about. Enna Racyne had never given up the candidacy. She had every intention of winning and pushing her own obsessive agenda through, using Erenia as a front to be controlled. Her outrage spiked. This was going to end right now.

"You know something, Enna? You're right. Eulos' death clears a big liability out of my way. More Reformers will support me now. I'll get many sympathy votes from the public. I no longer have to worry about Eulos reverting back to form and engaging in bloody brawls, even though he gave up the booze and stayed sober to help me realize a cause he didn't share. Any ties I might have had to arena fighting are now gone. My chances of winning are pretty good.

"But listen to me, Enna Racyne: I will not be a puppet for anybody, not you, not Parmen Warsas, not anybody. If I am elected, it will be on my own terms, and I will perform the duties of the office in the way I see best."

Enna Racyne's expression remained neutral. "Of course, as you see best."

This seeming indifference didn't fool Erenia. "That's right, and since it is in your best interest that I be elected, I will have the support of you and this temple, and through that the support of the other temples throughout Talgourge. Make sure I can count on it."

Erenia made an attempt to bridge the chasm between her and the woman she had once called friend. "Enna, we have a good chance of realizing our goals. We must keep that in mind and work together."

"Of course we must work together," Enna said with as much warmth as a glacier. The priestess stood rigidly, her eyes imperious, her body language announcing that the meeting, and their friendship, was over.

Without another word Erenia left, envelope in hand.

Norn Sanna waited for her in the main body of the temple. "How did everything turn out?"

Erenia sighed. She felt hollow. "I'm still in. I've got a flight leaving for Talmount in a few hours. I have to get ready."

Sanna nodded. "I'm not going to lie to you, Erenia. I know you wanted out, but I'm glad the priestess talked you into staying in the race. I know you can win."

"Don't talk to me about the priestess right now."

Sanna's eyes widened at the bitterness in Erenia's voice. "What happened in there?"

"I told you, I don't want to talk about it. Now excuse me, I don't have time to stand around."

Sanna held up his hands. "All right, take it easy." He paused. "Would you like me to come with you to Talmount? I'm sure I can get a ticket on the same flight."

Erenia's features softened. "Norn, you're the one who's kept me going during this horrible week. I can't thank you enough, but I have to make this trip on my own. Please understand."

Sanna frowned, but nodded. "All right, Erenia, but when you get back, there are some things we need to talk about."

Erenia didn't answer. She knew Norn was right.

CHAPTER 23

Ocelot wiped her eyes. "I know this is what you do for a living. I know I can't ask you to give it up. This is part of who you are, and I have to accept it." More tears ran down her cheeks. "But I'm having a much harder time than I thought."

Kyu didn't know what to say. This was, as Ocelot had conceded, a part of who he was.

Yuv had called with news of another match. To make it worse, it was an away match, at Plaii Arena in Urigor. It was, however, another large pot – two million marks. He was confident Kyu could command up to five million marks for future matches, much more than any other fighter was getting. Yuv couldn't hide his excitement, especially since he was getting a healthy cut of all that money. Also, the Arena Commission was considering establishing a Championship Tournament, with Kyu as one of the top contenders. They, Yuv had gushed, would become the wealthiest fighter/manager combination around.

Looking at the woman he loved weeping inconsolably, Kyu could not match Yuv's enthusiasm.

"When is this… thing… going to be?" Ocelot asked.

"Two more weeks, at Plaii Arena."

"That's so far away."

"I'm taking Aest. You could come with us."

"No!" Ocelot stiffened with anger. "I will not watch you fight. Don't ever ask me to watch you fight." Ocelot sobbed and ran from the room.

Kyu never felt so miserable and helpless in his life. He was angry at himself and, yes, angry at Ocelot as well. Knowing his anger was selfish did not stop it from coming.

He wanted to go after Ocelot to explain to her that everything was going to be all right, that he would come out on top as he always did, and that the money he would get, now and in the future, would give them financial independence for the rest of their lives. What stopped him was a strong, knowing voice within that told him going after Ocelot right now would be a big mistake. They needed time apart to do some inner searching. Then they needed to see if their findings were compatible.

#

Ocelot, her throat squeezed to the size of a pinhead, sat on the bed and tried to stop crying. She had known this was going to happen, but now that it was here, it was so tough to take. *Mother, how do they do it? How do they cope with so much pain?*

#

Several gloomy hours passed. Kyu sat morosely in the living room, listening to Ocelot cry in their bedroom. Aest lay quietly in a corner, wisely avoiding them both.

Ocelot, he knew, had to approach him first. When she finally did, his hands were clammy and his mouth was dry. The living room was dark; Kyu had no desire to put on a light. Ocelot didn't bother, either, as she sat in a chair opposite the sofa.

She sighed. "In my heart, I'll never be able to support what you do. The money you get from this does not matter to me in the least. I know how good you are, but every time you step into an arena it results in a life cut short, and I will always be afraid it will be yours.

"I don't support arena fighting, but I support you. I love you, Kyu, but I warn you right now that I will do everything in my power to get you to give up this career. You've said before how you never liked Erenia doing that to your friend Eulos, but now I intend to do the same to you. I won't issue ultimatums, but you'll always be aware of how I feel. Will you be able to deal with that?"

Kyu said nothing at first. He couldn't. His throat was too tight, but the words finally came. "We've always been honest with one another. I don't intend to stop now. I've agreed to this match, and I'm going to see it through. I wish I could tell you not to be worried. I do have confidence that I will win, but there is always the chance I won't.

"I know you won't go with me to Plaii, and I understand. However, I hope you will travel with me as far as Talmount."

"Why? What's in Talmount?"

"Two things: one, I want you to meet the Empress, my aunt. And two…" Kyu had to work some saliva into his mouth. "I know this is sudden, and if you say no, I'll understand, but maybe we can go to the Sysseran temple there." He took one final swallow, then the leap. "Ocelot, will you marry me?"

Silence ensued. The darkness of the room hid everything. Kyu was certain his heart had stopped beating.

Ocelot got up and walked to an end table. A lamp clicked on, bathing Ocelot's face in a soft glow. Her dark eyes were large and wet. She sat next to Kyu. "Are you sure about this?"

"Yes, more than anything."

Fresh tears spilled down Ocelot's face. "Me, too. I will marry you, Kyu."

They embraced, and would have stayed that way the entire night if Aest hadn't shoved his large nose in between them and barked. *I'm glad everything has worked out, but I've been ignored for most of the day, and I'm getting hungry. Feed me!*

Kyu and Ocelot laughed a great, healing laughter that went on far too long in the opinion of an indignant and hungry ravener.

CHAPTER 24

The vaulted ceiling of the vast convention chamber within the Talmount Government Building was home to hundreds of lights. It was supported by two rows of white polished marble pillars, the stone run through with blood-red veins. On the walls hung portraits of past Talgourgese Regents, going back almost to the time of the Unifier. Their dead gazes watched over the chamber with stony silence, passing unspoken judgment on all they saw.

Thousands of seats, both on the floor and in upper balconies that horseshoed around the main dais, encircled the outer periphery of the chamber, for those citizens who had an interest in what was being discussed at any given time, or who were curious of how government worked. Large sections near the front were reserved for the media, except during Seats when they were relegated to the back and the balconies.

An open area surrounded the inner circle of the chamber, with cordoned-off walkways branching out to access doors. During sessions this area was patrolled by an armed, elite security force called the Empress' Guard. Beyond this was a semi-circle of one hundred seats, separated into groups of twenty-five, one section for each Territory for those times that Talgourge had the Elder Regent and the Seat was convened there. The seats faced a raised dais, where four chairs faced them from behind a short, ornate palisade rail where the Regents for the Territories sat. Behind these chairs, elevated even more, was a huge throne, intricately crafted from Ormnian mahogany, that was reserved for the Empress... a seat many doubted had ever been filled.

Erenia Baak had seen this chamber before, but as always was awed by its magnificence and importance, at all of the history that had occurred within this room. Soon, history would be made again. In a matter of months, the Seat would be hosted here, as the Elder Regent was Parmen Warsas of Talgourge, the man Erenia was here to meet.

From a balcony, Erenia looked down at the Councilor seats. Would she fill one of those seats when the time came? Did she dare imagine it?

A young page approached her. "Mrs. Baak? The Regent will see you now."

Erenia banished her musings and followed the girl through numerous corridors. The Government Building was the largest structure per square feet in Talgourge. If Erenia was elected, she would have an office here and have to learn the building's intricacies.

The page led her to the Regent's office and quietly slipped away. Within the office vestibule an Empress' Guard passed a scanner over Erenia and made her walk through a metal detector. She was then ushered into the Regent's office.

The office was large, with photos, honors, and plaques festooning the walls in a celebration of accomplishment. The room was dominated by a monstrous desk of dark, polished wood, with a surface area as big as a dining room table. Behind the desk, smiling at Erenia, was the Elder Regent, Parmen Warsas, an athletic-looking man of late middle-years with perfectly groomed silver hair.

The man was an important ally. Without his help, chances were slim she would get elected. Unfortunately, impressions didn't care about any of that, and Erenia's impression of Warsas was of a vain, pompous asshole.

Regent Warsas rose from his padded leather chair and took Erenia's hand in both of his dry, cold ones. He pumped her arm as he would a hydraulic jack. "Erenia, it's a pleasure to see you. First off, let me offer my condolences for the passing of your husband."

Erenia managed to smile. *Be nice, you need this guy.* "Thank you, Regent."

Warsas finally released her hand and sat back down. Erenia remained standing. "You are a strong woman to carry on."

Erenia's bile rose at the patronization. To move things along, she handed the sealed letter from Enna Racyne to the Regent.

"Ah, Enna's regard of your exemplary character, I am sure." Parmen Warsas opened the envelope with a slim silver knife and extracted two hand-written pages. The Regent perused them quickly, twice looking up at Erenia with an unreadable expression. The familiar tone with which the Regent had said Enna's name had not been lost on Erenia.

Once he was done, the Regent folded the papers and slid them into a desk drawer. He looked up and seemed to notice for the first time that Erenia was still standing. "Where are my manners? Please, Erenia, have a seat. This whole business of preparing for the Seat has scattered my wits. Temporarily, I assure you!" Parmen Warsas laughed at his own humor.

Erenia sat in the uncomfortable chair in front of the desk and forced herself to chuckle at the joke. Despite his vainglory and ridiculous attempts at self-deprecation, Erenia knew Warsas was a man with drive, intelligence, and an agenda he wasn't revealing to anybody. She couldn't dismiss anything the Regent said as foolish and irrelevant. She needed to pay attention to every nuance.

Warsas sat back. "Many of the incumbent Councilors are running out of ideas. We need some fresh input, so, Erenia, if you're elected… wait, I mean when you're elected, what exactly are your plans?"

Erenia sensed the tonal shift of the meeting to a formal interview. "To serve the people of Talgourge the best I can, by advocating and supporting programs and laws that are beneficial to the Reformist movement, and therefore to the people of Talgourge and, hopefully, all four Territories as a whole." Erenia knew immediately it was a bad answer.

Warsas smiled condescendingly. "Yes, of course. That's what all of us who share the Reformist philosophy are trying to do, but what I want to know is what are your specific ideas and plans once you take office?"

All right, fine. "The Reformers have the right idea, but sometimes they lack focus. The changes they… we… propose are profound, on a cultural, sociological, and economic level, and that is never easy or quick. People are resistant to change. Look at what's happening in Ormnia. The Reformers there are too impatient, too unrealistic in their short-term expectations, and it has led to violence and loss of life.

"Change is needed, but it has to be gradual. It needs to be realized through education and communication, and that takes time. One of the things I would propose is an exchange of students between the Territories, to give them exposure to differing cultures and societal values, which will, hopefully, lead to dialogue and form cooperative groups that strive to bridge perceived gaps between sets of beliefs.

"I also hope to encourage meetings between the temples of Syssera and Syrra. There is a schism between them that, I believe, is purely political. If the two temples could resolve their differences and work together, it would be a huge step toward true Unification. I want to correspond with the Sysseran High Priestess in Talmount and the Syrran High Priest in Plaii to see if something could get started.

"Speaking of communication, I would strive to establish talks between myself and Councilors from other Territories, especially Traditionalist ones. I would float the idea of Councilors being able to meet without the presence of our respective Regents. I believe, in a more intimate setting without our Regents looking over our shoulders, we can truly discuss and hammer out legislation that may otherwise founder and die. I'm not saying we should do away with the Seat; I just want to include a 'Councilors only' forum for less partisanship and more relaxed talks.

"As for bigger divisive issues, such as arena fighting, we as Reformers know this to be a Korl-controlled blood sport, and we agree it needs to be outlawed. Yet arena fighting has been around since the time of the Unifier, if not before, and, let's be honest, it's very popular. It's also a huge moneymaker, a significant boon for local and Territories-wide economics. While, personally, I would love to see all the arenas shuttered today, the immediate loss of revenue and jobs would hurt a lot of people.

"So, how do we change something as established and entrenched in our society as arena fighting? Through a gradual change in our values. This is not as improbable as it sounds. The general culture of the Territories is stagnant, and it has been for centuries, despite the technological advances we have had. Deep down, the people realize this. Whether they are willing to admit it or not, they are ready for change. Part of this will be the promotion of other sports, more competitive ones, where the participants actually return for rematches, instead of dying, and have the opportunity to form true fan bases.

"As Reformers, it is up to us to stay the course and show the way, to give those who strive for change the support they need. We need to be patient. We are not doing this for now; we are doing this for future generations.

"Do I have all the answers? Of course not; I am just one part of this. This will need to involve all of us, with all of our diverse talents, but I know where to start – with the young, with education and communication that will support short-term goals and build toward the larger, more important long-term goals.

"These are my ideas, Regent Warsas."

The Regent smirked and shook his head. He clapped his hands mockingly. "Bravo. We have an idealist." He leaned forward. The smirk disappeared, all traces of humor and contrived charm gone. "The problem with idealists is that they believe their way is the only way. You are new to the world of politics, Erenia, which means you know nothing. All of your grand ideas will not work in the real world. Idealists are loners. Our cause is a team effort. We will not countenance any loners within our ranks.

"The letter from Enna Racyne confirmed what you just showed me. You are resistant to authority. You want to make up your own rules to a game that has been established for centuries. Arranging meetings with Councilors from other Territories without Regents present? Indeed."

Erenia sat in silence, seething. From start to finish, this had been a set-up. The Elder Regent and Enna Racyne were obviously intimate on a level that Erenia had not been aware.

Warsas continued. "In this race for a Council seat, you will win or lose on my sufferance. Do not kid yourself otherwise. If you want my support, you will toe the line. Once elected, you will support, and vote favorably for, any initiatives or bills that I, or someone I sanction, put forth, whether you personally agree with them or not. You will not go off on your own tangents. Do we have an understanding?"

Erenia felt physically sick. She couldn't believe she had been taken in like this. Parmen Warsas was a political animal, in every sense of the word. His public persona of a charming, slightly buffoonish but dedicated Reformer masked a hard, autocratic personality. She nearly lost her resolve. Her soul screamed at her to walk out of the Regent's office and leave behind the brutal, disingenuous world of politics.

Erenia looked across the ocean of a desk at Parmen Warsas, whose eyebrows cocked arrogantly as he awaited her acquiescence. Her anger grew, and with it her determination to see this through. Yes, she was an idealist, and proud of it. Yes, she would toe the line, though her bile rose at the thought of it, at least until she was filling a Councilor's seat.

Erenia fixed the Elder Regent with a steady gaze. "I understand perfectly."

Warsas studied her a moment then nodded his head. "I certainly hope you do. There is no reason why you shouldn't have a successful career in politics, Erenia, but you must always defer to those who have more experience than you. Public service is a cutthroat world, and it devours those whose egos are bigger than their abilities. Never forget that.

"Go back out and campaign. In a month, I'll see you here again, being sworn in as one of the new Councilors of the great Territory of Talgourge."

With these words, she was dismissed. With a curt "thank you," she rose and walked out.

Erenia found a cafeteria and bought a coffee. The cup shook in her hands as she sat at a table. She was shocked to realize that much of what Parmen Warsas said was true. Her own naivety appalled her. She had been so caught up in the campaign and the promises she had made to herself that she hadn't taken the time to think through the realities of the situation.

Still, she couldn't get over her bitter disillusionment. The Reform party, which Erenia had thought stood for everything good and right, was just as rigid and self-serving as every other political system. What had she gotten herself into?

With a deep pang, she realized she needed Eulos by her side. The guilt hit her with shocking force. She had mistreated and ignored him, even when it was obvious he was trying to change his ways in support of what she believed in.

The guilt quickly spun into fury at the thought of the circumstances of his death. Eulos had been in the company of that awful Kyu, The Unknown who, despite knowing Eulos' drinking problem, had taken him to a bar. If it weren't for Kyu, Eulos would still be alive. Erenia was certain the gunman had been after Kyu. Eulos just happened to be in the way. The thought that Kyu had survived while her husband had been killed curled Erenia's hands into tight fists. Tears spilled down her cheeks. Her rage at Kyu, The Unknown mixed with her humiliation at how callously she had been handled by the Regent.

Resolve solidified under her feet. Erenia wiped away her tears with a brisk hand. She would not surrender.

CHAPTER 25

It was nearly midnight when the Ormnian Regent, Fey Gherren, walked into her bedroom in the thirty-room mansion she owned outside of Ormount. It was tastefully, if sparsely, adorned with a simple dresser, an enormous bed, and a full-length mirror. The bed was there for two reasons: for sex and for show. Fey Gherren never slept.

She stood in front of the mirror and removed her clothes, one article at a time, admiring herself as she always did. Her nude body was perfect, of course. She wouldn't have it any other way. Still, the face was older than she would like, and that hair was much too short. Asrath abandoned the Fey Gherren façade and allowed her hair to grow. Long black locks sprouted from her head and flowed down her naked back. That was better.

It grated against Asrath's pride to have to masquerade as a human when she was so much more. She was a Diaboli Domini, and Queen of the succubi. Humans were foolish and contemptible, although, Asrath conceded, their souls were quite tasty.

Asrath had dined well recently. The riot in Erat, after Kyu had killed Havla Cort, had been delicious. Once she, as Fey Gherren, made her announcement at the upcoming Seat, there would be much more upon which to feed. Asrath felt tremors roll through her as her brethren on the other side of the Curtain clamored for their share of the coming feast. *Soon,* she promised. First she had a few loose ends to tidy up, the biggest one being her son.

Asrath had spent a thousand years trapped behind the Curtain after being banished by her human seed-giver, Harra Ardrassis. This time, she made sure that mistake would not be repeated. Too bad the oaf she had sent to do the job hadn't finished it, but then, when dealing with a half-Infernal, no human really stood a chance.

After Asrath's banishment, the Sorceress had taken her son Kyu and stored him in a reality that had no time. Asrath had been patient, knowing that the Sorceress, who now called herself the Empress, had plans for Kyu. It was only a matter of time. Once the Empress brought him back, Kyu's presence provided Asrath the means to return.

Kyu had to grow to adulthood in the normal, human way. Asrath used this time to establish herself as Fey Gherren and start her rise to power. Humans were easy to manipulate, and her ascension in their politics was pitifully simple. Asrath knew her physical looks had to age as the years went by. She grudgingly allowed it to happen, at minimal expense to her beauty and sexual allure.

All of Asrath's plans had been carried off flawlessly. Everything was in motion. It had been so easy.... except for one thing – the seduction of her son. Asrath couldn't believe Kyu had turned her down. She had radiated sexuality that no one should have been able to resist, but Kyu had backed away. It was more than Kyu being half-Infernal, Asrath knew. It was the nascent awareness that he had inherited from his aunt.

If Asrath had succeeded in getting Kyu's seed, the resulting offspring would have been nearly all Infernal, with just enough human blood to keep it in this world. The child wouldn't have been just a doorway for those beyond the Curtain; it would have been a gaping rift. Alas, that was not to be, at least not yet. For now, she had another's seed within her, and this seed-giver was satisfactorily dead.

Asrath's thoughts turned to the Sorceress. She was up there, on her damned mountain, and she would do everything in her power to thwart Asrath. After millennia of non-corporeal existence, however, the Sorceress' powers had diminished almost to nothing. She was a shade now, in every sense of the word. She knew where Asrath was, but was unable to do anything about it. She was not a threat, but her son was, and the Sorceress was manipulating him. Kyu had no idea just how much his newfound aunt was pulling his strings. That would need to be dealt with.

CHAPTER 26

Outside Talmount Airport, Kyu rented a car. He, Ocelot, and Aest drove to the hotel he had stayed at before. The concierge was the same, and recognized Aest. "Excuse me, sir, but is Kyu, The Unknown returning?"

Kyu, not wanting to lie, paused, and Ocelot came to his rescue. "We are friends of Kyu, The Unknown, and we are watching over his pet. He wants you to extend the same courtesy of having us stay here as if he were here himself."

The concierge hesitated only a second. "Certainly. One room or two?"

"One room," Kyu said. "Please see our luggage up when the room is ready. We'll be back in a few hours."

"Very good, sir."

Ocelot flashed the concierge a dazzling smile as they walked out. The man blushed.

"Well, that's it," Kyu said once they were outside. "You had to go and smile at him. Now you own him."

"I don't want to own him. The only one I want to own is you." Ocelot poked Kyu in the ribs.

"You've owned me from the first instant I saw you."

"What a sap you are. Now let's go and make this ownership official."

Their first stop was at an upscale jewelry story where they purchased two gold and diamond rings. Kyu winced at the cost, but they were worth it. She was worth it.

Their next stop was at a men's formal wear shop, where Kyu purchased a white tuxedo with black trim. They then went to a bridal boutique, where Ocelot spent two hours picking out her wedding dress. She chose a classic strapless column gown, white with raised floral designs running across the breast and down the back. Ocelot held it out to show Kyu, refusing to put it on with him watching. She insisted it wouldn't be right for him to see her in it before their wedding day.

Each shopkeeper had looked more than a bit concerned with Aest's presence, but Ocelot's insistence that he be there, plus the generous amount of money Kyu was leaving at each place, convinced them that an exception could be made to their no pets policy.

Their fourth stop was at the Sysseran Temple of Talmount, run by the high priestess of all Sysseran temples. Shalyse Goranna, a pleasant, plump woman about sixty years of age, delightfully agreed to marry them, for a slight fee for the temple, of course. Her schedule was tight, but she had an opening in three more days in which to perform the ceremony.

After they left, Kyu did the math in his head and concluded that his bank account was close to twenty thousand marks lighter. He didn't mind.

Their fifth and final stop was at the base of Empress Mountain. Exiting the car, Ocelot looked dubiously at the imposing mountain. "Don't tell me we have to climb that thing."

"I hope not. Let's see what happens." Kyu emptied his mind of thoughts and allowed awareness to expand within him. He sent a silent call to his aunt that they were there. He nodded at Ocelot and Aest, and they stepped forward into a beautiful wooded glade.

Ocelot, her face frozen in wonder, looked around at the stately trees, the multi-colored flowers, the grassy trails and sparkling, running streams. The contented chirping of birds accompanied the flashes of deer and other forest creatures.

"This is so incredible!" Ocelot walked to a patch of bright yellow flowers and ran her fingers through the silken petals. "Suncups! These are my favorite flowers." She continued to look around. "I've never seen such beauty in my life."

"I'm glad you like it." The Empress, Haena Ardrassis, appeared seemingly from nowhere, gathering herself in a corporeal form. "I've had this all to myself for the past thousand years. It's nice to finally be able to share it with others."

Ocelot stared at the Empress, her mouth open. "You're Kyu's aunt?"

"I am indeed."

Kyu felt he should say something. "Uh, Aunt Haena, this is Ocelot."

The Empress smiled. "I am very glad to meet you, Ocelot." She took Ocelot's hand in both of hers.

"You as well."

Haena turned to Kyu. "I am very glad to see you have taken my words to heart and have embraced the other, truer side of yourself."

Kyu smiled. "So am I."

The Empress addressed Aest. "And you, Aest, I trust you are well?"

Aest barked. *Can't complain.*

The Empress laughed. "I'm glad. Too many complain about the most trifling things." She gestured, and a heavy wooden table with four high-backed chairs appeared next to the patch of suncups. On the table was a bowl filled with succulent, dew-kissed fruit. Four wooden plates were placed in front of each chair, all empty except for one which held a thick cut of roasted meat. "Let us sit and eat."

Aest's knob vibrated and he bounded enthusiastically to the chair he knew to be his. The meat was gone before the others had a chance to pull out their chairs.

"Great table manners, Aest," Kyu said.

Aest belched in reply and jumped to the soft grass, where he made himself comfortable.

Ocelot took one of the fruit and bit into its golden skin. Her eyes widened in amazement. "This is beyond delicious! I've never had anything like it. What kind of fruit is this?"

"It's a hybrid I created centuries ago," the Empress said. "Some mangoes, guava, dwarf watermelons, sweet oranges, and others I managed to crossbreed just right. The animals here like it as well, and it is plentiful."

Kyu bit into his own fruit. The sweet juiciness begged to be swallowed, and once it was it traveled to all of his nerve endings in a jolt of pleasurable energy.

The Empress did not reach for any fruit. Ocelot asked her why.

"Because I have no mortal body, dear. My body died a thousand years ago. What you see before you is a composite of atoms from the surrounding atmosphere, formed into molecules which in turn are banded together into this quasi-physical construct shaped by my will. Even if I could eat the fruit, I would not be able to taste it." The Empress looked away. "You have no idea how much I wish I could share this meal with you."

Ocelot put down her fruit and covered the Empress' hand with her own. "I am so sorry! If I could, I'd give you the ability to taste this delicious fruit." Ocelot's fingers curled around the Empress' palm and squeezed.

A confluence of emotions crossed Haena's face. She looked like she wanted to cry, but no tears would come. They couldn't. With a shock Kyu realized just how lonely Haena must be, alone for a thousand years.

The Empress composed herself and smiled at Kyu. "So, what brings you here? I love having you here, but I know this isn't purely a familial visit."

"You're right. We're not in Talmount just to visit. Ocelot is my betrothed. We're getting married in the Sysseran temple here in three more days."

Light bloomed in Haena's face. "That's wonderful, Kyu!" She turned to Ocelot, who was smiling shyly. "And to such a beautiful, charming girl. Congratulations to the both of you."

Ocelot blushed. "You're so sweet. It must be an Ardrassis trait." Her eyes widened and she gripped the Empress' hand harder. “You must come! Please say you’ll attend our wedding. It’ll be at the Sysseran temple here in Talmount.”

For a moment the Empress’ smile faltered, and Kyu knew why. Despite Haena’s resiliency over the past millennia, Kyu was not sure she could materialize off this mountain.

Haena’s eyes briefly met Kyu’s, and then she turned back to Ocelot, her smile back in place. “How can I refuse my nephew’s betrothed? Of course I’ll be there.”

Ocelot jumped up with a delighted squeal and embraced the startled Empress. “Thank you!” Ocelot kissed Haena on the cheek. “This means so much to me.”

The Empress returned the embrace, but Kyu detected a silent sadness in her eyes.

“Your home is so beautiful,” Ocelot said. “Do you mind if I walk around and explore?”

“Not at all, dear. Don’t worry about getting lost. You will always find your way back to me.”

“Come on, Aest,” Ocelot called out. “Let’s see what we can find and allow Kyu and his aunt some time to catch up.”

Aest jumped up from the grass and followed Ocelot.

Kyu turned to the Empress. “I was surprised when you told Ocelot you would attend our wedding. You told me you have trouble materializing off this mountain. I must say,” Kyu paused. “I have a good idea how weak you are. You have difficulty materializing even here, don’t you?”

Haena’s face was grim. “One cannot cheat death forever, Kyu. I have kept myself in this world for only one reason, and that reason is almost complete. Once I am done, I will have no choice but to move on to my next level of existence.” The Empress sighed. “Truth be told, I am just as glad. I’ve been here too long. It’s time to go.”

Kyu took a few minutes to consider this. “What will happen to this world when you’re gone?”

“It will carry on, as it always has.”

Kyu looked at his aunt and saw how tired she was. "Will you be able to appear at our wedding without harming yourself?"

The Empress nodded. "I'll find a way. I won't disappoint your dear bride. I need the practice, anyway."

"Practice?"

Ocelot and Aest stumbled back into the clearing, soaking wet and laughing. She laughed harder at Kyu's incredulous stare. "We came across the most wondrous spring. The water was so clear, and there were tiny silver fish darting around in it. We couldn't resist jumping in and joining them, could we, Aest?"

Aest gave an embarrassed bark. *Yeah, I was caught up in the moment.*

Kyu shook his head and smiled. Ocelot was naturally impulsive, but this place was really bringing it out in her, not to mention Aest!

The Empress chuckled. "I'm sure the fish enjoyed it as much as you."

Kyu stood. "Now that my fiancée is dripping wet, I guess we should return to our hotel."

The Empress stood as well. "Three days hence then, at the Sysseran temple."

"Don't forget, Auntie Haena," Ocelot said.

Auntie Haena? "Should we gather together so you can send us back?" Kyu asked.

"Why should I send you back when you are fully capable of doing the job yourself?"

Kyu paused and looked at Haena. "I can do that?"

"Of course you can. Your awareness is every bit as potent as mine. You just haven't tried to see what you can do. Gather Ocelot and Aest around you."

Ocelot and Aest stood next to Kyu.

"You can travel anywhere you wish. You can return here anytime without having to drive or take air transport. It may be easier to focus if you close your eyes. That's it. Now, visualize the flower bud within your mind and will it to open. Feel the petals soak up the sunshine and gather strength."

Strength surged through Kyu as he followed his aunt's instructions, more powerfully than he had ever felt it before. Even with his eyes closed, everything and everyone around him was visible in precise, crystalline detail. He saw how every individual atom was in constant motion, eager building blocks waiting for transformation, either into something perceivably physical or into more complex tasks, such as instant, long-distance travel. Kyu felt life as never before.

"Visualize your car at the base of the mountain." Haena's voice tinkled through his mind like chimes. "Will the three of you there."

Kyu saw his rental car, parked where he had left it at the end of the road. He projected his will… The three of them stood in front of the car.

Ocelot looked up at the mountain, then back at Kyu in wide-eyed amazement. "That was incredible. You did it!"

Kyu took mental stock of his own body. Everything seemed to be in order. "Are you all right?" he asked Ocelot.

"I'm perfectly fine."

"Aest?"

Aest barked. *I'm all here. You did well.*

Ocelot grabbed his arm. "Don't start doubting yourself, Kyu."

"That's what Haena told me on my first visit."

"After a thousand years, don't you think she knows what she's talking about?"

Kyu chuckled. "Well, at least this will save a lot of money on travel bills."

"True, but then you'd have to explain how you keep appearing unexpectedly everywhere. I know your aversion to lying; it's one of the reasons why I love you. You may want to keep this ability low-key, at least for now."

Kyu sighed. "I suppose you're right."

"Of course I'm right."

Kyu looked at her. “Are we already married and I don’t know about it?”

Ocelot playfully slapped his shoulder. “Don’t get smart. You haven’t seen anything yet.”

“That’s what I’m afraid of.”

She offered another slap, a bit harder this time.

Kyu looked to Aest. “A little help here?”

Aest barked. *You’re on your own.*

CHAPTER 27

Kyu stood fidgeting in the nave of the temple, Aest at his side. He appreciated Aest’s presence, but he felt a deep need for Eulos and his solid gruffness. Not since the funeral had he felt the loss of his friend so keenly.

Ocelot was in a back chamber with the high priestess and an acolyte. The high priestess had been scandalized at first by Aest’s presence, but through the insistence of both Kyu and Ocelot, not to mention a sizable donation Kyu had made to the temple’s coffers, things had been grudgingly ironed out.

Another concern of Kyu’s was the nonappearance of the Empress. He had grave misgivings that his aunt would not be able to materialize. Ocelot would be terribly disappointed if that were the case.

The high priestess finally came out and beckoned him to the altar. Kyu and Aest stepped forward.

Shalyse Goranna was dressed in a pure white robe, with a blue sash around her shoulders. She leaned toward Kyu. “Is there anybody else coming? Or is it just you and…” She looked with distaste at Aest. “…Your friend.”

“Well, I’m not really…” The front door of the temple opened. Haena Ardrassis walked in, dressed in a smart, dark-blue contemporary dress. “It appears that my aunt was able to make it, after all.”

The door to the back chamber cracked open, and the acolyte gestured to the high priestess that the bride was ready.

"All right, if everybody is here, and we are ready to proceed." Shalyse Goranna nodded to an organist, who began the opening notes to the traditional bridal march.

Ocelot stepped out, escorted by the acolyte. Kyu thought his heart would burst in his chest. The white dress fit her like the sparkling smile he could see through the pale translucent vale.

The high priestess turned to Haena. "Are you to stand with the bride?"

"Yes, of course, if she wishes."

Ocelot glided over and grasped the Empress' arm. "Auntie Haena," she stage-whispered delightedly while bouncing on the balls of her feet.

"Ahem!" The high priestess tried to retain some decorum. "Positions, please."

They gathered in front of the altar, Kyu and Aest on the right-hand side, Ocelot and the Empress on the left.

"Under the sight of Syssera, goddess of marriage, family, and home…"

Kyu did not hear the rest of the marriage blessing. He was captivated by Ocelot. He could not believe how lucky he was to be standing there, marrying this marvel.

Shalyse Goranna presented the two rings, sanctified earlier by the high priestess.

"With these rings, blessed by Syssera, a union is formed, the eternal circle of life is realized, and love without end is bestowed upon this couple. Let their lives forever merge as they consecrate their acceptance, freely and joyfully, of each other."

The high priestess nodded. Kyu and Ocelot took the rings and slipped them on each other's fingers.

The Empress reached out and removed the vale from Ocelot's face. Her lips trembled slightly, and her brown eyes were moist. Her smile nearly made Kyu's knees buckle.

This is perfection. I will never have another moment like this.

"Under Syssera, you are joined in matrimony." A smile finally cracked the high priestess' stern face. "You may now kiss."

Their lips met, and Kyu realized he had been wrong. This was the perfect moment. Then, just like that, it was over. Kyu and Ocelot were married. The organist played, and the four of them walked out of the temple.

Outside, the sun was startlingly bright. Kyu looked at the Empress, and with a shock realized he could see right through her. "Thank you for coming, Aunt Haena, but I think you'd better get back to the mountain."

Ocelot looked, and her features turned from affection to sharp concern. "Oh, no, are you all right?" Concern soon turned into guilt. "I'm so sorry I insisted you come! I had no idea..." Her eyes misted over.

Haena smiled reassuringly. "Don't worry, dear. Once I get back, I'll be just fine."

Kyu looked at his aunt and realized that aversion to lying did not run in the family.

"I wouldn't have missed your wedding for anything," Haena continued. "After a thousand years, I finally have a family again. Before I return to the mountain, I must give you my wedding gifts."

Kyu was surprised. "Wedding gifts? You didn't have to do that."

The Empress turned serious. "Yes, I did. You are the last Ardrassis by blood, and Ocelot is the last by marriage, therefore..." She produced two small polished wooden boxes, well-preserved but obviously of a great age. She gave one to Ocelot and the other to Kyu.

Kyu opened the hinged lid. Inside, on a bed of purple silk, was a large, beautifully crafted gold ring, engraved with archaic writing. Set in the middle was a pearl that shone with the greens and blues of the ocean's depths. He was stunned by the beauty of the ring and understood that some matter of significance was involved.

Ocelot gasped. Kyu looked over and saw an identical ring in her box, only slightly smaller. "This is beautiful. Where does it come from?"

"Those are family heirlooms. Before the Territories were unified, they were sovereign entities ruled by royal families and their nobles. The House of Ardrassis was the royal family of Talgourge. Their line went back several centuries into antiquity. These rings are nearly two thousand years old and have been worn by every king and queen in the Ardrassis family. The engraving is in an ancient dialect, long dead, that eventually evolved into Old Talgourgese. It is the Ardrassis name and motto: *'Kai vloma beel, estragyko'*. Translated, that means 'For the weak and the strong, we protect'. The pearl is the traditional stone of Talgourge, and its color is symbolic of the Talgourgian ocean-going spirit.

"My parents, Kyu's grandparents, were the last ones to wear these rings. My brother never wore the king's ring after our father died. He understood that such an obvious display of Talgourgese authority would hinder his efforts to unite the Territories. Of course, because of Harra's success and my posthumous restructuring of all the disparate governments under a central one based on democracy and representation, the concepts of nobility and royalty were rendered obsolete."

The Empress smiled. "Even though it's an empty title, by virtue of blood and marriage, you, Kyu, and you, Ocelot, are the unquestioned King and Queen of Talgourge."

Kyu was stunned. Him? A king? He looked at Ocelot. Her eyes and mouth were so wide they seemed to take up her entire face.

"I… I don't know what to say," Ocelot said, her voice quivering. "This is beyond anything I've ever imagined. A queen? Me? Really?"

The Empress nodded. "Really."

Kyu took the ring out of the box. It was heavy; solid gold, for sure. He slipped it on the ring finger of his right hand. The fit was perfect.

Ocelot did the same, tears running down her face. Her ring was a perfect fit, as well.

"I must return home." The Empress smiled and bowed. "By your Majesties' leave, of course."

"Oh, please, no, don't say that." Even though Kyu knew Haena was joking, the reference to royalty made him uncomfortable. He felt like an imposter.

Haena straightened up, smile still in place. "Feel free to come visit me anytime. Until then, farewell." She disappeared.

Ocelot turned to Kyu. "Is she going to be all right?"

"I don't know. I hope so."

Ocelot looked down. "It's my fault. I should never have insisted that she come."

"Stop it," Kyu told her. "Stop it right now. You are not to blame. My aunt had every intention of coming. I think she felt she needed to, and not just because we're her family."

"What do you mean?"

"I'm not sure. It was something she said when we were there – something about needing the practice."

They were silent for a moment. Ocelot gazed at the ring on her finger. "It's so heavy."

Kyu looked at his. "It's nice, to be sure." He lifted his left hand, fitted with the marriage ring. "This one means so much more, though."

Just when Kyu thought Ocelot's smile couldn't get any brighter, it did. She flung her arms around his neck and gave him a long, passionate kiss, right there for every passerby to see. Neither of them cared. Aest, nonplussed, wandered about, trying to look like he wasn't intruding.

Ocelot finally broke off and rested her head on his shoulder. "What a sap you are. Never stop being a sap."

"I promise. Shall we return to our hotel, Mrs. Ardrassis?"

Kyu and Aest turned to go. Ocelot did not follow. Kyu looked back to see wonderment on her face.

"I am Ocelot Ardrassis now, aren't I?"

Kyu nodded. "Yes."

Aest let them know his patience was growing thin with a bark. *This is all very nice, but I'm getting hungry.*

"Oh!" Ocelot laughed. "We're sorry, Aest. We can't keep your belly empty, can we?"

"We're newlyweds, Aest. This is supposed to be our honeymoon. You're cramping our style."

Too bad. Feed me!

Kyu and Ocelot laughed. "Thus family life begins; you, me, and Aest, with occasional visits to Aunt Haena."

"Neither of us would have it any other way."

Kyu could only agree.

CHAPTER 28

The limousine with Urigish plates glided silently down the night-darkened streets, through a section of Shaelmount thick with shadows and debris. Windows on buildings to either side were either boarded up or protected with thick iron bars. Disheveled shapes shifted and stared as the black vehicle drove past. Nobody approached the car, even when it stopped at traffic lights. The denizens were under orders not to attempt any depredations. The limousine was off-limits.

The car pulled up in front of a large warehouse with a corrugated metal roof over chipped brick walls. Multi-colored graffiti covered most of the outside surface. An electric motor hummed within the warehouse and a metal overhead door rolled up, providing the limo enough room to drive in. Orange light from overhead sodium-vapor lamps lit a bare and dusty interior. Once the limo was inside, the door rattled down. The car stopped in the center of the cement floor and the engine shut off.

The limo doors opened and five large, armed men dressed in dark suits piled out, their eyes scanning in every direction. They all had blonde or reddish-brown hair and the pale skin on their faces was slick with sweat from the unaccustomed heat. When they were satisfied there were no threats in the immediate vicinity, one nodded to the occupant in the rear seat.

The man who got out was an inch shy of six feet in height, short for an Urigish. He was slim and wore a suit that fit his frame perfectly. His once-blonde hair was now mostly white, and his eyes, set in a lined, stern face, were pale almost to the point of being colorless. Regent Nevin Ghat wrinkled his nose. The stench of decay was everywhere in this city. Why it was insisted the meeting be here, in this filthy, squalid building, he couldn't understand.

A group of Shaeldori men, equally well-dressed and armed, stood nearby. Their dark skin showed no signs of sweat or discomfort from the heat. They parted, and a small figure stepped forward.

Councilor Thei Porrso was shockingly young – not yet thirty – and Ghat had to admit, quite attractive. Dark coffee skin accentuated high cheekbones, and the sharp eyebrows complimented her shining brown eyes.

Councilor Porrso nodded. "Regent Ghat, thank you for coming."

Ghat stopped himself from brushing imaginary dust off his sleeve. "Why do we have to meet in this ghastly place?"

Porrso's smile was grim. "There are eyes and ears everywhere, Regent. This section of Shaelmount is my old neighborhood. I have nothing but friends and family here. Nothing will disturb us. No word will leak out about this meeting."

Ghat was still unhappy, but grunted his assent. "Fine. Let's get this done."

Porrso's eyes filled with mocking amusement. "Why are you so tense? We're on the same side."

"Let's just say I am uncomfortable."

"Does it bother you to be surrounded by poverty and want, instead of status and privilege? Welcome to the reality the rest of us come from… well, not all of us. Our exalted Regent, Mabb Youri, is, like you, a man born to wealth."

Anger flared in Ghat. "Do not compare me to that man."

"Then stop acting like him," Porrso snapped back.

"You don't see me in bed with the Ormnian whore Fey Gherren, do you?"

Thei Porrso's eyes blazed and the men around her stiffened. The Urigish guards made subtle moves for their weapons.

"Stop!" Nevin Ghat turned to his men, who reluctantly dropped their hands. Ghat looked at Porrso. "All of this posturing is counterproductive. As you said, Councilor Porrso, we are on the same side. Something needs to be done about Gherren and Youri, and we need to make sure that Parmen Warsas has no power to interfere. What are your suggestions?"

"That depends."

With effort Ghat tamped down his impatience. "Depends on what?"

"On just how far you are willing to go for what we know is right."

Ghat met Porrso's fiery gaze with ice. "I am not a timid man, Councilor. I am the Regent of Urigor. I do not quail from what needs to be done."

Porrso pushed back a lock of dark hair and smiled. "Is that so? Let's find out."

She turned to a shadowed corner and nodded. A slim figure, previously unseen, detached itself from the darkness and glided forward. It was a Shaeldori, with piercing black eyes that reminded Nevin Ghat of the fierce, giant raptors that soared the skies over the deserts of this Territory. Ghat, who had been in the presence of dangerous men before, knew he was in the presence of one now.

The Shaeldori stepped silently into better light. His face was as thin as his body, with tight skin pulled over his cheekbones. His hair was brilliant silver.

Thei Porrso smiled at Nevin Ghat's attempts to conceal his unease. "Regent Ghat, this is Argenta. Argenta has several skills, many of which we can put to good use. His services are quite expensive. This is where you come in."

Ghat gave Porrso a sharp look. "He's an assassin?"

"Among other things."

"Putting an end to that Ormnian bitch is something I can go along with."

Porrso laughed, which irritated Ghat. What had he said that was so funny?

"My dear Regent…" Porrso condescending tone had Ghat's face flushing with indignation. "For a man of your position, you certainly think small. I have a much bigger picture in mind."

Ghat's temper snapped. "Enough! Speak plainly."

Councilor Thei Porrso did.

Ghat was astounded at the scope and audacity of Porrso's plan. It was well beyond what he had expected, but as he thought about it he knew it was the only acceptable course of action. The two million mark price tag made him cringe, but he knew there were many ways of providing the money without any of it being traced back to him.

Sitting in the limo as it left the forlorn building to return to Urimount, Nevin Ghat turned everything he had been told over in his mind. The intelligence and ruthlessness of Thei Porrso, despite her youth, left a lasting mark on him. She was going to make a valuable ally.

CHAPTER 29

Staring up at a ceiling she could barely see, Erenia knew that sleep would be long, if ever, in coming. One of the reasons for that snored softly next to her. Erenia looked at the broad, strong back of Norn Sanna, who had no problem sleeping at all. Then again, he didn't have guilt twisting at his guts – unreasonable guilt, she knew, but there nonetheless.

Erenia traced a gentle finger along the lines of muscle on Norn's shoulder. *So similar to Eulos*, she thought, and was immediately hit with shame. *It's impossible to cheat on the dead.* Tears streamed down her face and she took her hand away. Maybe it was too soon. It had only been a month, after all. She should have insisted on more time.

Erenia couldn't accept this argument, either. She and Sanna had been emotionally, if not physically, intimate for several months now. To feel guilt that their relationship had finally become physical was hypocritical. Sanna was a strong, decent man who deserved better than her continued vacillation. It was time to let Eulos, and her old life, go.

She leaned into him, her breasts pressed against his back. Her arm slid underneath his and grasped his hand. He jostled a bit and murmured. Then he took her hand and fell back into slumber. She rested her head against him and inhaled his scent. Her mind made up, Erenia finally relaxed and took comfort from the body next to her.

She thought about the election, only two weeks away. It was now quite certain she would be elected. Nia Kalla was ecstatic about her numbers in the polls. Regent Warsas' promotion of her had been the deciding factor.

The thought of Parmen Warsas darkened Erenia's mood. Despite what she had implicitly promised the Elder Regent, Erenia would not be an obedient little girl, blindly supporting what her 'more experienced colleagues' told her to support. She would not be a puppet, even for those in whose cause she shared. It was her intention to forge her own way, doing what she knew was right. She would create bills for improved education and economic development with the exchange of students and businesses between Territories. She would be a tireless advocate for the elimination of arena fighting, supporting other sports – showcases of skill, ability, and competition that did not result in ending a human life. It was time to take Talgourge out of the darkness of its past and into the brilliance of a new day.

Erenia knew trouble would come from Parmen Warsas, once he realized she wasn't following his plan. She pushed back her trepidation and grasped for resolve. She would do what she knew was right. She may not succeed, and her career as a Councilor may be a short one, but to do otherwise was unthinkable.

Norn knew of her plans and had pledged his unequivocal support. She hugged his sleeping form tighter. She had to start her new life somewhere, and she couldn't think of a better place than here.

CHAPTER 30

Kyu, The Unknown crossed the border between Talgourge and Urigor at thirty-seven thousand feet. Looking out the aircraft window, he watched as the mountains grew from unimpressive foothills to towering, white-capped crags in the western distance. His hands were now claws, the shadow was back over his face, and Aest rested in the seat at his side. He considered the claws. For the first time in his life, they were strange to him.

He enjoyed being Kyu Ardrassis, the loving husband of Ocelot Ardrassis. The arena fighter, Kyu, The Unknown, was beginning to feel like an unnecessary weight around his neck. Unfortunately, Kyu Ardrassis made no money. Kyu, The

Unknown made a ton of it. For now, the real world would win. The most wrenching aspect was that Ocelot understood. She didn't like it one bit, but she understood.

Kyu marveled at her forbearance and strength. There had been tears when they had parted in Talmount, but all she had said was, "Just come back."

Kyu had wanted to send Aest home with Ocelot, but she had refused, insisting Kyu would need him.

Ocelot was taking the king's ring home, but he still wore the marriage ring. Kyu refused to take it off. He knew the media would be waiting for him at Plaii Airport and would notice it immediately. He didn't care. He wouldn't give them any information, but knew they would track down Ocelot soon enough. He and Ocelot had talked about it before he left. Surprisingly, she showed no concern.

"Bring them on," she had said with a defiant smile. "I know it will be intrusive, but I don't care. Besides, after a week or two they'll find some other shiny object to fixate on, and leave us alone."

Kyu hoped she was right.

He had talked to Yuv before he left, and learned his earnings from this match would be even more than earlier quoted. Providing he survived, which Kyu had every intention of doing, he would get two million, seven hundred and seventy-five thousand marks. It would be a very nice payday, especially compared to what Kyu had earned for his first match – a measly two hundred marks.

A few hours later, the plane landed in Plaii. As usual, a chauffeured limousine, with Yuv in the back, was waiting for him.

At an altitude of over six thousand feet above sea level, the city of Plaii, while surrounded by breathtakingly beautiful mountains, had cool, brisk air even during the summer months. Now that it was autumn, the air was frigid. A furless Aest shivered next to him as they walked toward the limo.

The driver took the bags and put them in the back. Kyu's first instinct was to hold on to his sword, but now that he knew he could call it to himself, he allowed the driver to put it away in the trunk.

Kyu and Aest climbed into the back of the car, where Aest began to growl at Yuv.

"Syrra's balls, Kyu, can't you leave that fucking thing at home? Does it always have to travel with you?"

Kyu laid a restraining claw on Aest, though he wouldn't have minded letting him take a chunk out of Yuv. "Yes, Aest goes everywhere I go. Get used to it. If you ever refer to him as 'that fucking thing' again, I'll let him chew you a new asshole."

Yuv held up his pudgy hands. "Take it easy, Kyu. I don't know why you're so pissed off, but save it for tomorrow night. It's just that your... friend... obviously doesn't like me, and that makes me nervous."

Kyu reined in his anger. "Speaking of tomorrow night, who am I going up against?"

Yuv looked at Kyu, aghast. "You don't know? It's been in all the papers and sports reports on television. Where have you been the last couple weeks?"

"I've been busy. Besides, that's why I hired you; to inform me of details like this."

Then, as Kyu knew he would, Yuv noticed the ring on his finger. "What the fuck is that?"

"What the fuck do you think it is?"

"It looks like a marriage ring, but that can't be."

"Why can't it be?"

Yuv face shifted from puzzlement to amazement. "Are you fucking serious?"

"I am quite serious."

"When the fuck did this happen?"

"Last week."

"And I wasn't invited?"

"It was a private wedding, Yuv."

Yuv was silent a moment. "So, who is she? Anyone I would know?"

"No, no one you would know."

"One of your groupies, like your late buddy Eulos?"

"No," Kyu said flatly.

"Isn't this awfully fucking sudden? I had no idea you were serious with anyone. What's her name?"

"You ask a lot of questions. You're not involved in my private life, Yuv. I want to keep it that way."

Yuv looked at Kyu in shock. "What the fuck has gotten into you? You suddenly get married, and then you get pissed off because I'm curious about it? I don't know what your fucking problem is, Kyu, but if you don't want me asking any more questions, fine. I hope you realize that the media will spot that ring immediately, and they won't take 'no comment' for an answer. They'll find out who you're married to. They'll stake out that cave you call a home and stay there until they get plenty of photographs and interviews from both of you. You've just turned your life into a fucking circus."

"I'll deal with it."

"I bet you will. The question is, how will your new bride deal with it?"

"Can we get back to business? Who am I facing tomorrow night?"

Yuv settled back into his seat. "The name of your opponent is Shair Marei. Does the name sound familiar?"

"No. Should it?"

"You really have to get out of your cave more often. Of course, being a newlywed, I can understand why you haven't seen daylight for a few days, but I fucking digress. Shair Marei has twenty victories, which is almost unheard of."

"Of course it's heard of. Plenty of fighters have twenty or more victories."

"Not female ones… with her last seven victories being against men."

It was Kyu's turn to be shocked. "Shair Marei is a woman?"

"You catch on quick."

No wonder this fight had been getting so much coverage and that Kyu was getting a bigger paycheck. Sponsors must have been falling over themselves, paying big money for a chance to associate their names to the match. As distasteful as Kyu found Yuv, he had to admit his manager had scored a major coup with this.

Yuv gave Kyu a grin that held more than a little malice. "Oh, and by the way, they're bringing back the dragons for this one."

"Dragons? The Arena Commission banned them after that incident in Shaeldor."

"That was before they put acrylic glass between the crowd and the fighters. For this fight, the glass has been treated to make it heat-resistant. The sponsors and the networks carrying this want the biggest bang for their bucks. Bringing back the dragons was unanimously agreed upon."

"The Commission is going all out to counter the rising shift toward Reform in politics," Yuv continued. "These elections will see a lot more Reformers elected than ever before, even here in the West. The Commission has been in talks with those in all four Territories who still support arena fighting, including Ormnia. It's been agreed that a Championship will be created. This idea had always been defeated before due to bad blood between the Territories, especially the East and the West, but that has changed. Reformers want to eliminate arena fighting, and the best way to battle that is economically, so a Championship Tournament is being planned. This way, even if that bitch Fey Gherren succeeds in outlawing arena fighting in Ormnia, once the citizens there see how much money they are losing, not to mention the loss of honor because none of their fighters are involved, there will be a popular outcry to reinstate it.

"Thirty fighters from each Territory will be paired off to fight regionally, with each winner facing one from another fight the following week. Eventually it will come down to one Regional Champion from each Territory. A city will be drawn by lottery to host a four-way battle royal, with the last fighter standing crowned Champion."

Unless all four manage to give each other mortal wounds. Kyu had been in a couple battle royals early in his career, and hated them. While facing off against one opponent, a sword thrust from behind could come at any moment. Winning a one-on-one fight took skill; winning a battle royal took as much luck as skill. A lesser fighter could easily kill you. Although there was no doubt the fans would love it, the idea was an awful one for determining a Champion.

"Between sponsorships, merchandising, ticket sales, television revenues, and gambling, this is big money, Kyu; very big money. After you win here, you'll be the favorite to win the Championship. You'll be made top seed, so you won't have to fight until the semi-final rounds. The money you stand to earn from this will make you one of the wealthiest people in the Territories. Your victory as the first Champion will immortalize your name forever." The money and fame Yuv would garner wouldn't be miniscule, either.

Despite himself, Kyu felt some excitement at the prospect. A Championship had been talked about for years, but nothing had been attempted. Now, in the face of threats from Reformers, it was going to happen.

Ocelot will hate it. Kyu's excitement fluttered and died.

#

Unlike in Ormnia, nothing untoward happened in Urigor. The Urigish were very rabid fans of arena fighting and welcomed all fighters, no matter from where. Kyu couldn't step out of his hotel without being mobbed by legions of adoring fans. Dozens of groupies offered to share his bed. The marriage ring didn't dissuade them. Kyu politely but firmly turned them down.

Kyu knew his marriage was now common knowledge, but so far the media hadn't approached him for a story, aside from a few shouted questions that he had ignored. He knew they would be feverishly digging behind his back to find out who his wife was and get the scoop. He hoped Ocelot would be able to handle it.

#

On the night of the match Kyu and Aest were driven to Plaii Arena, a domed stadium that was the biggest in the Territories. It sat over fifty thousand people and had four gigantic video screens that allowed everyone a close-up view of the blood-letting.

Aest was escorted to his private booth, and Kyu was led by a smiling attendant to his dressing room. He hadn't spotted Yuv yet, but knew he couldn't be far. The fat manager was probably stoking up the media for the dreaded interview once the match was over.

Kyu heard the roar of the crowd through the walls of his dressing room as he changed into his black armor. There were four other matches scheduled before his, and the fans were getting into it.

He unsheathed the red sword. Even now, Kyu marveled at its beauty. He returned it to the scabbard then emptied his mind. The collective bloodlust of the crowd was nearly its own sentient creature, gaining power with every blow that found its mark on the arena floor. Spilled blood from countless fallen combatants collected in a reservoir beneath the stadium, claiming everything above it as its own.

The crowd's roar swelled to a sudden crescendo. The last kill had been made. Time was needed to clean up the remains of the loser, but the Urigish crew was quick and efficient. Within fifteen minutes there was a knock at Kyu's door, which then cracked open. "Time, Mr. Kyu," called a voice, and the door closed.

Kyu walked out to the waiting man, who led him through a labyrinth of corridors until they reached the gates that opened to the arena floor.

Yuv waited there, a lit cigar between his teeth. Dressed in a gaudy gold and white suit, he clamped a heavy hand on Kyu's shoulder. "Ready, champ?"

Kyu ignored him.

The announcer built up the crowd's excitement. Finally, Kyu's name was called and the gates swung outward. Yuv strode out first, smiling and waving to the fans. Kyu tossed the scabbard to the attendant and ran past Yuv to the center of the arena. The floor was granite, with a fresh layer of sand thrown on top to help soak up the blood. The noise of the crowd was beyond deafening. He saluted the fans with his sword. The mob exploded with adulation. Not even in Cyphus Arena had Kyu gotten an ovation this intense. Urigor was, truly, the heart of arena fighting. He looked up at one of the giant monitors; his sword, blood-red steel, hovered above tens of thousands of fans like a deistic obelisk. It was family night at the arena. Several thousand children held up plastic swords to return his salute.

Kyu lowered the sword and took in his immediate surroundings. The arena floor was oval-shaped, about one hundred feet long. Five long, metal tubes were stationed an equal distance apart along the rim. Each was connected to a circular base that could swivel and were attached to torque reaction arms that could extend and retract. Metal flex lines ran from enclosed tanks to the base of each tube, where an ignition switch was ready to turn natural gas into a long, intense blue flame – the dragons.

Kyu's breath was sharp. He knew the advantage lay with his opponent, whose body was acclimated to this low-oxygen altitude. He needed to make this kill as quickly as possible.

The announcer began his introduction of Kyu's opponent. The crowd hushed, collecting itself. Kyu turned to the gates on the other side of the arena floor. The excitement was a living, breathing thing that engulfed all, including Kyu.

Voice rising, the announcer yelled out. "Here she is, Urigor's own Shair Marei!"

The gates swung open. It was as if a flame had been introduced to a powder keg.

The Urigish fighter bounded out to shattering acclaim. The torque arms pushed the tube openings skyward and flames roared out of each as the woman warrior saluted her brethren.

Shair Marei was tall like most of the Urigish. Her torso was clad in boiled leather adorned with simple designs and crisscrossed with slashes and dents. Her arms and legs, heavily muscled and laced with scars, were bared for ease of mobility. Underneath her leather helmet, white-blonde hair was cut short, most likely in respect to the danger of the dragons rather than any affiliation to the temple of Syssera. Her facial features were broad, with a long, jagged scar running down the left side of her face, from hairline to jaw.

Shair Marei's weapon of choice was a six-foot wooden pole arm, with foot-long, double-edged blades attached to either end. The wood beneath the sharpened steel was strapped with iron to prevent them from being chopped. Marei spun the weapon over her head like a quarterstaff. The mob went nuts. Finally, she faced Kyu. The crowd settled in eager anticipation.

Kyu advanced cautiously. He imagined that many of Shair Marei's former opponents had underestimated her because she was a woman. Kyu would not make the same mistake. His attention was also on the dragons; while this took away much of his focus, he realized that Shair Marei had to be doing the same.

Marei darted forward, the pole arm swinging. One of the blades sliced down at Kyu's head. Kyu raised his sword just in time to block the blow.

Fuck, she's quick!

With a shock, Kyu realized Shair Marei was behind him. He spun around, just in time to deflect another blade. Marei danced away, a tight grin on her face.

Click.

Kyu had a half-second to realize the noise was an igniter going off. He felt more than heard a sudden roar behind him. Kyu somersaulted to the side as an intense blue flame seared the area where he had been standing.

Shair Marei loped forward, but flame from another dragon made her back up.

Enough of this. Time to take the offensive. Kyu strode forward and jabbed at Marei with his sword. She knocked it aside with her blade, as Kyu knew she would. His arm continued with the motion.The steel spun over his head and sliced downward.

The pole arm was there, the iron strapping catching the red blade with a loud *clang!* Shair Marei reversed her hold and thrust a blade at the darkness that hid Kyu's face. He jerked his head aside, but the blade kissed his cheek, leaving a shallow slice. Shair Marei's blue eyes lit up as drops of blood fell out of the darkness and onto Kyu's armor.

The roar of the crowd as they, too, saw Kyu's blood on the giant video screens shook the arena. Kyu heard none of it. He was too busy trying to stay alive.

Click.

Before Kyu could discern from which direction the flame would come, Shair Marei spun her pole arm in a whirling blur and struck at Kyu. He knocked the blade away as the dragon on his left erupted.

Kyu staggered back. The flame had caught his forearm. Most of it had been stopped by the vambrace; however, enough of the heat had reached his upper arm to do damage. The hairs were scorched, the skin turned red and began to blister. Kyu willed himself to shut away the pain.

Again, Shair Marei was behind him. Kyu turned, his sword held in a defensive position. He wasn't quite quick enough. Instead of striking high, Shair Marei aimed low. She slashed at his leg, opening a deep wound in his right calf.

Miraculously, the blade missed the tendon. Kyu was able to remain on his feet, but he was losing a lot of blood, depleting his body of already-scarce oxygen. He drew in ragged gulps of breath and tried to fight off the lightheadedness that threatened to overwhelm him.

Shair Marei smiled, but was delayed in delivering the final thrust when she had to jump out of the way of a spitting dragon. She took a second to collect herself and, with lightning speed, thrust a blade at Kyu's exposed throat.

Kyu dropped to the arena floor. As the blade sliced through empty air, he swung his sword and caught the pole arm dead center. There was no iron strapping there, and the wood snapped in half. The severed section of the weapon hit the granite floor and bounced away.

Shair Marei, stunned, looked at the remains of the weapon she still held. She quickly recovered, reversed her grip, and swung the blade down at Kyu.

The moment's hesitation was all Kyu needed. Deciding to return the favor, he opened up Marei's lower leg with the red blade, making sure the tendon was severed. With a cry, Shair Marei collapsed to the arena floor. Kyu regained his feet with some effort.

Unable to stand, Marei swung the weapon she had left, desperately trying to keep Kyu at bay. Kyu flicked his sword and knocked the blade out of her hand. He then plunged the red sword through the boiled leather armor and straight through Shair Marei's chest.

The crowd's roar blotted out everything. As opposed to Erat Arena, this response wasn't hostile. It was wholehearted approval. It didn't matter that their local favorite had lost; for them, two superior fighters had given it all, and the better one came out on top.

Kyu looked down at his defeated opponent, and was surprised to see she was still alive. The blade had missed her heart; a major artery had been severed, however, and she was bleeding out fast. She was less than a minute from death.

Shair Marei knew it. Despite her mortal wound, she had a light of clarity in her eyes. In them Kyu saw regret – regret at a life wasted, cut short for the amusement of the bloodthirsty masses.

Kyu's blood curdled as he realized he had seen this exact same regret on the faces of all he had defeated in the arena. Shair Marei coughed up blood. A single tear slipped from the corner of her eye, rolling down her face until it reached the scar then following the line of the old wound until it dripped to the blood-soaked sand beneath her head.

No… no…

His new gift surged through Kyu, bringing every cell to sentience, blasting away the hate and savagery around him. It flowed through his hands, down his sword, and entered Shair Marei's torn body. Kyu commanded the staca to heal what it had damaged.

Ripped flesh knitted together and the artery closed as Kyu slowly drew the blade from Shair Marei's chest. He urged her body to produce more blood. The healing was also happening to his own body. The shallow cut to his face disappeared, and the deep slash in his leg shut and scarred over.

Shair Marei gasped as bones snapped and fused together as the blade was pulled through her shattered ribcage. The tip emerged from her body.

It was not enough. Too much blood had been lost. Shair Marei shivered. Her eyes glazed over, her body settled into stillness. Kyu looked down at the life he had taken and felt profound emptiness, desolation he thought would cripple him.

The mob chanted his name. Bile rose in his throat. He stalked off the arena floor and out of sight of the crowd who, not receiving their expected salute, began to boo.

Kyu didn't want to stay in the stadium, or Urigor, a minute longer than he had to. *Fuck Yuv and the media.* He retrieved Aest then took his friend to the access tunnels beneath the stadium.

Aest looked at Kyu without barking. *Is this it?*

Kyu nodded. "Yes, it is."

Good.

Kyu smiled and felt immense gratitude that Aest understood.

Avoiding the stadium staff, Kyu entered his dressing room and locked the door. He banished the shadow and the claws then quickly changed into regular clothes. He inspected the leg wound that Shair Marei had given him a few minutes earlier. Nothing remained but a thin white scar.

The knob rattled, and pounding shook the door. "Open the fucking door, Kyu!" Yuv bellowed out.

Kyu turned to Aest. "We're going back to Cyphus now."

Holding his armor and his sword, Kyu willed it. He and Aest disappeared from Plaii Arena.

#

Ocelot sat on the bed, twisting the marriage ring on her finger and staring off into total darkness. Unable to take not knowing any longer, she put on the television for news of Kyu's match. It had just ended. He had won.

Her relief was quickly replaced with dread. Soon there would be another match, and another… She shut off the set, turned off the lights then sat on the bed, twirling and worried. *So many limitations, Mother; so much doubt. Still they persevere. They are stronger than we give them credit.*

There was a sudden shift in the air around her. A new presence was in the bedroom. Ocelot sat still and held her breath.

The light flicked on. Kyu stood there with Aest. He dropped his armor and sword to the floor then looked at her. His eyes misted over but he said nothing.

Ocelot understood. The terrible burden of anguish was lifted from her heart. She rose from the bed and held his face in her hands. She felt Kyu's need for salvation as he wrapped his arms around her, and she gave it to him. His tears ran free, dampening her dark hair that now reached her shoulders. Aest nuzzled against the both of them, and they welcomed it.

Outside, the sun rose and chased away the night.

CHAPTER 31

The following week was among the worst of Kyu's life.

Yuv called at least twice a day. Each time, Kyu let it go to the answering machine. The messages became increasingly heated and malicious.

The media camped outside his underground home, wanting to know how and why Kyu had disappeared so completely from Plaii Arena after his victory. They also demanded to know about his wife and for both of them to come out for interviews and photographs. The police were there to preserve order, but after several days even they were calling on Kyu to say something so everyone would be satisfied and leave.

After a week of being trapped in their home, Ocelot finally convinced Kyu to do what had to be done. Kyu picked up the phone and called the police. "Tell the media that I'll give a statement at noontime." Kyu hung up, his mind heavy with misgivings.

"If we are to have a chance at a normal life then it has to be done," Ocelot told him.

"I know, but that doesn't mean I have to like it."

"Look at it this way: the Council elections happen next week. The media will shift its attention to that, and we'll be left alone."

Kyu shook his head. "Somehow I doubt that. Look, you don't have to go out there with me."

"Yes, I do." Ocelot touched Kyu's arm. Her voice softened. "I need to be seen with you, and you know it. The media won't be happy until they know who I am. They'll find out eventually. It's important that we cannot be seen to be hiding. If we do, we'll never know a moment's peace. I don't like this, either, but it has to be done."

Kyu nodded reluctantly. "Okay. Let's get this over with."

#

Precisely at noon, the heavy wooden door opened. Kyu, with his face hidden in shadow and his hands as claws, stepped out with Ocelot at his side.

The reporters and onlookers, several hundred of them from all Territories, strained against the line of police. A cacophony of voices rose, slinging questions and demanding answers. Lights and cameras fastened on Kyu and Ocelot, along with a lightning storm of flashes from photographers. All major television news networks were there.

Kyu wanted to turn away, but Ocelot's hand tightened on his arm. He proceeded forward. A podium had been set up, bristling with microphones and cables. It was wide enough for two people; Kyu and Ocelot stepped up to it. He held up a clawed hand, and after a few minutes, the crowd fell into an expectant, low-buzz silence.

Kyu took a deep breath. "I have a number of things to say. I would appreciate your courtesy as I speak. Please do not shout any questions; I will not answer any beyond what I say here now.

"First: I am married. This is my wife, Ocelot."

The full force of the media attention shifted to Ocelot like a massive, hungry carnivore eyeing a lone deer. Despite Kyu's earlier request, questions rang out at Ocelot, who blanched but said nothing and kept smiling.

#

In the home she now shared with Norn Sanna, Erenia's mouth hung open as she watched the television.

Sanna pointed at the screen. "Isn't that the acolyte who left the temple recently?"

"Ocelot," Erenia murmured. "She's married to that maniac? It can't be!"

Sanna grunted. "You never know, do you? She must be as twisted as he is. No wonder she left the temple."

Erenia shook her head and kept watching.

#

Kyu held up a claw. Once it was clear Ocelot wasn't going to speak, the media silenced.

"Second: I am Kyu, The Unknown no longer." The shadow disappeared from Kyu's face. His claws became normal human hands.

A stunned silence was followed by an explosion of questions and camera flashes. Reporters surged forward once more. It was several long minutes before the crowd settled enough for him to speak.

"My name is Kyu Ardrassis."

A question was shouted from the crowd. "Are you claiming descent from the Unifier, Harra Ardrassis?"

Despite his earlier promise not to answer questions, Kyu did so. "Yes."

The noise level rose. "Impossible," someone yelled out. "Harra Ardrassis had no heirs."

"He had one who was commonly thought to have died as an infant. That child did not die, and I am descended from that line." Kyu marveled that he had gotten through the half-lie as easily as he did.

The reporters murmured skeptically.

Kyu held up the King's Ring. "This is the ring that Ardrassis kings have worn for generations. To prove it, I will allow historians from Cyphus University to study it and verify that it is, indeed, what I say it is."

"Does that mean you're proclaiming yourself King of Talgourge?"

Kyu shook his head. "No, of course not. I would never do such a thing. I'm an ordinary citizen, like you."

"A citizen, maybe," the reporter said. "But hardly ordinary!"

Bursts of nervous laughter ran through the crowd.

#

In her guise as Fey Gherren, Asrath watched her son on television and smiled. "You do realize what he's going to say next, don't you?"

Padanor Syche fixed his cold eyes on the Regent. "Why don't you enlighten me?"

Asrath smiled and looked away. "Let's just say that you're going to be left financially stranded on an institution that will die off without him."

Syche's gaze darkened. "How do you know so much about him?"

"We go a long way back." She turned her attention back to the television. "He's actually quite pitiful. You honestly thought he would have succeeded in killing me?"

The Korl leader shifted uncomfortably. How did this woman know so much? "That was before I realized your interests coincided with mine."

Asrath laughed. "They may coincide at the moment, but my ultimate interest goes far beyond yours."

Syche frowned. "As long as you don't prove a hindrance, I don't care what your interests are."

"Threats again, Padanor? We've only just become friends."

Syche turned back to the television.

#

"Third, and lastly: the match in Plaii Arena was my last. I am no longer an arena fighter, nor will I take a position with the Arena Commission or at any of the Combat Academies. I am out of that business, completely.

"This concludes my statements. I will not answer any more questions. I now ask all of you to leave and extend the courtesy of privacy to my wife and myself. Thank you."

#

Erenia stared at the screen, stunned.

Eulos is dead because of you, Kyu. You don't get off that easy.

#

Padanor Syche seethed as the Ormnian Regent sat back and laughed. Fey Gherren had been right. Kyu, The Unknown had up and quit. The biggest moneymaker the world of arena fighting had ever seen was walking away and leaving everyone involved, including Padanor Syche, with nothing but their dicks in their hands.

Kyu had just become a big embarrassment and a liability.

#

The bellow of outrage and fury that blasted through Yuv's office sent Shanna running for cover. She was a quarter-mile down the street before she slowed. Thankfully, there was nothing in the office worth going back for.

#

Inside their home, Kyu stood in the bathroom and looked at the face in the mirror. Ocelot walked up behind him and rested her head on his shoulder. She stared into the mirror with him.

"All my life I've hated mirrors. Normal people could gaze into them to see what they looked like. They could see what needed touching up to make them look better. I was always denied that. All I saw was darkness. I knew I had a face, but couldn't see it. And, since I had claws for hands, I figured the darkness was there to hide something truly hideous. I was scorned and made to feel ugly, so I felt it was all right for me to do ugly things. After all, I was a monster. It was to be expected."

Ocelot ran a hand down his face. "But now you know you're not a monster. You're not ugly at all, inside or out. You're a decent man, and although you have a heritage you can't change, you can control what you do with it."

Kyu was silent. Ocelot stood in silence with him. He took her hand into his own and squeezed. "You are the one who makes me decent. I love you so much."

#

Up on Empress' Mountain, Haena Ardrassis nodded wearily. It was all going as planned. A terrible sadness settled over her.

CHAPTER 32

It was election day in the Territories. The media buzzed with excitement: Reformist candidates were expected to gain a lot of ground in Talgourge and Ormnia, and were even expected to have a sizable minority in Shaeldor. Urigor, as always, would be almost all Traditionalists, but two or three Urigish Reformist candidates had made a serious push to be elected. Everywhere, hope and tension ran high.

Kyu Ardrassis stalked the streets of Cyphus, the elections the least of his concerns. He had unpleasant business to resolve. People recognized him with his now visible face, but would-be autograph seekers were warned away by the fury that radiated from his taut body.

After his statements to the media, the mob had stayed around for the rest of the day, hoping for more, moving on only when the police threatened to arrest them for loitering. The calls from Yuv, however, did not stop. With each succeeding day they got angrier and uglier. Enough was enough. Leaving Aest home with Ocelot, Kyu left to settle the matter once and for all.

Kyu got to Yuv's office and barged inside. He was surprised to see Shanna wasn't there, but he had no time or inclination to wonder about that. Feeling the weight of the gun underneath his jacket, he pushed open the door to Yuv's office and strode in.

The air was nearly unbreathable with pungent cigar smoke. The ashtray on Yuv's desk overflowed with mounds of gray ash and dirty brown stubs. Yuv sat back in his massive leather chair, a fresh-lit cigar jutting from his mouth. He looked relaxed and grinned when Kyu stormed in.

"I knew I could get you down here, given enough calls," Yuv blew out a choking cloud of smoke. "We have business, you and I, and we need to get down to it."

"We have no business together.Your services as manager are no longer required. Consider yourself fired."

Yuv chuckled and shook his huge, bald head. "Kyu, Kyu. Do you honestly think you can just walk away from this? That you have a job like all the other shitheads out there who can say, 'I quit', and do just that? No, Kyu, it's not that easy for you. You are beholden to a lot of powerful people who will not take 'no' for an answer."

"They have no choice. I'm through with arena fighting, and I'm through with you. Stop calling my house or I may just drag you out to the arena for my final match."

Yuv rested his hands on the desk and worked the cigar to the corner of his mouth. "So this is what you look like without that shadow. It was pretty clever of you to keep this ability a secret for all this time. No wonder you got out of Plaii Arena without being seen, though I don't know how you did it with that animal of yours, nor do I know how you got back to Cyphus so quickly."

Kyu was not about to enlighten him.

Yuv shook his head and leaned forward. "Now you've got a sweet young wife. Tell me, Kyu, is that fucking cunt the reason you've suddenly gotten soft?"

Fury seized Kyu. The red sword appeared in his hand. Before Yuv could react, Kyu thrust the tip of the blade between his second and third chins, pinning the fat man to the chair. Yuv's eyes widened in shock and the cigar fell from his mouth onto his stomach. A trickle of blood ran along the folds of flesh and soaked into the collar of his shirt.

Kyu's rage nearly overcame him. He wanted desperately to take Yuv's head off his shoulders. "If you say anything like that about my wife again, if you even dare to say her name, I will kill you. Am I understood?" Kyu pushed the blade a quarter-inch deeper into Yuv's fat.

"Argh!" Yuv sputtered, unable to get away from the steel. "All right! I'm sorry, okay? Just take that thing away."

Kyu pulled the sword back, but kept it in his hand. Yuv grabbed a white handkerchief and pressed it to the shallow wound in his neck. He plucked the cigar off his stomach before it burned through his shirt and stubbed it out in the overfilled ashtray.

Yuv's face was a mask of anger. "That's a nice trick. Now I know how you won that match with Havla Cort. It would have come in handy for the Championship Tournament that's coming up, the Tournament that was created to showcase you, the Tournament that would have made you immortal in the annuls of arena fighting, not to mention several million marks wealthier. Are you actually going to throw all that away?"

"Yes."

Yuv's meaty fists came down like twin hammers on his desk. "By Syrra's balls, why? What's happened to you, Kyu? You were always glad to chop someone up in the arena, for a lot less than that. Could you at least tell me what the fuck is going on?"

"It's just over, Yuv. Accept it and leave me alone. There are plenty of up-and-coming fighters out there to make famous and make you rich."

"None of them are Kyu, The Unknown. You are the only one who can generate enough interest to bring in the big sponsors and cause money to flow like rivers for the Arena Commission."

"I'm no longer Kyu, The Unknown. He's gone and not coming back."

Yuv's gaze was cold. "If you walk away from this, that magic trick with your sword won't help you when the Korl comes to pay you a visit."

"You can tell Padanor Syche for me that any move he makes against me will be his last."

Yuv barked out a laugh. "You're no longer in the arena, Kyu. This won't be a fair fight between two evenly-matched opponents. You won't see them coming until it's too late." He leaned forward. "Don't think they'll spare your pretty wife or sidekick beast, either. By quitting, you're putting them in the line of fire. Can you handle that, known Kyu?"

Kyu's rage almost got the better of him again, but he knew the truth of Yuv's words. "I'll do what I have to do to protect them."

Yuv shook his head. "It won't be nearly enough." He sat back and pulled out another cigar. "What a fucking waste. You could have had it all. Soon you'll have nothing."

"Goodbye, Yuv. Why should you worry? It's not your problem." Kyu turned and walked out.

#

Yuv lit his cigar. To an empty room, he said, "You're wrong, Kyu. It is my problem."

#

In the Cyphus temple of Syssera, Erenia, Norn Sanna, Nia Kalla, and a dozen excited acolytes watched on television as the final results from the polls came in. Erenia Baak was now a Councilor for the Territory of Talgourge. Nia hugged her. The acolytes squealed in joy and embraced her. Norn took her hand and squeezed it, his eyes reflecting pride. One person was conspicuously absent. Erenia excused herself and went to the priestess' chamber.

Enna Racyne sat at her desk and looked at Erenia with unsmiling eyes. "Congratulations." Her tone was flat.

Erenia shook her head. "Is that all you can say? This is what we've worked so hard for."

"No, this is what you've done for yourself."

It saddened and angered Erenia to hear the bitterness in Enna Racyne's words. "Who talked me into this in the first place? You did. Who convinced me to stay in the race when my husband was killed and I wanted to drop out? You did. You provided me with the funds and support I needed to make myself known. You were adamant that I win. It was an obsession with you, but now that I've won, you're acting like it's something terrible. Why, Enna? Please, talk to me."

"There's nothing to talk about. You won. I just hope you know what to do now that you're in office."

Erenia's anger flared. "You're envious, aren't you? You pushed me to win, running this race vicariously through me because you couldn't do it yourself, but deep down, you always thought I was undeserving. When I showed I had a mind of my own and that I wasn't going to be your puppet, you finally realized this was no longer your campaign, and you did your best, along with Regent Warsas, to bring me under your control.

"It's not going to work that way, Enna. I've won, and I will fulfill my duties as Councilor as I deem best."

Enna Racyne's face reddened as she stood from her chair. "You stupid, foolish girl! You think you have such grand ideas. What do you know?" The priestess was shouting. "You are nothing but a newborn in the world of politics. You think you have all the answers, and that everyone will listen to you. You're going to ignore the advice of those who know better.

"Do you know what will happen?" Enna's eyes glittered. "You'll get flattened like an insect and brushed out the door, you ungrateful, headstrong bitch!"

Erenia stood in shock. The priestess, who was once her closest friend, was gone. In her place was someone consumed with bitterness and hate. "Enna, what has gotten into you? Our ideals are still the same."

"Idiot!" Enna spat at her. "I'm warning you, Erenia Baak, either you keep your mouth shut and follow the counsel of Regent Warsas and myself, or you're going to wish you were still fucking arena fighters."

Erenia had enough. "Don't you dare threaten me, Enna. I will fulfill the duties of my office the way my conscience tells me to, and neither you nor the Regent will stop me. This may be my only term in office, but at least I will know that I did what I promised to do for the people who voted for me."

Erenia stalked to the door then turned around. "One last thing, Enna: I will always be a follower of Syssera, but I am no longer an acolyte at this temple. Goodbye."

Erenia gave each acolyte a tearful hug before leaving. She conferred briefly with Nia Kalla, who assured her that her office at the Government Building in Talmount was ready for her, along with a local office in Cyphus whenever she needed it. Nia had already agreed to stay on as Erenia's chief aide.

Erenia grabbed Norn's hand and pulled him out of the temple, whispering furiously about her confrontation with Enna Racyne.

At the exit, Norn turned to the remaining acolytes. "Tell the priestess she has lost me as an acolyte, as well."

#

After the elections there was much buzz about the results. The Reformers had made significant gains. Ormnia was now completely Reformist. The Council, urged by Fey Gherren, passed a law that officially banned arena fighting, and shut down all Combat Academies in the Territory.

The Korl was surprisingly quiet about this development.

#

Talgourge was now a solid three-fourths Reformist. Councilor Erenia Baak wasted no time. Less than a month after the elections, she initiated studies that laid the groundwork for inter-student transfers between the Territories, conferred with educational leaders to revamp the school system with teaching programs that focused on comprehension rather than memorization, and reached out to poverty-stricken communities to ensure their children got the same education as those whose families were financially better off. Erenia contacted business leaders and tried to sell them on the labor pool and resources available to them if they constructed office and manufacturing sites in Talgourge, and she drafted a bill that would give tax breaks for companies that did just that. She was an active sponsor of the arts, and promoted the many non-lethal sports while proposing legislation that would follow Ormnia's lead and banish arena fighting for good.

Many of the other Councilors were attracted to Erenia's energy, passion, and leadership. Within weeks of taking office, she had a solid core of supporters.

#

Shaeldor was still held by Traditionalists, though the Reformers had made some surprising gains. Councilor Thei Porrso considered this an abomination, and knew just where to lay the blame: Regent Mabb Youri and that Ormnian whore, Fey Gherren

No matter, she thought to herself in her darkened office. Soon enough, it would all be corrected.

#

The Traditionalist stronghold of Urigor had remained intact. The Urigish looked upon their eastern neighbors with contempt, and their southern neighbor, supposedly an ally, with a hint of betrayal.

Regent Nevin Ghat did his best to foster these feelings. He wondered, not for the first time, whether he could trust Thei Porrso. She had cost him a lot of money. The return on that investment had better be worth it.

CHAPTER 33

Now that Kyu was unemployed, Ocelot insisted on getting a job, despite her husband's protests that they were in decent financial shape. "Maybe you're happy sitting around all day watching television, but I've done too much of that already. I have to go out and do something or I'll go nuts. No offense, dear."

Ocelot went to the Ocean View, the seafood restaurant where she and Kyu had gone on their first date. She applied for, and got, a position as a hostess. With her charm and effervescent personality, she quickly became a favorite with her co-workers and customers.

It was several miles between the restaurant and their home. Ocelot told Kyu she would take public transportation to work and back. Kyu told Ocelot that with the money they had, they could afford a car. They went to a dealership and Ocelot chose a small car that resembled a bubble on wheels. After driving it for a week she lovingly named it her 'bumpmobile'.

A month later, Kyu found her sitting alone in the living room. Tears streamed down her face.

Alarmed, Kyu went to her. "What is it? What's wrong?"

Ocelot remained silent. Then she grabbed Kyu's hand and squeezed it tight. She turned to him and, through her tears, gave him the most brilliant smile he had ever seen. "Nothing's wrong… Daddy."

It took a full five seconds for Ocelot's words to sink in. When they did, Kyu's world shifted. He opened his mouth, but no words came. He was happy, incredibly so. He saw the rapturous joy in Ocelot's eyes. After growing up as orphans, he and Ocelot would now be part of a true family.

Kyu put his hand on Ocelot's stomach, which was still flat. She rested her hand atop his.

Kyu, a father; he knew it would take time for that concept, and all it entailed, to settle within him. He felt a rare flash of uncertainty. Having no role models of his own, he hoped he was up to the responsibility, but as he looked upon his beaming wife, he knew this would be a partnership in the truest sense of the word. They would support and be supported by each other as they brought this new life into the world.

"When is the baby due?" Kyu asked.

"The doctor told me about seven and a half months. I'll be seeing an obstetrician during this time."

Kyu sat with Ocelot in silence while several thoughts whirled through his head. A few were not pleasant.

It had been three months since Kyu had announced his separation from the world of arena fighting, and ever since he had been in a high state of alert for retribution from the Korl.

So far, nothing had happened, but Kyu knew it would be foolish to think they had forgotten about him.

A bigger concern was Asrath. Kyu had kept a careful eye on his mother. After her failed seduction, she no longer seemed interested in him, but he knew she wasn't done yet. Fey Gherren had become a powerful, polarizing figure, who seemed to have reached a truce with the Korl. Kyu didn't know what sort of alliance she had made with Padanor Syche, but whatever it was would not be for the benefit of the Territories.

During one of his daily meditations, Kyu projected his consciousness to Empress' Mountain while keeping his physical body in Cyphus. Once there, he discussed Asrath with his aunt.

"Is there any way I can banish Asrath back beyond the Disian Curtain, like my father did?"

It's possible, Kyu, though I don't know for certain. You do have a physical connection with her, though not in the traditional way by giving her your seed. This would be unprecedented.

"Why don't I go to Ormnia and try?"

I don't encourage that, for three reasons. One: I don't feel your skills are strong enough yet to face her or banish her. Two: we need to see what machinations she has set in play, so we can take steps to counter them. Three... there is something different about her now. She has something that I believe would defeat any attempt by you to banish her.

"What does she have now that she didn't have before?"

The Empress shook her head and remained silent. Kyu's physical concentration faltered and his consciousness returned to Cyphus.

He worried constantly about Ocelot when she went out alone. There was nothing he could say that would stop her from doing so. In truth, Kyu had to admit that if he were in Ocelot's position, he would do the same. If they wanted a shot at normal lives, then they had to do normal things, like go to work, make friends, and sometimes go out with those friends, as Ocelot did.

Their situation, however, had altered dramatically. A new, young life was coming – a life that needed protection and stability.

“The baby can sleep in our room at first, but eventually will need his or her own room. I think the weapons room will work out fine, once the weapons are gone, of course.”

Kyu brought his mind back to the present. “My weapons are going?”

“Of course they are. You don’t need them anymore. I don’t think you needed them at all.”

“Where will they go?”

“I think the landfill outside of Cyphus is the perfect place for them, but I’ll leave that final decision to you. You can keep your sword, of course, and that stupid handgun if you insist, but the rest have to go.”

Kyu had a spot in mind. He had found it during a session with his awareness. “I know the perfect place for them.”

CHAPTER 34

Alone in her office in Ormount’s Government Building, Fey Gherren allowed herself to become the Diaboli Domini Asrath.

She had accomplished a lot over the past few weeks. Ormnia was now, realistically if not officially, a sovereign Territory, and Fey Gherren was its absolute leader. The entire Ormnian Council bowed to her in all matters. Only one Councilor, an old incumbent, had spoken against her. A few hours later he had been mugged outside his home by a gang wielding clubs and hammers. His face had been pounded into unrecognizable mush, but police were able to identify the body through paperwork in his wallet which had, remarkably, been left untouched.

The message had been missed by no one.

The Korl was now firmly under her sway. Through them, Asrath had made contact with the denizens of Xiaroc Isle. The criminals there had a unique social structure and, amazingly, had created a crude but stable form of government. Their main occupation was agriculture, with a number of crop fields on the inhabitable section of the island.

Half of the crops consisted of foodstuffs, the other half vorchals. Native to the island, they were long-stemmed flowers with bright red and yellow petals which produced nectar that contained strong narcotic properties. The nectar was harvested and chemically distilled to a fine yellow powder, which was then cut and expanded to become a powerful and highly addictive opiate called Vortex.

The Isle Patrol was tasked to watch over Xiaroc Isle. They brought over condemned prisoners and humanitarian supplies, and made sure none tried to escape, but like many government agencies, they were understaffed, underpaid, and prone to corruption. The Korl controlled several vessels and aircraft of the Isle Patrol. They brought weapons and luxury items to the Isle's rulers, and smuggled Vortex back to the mainland.

Once in Ormnia, the drug was cut down even further then sold, making hundreds of millions of marks for the Korl, and an ever-increasing number of addicts in all four Territories.

Asrath smiled. Pretty soon the drug plague would be the least of the humans' problems. Through her meticulous manipulation, everything was in place to tear the Unification apart. Large-scale hatred had been sown, and warfare would be harvested.

The coming violence and misery would feed the denizens beyond the Disian Curtain. Asrath marveled that the humans paid no attention to the Curtain. As far as they were concerned, the Curtain had always been there, since before the time of Harra Ardrassis. For them, it was like the sky and the ocean; a constant in their world. Since it was never seen to move, it was never thought about.

The Curtain, however, was moving. It always had been, bit by bit, coming ever closer to the large continent that was the humans' only bastion on this world. Only two things had ever held it back: the conjoined faith of the Parents, Syrra and Syssera, and the presence in this world of an Odigos. Humans, though, could not help being humans, so they mixed what should have been an inseparable intimacy, a single Faith, with their politics and polarized their worship of the Parents, separating them and making them weaker. The hostilities to come would widen the schism and make it unbridgeable.

The Odigos was helpless to do anything about it. Her very existence was coming to a close, and the plans she was desperately making to prevent the destruction of this world were doomed to failure.

The edge of the Disian Curtain had already reached Xiaroc Isle's eastern coast and begun its subjugation of the island. It hadn't reached the penal colony on the island's western edge yet, but the humans would soon realize that their tropical prison was now their damnation.

Asrath felt the clamoring of her brethren beyond the Curtain, their yearning for human souls. She felt the power of the other Diaboli Domini as they schemed and fought for dominance of worlds beyond count.

This world, though, belonged to Asrath, and she would not give it up to another. Besides, the more powerful Diaboli Domini were vying for dominance of Dis itself. Asrath kept on the outside of this. She had no wish to cross the Son of the Morning, and felt the others were fools for even considering it.

The Infernal laughed. She had everything she needed. She patted her stomach, where life squirmed and grew. Once born, it would allow its mother unquestioned sovereignty over the entire planet.

CHAPTER 35

After incessant badgering by Norn, Erenia finally conceded that she was exhausted and needed a few days of rest. She had thrown every bit of herself into her office since the election two months earlier, and had accomplished more than she dared hope. Most of the other Councilors, including many of the senior ones, had responded to Erenia's passion and drive, and had tacitly given her the lead.

Unfortunately, but expectedly, her biggest distractor was the Elder Regent. Parmen Warsas had tried to rein her in any number of times. Erenia knew a confrontation was coming, and she wasn't looking forward to it.

She resolved that for the next few days she would relax, enjoy herself, and spend some much-needed time with Norn, whom she knew felt abandoned as of late. What a Syssera-blessed man he was. His support was unflagging, and he never complained about the long hours Erenia put in. He had insisted on this mini-vacation only because he had seen how close to collapse, physically and mentally, she was.

Norn was right. She needed time to rest and recharge. There was still much to do, and she had to conserve her energy for where it was needed.

Erenia reclined in a large, comfortable chair, savoring its warmth and softness. Her eyes were almost closed when something cold was placed in her hand. Surprised, she looked at the glass, filled with tropical fruit juice and lots of ice.

"I made that especially for you" Norn settled into another chair, his own drink in his hand. "It has a bit of kick added."

Erenia raised the glass to her lips and took a sip. She tasted strawberry with a touch of mango. She took a bigger swig. The kick set in almost immediately. She could taste the rum, but it blended so well with the other flavors it didn't overpower the drink. She took another, deeper pull.

"You'd better not do this too often, Mr. Sanna. I could get used to it."

Norn laughed and drank. "Anything for you, Madame Councilor."

Erenia took another sip. A pleasant lassitude settled over her. "Do me a favor, Norn. For the next few days, don't say the word Councilor."

"Your wish is my command." Norn got up and gave Erenia a full, heartfelt kiss.

Erenia's nerves tingled, sending a rush of pleasure through her. She noticed a prominent bulge in Norn's pants. Her hand cupped it and caressed it softly. Norn's eyes closed and he moaned.

"I've been ignoring you terribly lately, haven't I?" Erenia unfastened Norn's pants.

#

They laid in bed, spent, their naked limbs pleasantly entwined, staying that way for an hour without speaking. Erenia broke the silence. "I wish we could stay like this forever."

Sanna grunted. "No, you don't."

Erenia sat up. Sanna reached for a breast but she swatted his hand away. "What do you mean, I don't?"

Norn settled back in the bed. "I can feel you getting restless. It's only been one day, but you're already itching to get back to your office."

Erenia turned away, an angry retort frozen on her lips. Norn was right. There was no denying it.

Sanna's hand took hers. "This is one of the reasons why I love you. Needed change is going to happen because of you."

Erenia looked at him. "You think a lot of me. I hope I can justify your faith."

"You already have." Norn sat up and embraced her. "You've given me meaning and happiness." Norn broke the embrace and looked Erenia in the eyes. "I want to marry you. Will you marry me, Erenia?"

Erenia hadn't believed she could be surprised by anything. This, however, succeeded. She loved Norn Sanna, but was still reeling from the memory of Eulos; both their fractured marriage and his sudden, violent death. It was the type of death Norn could easily suffer, given his position in law enforcement and the number of violent, amoral criminals he encountered.

Erenia looked into the eyes of the man she loved – eyes filled with pleading. This was a chance that needed taking. She placed a hand on the strong line of his jaw. "Yes, Norn, I will marry you." They embraced again.

Despite her happiness, two thoughts troubled Erenia. One: she wanted to get married in a Sysseran temple, but not the one here in Cyphus. Erenia wanted nothing whatsoever to do with Enna Racyne. Two: before she could put Eulos behind her for good, there was a certain bit of business she had to attend to.

CHAPTER 36

In the third month of Ocelot's pregnancy, Kyu got a notice from the Tax Collector's office. The troubles began.

"Audited?"

Kyu could tell that Ocelot was beginning to feel her condition. So far, she had avoided the morning sickness that plagued many other expectant women, but she tired easily and was prone, to Kyu's dismay, to sudden mood swings.

When Kyu had received the envelope, Ocelot was in a particularly foul mood. That one word did not improve it.

"What are you talking about? What do you mean 'audited'?"

Kyu handed her the notice. "Read it for yourself."

Ocelot snatched the paper from his hand and perused the contents. "We're being audited!"

"Didn't I just say that?"

"Don't get smart. I'm not in the mood."

What else is new? Kyu thought but wisely did not say.

Ocelot looked up from the notice. "What are we going to do about this?"

A thought occurred to Kyu. He pulled a card from his wallet.

"What's that?"

"I don't know if he can help or not, but I suppose it won't hurt to call and ask. When I had been taken into custody after Eulos was killed, Yuv sent a lawyer to get me released, a man by the name of Kelvin Varaii. He seemed competent enough. Maybe he can help us out with this."

"But if he's associated with Yuv, can you trust him?"

It was a fair question. "I don't know. I don't know who else to turn to, though."

Ocelot thought about it, then nodded. "All right, call him."

Kyu dialed the number. A female voice answered. "You have reached the office of Handos and Varaii. How can I help you?"

"I need to speak with Kelvin Varaii."

"Whom may I say is calling?"

"Kyu Ardrassis, though he may remember me as Kyu, The Unknown."

"Certainly Mr. Kyu. Please hold."

Why did everyone still insist on calling him "Mr. Kyu" instead of "Mr. Ardrassis"?

Insipid music played for a few minutes until the line was picked up. "Mr. Kyu! Kelvin Varaii here. How can I help you?"

Hoping he was doing the right thing, Kyu explained about his upcoming audit, and asked if he could do anything about it.

"I'm sorry, Mr. Kyu, there's nothing I can do about a tax audit. However, I do know an accountant who knows the tax laws inside and out. He has helped others in your circumstance. Would you like his number?"

"Yes, thank you. I'll take any help I can get."

Varaii gave Kyu the number, promised to call the accountant ahead of time to inform him of Kyu's situation, and wished him the best of luck.

Kyu told Ocelot what the lawyer had said.

"If this accountant can help us, I suppose we should contact him," Ocelot agreed. "I take it you've never had this happen before?"

"Never. I've made a lot of money, but I always made sure to pay my taxes."

"So why are they auditing you now?"

"There are a lot of people who have it in for me, but only one who has the power to push this sort of thing."

"Who?" After a few seconds of thought, Ocelot's mouth dropped. "You mean Erenia Baak?"

"Who else? She still blames me for Eulos' death." *As do I.*

"This would be a flagrant abuse of power! Why would she risk her career just to get back at you?"

"What exactly is she risking? People get audited all the time. She just made sure it was my turn, hoping I was stupid and greedy enough to try to hide some income."

"But you haven't. You shouldn't have anything to worry about."

"Unless she made a special request for the auditors to find something that isn't there."

"Would she actually go that far?"

"I don't know. That's why we need this accountant."

#

As it turned out, Kyu didn't call the accountant. The accountant called him. The next day he was at their home. Jerrid Handos was the brother of Kelvin Varaii's partner at the law firm. He was a small man, with thinning hair and bright hazel eyes.

Aest, who had been kept on hand to appraise the man's character, sniffed the nervous accountant's hand. His knob vibrated and he turned his head to Kyu and Ocelot.

He seems all right to me. I'm going to finish my meal now. Aest scampered off to devour the rest of the meat Kyu had put out for him.

Once Aest was gone, a relieved Jerrid Handos shook hands and asked for their financial records for the past three years. Ocelot had organized everything ahead of time and handed it to the accountant, who dug into the papers like a prospector seeking gold.

Three hours later, he was finished. "This is everything?"

"Yes," Kyu affirmed.

"Then I see no problems. When is the audit scheduled?"

"Next week."

"I shall be there by your side, if you wish my services."

"How much are your services?"

Jerrod Handos told them. Kyu winced at the price, but he wanted the accountant there to help him face the auditors.

"Can I claim your fee on next year's taxes?"

Jerrid Handos smiled. "You could, but it would be an illegal deduction. Let's keep your record clean, shall we?"

#

At the appointed time, Jerrid Handos, the unlikely champion of the king and queen of Talgourge, accompanied Kyu and Ocelot to the Tax Collection office in downtown Cyphus to slay the bureaucratic dragon that threatened them.

The auditors were cool and professional. Briefcases were opened on both sides, and pens were drawn. Battle commenced.

It took several hours, with Kyu and Ocelot losing their way more than once through the financial jargon, but their champion prevailed. The battle was over. Kyu and Ocelot were in the clear.

Walking out of the office, Ocelot shivered. "I feel like I've just been violated."

Kyu hadn't been too keen on the experience himself. Still, it was a victory. *You'll have to do better than that, Erenia.*

#

Two weeks later, the police raided their home. Norn Sanna himself led the way, armed with a search warrant for illegal firearms Kyu was suspected of having – a suspicion that was, of course, well founded.

Aest was beside himself. Ocelot had to hold him in another room to prevent him from attacking the hostile invaders. The police tore the place apart. Kyu stood in restrained rage as they went from room to room, ripping furniture, upending containers, and leaving everything in shambles.

After more than an hour, the leader of the five-man team reported back to Sanna. "Nothing has been found, sir."

Sanna's face darkened. "There are weapons here. I know it." He turned to Kyu. "I've heard this place has secret passages. Show them to us, or things will go harder for you when we find them ourselves."

Kyu gave them the tour. He showed them two additional passages they had missed, keeping the other secret. He then led them to the arsenal room and ushered them in. It was empty. "Satisfied?"

Sanna gave him a baleful look. "This isn't over, Kyu. You were obviously tipped off that we were coming and found a hiding spot for your weapons." The Chief Detective pushed his face to within inches of Kyu's. "We both know who and what you are. Soon enough this respectable citizen ruse will fall apart, and I'll be there to see you shipped to Xiaroc Isle. In the meantime, I know you carry a handgun. Hand it over."

"I have a legal permit to carry it."

"Not any more. The permit's been revoked. Give me the gun."

Glaring at Sanna, Kyu pulled the gun from its holster and handed it over. Sanna snatched it away and handed it to one of his men. "Now the sword. Since you say you're no longer an arena fighter, you have no need for it. Give it up."

Kyu's eyes were flat. "I don't have it."

"Don't hold out on me. Give me the sword."

"I told you, I don't have it."

They locked eyes. The tension between them nearly sparked into something more.

"This isn't over, not by a long shot." Sanna turned to his men. "Let's go."

On the way out, Sanna was stopped by Ocelot. "I heard you and Erenia got married recently."

Sanna, taken aback by the unexpected remark, stared at Ocelot for a few seconds. "Yes, we did."

"Congratulations."

Sanna, confused and wary, remained silent.

"Erenia has done much good since being elected," Ocelot continued. "Everything she's achieved in the short amount of time she's been in office is commendable. Tell her I said so. Also tell her that this continued harassment of my husband and myself is petty, destructive, and very much beneath her. We just want to live our lives as well as we can. Remind her she's a follower of Syssera, as am I." Ocelot looked pointedly at Sanna. "So are you. Defiling another's home is no way to honor the goddess, and you know it."

Ocelot paused and wiped away a tear. "I know you and Erenia don't like us, but I ask that you respect the lives we are trying to live. Now if you'll excuse me, I have a lot of cleaning to do." Ocelot turned and walked away.

Sanna watched her go, an odd look in his eyes. He turned, nodded gruffly to his men, and they left.

Kyu started to clean alongside his wife. "Nice little speech. I hope it does some good."

Ocelot was quiet a moment. "So do I."

"I can take care of this." Kyu looked with concern at Ocelot's swelling belly.

"I'm not that delicate!" she snapped then closed her eyes. "I'm sorry. I've been terrible lately, haven't I?"

"Well…"

Aest walked in the room and barked. *Ocelot, we love you, but you've been a real terror lately.*

Ocelot gave a rueful laugh. "Whenever I need a dose of reality, I turn to Aest." Ocelot paused. "He's right, though.I apologize to the both of you, for my past and for my future bitchiness."

Aest licked her face at the same moment Kyu leaned in for a kiss, which sent Ocelot into uncontrollable giggling. "Does this mean I'm forgiven?"

"You never had anything to be sorry about… and before you say it, yes, I'm a sap."

Ocelot smiled then turned serious. "Where did you put all of your weapons?"

"The same place my aunt held me for a thousand years."

"That timeless place you told me about? You know how to get there?"

"It took some experimenting, but I found it." Kyu finished refilling the bureau drawers in their bedroom.

Ocelot remade the bed. "Why don't you just get rid of them?"

Kyu thought about the Korl. "Hopefully, I'll never need them again, but if something happens, it's nice to know they're within reach."

"You sound like you expect something bad to happen."

"You know the enemies I've made, Ocelot. I hope they leave us alone, but I can't count on it."

Ocelot rubbed her stomach. "Are we really ready for this child?"

"We have to be. We can't stop living our lives. We can't be paralyzed by 'what if's'."

Ocelot nodded. "You're right." She wrapped her arms around Kyu's neck. "I wouldn't give this up for anything." They kissed, first tenderly, then with more passion.

Aest, reading the signs, wandered off to look for something to eat.

#

Two weeks later, a building inspector paid an unannounced visit. Walking through each chamber, the man checked off items on a clipboard as Kyu and Ocelot followed. The inspector voiced his displeasure at everything he saw with an annoying cluck. Going from room to room, he clucked a lot.

When he was finished, he turned to Kyu and Ocelot. "I'm afraid you need new living arrangements. This dwelling is unsafe for habitation."

Kyu couldn't believe what he was hearing. "What do you mean, 'unsafe'?"

"For one thing, the residence is not structurally sound."

"Not structurally sound? It's a fucking hill! It doesn't get any more sound than that."

Ocelot laid a restraining hand on Kyu's arm.

Unfazed, the inspector continued with his assessment. "The residence is also a fire hazard."

"What? The walls are made of stone, which, last I checked, doesn't burn. Besides, if any of the furniture or wood trim ever catches on fire, there are numerous exits."

The building inspector went on. "The air is unhealthy."

"I showed you the ventilation and air circulation system. The air here is fine. I demand a proper testing to prove I'm right."

The man shook his head. "You'll be allowed a hearing with the Cyphus City Board to voice your opinion on this matter."

"When?"

"If you make an appointment now, you may get a hearing in six months."

"Six months? That's fucking outrageous!"

"That cannot be helped. There is quite a backlog. In the meantime, you will need to find somewhere else to live. This property is condemned."

The infernal rage nearly overtook Kyu. The pressure of Ocelot's hand was the only thing that kept it from spilling over. The police were called. Kyu, Ocelot, and a restrained Aest were escorted out of their home.

Driving the bumpmobile to a cheap motel, Kyu turned to Ocelot. "It looks like your message to Erenia was ignored."

Ocelot remained silent.

CHAPTER 37

Erenia looked at the name embossed on the door to her Cyphus office. It read *Erenia Baak*. It would need to be changed to *Erenia Sanna*.

She and Norn had gotten married by high priestess Shalyse Goranna at the Syssera temple in Talmount a month earlier. As the ring had gone on her finger, Erenia had an epiphany. Her old, uncertain life was gone for good. A new life, full of promise and fulfillment, lay ahead. It had felt like sloughing off dead skin for a fresh, vibrant one.

Not that this new life was without its share of problems. The Regent was getting more displeased with her by the day, and the few Traditionalists on the Talgourge Council could still garner enough of a vote to defeat bills she introduced, or demand that amendments be added that pushed their agenda. Even so, she had the utmost confidence in her own abilities to make a difference, despite the obstacles that stood in her way.

No sooner had Erenia sat at her desk and started in on the morning's reports when someone knocked on her door. Nia Kalla poked her head in.

"I'm sorry to disturb you, Erenia, but someone wants to see you. She has no appointment, but she's very insistent."

"Who is it?"

"It's Ocelot Ardrassis." Nia made an apologetic face. "Shall I have security escort her out?"

Erenia's first instinct was to say yes, yet she found herself saying, "No. Send her in."

Nia was shocked. "Are you sure this is wise?"

"No, I'm not, but send her in."

"Shall I have security standing by, just in case?"

"In case of what? That she's here to assassinate me? If this was her husband, that might be the case, but I don't see her doing that. Besides, she's been scanned for weapons already, right?"

"Yes, like every other visitor."

"Then security won't be necessary. Send her in."

Nia frowned but nodded her head. "As you wish."

A minute later, Ocelot Ardrassis walked through the door. The young woman had blossomed since the last time Erenia had seen her. She had allowed her hair to grow since leaving the temple. The dark locks now flowed past her shoulders. Her manner and bearing, once timid and shy, was now mature and confident. The soft brown eyes made direct contact and showed no fear. Erenia also noticed that Ocelot was at least six months pregnant.

Erenia indicated a chair with a cool wave of her hand. Ocelot remained standing.

"Why are you doing this to us?" Ocelot asked without preamble.

Erenia settled back in her chair. "Your husband has destroyed many lives. He was never punished for it; indeed, he was put upon a pedestal. Then he made himself more of a hero with that farce of a news conference he gave, showing his face and announcing his retirement from arena fighting.

"I don't know what you saw in him to make you want to marry him. I don't want to know. I know your husband to be the vicious, murdering animal that he is, and I don't believe for a second that he's changed his ways.

"Now I'm doing something about it. I'm sorry, but you made your decision to share his fate when you married him. I want him out of Cyphus. I want him out of Talgourge altogether. The two of you can go live in Urigor, where creatures like him are welcomed. He's no longer wanted in this Territory."

There was pain in Ocelot's eyes, but she kept her composure. "Did you love your husband, Eulos?"

Erenia blinked at the unexpected question. "What? What does that have to do with anything?"

"Please, did you love your husband?"

Erenia was silent a moment. "My marriage to Eulos was falling apart, mainly because he remained under the influence of people like your husband."

"That doesn't answer my question. Did you love Eulos?"

Erenia turned away.

"You did," Ocelot said. "I can see the pain in your eyes when you think about him."

"Enough of this!" Erenia snapped, facing Ocelot again. "It doesn't matter. Eulos is dead, and your husband is the reason why."

"I know. Kyu told me. He blames himself as much as you blame him. I'm not sure he will ever come to grips with it."

Erenia's eyes darkened. "I don't want to hear this. If that's all you've come to say, then you've wasted my time and yours."

"When you were away from home, campaigning, what do you think Eulos was doing?"

Erenia shook her head in impatience.

"Eulos realized that your campaign was being hurt by his image so he took steps to change. He quit drinking and fighting. He tried his best to act in a way that would be respected by those you were trying to win over, even though he did not personally agree with your political stance."

Erenia knew this to be true. "How do you know all this?"

"Kyu told me. He supported your husband in this endeavor."

Erenia's anger spiked. "By taking him to a bar, where he got killed?"

Ocelot remained calm. "Eulos drank soft drinks at the bar. Kyu told me. He also told me the topic of their conversation. It was about me and you. Eulos told Kyu how much he loved you, and how he wished the changes he had made with himself would be enough. He wasn't just talking about the election. He was talking about your marriage, as well."

A hot crack opened within Erenia's chest. She didn't want to listen anymore.

"People can change, Erenia. Sometimes situations give you insights to yourself, and you don't always like what you see. Eulos saw the harm he was doing to you, both personally and professionally, so he strove to do something about it.

"Look at the change in yourself. It wasn't all that long ago your hair was long and you thirsted for the sight of spilled blood. You can't deny that's who you once were. Yet that misguided girl is gone, eradicated. Look at who and what you are today.

"The same is now happening to Kyu. You have no idea the obstacles he has overcome and continues to face, obstacles he will have to deal with for the rest of his life. He's sick of his old persona. Yes, he's taken lives in the arena, but despite that, he's a decent, loving person who's trying to make a complete change with his life.

"I know you don't like him, and I imagine you never will, but what's done is done. Nobody can change the past. All I ask is that you leave us alone. Look at me, Erenia. I will shortly give birth to a child, and we have no home to raise that child in. We are both followers of Syssera. Nothing is more sacred to the goddess than family and home."

Ocelot, tiring, took the chair that had been offered. "Please, if not for Kyu and myself, then for the sake of our child, give us back our home. You've done so much good in the short time you've been in office. Please, for the sake of Syssera, put aside your personal vendetta, and let us live our lives in peace." Ocelot bowed her head. She had no more words.

The silence stretched. Erenia finally sighed and spoke in a soft voice. "It may take a week or two, but you'll have your home back."

Ocelot said nothing. Fresh tears spilled down her face.

"Does Kyu know you've come to see me?"

"No. He thinks I've gone to see the obstetrician, which I will actually be doing once I leave here."

"The baby is healthy?"

Ocelot nodded. "So far, so good."

"Do you know whether it's a boy or a girl?"

"I'm hoping to find out today."

"You'd better get going. You don't want to be late." She paused. "Good luck, Ocelot."

Ocelot smiled, and Erenia was struck by its beauty. She thanked Erenia, turned, and left.

After Ocelot was gone, Nia poked her head in the door. "Is everything all right?"

"Yes, Nia. Thank you."

Nia nodded uncertainly and the door closed. Erenia felt uncertain, as well. She wondered at herself, at her reaction to Ocelot's words. She still despised Kyu. Ocelot, however, struck her as strong, confident, and decent. She also carried Kyu's child.

Erenia shuddered at the thought of another Kyu in this world then scolded herself for branding the unborn baby a villain. No matter what, the child was an innocent.

That, of course, was the crux of the matter. Neither the baby nor Ocelot deserved to pay for Kyu's crimes. No matter one's personal feelings, depriving a family of their home was itself a crime. Erenia would always hate Kyu, but she had much more important matters in which to direct her energies.

Erenia sighed. Another, deeper issue had led her to unexpectedly bond with Ocelot. She had missed her last period. That may not mean anything, but her menstrual cycles had always been regular. Erenia tried to keep her hopes from rising, but after years of trying and failing with Eulos, could this actually have happened so soon after becoming intimate with Norn?

Erenia called her doctor to make an appointment for a blood test.

CHAPTER 38

Erenia's promise came through quicker than anticipated. Within five days, Kyu, Ocelot, and Aest were back in their home. Ocelot had told her husband about the visit to Erenia. He had been angry at first, but conceded that this was their only way to return to normalcy.

Once they were settled back home, they discussed baby names.

"I don't think Eulos is a good name at all to give our child."

Kyu was disappointed. "Why not?"

"Because that's a terrible name to give a girl; we're having a daughter."

"Oh!" Kyu felt ashamed for automatically assuming the child would be a boy. As he thought about it, the idea of a daughter appealed to him. "Well, I'm stumped for a girl's name. Any ideas?"

"Well, I was looking through the history of the Ardrassis family. The last official queen of Talgourge, Harra's mother, was named Rhigh. I think that's a pretty name, and a good way to honor your heritage. What do you think?"

Kyu liked the name immediately. "Rhigh Ardrassis it is."

Ocelot grasped his hands. Kyu felt a tightening in his throat. The baby, until then, had been an abstraction. Now that a name had been given, 'it' was now a 'she'. Little, unborn Rhigh Ardrassis was now an integral part of the family. The old arsenal room had a cradle, dresser, and a changing table. It was now time to decorate it with Rhigh in mind.

Ocelot settled into his arms. Aest jumped on the couch to join them. Ocelot put her arms around the ravener's thick neck and kissed his head.

A profound sense of peace settled over Kyu. Yet, like a dark spider crawling in under the door, he could not help but wonder how long it would last.

#

Haena Ardrassis materialized in the dark room. A soft glow emanated from her essence, creating a moonlit effect on the smooth stone walls.

She looked toward the bed. One form, wrapped in a blanket, snored softly. The other sat up and looked at her.

Ocelot's expression was one of expectation, not surprise. Her mouth twisted up in a melancholic smile. "Hello, Auntie Haena."

Haena gave a minute bow of her head. "The time is getting close, Daughter." The Empress looked at Kyu's sleeping body. "I am sorry."

Ocelot's face tightened. "I didn't know what to expect. These feelings, these emotions…" She shook her head then looked at Kyu. "I didn't know I would come to love him this much. Now…" Tears sprang from Ocelot's dark eyes.

"Yes, now it is time."

Ocelot turned back to Haena. The Empress saw something shift within the young woman, an assertion of power that transcended the flesh that housed it.

"Is everything set?" Ocelot asked.

"Yes, Daughter. All is in preparation."

"Then may Mother and Father protect and guide us." Ocelot looked back at Kyu and laid a hand on her swelling stomach. Haena felt the Daughter's pain, so alien to her, and wished she could do something to ease it, but the pain needed to be real. Too much was at stake.

CHAPTER 39

The summons to the Regent's office came, as Erenia knew it would. Norn had wanted to accompany her to Talmount, but Erenia told him to stay behind. She had to prove to herself that she could confront the Regent with no support other than her own fortitude. Although, strickly speaking, she wouldn't be flying to Talmount alone. Erenia smiled and rubbed her stomach.

As the jet climbed into the clear Talgourgese sky, Erenia mused about her situation. Norn's reaction to her pregnancy had been unsettlingly mixed. In his job with the Cyphus police, he was exposed daily to the worst humanity had to offer. Violence and depravity were the foundations of his professional life, and he saw it in all shapes. He had assured Erenia that he was happy to soon be a father, but he also told her he was uneasy bringing a child into this world. Maybe Norn was right. What kind of a world were they bringing their child into?

Three hours later, the jet landed in Talmount. As Erenia exited the airport, she spied the government car waiting for her. To her horror, she also saw hordes of reporters and photographers waiting for her arrival.

Bracing herself, Erenia ignored the blinding lights and cacophony of shouted questions as she made her way to the car. A burly driver got out and ushered her into the back seat. The closing door muffled most of the noise, and the window glass was thankfully tinted. Erenia did her best to compose herself as she was driven to the center of the city, the media close behind.

The car pulled to a side entrance of the immense Government Building. Erenia exited the car and practically ran inside before the media had a chance to organize. The Empress' Guard was expecting her and ushered her to the Elder Regent's office; she was to be given no time to refresh, never mind compose some sort of defense for what was coming, after her flight.

Parmen Warsas sat behind his gigantic desk. The friendly smile of their first meeting was gone. With a frown, he nodded to Erenia to take a seat. Once Erenia was settled in the chair, the Elder Regent leaned forward. "You've been very busy since I've gotten you elected, haven't you, Erenia?"

With that phrasing, Erenia knew this was going to be bad.

"Energy and conviction are good things," Warsas continued. "But when they're used in a misguided way they not only defeat their own purposes, they do considerable harm... as you are doing now."

"I'm sorry you feel that way, Regent." Erenia spoke quickly. "I think I've made great strides for our cause."

"How can you, when you don't even know what that cause is?" The Regent's eyes were dark slits. "You are guided purely by ego and ignorance, which you mistake for wisdom. You refuse to listen to those who know better. Even worse, you've managed to convince a handful of empty-headed idiots that you have all the answers. They follow you like dogs and convince other idiots of your so-called sagacity."

This, Erenia knew, was the heart of the matter – power. Erenia's base was building, while the Regent's eroded.

"You consider me and many members of the Council to be 'empty-headed idiots'?"

Parmen Warsas gave her a look of disdain. "You have no idea how government works, or the nature of inter-Territorial politics. You are a child with a loaded gun, and you are firing without discrimination in all directions, unaware of the damage you are doing. Do you at least follow the news? Have you any idea as to the state of relations between the

Territories? There is a schism between East and West that is widening by the day, and your foolish convictions do nothing but drive a wedge in that gap. We have to work with these people, not tell them they have to change.

"You're becoming a firebrand, just like that insane bitch down in Ormnia. Fey Gherren has torn her Territory apart, and now she's practically declared Ormnia to be a sovereign state, and a lawless, Korl-ridden one at that. Is that who you're trying to emulate?"

Erenia's anger flashed. "Don't you dare compare me to that woman. I am not at all like her. Everything I've done has been within the parameters of the law, both Talgourgese and Territorial. I've promoted financial stability and security for every Talgourgese citizen. I've pushed for education and tolerance. Yes, I am against arena fighting, as the Ormnian Regent purports to be, but I am pursuing legal avenues and gradual cultural readjustment to eliminate it, not despotism as she has done.

"Yes, I follow the news. All reports I've seen have said that the work I have done so far is approved by two-thirds of the population of Talgourge. I'm not one to shout my own praises, but I will defend myself if I am attacked, Mr. Regent."

As Erenia was stating her case, the Regent had been shaking his head. Now that she was done, he rounded on her. "How long have you been a Councilor? Six, seven months?"

Erenia said nothing.

"I've been doing this for thirty-five years. I've seen idealists like you come and go. When they go, it's never pretty. Despite all their good works, what have they accomplished in the end? Nothing, absolutely nothing. Once people find someone new to latch onto, their former heroes are quickly forgotten, so don't think you're someone special, Erenia Sanna. You will fail, as all those like you have failed."

Parmen Warsas sat back. "Why am I telling you all this? Why aren't I just letting you crash in flames, as you will surely do? Because it's not too late for you. Your energy and determination can be a great asset, if it is guided by those who know how to channel it. You can reverse this self-destructive trend and do a lot of good, if you accept the wisdom of those who know what they're doing."

Erenia's anger and indignation solidified into a molten core deep within her.

"The Seat is scheduled to convene in two more months," the Regent continued. "Since I am the Elder Regent, it will be here, in Talmount." Warsas leaned forward, hardness in his eyes. "As Regent of the host Territory, I will not be embarrassed by a thick-headed, rogue Councilor and her foolish followers. You will be brought back in line, and you'll talk and act only as I direct. Am I understood, Councilor?"

Erenia had heard the term 'seeing red', but had never experienced it until now. She stood from the chair, shaking with rage. "Understand this, Elder Regent. I will not be your pawn. I will not sell out what I know is right, to assuage your ego. Yes, your patronage helped get me elected, I admit it, but that doesn't mean you own me. I answer only to the people I represent. While I am here, I will do all that my conscience dictates, with as much energy as I can muster.

"I don't believe there is anything left to say. I can see my own way out." Erenia turned to the door.

The Regent's laughter stopped her cold. "Do you really think it's that simple? That I will let you off this easy? You really are ignorant. Have a seat. I have something to show you."

The pit of Erenia's stomach dropped. She sat back down and tried to brace herself for whatever was coming.

"You were quite wild in your younger days, weren't you?" he asked with a malicious grin.

"You're threatening to use my past against me? I've never hidden my past from anyone. You're wasting your time."

The grin grew wider. "Hearing about someone's past is one thing. Seeing it is quite another." The Elder Regent opened a drawer in his desk and took out a large envelope. He opened it, removed the contents, and pushed them across the desk for Erenia to see.

The photos were grainy but it was clear that the girl with the long dark hair and blonde strands was Erenia. She had a sloppy, lascivious grin, and her eyes were half-shut on some sort of drug high.

She must have been really high. Erenia didn't remember these photos being taken. In the photos the young Erenia was totally nude. Along with her were two muscular, scarred men, obviously arena fighters. Erenia didn't recognize either one. The remainder of the photos showed shockingly graphic, brutal sex. The worst part was that the girl seemed to enjoy it.

Coldness froze the marrow in Erenia's bones as she numbly shuffled through the photos. Her hands shook. She thought she would vomit. Erenia lifted her burning eyes to the Regent. "You sick scumbag fuck."

Warsas laughed. "Hey, that's not me getting pounded in the ass, sweetheart."

It took all of Erenia's willpower to keep from striking the Regent. She crumpled the photos in her hand and stood, trembling with rage.

"Don't worry, you can keep those. I have more where they came from."

Erenia shoved the crumpled ball into a jacket pocket. She would burn them the first chance she had. "If you think this is going to stop me, you're wrong."

"How brave you are, not caring if strangers see that, but I wonder how you'll explain it to your new husband when I send him copies?"

Erenia's face drained of blood. She felt faint.

Parmen Warsas' perfect white teeth looked bared for flesh. "Your reputation will be shot, and your new marriage will probably be over, but that won't be the end of it. Oh, no. Then I will have you thrown out of office."

Erenia, in shock, said nothing.

"How, you ask? The abuse of power in the unlawful persecution of an upstanding Talgourgese citizen would do it."

Erenia finally found her voice. "What?"

"Kyu Ardrassis, of course: first you arrange to have him audited by the Tax Department. He came up clean, as you know. Then your husband leads a raid on his home, on the pretense that there are illegal weapons inside. None are found. And now you've had him and his pregnant wife thrown out of their home.

"What do I care about any of this? Personally, I don't, but when Kyu Ardrassis held that news conference, his popularity jumped significantly. By finally revealing his face, declaring his love for his wife, and announcing that he was quitting arena fighting, he gained the admiration and respect of many people who, by the way, voted for you. What would these people think if they found out you led an illegal crusade against their newfound hero? I think they would demand your head. Guess what? I would be very happy to oblige. That's not all. Your husband was obviously in on this. Once this gets out, he'll be investigated, suspended, and probably fired from the police department. Then the criminal prosecutions begin."

All of Erenia's rage drained from her, leaving an empty desolation behind. It didn't matter that she had a change of heart and had given Kyu and Ocelot back their home. She had acted from an old, useless animosity which had blinded her otherwise good judgment. The damage was done, and the Regent was right. If her constituents found out, they would demand her immediate removal from office, despite all the good she had done.

She would deserve it. Yes, Kyu was a killer, but what she had done, to him and his pregnant wife, was inexcusable. *Syssera, please forgive me.* Erenia closed her eyes. No matter what, she was not going to shed tears in front of the Regent.

Warsas smirked. "I think you understand your position now. There is a way to save your career. I can make sure that none of your transgressions against Kyu Ardrassis ever see the light, but for that to happen, there is something you need to do."

"I don't want to save my career," Erenia said in a hollow voice. "You can have my resignation."

"Oh, no, that's not an option anymore. You've become very popular, Erenia. I've no intention of allowing you to become a martyr. If you resign, all of this information comes out. No, I have other plans for you. I intend to use your popularity to solidify my standing as Elder Regent and host of the Seat.

"I'm sure you noticed the sizable media contingent that followed you here from the airport. They are here because I told them we would make a joint statement. They're waiting for us now. You are going to tell them that, after our congenial meeting, you have decided that all of your future endeavors will be joint ventures with me, as you fear you have taken on more than you can handle and need my experienced, guiding hand to help you along. You will defer to me on all matters of import. I will then speak, assuring our continued dedication to moderation and smoothing the waves you've caused over the last few months. It will be made very clear that I am in charge, and that your independent actions are over. Is that understood?"

Erenia, feeling sick to the depths of her soul and wishing she had never agreed to enter the horrible, twisted, filthy world of politics, nodded.

"Good. Let's go."

Accompanied by several Empress' Guards, they went to an outdoor balcony that overlooked a wide courtyard. Within the courtyard the media frenzy was intense, with cameras being set up and reporters jockeying for position. A number of Empress' Guards were on the ground, keeping the overzealous back.

Erenia and the Regent stepped up to a bank of microphones. The buzz of activity below settled to a low murmur. Giving the cameras his most photogenic smile, Warsas spoke first.

"Thank you for coming today. Councilor Sanna and I have had a most enlightening and productive meeting, and we have some statements we would like to make. Councilor?" Parmen Warsas gave Erenia his warmest smile and stepped aside.

Swallowing her bile, Erenia stepped forward. She scanned the crowd of expectant faces as the Regent stood to the left and a step behind her. Erenia wanted to scream when she felt the unexpected pressure of his hand on her lower back.

"Keep your composure," Warsas whispered too softly for the microphones to pick up. "Just say what I told you to say. Don't fuck this up." He removed his hand and stepped back.

Erenia gathered herself. Someone pushed their way to the front of the crowd. It was a woman, and once she got to the line of Guards she was forced to stop. It took a moment for Erenia to recognize her as Enna Racyne. The priestess' face was twisted with black hatred. Enna undoubtedly knew what this media circus was all about, but she didn't look pleased. She looked like someone ready to explode.

There was nothing to do but get it over with. Erenia opened her mouth to speak. The media fell to silence, awaiting her words.

"Whore!"

The shout was loud and stunning. For a second, everything froze.

Erenia heard a grunt of surprise behind her and turned. Warsas was staring down at Enna Racyne. He looked shocked to see her there.

"She's a liar, Parmen!" Enna shouted out. "The whore can't be trusted. I know her better than you. She'll wiggle out from under you and continue her pigheaded ways. She needs to be dealt with permanently!"

The Elder Regent shook his head. "Enna, why are you here? Everything is fine."

"No, Parmen, you may think everything is fine, but it isn't, and it won't be until the whore is dead." Enna Racyne pulled out a gun from beneath her clothes and pointed it at Erenia. A collective gasp rose from the crowd.

Erenia stared down the black barrel of the gun. She couldn't move. The distance between her and the priestess seemed to close. She saw Enna's finger tighten on the trigger. In that instant she knew she was going to die, along with her unborn child.

Below, the arm of an Empress' Guard shot out. There was a flash and an explosion. Erenia felt something tug at the fabric of her blouse at her left shoulder. Her skin burned. Behind her, Parmen Warsas let out a sudden exhalation of breath. A half-dozen Empress' Guards drove Enna Racyne to the ground and disarmed her. The cameras caught it all.

Erenia looked behind her. The Regent's face was ashen. He clutched his chest. Blood spurted between his fingers. Parmen Warsas looked at her, an expression of bewilderment on his face. He opened his mouth as if he had a very important question to ask. No sound came out. His legs buckled, and he collapsed.

"The Regent! The Regent's been shot!"

Chaos erupted. Empress' Guards were everywhere. The media pulsed like an electrical charge.

There was a cry of desolation. "Parmen! No!" Enna Racyne had been brought to her feet, her arms bound behind her. Another scream tore from her.

Erenia was grabbed by several of the Empress' Guards and ushered into the building. Medical personnel, surrounded by Guards with weapons drawn, swarmed over the motionless Regent.

Before she was brought inside, Erenia heard Enna Racyne scream in a voice filled with hate and bright, shining insanity. "I'll kill you! I'll kill you, you fucking whore! I'll…" The rest of the threat was lost as the door closed behind her.

Erenia grew cold and numb. Everything became a blur. She found herself in an infirmary within the Government Building. She was lying on a gurney, with her feet raised on a folded blanket. A physician had bandaged her shoulder, and was now in quiet conversation with a high-ranking Empress' Guard.

Erenia sat up, and the physician quickly came over.

"You shouldn't get up, Councilor. You're still in shock."

Erenia touched her shoulder, and pain flared. "Am I badly hurt?"

"No, it's just a graze. You're very lucky."

"What about the Regent?"

The physician shook his head. "The Elder Regent was not so lucky. I'm afraid he's dead."

Erenia's head swam. Parmen Warsas? Dead? The full implication had yet to sink in, but this much did: Erenia had been given a second chance. Despite the physician's protests, she stood from the gurney and approached the Empress' Guard. She identified his rank from his insignia.

"Major, I need to go to the Regent's office, right now."

"I can't allow that."

"Why not?"

"The building is under shutdown. All non-essential personnel are to stay where they are."

Erenia, who was a full six inches shorter than the Guard, fixed him with unblinking eyes. "You do know who I am, don't you?"

The Major fidgeted. "Yes, ma'am."

"Are there any other Councilors in this building?"

"No, ma'am."

"Then I am taking charge until order is restored. Take me to the Regent's office. Now."

The Guard grimaced but gave in and led her down the corridor. Empress' Guards swarmed everywhere, the crackle of radio chatter indicating rooms being cleared one at a time.

They reached the Regent's office. "Wait here," Erenia instructed the Guard.

She closed the door behind her and searched the massive desk. One drawer was locked, but in another was a set of keys. Erenia tried them. The drawer opened.

Within an envelope were more photographs of a young Erenia with the arena fighters. She searched further but couldn't find any negatives. Erenia prayed to Syssera they would never turn up. She ran the photos, along with the ones in her pocket, through a paper shredder, knowing that anything the Regent shredded was thrown, sight unseen, into an incinerator.

Once she was done, she opened the door and gestured for the Major to follow her. It was time to bring the Government Building back under control.

CHAPTER 40

In his office in the Government Building in Shaelmount, Mabb Youri watched with disbelief the events unfolding in Talmount. The television cameras had caught the Talgourgese Regent taking a bullet in the center of the chest and collapsing like a marionette puppet with cut strings. Even before the official announcement, Mabb Youri knew that Parmen Warsas was dead… which meant that he was now the Elder Regent.

Youri shook his bald head. This complicated things. He would have to be very careful, watch every step he took with the utmost vigilance. For in a Territory that was decidedly Traditionalist, Mabb Youri was a secret Reformer, though, he reflected morosely, not as secret as he would like.

Youri had always had a taste for women – more than a taste, it was a ravenous hunger. Yet none of the thousands he had bedded over the past forty years compared to Fey Gherren. That woman knew every inch of his body, and knew exactly what to do to turn the act of sex into something that transcended all other experiences.

Not only did Fey Gherren know his body, she divined exactly what was in his mind. She had immediately discerned his private Reformist sympathies and had used all of her considerable charms to convince him to announce his true political position at the upcoming Seat. She had assured him of support, not only from herself, but from members of the Shaeldor Council.

In the heat of the bedroom it had seemed like a good idea, a liberating one that would help put Shaeldor on the path to Reform. Youri barked a bitter laugh. He knew better now. He had watched Fey Gherren tear Ormnia apart, and knew that members of his own Council, especially that rabid Traditionalist extremist Thei Porrso, would tear him apart, probably quite literally, if he gave even a hint of Reformist rhetoric.

With Parmen Warsas gone, the Territories would now look to Youri for stable leadership. He thought of the Talgourgese Councilor who had been the obvious target of the assassination, Erenia Sanna. Mabb Youri had looked into her career, and she seemed like an intelligent woman, passionate yet level-headed, much more so than Fey Gherren. Maybe he could contact Councilor Sanna, work with her and possibly form a low-key alliance to help the Territories transition into something better than what they were now.

"You're not having a change of heart, are you, Mabb?"

Youri's breath froze in his chest. He spun around. Fey Gherren was standing there. How had she gotten past his Empress' Guards?

"That just wouldn't do," Gherren continued, gliding into Youri's office. Her lips were split into a red, vicious smile. "It's not nice to break a promise."

"What are you doing here?" Youri demanded. "How did you get in here?"

Gherren reached out and placed a finger on his bearded cheek. "Oh, I have my ways."

Mabb Youri grabbed her hand and pulled it away. "Do you know what will happen to me if you're seen here?"

Fey Gherren's smile disappeared. Her dark brown eyes emptied into pools of desolation. Sudden fear bloomed within

Mabb Youri. "Nothing as bad as what will happen to you if you take the coward's way out and break your word with me."

Youri shook his head in an effort to dispel his fear. He couldn't look at those terrible eyes. "Things have changed. In case you haven't been watching the news, I'm the Elder Regent now."

"How does this change things?"

"Get in touch with the real world, Fey. If I come out as a Reformist now, my own Council will ship me to Xiaroc Isle… if I'm lucky."

The bright Shaeldori sunlight streaming through the office windows suddenly dulled and leached away. Darkness gathered around Fey Gherren like a cloak, and she transformed into something that was not human. Her body bloated like undercooked dough and her skin changed from an olive complexion to a sickly, mottled white. Her eyes swirled with malevolent hunger. She smiled, revealing long, razor teeth that were as black as a closed tomb.

The creature that had been Fey Gherren reached out and grabbed Mabb Youri's face, her sharp claws sinking into the soft skin of his cheeks. "Your so-called Council is nothing." The alien voice was carried on a breath that stank of a slaughterhouse. "I can do far worse to you than even you can imagine."

Mabb Youri's blood ran ice cold. A fear he had never felt before, that blotted all rational thought and blasted from the animal part of his brain, screaming at him to flee, lit up every nerve ending like a massive electrical charge. He tried to move, but his limbs were frozen. It didn't matter. There was no place to run. The darkness was complete. Rot and putrescence surrounded Mabb Youri like a mist. His vision was limited to twin orbs of oblivion.

"You will not fail me," said the awful voice again. "You will do as you are told."

"Yes!" He screamed. He would say anything to get back to the light.

Normalcy returned. The darkness and death smell were gone. Sunlight once again flowed into his office. Youri was prostrate before Fey Gherren, who gave him a carnivorous smile.

"That's how I like my men, Mabb; on their knees."

She walked calmly to the door, as if nothing had happened. Taking the knob, Fey Gherren turned around once more. "Even though you're now the Elder Regent, make the announcement that the Seat will still be held in Talmount. That will work best for me. Do not disappoint me again, Mabb." Gherren's eyes flashed once more, and she was gone without having gone through the door. She winked out, right before Youri's terrified eyes.

The Shaedori Regent began to shake, and couldn't stop. Unable to rise to his feet, he buried his bearded face in his hands and, for the first time since childhood, prayed. He beseeched both Syrra and Syssera, but felt nothing but emptiness. He was lost, and he knew it. He had struck a bargain with an Infernal, for he now knew this was what Fey Gherren was. As a child, his grandmother had told him stories of these fiends, who existed only to corrupt humans and feed upon their souls. As he had gotten older, Mabb Youri had scoffed at his grandmother's words as nothing more than superstitious nonsense. Now, much too late, he knew his grandmother had been right.

CHAPTER 41

Five days after the death of Parmen Warsas, Erenia and Norn Sanna stood together at his funeral. Security was tight; Empress' Guards were everywhere. Norn, knowing the bullet that had killed the Elder Regent had been meant for his wife, refused to leave Erenia's side.

The other Talgourgese Councilors were there as well, having arrived in Talmount from the towns and cities where they had their local offices. Of course, the media was there, kept at a distance by the Talmount police but still focusing most of their attention on Erenia Sanna. Conspicuously, the Regents from Shaeldor, Urigor, and Ormnia did not attend, nor were there any Councilors from the other Territories.

Shalyse Goranna, the high priestess of the Talmount Sysseran temple, officiated. She sang the praises of the Elder Regent as his family stood and wept. Erenia kept a solemn face but wanted nothing more than to spit on the casket.

Fucking pig. If Syssera is just, she'll sink your soul in raw sewage.

Once the service was over Erenia and Norn moved away. He used his bulk to shield her from most of the media, and his eyes swept everywhere as he locked himself into full protection mode.

Over the past five days the media had desperately tried to get Erenia's reaction to what had happened. She made one appearance, issuing a statement that, despite their less-than-cordial relationship, she had no idea Enna would try to kill her. She expressed the obligatory sorrow to the family of Parmen Warsas then ended her remarks by saying that the investigation was continuing.

Walking away from the service, Erenia turned to Norn. "Anything?"

Sanna shook his head. "Nothing. I talked to all the acolytes, and while they said Enna had been in a permanent foul mood, they were shocked that she would do such a thing. Maybe her familial connection to the Korl isn't all that distant, after all, but there's no evidence they helped her in any way. The gun she used was reported stolen in, of all places, Ormnia, but how it came into Enna's possession is still a mystery."

Erenia and Norn were approached by a large group of Councilors, led by the senior Councilor Aden Norrle, one of Erenia's biggest supporters. Norrle adjusted his glasses and patted down a few errant strands of his gray hair. He smiled warmly at Erenia and took her hand. She smiled and squeezed back; he was a good man and a valuable ally.

The older man shook his head. “Such events happening in the world today; everywhere you look – insanity. It grieves me to see it touch someone such as yourself.”

Erenia nodded. “This is why we are doing what we can to bring about stability and reason.”

Norrle glanced at the casket. “It is a shame about our Regent, though.”

Erenia remained silent.

Aden Norrle noted this and chuckled. “Maybe I shouldn’t say this, but perhaps it’s not much of a shame, after all. He was going to destroy your career, wasn’t he?”

Erenia nodded. She was not going to give out any details about her meeting with the Regent. Not even Norn knew exactly what had transpired.

Norrle cleared his throat and continued. “What are your plans now?”

“To continue what I’ve been doing.”

“We’re going to need a new Regent.”

Erenia laid a fond hand on the older man’s shoulder. “It will surely be you. Who else could it be?”

“You.”

Erenia backed up a step, not certain she had heard right. “What did you say?”

Norrle stood his ground. “True, you have been a Councilor for only a short time, but you display uncommon leadership and initiative. You have intelligence, passion, and, most importantly, good common sense. Many Councilors don’t achieve what you have already done, even after years of service. The way you took control of the Government Building during its moment of crisis, and the way you have kept everyone together and focused over the last few turbulent days is inspiring. Plus, you have youth and energy, which I no longer have. You have my vote for Regent, Erenia Sanna, and I am not alone.”

Erenia looked at the Councilors behind Aden Norrle, all supporters of hers, nodding their heads in agreement with the senior Councilor. In total, there were fifteen of them – a majority vote.

Norn had been following the conversation intently. He nodded toward a small knot of people a short distance away, watching them and muttering amongst themselves – the other nine Councilors. "What about them?"

Norrle shook his head. "They are not enough. Your wife has a majority. All she needs to do is accept."

Erenia looked over at the nine Councilors, followers of the late Parmen Warsas, now cast adrift. They were a minority, but they could still cause her trouble.

She turned back to Norrle. "Please give me a few minutes while I discuss this with my husband."

"Certainly." Aden Norrle walked off, followed by the others.

Erenia's mind was whirling. A few days ago she had been ruined, her life and career about to be shattered. Now she was being asked to become Regent of Talgourge. "I don't know, Norn. This is so much. I can't believe they want me as Regent. I don't know if I'm up to that challenge."

"Why not?" Norn said with his usual gruffness. "You never wanted to become a Councilor, yet here you are, doing a fantastic job of it. Don't lose your confidence now."

"This is different. I'll have so much more responsibility. I'll be made an equal with the other Territorial leaders."

"We've seen what a great job they've done so far," Norn snorted. "Fey Gherren is a despot who is tearing Ormnia apart, Mabb Youri thinks with his dick more than his brain, and Nevin Ghat isolates Urigor from the other Territories more every day. If you ask me, you'll be the smartest and most competent one in the bunch, not to mention the sanest."

Erenia smiled and took Norn's arm. "What about you? If I become Regent, I will have to move my permanent office to

Talmount. You still have your position as the Chief Detective in Cyphus. I don't want us to be separated."

"Don't worry about me. Honestly, I'm getting tired of my job. I have enough years to put in for retirement with a decent pension. If I get bored, I'm sure I could find some sort of position with the Talmount police."

Despite herself, a spark of excitement lit within Erenia's chest. "Are you sure?"

Norn embraced her. "Of course I'm sure. Now, go accept your new position, Madame Regent."

Wiping away tears, Erenia released Norn and walked back to a waiting Aden Norrle.

CHAPTER 42

Dusk quickly gave way to nightfall. In her office in the Government Building in Shaelmount, Thei Porrso did not turn on any lights. She allowed the darkness to envelope and succor her. Darkness was where she was at her best.

Interesting, she reflected, how events were playing out. The Talgourgese Regent shot dead. The new Elder Regent, Mabb Youri, announcing that the upcoming Seat, one week away, would still be held in Talmount, explaining there was no time to switch everything to Shaelmount.

Porrso smiled. Just as well. She hated last minute plan changes.

She had confirmed that everything was still a go with Argenta, whom she trusted more than anyone else. After all, if one could not trust one's father, who could one trust?

Then came the news that Erenia Sanna would be voted in as the next Talgourgese Regent. Things couldn't have worked out any better.

Nevin Ghat provided her with the money she needed, thinking he knew what it was for while remaining unaware of the true scope of what was to come.

It was time for Shaeldor to tear away from the Unification and the Reformers who sought to rule it. It was time for Shaeldor to be a sovereign nation once again, run by Traditionalists who would not be held under by Eastern Reformers.

Total darkness engulfed the office. Thei Porrso basked in it.

CHAPTER 43

Ocelot, entering her eighth month of pregnancy, waddled to her beloved bumpmobile in the parking lot of the Ocean View restaurant. She opened the door and was struck with a sorrow so profound it nearly buckled her knees.

It's finally time. Mother, please give me strength.

She got in and, numb, started the car. Something shifted in the backseat, and Ocelot felt a hard, cold object press against the back of her skull.

"Drive." A harsh, stale breath washed over her shoulder. "It's time to see your husband."

CHAPTER 44

Erenia Sanna was restless and short-tempered. She didn't mean to be, but she couldn't help it. The Seat was set to convene in a few more hours, and her nerves were threatening to give out.

Security was high. Armed Empress' Guards were at each corner, in every corridor. They patrolled outside, and on top of, the Government Building. Within the convention chamber they were as numerous as newly-hatched spiders.

One hundred Councilors would be present. Erenia's replacement in the Council was a woman who had finished twenty-sixth in the general elections, the usual procedure in a situation such as that.

For the umpteenth time, Erenia checked herself in the mirror. Both Nia Kalla and Norn had done their best to assuage her anxiety, and she appreciated their efforts. As she sat alone in her office, however, the tension came back with a vengeance.

Erenia still marveled as she looked around at her new office. It was Parmen Warsas' old office. The huge, ostentatious desk was gone, replaced with a smaller, more practical one, which had the effect of making the room seem larger and more receptive to visitors.

As Host of the Seat, once everything started Erenia would be required to walk down the main corridor of the convention chamber, escorted by an elite unit of Empress' Guards, be the first to take her place in a Regent's chair, and would formally announce the Seat was convened. It would all be televised. The eyes of the Territories would be upon her.

Erenia bowed her head. *Dear Syssera, help guide me through the trials I will soon face. Do not let me lose my strength, and let me be worthy of my new responsibilities.*

#

The Empress' Guard rubbed his eyes. Fatigue was wearing on him. Despite his superb physical fitness, he was feeling his age. It was getting harder to stay awake for days on end.

None of that mattered, he thought to himself as he stared across the convention chamber at the hustle of hundreds of moving bodies. Councilors, aides, reporters, and other Empress' Guards dashed to and fro. The acoustics of the round room echoed much of the noise back onto itself, making murmured conversations much louder and clearer than they would be otherwise.

Someone jostled his shoulder. A Councilor, an attractive young woman and a Shaeldori like the Empress' Guard himself, kept walking as if no contact had been made.

The Empress' Guard's black raptor's eyes followed his daughter as she joined the rest of her Council.

CHAPTER 45

At home, Kyu watched the news coverage on the Seat. He was still in shock that Erenia was now the Regent of Talgourge. He couldn't help but wonder what Eulos' reaction would have been to that.

Aest barked then growled. Kyu looked over. Aest's attention was on a security monitor. Glancing at it, he saw the bumpmobile pull up. Aest was usually happy and excited when Ocelot returned home from work. Now he was tense, his knob quivering with alarm. Something was wrong.

Kyu shut off the television and gave his full attention to the monitor. Ocelot got out of the car. So did a man he had never seen before, holding a gun to her head. Ocelot looked up to the security camera, her moist eyes imploring.

"Go out the exit on the northwest side of the hill, near the big rock," Kyu commanded Aest. "Position yourself behind the rock. Once I get Ocelot out of danger, go in fast."

Without a sound, Aest was gone.

Kyu ran to the main entrance, cursing himself for growing lax over the past several months. Padanor Syche had waited patiently before he made his move, and Kyu was caught unaware. Because of his carelessness, Ocelot and their unborn daughter were in danger.

Kyu opened the heavy door and stepped out, holding up his hands to show he was unarmed. The man with the gun saw him and turned, putting Ocelot in front of him. She made eye contact with Kyu but said nothing. She was holding up exceptionally well.

Kyu moved to the right, forcing the man to track his movements and put his back to where Aest was hiding. He quickly scanned the bumpmobile and the immediate surroundings. It appeared the man was alone. Kyu fervently hoped so.

He considered, and quickly dismissed, using his awareness to free Ocelot. The gunman had her in too close of a grip; if Kyu made even the slightest mistake, Ocelot would die.

"Stop right there, asshole," the man commanded. He still held his gun to Ocelot's head.

"Let her go." Kyu held out his right arm, as if in supplication. "You're after me, right? No need for her to be involved anymore."

Kyu could see the gunman thinking. He detected a slight movement behind the man as Aest moved into position.

"Where's your beast?"

"What beast?"

"Don't play fucking stupid with me!" The man dug the barrel of the gun into Ocelot's temple, making her cry out. "That thing that looks like a hairless wolf, with all sorts of sharp teeth. Where is it?"

"He's inside, he can't get out." With his wife's life in danger, Kyu found he could lie quite easily. "You have me, right here. Just let her go."

Kyu knew the gunman had plans to kill both him and Ocelot, but he hoped the man would see him as the greater threat and try to kill him first.

In a sudden, savage movement, the man pushed Ocelot to the ground and swung his gun on Kyu.

Kyu opened up his mind. His right arm still extended, he reached into the timeless place where he had his weapons. He grasped his shotgun and pulled it back.

The gunman's eyes widened in shock when he saw the shotgun appear, as if by magic, in Kyu's hand. He hesitated.

That was all Kyu needed; he pulled the trigger. The shotgun roared, but Kyu's aim was off. Instead of a center chest killing shot, the blast caught the gunman's left shoulder. Bone and meat flew everywhere, and the force of the blast spun the thug around. The man's left arm flapped uselessly, connected to his torso by only a few tendons, bloody and glistening in the sunlight. Somehow, he still held his gun in his right hand.

Aest launched his attack. Charging, Aest grabbed the dangling arm with his powerful jaws and yanked it free. The man screamed and aimed his gun at Aest. Kyu tightened his finger on the trigger for the shot.

Like a crazed animal, Ocelot jumped on the gunman's back to keep him from shooting Aest. The man cursed and tried to knock Ocelot away with his remaining arm. She stayed on him, screaming in fury, not realizing she was preventing Kyu from finishing off the gunman.

Aest attacked again, sinking his teeth into the man's leg. The thug swung his gun down and struck Aest on the knob. Aest immediately released his hold, disoriented and in pain.

With a final effort, the man pushed Ocelot away. Almost dead from loss of blood, he pointed the gun at her.

Kyu aimed again and squeezed the trigger. There was a quick pop. His shotgun erupted with metal and death. The gunman's head exploded in a geyser of blood, brain, and bone. The headless corpse stayed on its feet a moment longer then collapsed into a heap of gore.

Ocelot lay on the ground. Kyu dropped the shotgun and ran to her. Her eyes were wide and bright; her breath came in short gasps. Blood soaked through the fabric of her shirt.

Kyu went numb. He had been too slow. Without thinking, his consciousness dove into Ocelot's body. The bullet from the man's gun had missed her heart, but had sheared through an artery. The blood loss, even in this short amount of time, was staggering.

He tried to heal the damage, but it was like trying to hold back flood waters with his hands. *No, Ocelot, please don't die. Please.*

Her hand grasped his, breaking Kyu's harried concentration. "The baby is coming!"

No! Kyu shifted his attention to Ocelot's womb. The baby, as if sensing her mother's mortal condition, was birthing herself. Kyu fought off the shock that tried to sink its claws into his mind. Aest, recovered from the blow, stood nearby, whining with worry.

Ocelot's eyes met his. She spoke through ebbing strength. "Your aunt. Take me to your aunt."

Realizing this was their only chance, Kyu willed it. He, Ocelot, and Aest were transported to Empress' Mountain.

CHAPTER 46

There was some time before she was scheduled to convene the Seat, but Erenia, per the advice of Nia Kalla, walked about the chamber, greeting people informally, shaking hands and smiling, doing her best to look like she wasn't a nervous wreck. Her pregnancy was mid-term, and after an hour of diplomatic socializing she was ready for a quiet room and a soft chair. Still, she was meeting some interesting people, and every introduction was a learning experience.

The Urigish Regent Nevin Ghat was cool and marginally courteous when Erenia made his acquaintance. He reminded her of Parmen Warsas; she took an immediate dislike to him, which she hid behind a mask of courtesy.

Erenia next met the Shaeldori Regent, Mabb Youri. She was surprised at how ghastly he looked, as if he were in the grip of a dire illness. She asked the Elder Regent if he was all right; he gave her a wan smile and nodded. Youri's eyes widened with what looked like panic as he saw something beyond Erenia. With a sudden movement, he turned without another word and walked away quickly, knocking people aside with his bulk. Erenia watched the Elder Regent flee with bemusement. This was not going at all like she expected.

She caught a whiff of a subtle yet exotic scent, which raised an unexpected arousal in her. Erenia turned and found herself facing Fey Gherren.

Many male eyes, and more than a few female ones, were drawn to the Ormnian Regent. An attractive woman, Fey Gherren drew smoldering attention as if it were her due. Standing next to her, Erenia felt an aura of carnality and power pulse from the olive-skinned woman. Television did not do her justice. Nor did it do justice to the depths of intelligence and ruthlessness in those dark brown eyes. Fey Gherren was a very dangerous woman. Whatever was discussed here would have to be said with the utmost caution.

Belying her initial menace, Fey Gherren smiled warmly and extended a slim hand. "I am very glad to meet you, Regent Sanna."

Erenia composed herself and took the offered hand, which was cool and dry. "Thank you. I am glad to meet you as well, Regent Gherren."

Fey Gherren leaned closer. "How about we dispose with the formalities? Call me Fey, and if you'll allow me, I'll call you Erenia."

The scent of the woman was intoxicating. Despite herself, Erenia felt herself tingle and she desired… she flushed and took a step away from Fey Gherren. "Certainly," Erenia croaked.

The slightest of smiles cracked the Ormnian Regent's face. Fey Gherren knew what effect she had on other people, and clearly enjoyed their discomfort and arousal. "Is there anything wrong, Erenia? Are you ill?" Gherren's white teeth bared like daggers.

Control yourself, Erenia commanded herself. Her anger flashed, and it helped. She forced herself to smile back. "No, I am fine, thank you; just the excitement of the day catching up to me a bit."

Fey Gherren chuckled as if in sympathy. "Yes, it must be extraordinarily difficult for you to be suddenly named Regent and then thrust into the position of Host for your very first Seat. You've had no time to ready yourself, have you?"

The Ormnian Regent didn't bother to mask the condescending tone of her words. Erenia's anger grew. "As I said, Fey, I am fine, thank you. I foresee no problems with this Seat."

Gherren glanced at Erenia's stomach. "And you're expecting, no less! You really have been keeping busy, haven't you?" The Ormnian Regent smiled lasciviously.

Erenia forced herself to keep her anger in check. Fey Gherren was trash, but she was also powerful and needed to be dealt with carefully. "If you'll excuse me, Regent Gherren, there is much that needs my attention before everything starts."

Erenia turned to walk away, but before she did she saw a depth of emptiness, a hungry vacuum, deep in the Ormnian Regent's dark eyes. A chill ran through her, and Erenia instinctively put a protective hand over her unborn child.

A few minutes later, consternation erupted around the chamber when Fey Gherren suddenly disappeared.

CHAPTER 47

Haena Ardrassis was waiting for them when they arrived. She did not look surprised.

Kyu's panic made him nearly incoherent. The Empress laid a hand on Ocelot's shoulder, who at this point was barely conscious.

"I'll do what I can, Kyu, but I need to take her away. I'm sorry." The Empress and Ocelot faded as the Empress shifted them to another reality.

"What? No, wait! Take me with you!"

Ocelot turned her head to Kyu. Her voice was weak. “No, my love, you need to stay here. Trust your aunt.”

Then, before they faded away, she said, “I love you, Kyu.”

They were gone. Kyu looked in incomprehension at the empty space where Ocelot had lain. There weren’t even any blood stains to mark her passing.

Aest whimpered in despair.

Kyu searched the entirety of the four Territories, including Xiaroc Isle, in seconds, looking for the unmistakable life presence of Ocelot.

Nothing. He searched different realities outside the normal perception of the one he occupied. They were numberless, but Kyu cast out probes for Ocelot in a wide net that encompassed all he could see.

Each returned with nothing. It was as if Ocelot had never existed.

Kyu screamed in frustration and anguish. He paced the trails and meadows of the mountain top, oblivious to its beauty, a very worried Aest at his side. All track of time was lost.

The Empress materialized in front of him.

Alone.

“Where is she? Where’s Ocelot?”

The Empress shook her head, her eyes deep with sorrow.

“I’m sorry, Kyu. There was nothing I could do.”

Kyu felt the world, the very essence of his life, fall away from him. *No, it can’t be true. Oh, please, no.*

“Where is she?” Kyu shouted at the Empress. “What did you do with her?”

The Empress waved a hand. The scenery changed. They were still on the mountain, but now they were in a sunlit field which sloped down to a clear pool of water where shimmering silver fish swam. It was the same pool that Ocelot and Aest had jumped into on pure impulse when Kyu had first brought Ocelot here.

In the field, near the pool, was a freshly excavated hole.

A bundle, wrapped in white linen, lay next to the hole. The shape was unmistakably human.

Feeling horribly numb, Kyu approached the bundle. With shaking hands he carefully unwrapped the linen at the head.

It surprised him at how peaceful Ocelot looked. Her dark hair, carefully brushed. The splash of freckles across the bridge of her nose, standing out against the paleness of her skin.

Those soft brown eyes, closed forever.

Raindrops fell on Ocelot's still face. Kyu had never known it to rain up here.

Then he realized they were his tears.

Kyu's soul ripped open in an agony that made him scream. His grief was a molten flow that burned away everything else. A second scream tore from him, and then another.

Beside him, Aest cried and howled.

Kyu did not know how long he cried. Time was meaningless. Everything now was meaningless.

"My baby," Kyu croaked at the Empress, who stood by silently. "What happened to my daughter?"

"She passed along with her mother," the Empress said. "I wrapped them together so they would never be apart."

Kyu tore at the linen.

"No," his aunt softly commanded. "Don't do it."

Kyu rounded on her, his rage exploding through his grief. "That's my daughter, you soulless fuck! Don't deny me one glance at my daughter!"

"Please, Kyu, it would destroy you. Let her go."

Kyu didn't care. He turned back to the wrapping that held Ocelot and, somewhere, Rhigh.

She's right, came a voice in his head. *Let them go.*

Kyu spun to Aest, for this was who had spoken. Kyu's skin radiated heat from the fury that was consuming him. How dare Aest side with Haena? How dare they…?

Kyu desperately wanted to ignore the realization that sparked within him, that expanded and cooled the fires of his fury.

He could not. Haena and Aest were right.

Damn them for it, and damn himself. Yes, especially damn himself.

The Empress rested a hand on Kyu's shoulder. "Except for your own home, Ocelot loved this place more than any other. I cannot think of a better resting ground for her. She will remain undisturbed by man or beast."

The Empress held out her other hand and opened it. On her palm was the Queen's Ring.

Kyu shook his head. "No, it belongs to Ocelot."

"Ocelot insisted that I give this to you," Haena said. "She wanted you to keep it."

Fresh tears sprang from Kyu's eyes. Silently, he took the ring.

Kyu rewrapped Ocelot's face. He levitated her body and gently placed it in the hole.

The Empress waved her hand, and the grave filled with rich, black soil. Flowers sprouted from the earth, bright, yellow suncups. Ocelot's favorite. They opened their petals and shielded every inch of the grave.

Goodbye...I love you, Ocelot...

Kyu gasped for breath as more hot tears fell down his face. The molten core of his grief burned away what had been his life, leaving a charred, empty shell that filled with blood and fire.

Kyu raised his face to the sky and screamed his hate at Syssera and Syrra. A black, impenetrable shadow covered his features. Razor-sharp claws pushed through his fingers.

The staca appeared in Kyu's hand. The blade pulsated with rage.

Kyu, The Unknown looked down at Aest.

Aest barked. *Let's go.*

#

The Empress watched Kyu and Aest disappear.

Devastation tore at her, and not just from Ocelot's death. She had lied to her nephew. Necessarily, but it had still hurt to do so.

Kyu's destiny would now be fulfilled.

So would another's.

Haena knew she could not hold her presence in this world much longer. But there was one last thing she had to do before she could release her responsibility and move on.

CHAPTER 48

The Seat was due to convene in less than an hour, and Fey Gherren was nowhere to be found.

The Empress' Guards had searched everywhere. No one had seen her leave. Members of the Ormnian Council muttered darkly of foul play and cast suspicious glances at the Urigish and Shaeldori delegations. The Urigish and Shaeldoris ignored the scrutiny, thinking it beneath them to protest their obvious innocence. They had no idea what had happened, and treated the Ormnians rudely.

It was a bad situation that could only get worse. At least the Empress' Guards were making sure security remained tight.

Norn approached Erenia and stood close.

"Anything?" Erenia asked.

Norn shook his head. "Nothing. No one saw anything. It's like she disappeared into thin air."

Great. "Could the Ormnians be right? Could this be foul play?"

Norn considered the question, and then shook his head again. "I really can't see it. I know Fey Gherren has a bunch of enemies, but it would be foolish to try anything here. If the

Urigish or the Shaeldoris dared to try anything, it would be the end of the Unification and the start of a Territories-wide war."

Erenia grimaced. "That's exactly what I'm afraid of." Her hand went to her stomach.

Norn squeezed her arm. "You'll get through this. We all will."

She gave him a grateful smile. "Thank you."

"For what?"

"Just for being here."

Norn grunted, smiled, and walked off to continue the investigation into the disappearance of the Ormnian Regent.

A pall of dread settled over Erenia. Something very bad was on the verge of happening, and she didn't know what to do about it.

#

One of the Empress' Guards involved in the search was more anxious than the others, though he was careful not to show it.

Looking through another room, Argenta cursed under his breath. Everything depended on the Ormnian Regent being there.

Where had the fucking bitch gone?

#

In her seat among her fellow Shaeldori Councilors, Thei Porrso shifted uneasily. Everything would be for nothing if that Ormnian harlot didn't show up. It was as if she knew.

She cast a quick glance in the direction of the Urigish delegation. Nevin Ghat stared at her with accusing eyes. Porrso gave a minute shake of her head to show she had nothing to do with this and turned away.

Damn that woman!

CHAPTER 49

Yuv was sitting at his desk when Kyu and Aest materialized in his office. He did not seem surprised to see them.

Even through his rage, Kyu noted this. "You know why we're here."

"I tried to warn you, Kyu. You know I tried to warn you."

The red sword came down in a sudden arc and slashed through the center of Yuv's desk, cleaving through the hard wood as easily as slicing through butter. The two sides collapsed upon each other and fell to the floor.

Yuv pushed back in his chair. "Syrra's balls, Kyu!"

"My wife and daughter are dead, you piece of shit!"

"I'm sorry to hear that, but why are you blaming me? I tried to tell you that Padanor Syche would come after you."

Aest growled, low and deadly. Yuv glanced nervously at the beast. Beads of sweat popped out on his huge cranium.

"Yes, Padanor Syche sent the gunman." Kyu's voice was a match for Aest's growl. "But the gunman knew about Aest. I didn't bring Aest to this office when I met that slimy fuck, and Aest has never appeared on television with me. Yet the gunman knew all about him. How is this so, Yuv?"

Yuv remained silent as the sweat collected and ran down his jowls.

"I'll tell you how. It's because you gave Padanor Syche that information. You sold us out, Yuv, just like you sold me out in Ormnia. It was the Arena Commission and the Korl behind my poisoning, wasn't it? They hoped that if Havla Cort defeated me, arena fighting would become popular in Ormnia again, and you knew! I lived, so they created this Championship Tournament… but I walked away from that, and once I did, Padanor Syche put the screws to you, and you coughed me up."

"Damn it, Kyu!" Yuv yelled, fear in his voice. "I owed him money; a lot of money – money I would have had if you remained an arena fighter, but then you retired. I was stuck with my pants around my ankles. He was going to kill me, Kyu, but he offered to wipe the slate clean if I told him everything I knew about you. I had no choice. My life was on the line."

"So you put your fat ass in front of the lives of my wife and child." Kyu's sword went up. "Now, it doesn't matter. You're going to die anyway." Kyu never saw where Yuv pulled the gun from, but there it was in his pudgy hand, black and lethal.

"I know you don't believe me, but I'm sorry." Yuv pulled the trigger.

Kyu grasped the mechanisms of his biological time and sped it up, hundreds of time beyond its normal range. He watched the bullet erupt from the barrel and spin lazily in the soupy air, heading straight for his face. Instead of dodging the projectile, Kyu willed his body composition to change. Atoms reshaped, creating, for an infinitesimal amount of time, a space in the fabric of his physical being. The bullet passed through what seemed to be Kyu's face and slammed into the wall behind him.

Yuv's eyes widened with shock.

"That gun will do you no good, Yuv."

Yuv screamed and emptied the revolver. Five more slugs thudded into the wall. Kyu flicked the tip of the red sword and the useless gun flew across the room, along with Yuv's fingers.

Yuv gasped and clutched the bloodied stumps to his chest. His face turned white.

"Where's Padanor Syche?"

"He's in Erat! There's a fish processing company there called Railedge that fronts for his office."

Kyu's consciousness shot down to Erat. Within seconds, he found a building on the waterfront that had a 'Railedge' sign. An instant after that, he found Padanor Syche inside, along with twenty of his men. He brought his attention back to Yuv's office.

"You know where Syche is now." Yuv's eyes were red, his shirt soaked with blood. "Please don't kill me. I promise you'll never see me again."

"I know I'll never see you again."

"Please, Kyu! I'm begging you."

Kyu had heard enough. He turned to Aest. "He's all yours."

Yuv's eyes lit with panic. "No!"

With a snarl, Aest pounced. Yuv leapt out of his chair. Aest slammed into his massive body and drove him into a corner. Yuv fell and landed in a sitting position on the floor.

Aest dove between his legs. Yuv shrieked and tried to block the attack with his uninjured hand. He lost those fingers as well. With two useless paws, he tried to keep Aest away. Teeth gnashing, the ravener pushed through.

Aest tore through Yuv's pants and bit off his genitals. Yuv screamed and went into convulsions. The ravener chewed through the groin cavity, tearing away large chunks of flesh as he ripped into Yuv's bowels. His entire head disappeared inside the huge abdominal cavity, his teeth continuing their work.

Yuv remained conscious throughout. His screams got shriller as Aest dug deeper.

Aest's body shook as he tore at something tough. A tremendous spray of dark blood and viscera gushed from Yuv's ravaged torso. Yuv convulsed one last time. His huge body settled to the floor like melting wax.

Aest, his entire body dripping with gore, backed out of the eviscerated corpse. He swallowed whatever it was he had ripped free and licked himself clean.

Once Aest was finished, Kyu said, "We have more to do."

I know. Let's go.

Kyu and Aest left the blood-drenched office behind.

#

The Railedge fish processing plant sweltered under the humid Ormnian sun. The odor of brine and decaying seafood permeated every heat-warped plank in the building.

Kyu and Aest appeared outside the front doors. The area around Railedge looked abandoned. Kyu knew better, but he didn't care. He had nothing to return home to, and he knew Aest felt the same way. If they were killed in this attack, so be it. It didn't matter.

Splintering wood and shattering glass announced Kyu's arrival as he kicked in the front door. There were three men in the front office, armed Korl soldiers who stared wide-eyed as Kyu and Aest strode in. The closest soldier was three feet away from Kyu. The red sword flashed. The goon's head sailed off his shoulders before he had a chance to reach for his gun.

One of the remaining soldiers pulled out his gun while the other opened a heavy metal door that led to another room and called for help. Aest struck the man who had pulled the gun, his powerful jaws clamping down on the wrist. Bones crunched and the gun dropped to the floor. Before the man could scream, Aest's teeth sank into his throat and tore it away.

The last man, who had called for help, yanked his gun from its holster and fired. The bullet passed harmlessly through Kyu's body. Aest disemboweled the man before he could shoot again.

The metal door flew open, and a dozen Korl gunmen rushed in, guns blazing. Not a single bullet touched Kyu as he advanced upon them, his sword whirling. Heads and limbs flew from bodies. Aest, moving with incredible speed, never gave the gunmen a chance to aim. The ravener was upon them before they could react. Throats were ripped free and entrails spilled onto the floor.

Men screamed and died. Kyu lost himself in the carnage, and he welcomed it. He no longer held the red sword; he was the red sword. He sliced through soft flesh and quenched his thirst with hot blood.

One Korl soldier was left standing. His eyes wild with terror, he ran into the room behind the metal door, closing and locking it behind him.

Diabolical laughter and screams of hunger echoed through Kyu's consciousness. He knew they did not come from this side of the Disian Curtain. His Infernal side had taken over and opened his senses to his diabolical kin, feeding them with the horror and violence he was creating.

Kyu embraced it. He exalted in it. *Vengeance, vengeance!* The voices howled through his blood-red mind. *Feast on it! Make them all pay with their lives and their souls. Rip them into pieces!* Kyu's consciousness was a ravenous hurricane, his fury brighter than the sun, and he needed to feed, feed…

Kyu swung the staca and it blazed through the metal door, its reinforced steel construction no match for the living blade. The hinges popped from their sockets as the two halves collapsed with a heavy racket onto the floor.

The room beyond was smaller. Ten Korl soldiers, armed with automatic weapons, stood before a desk, blocking Kyu from its occupant. Their weapons opened up, spraying hundreds of rounds at him.

Kyu was well beyond the physical danger of bullets. His feet were light as he jumped into the room, his shadow-darkened face seeking out gunmen and his sword a bright, blood-red blur, taking off heads and slicing through spines and rib cages.

Aest stalked in and his sleek, lethal form launched itself into the storm of flesh and blood, his teeth tearing through clothing and ripping away groins and intestines. The gunmen shrieked and died. Thick, slimy entrails drenched the floor.

Within seconds, the ten Korl soldiers were reduced to quivering chunks of flesh and contorted faces whose lives were draining away.

Kyu mentally examined the building. There was no one left… except for the man behind the desk: Padanor Syche. He sat back in his chair and regarded Kyu with no fear whatsoever.

Even through his fury, Kyu knew something was wrong. Aest advanced, and Kyu stopped him with a gesture.

"You know I'm here to kill you," Kyu said.

The Korl leader gave a slight bow of his blonde head in acknowledgement, and then he smiled.

A door behind Padanor Syche opened, and a figure stepped into the room – the Ormnian Regent, Fey Gherren; Asrath, the Diaboli Domini from beyond the Disian Curtain: Kyu's mother.

The Infernal smiled at her son. "Well done, Kyu! Do you see what you can accomplish when you put your mind to it? Didn't it feel good?" The guise of Fey Gherren dropped away. Her skin stretched taut as her body expanded, taking on the white hue of death. Her nails grew into long, sharp claws, which were as black as the fangs that emerged from the gaping rift of her mouth. Her eyes were an oblivion that sucked at Kyu's soul. The staca blazed in response.

"Today you have finally become my son."

Kyu turned to Syche, who seemed unconcerned about Fey Gherren's change from human to monster. "Do you know what this is? Have you any idea what kind of creature you have allied with?"

Syche shrugged. "She's made me wealthy beyond my dreams and has, essentially, given me Ormnia."

Asrath advanced on Kyu. Aest growled, his muscles tensing to strike. Kyu held out a restraining hand.

"We could have had it all, you and I," Asrath said. "If you had joined with me when you had the chance, this pitiful little world would be ours. I would have shown you the peak of sexual gratification, and done for you things your weak little wife would have never dreamed to do."

Ocelot... Fury spilled out in a scalding geyser, burning away all fear. A scream tore from Kyu's throat and he swung his sword, cleaving the Infernal in half.

Laughter filled the room as the two halves swirled like smoke and reformed back into Asrath. "You're a fool, just like your father."

Kyu opened his mind. More laughter came from the Diaboli Domini.

"Now you're going to try some tricks your aunt, that weak little shade who calls herself the Empress, showed you? Don't you know she has used you right from the start to further her own ends?"

Kyu's heart lurched. His mother was a creature of lies, but he now could pick up an undeniable truth in what she said. He grasped his rage in desperation and unleashed it on Asrath.

The psychic blast, which had enough power to knock a building down, was cast aside by the Diaboli Domini as if it were nothing more than a down-filled pillow.

Asrath's face contorted. Her mouth opened, impossibly wide, her obsidian teeth dripping with poison and bile. Her tongue, black and serpentine, twisted as a shout exploded from her throat and struck Kyu with a merciless force.

Kyu flew back and hit the wall behind him with a velocity that cracked the thick wood and rattled every bone in his body. The red sword clattered away. Blood flooded his mouth as his teeth bit into his tongue. Kyu fell to his hands and knees, struggling to draw precious air into his lungs.

"Look upon me, and behold your heritage."

His head heavy, Kyu looked up. He could not comprehend what he now saw. The thing before him was bloated beyond any semblance of human form, the white skin splitting, oozing pus and black bile. It stank of death and corruption, and its eyes enveloped Kyu with a hate so pure that nothing else could possibly exist.

The soft, gangrenous flesh below the eyes parted, revealing a maw of putrid darkness. Unspeakable things squirmed within. The true manifestation of Asrath made an awful, nauseating sound. Kyu's stomach turned when he realized it was laughter.

This is my mother. This is half of what I am. Tears slid down Kyu's face. He felt unclean, corrupted. He had no business being in this world, masquerading as one of its inhabitants. Despair hollowed him out, leaving only shame and self-loathing.

A movement caught Kyu's eye. Aest was charging the horror.

"Aest! No!"

Teeth bared, Aest launched himself at the creature. A mottled, bloated arm shot out and hit Aest in mid-air. Bones crunched with the impact. Aest flew across the room and slammed into a wall. His sleek, hairless body fell lifelessly to the floor. Blood poured from his nostrils and mouth.

"Aest!" Kyu was up and running toward his stricken friend. Another blast from the Infernal knocked him off his feet and sent him back to the floor. Dazed, Kyu stared at the thing that was Asrath.

She held two large claws over her bulging stomach. "Say hello to your brother, Kyu." The talons dug into the doughy flesh and tore it open with a wet, sickening sound. The bared cavity quivered with yellowish, gelatinous organs. The stench of killing grounds and rotting graves poured out, so overpowering that Kyu could not help but bend over and vomit.

Within the cavity was a perverted form of a human uterus. The creature's claws sank into it and ripped it open. An odor more noxious than before wafted out.

That's where I was conceived and gestated, Kyu realized.

The tiny figure inside was human-shaped, except for its claws and the darkness that hid its face. It squirmed and turned to face Kyu. Its tiny arms opened, as if to give its older brother a hug. The shadow that covered its face disappeared.

Kyu recognized who it was, and the scope of the horror overwhelmed him. *Eulos. Dear gods, it's Eulos.* He lay on the floor, unable to move or think. The red sword remained where he had dropped it, a useless piece of metal.

It was all gone; every bit of it. He was empty, a hollow shell. His entire life had been nothing but a lie. Everyone he'd dared to care about had been destroyed. There was nothing, nothing…

Somehow the hilt of the sword was in his hand.

"Finish it," Asrath hissed from somewhere above him. "Release yourself from this world and join your true brethren."

The tip of the red blade pricked into Kyu's chest, just above his heart. A single drop of blood ran down his body. All he had to do was push, and the meaninglessness of his life would be left behind. His muscles tightening, Kyu prepared for the final thrust.

The words, coming from a nearly forgotten corner of his mind, started as a whisper then rushed into him, an epiphany that he had known all along. *The sword does not always need to kill.*

The staca flared, its brightness casting everything in a pure, regenerating hue. It pulsed with power and purpose, sending its essence deep into Kyu. Every nerve ending sparked with renewed life, each synapse sent a healing resolve to every part of his body.

Kyu's psyche, tattered and nearly defeated, rebuilt itself in an instant. Desolation was dispelled, replaced with clarity and strength.

Kyu stood, his body and mind tingling. He pulled the tip of the blade from his chest, which healed immediately. It was so clear now. Kyu had been attacking the Diaboli Domini the wrong way. Violence and hate merely fed the creature, made it stronger.

Kyu and the sword were one, but instead of an instrument of death, he was now an instrument of life. He settled into a calmness that banished all doubt, all hate. Kyu threw open the doors to his being and welcomed a surge of awareness that did not just encompass everything, it came from everything, giving him a true and complete perspective of all. Kyu now understood his purpose in this world.

He had tried to heal Shair Marei. He had tried to heal Ocelot. Both times he had failed, but instead of giving in to despair Kyu grasped determination and made it his. He was a healer, and he would not fail again, for now his responsibility was for the entire world in which he lived.

Kyu turned to Asrath, who was, he now knew, a cancer upon this world. The blade of the staca bathed the room with the clean tinge of healthy, life-giving blood. The obscene creature that was Asrath shrieked and disappeared.

Kyu could have followed her; he knew where she had gone. He noticed that Padanor Syche was no longer there; the Korl leader had fled when things had gotten interesting. Kyu knew he could find him whenever he wanted to, as well.

He turned to Aest, who had stopped breathing.

CHAPTER 50

It was time to convene the Seat, but there was still no sign of Fey Gherren. Erenia was at her chair at the base of the Empress' Throne. She glanced at Norn, who gave a minute shake of his head. She couldn't put it off any longer. Feeling queasy, Erenia approached the podium at the center of the dais and raised her arms over her head, the traditional call for silence by the Host; the Seat was officially convened.

The Talgourge Council fell to silence, as did most of the Shaeldor Council. The Ormnian Council, however, was having none of it. They shouted their outrage over their missing Regent, accusing all of misconduct, especially the Urigish, who fired their own accusations back.

Erenia's heart sank at the disaster unfolding before her. Empress' Guards tried to restore order, but it was clear the meltdown would not be stopped.

Damn that woman! Where is she?

There was a shout at the entrance to the chamber. All eyes turned, and silence finally fell upon the assemblage.

Fey Gherren walked calmly down the main aisle to the Regents' chairs, as if she were unaware of the near-disaster her absence had caused. She nodded to the Ormnian Council, who watched her with stunned disbelief and wary relief, and mounted the dais. She took her seat, between Nevin Ghat and Mabb Youri. The Shaeldori Regent, who had been acting strange all day, had a look of near-panic in his eyes and appeared ready to bolt.

Gherren turned to Erenia and smiled. Erenia gave the Ormnian Regent a dark look, which did nothing to erase the mocking grin. She turned back to the chamber.

All were silent, waiting on Erenia's words. Media cameras zeroed in on her with their unblinking, merciless stare.

Erenia began reciting the traditional opening statements from memory. "Under the eyes of Syrra and Syssera, by the benevolence of the Empress, I, Erenia Sanna, hereby open the Seat. I welcome all of you to Talmount. Let us begin."

After the Host, it was customary for the next senior Regent to speak. All eyes turned to Mabb Youri. The dark skin of his face had paled to a sickly gray. He made no move to get out of his chair. Fey Gherren, sitting next to him, did not take her eyes off of him. The moment stretched.

The discomforting silence was broken when Nevin Ghat stood and glared at Fey Gherren. "We all know what needs to be addressed today. It's the villainy of that woman!" Ghat pointed to the Ormnian Regent. "Because of her, the Territory of Ormnia is a cesspool of anarchy and Korl infestation. She is responsible for the inter-Territorial influx of Vortex, which is destroying not only individuals, but families and societies.

Because of her, the stability of the Unification is balanced on a sword's edge."

The Urigish Council cheered, and Nevin Ghat continued. "Fey Gherren is a danger not only to her own Territory, but to every Territory. She needs to be removed from office immediately!"

The Urigish Council thundered its approval.

Fey Gherren smiled faintly, as if Nevin Ghat's words did nothing but amuse her. The Ormnian Council rose to her defense and tried to shout down the Urigish Council; once more the Seat was disrupted.

Erenia raised her arms again in an effort to restore peace. She was soundly ignored. Despair pooled in her stomach as she realized just how little control she had.

In the midst of this political maelstrom, Mabb Youri stood and approached the podium. The Shaeldori Regent's eyes reflected a strength they had lacked all day, along with a grim gravitas that reminded Erenia of nothing more than a condemned man finally accepting his fate in front of the gallows.

Erenia moved away, allowing the big man the podium. He nodded his thanks and looked out over the crowd, who had once again gone silent.

"I have an announcement to make," Youri said, his deep voice carrying throughout the chamber. "Once I make it, I can't imagine my Council will accept me any longer as their Regent, but it must be said, and said now. I am a Reformer."

Erenia was shocked, along with the rest of the assemblage. Mabb Youri had always been known as a Traditionalist, albeit a moderate one. The media went electric with this sudden revelation. The Shaeldori Council hissed and muttered at their Regent. The only one who did not look surprised was Fey Gherren, who smiled as if she had expected this.

Youri continued. "I was supposed to follow that announcement with another one, but I cannot do it. In my weakness, I made a pact with evil, but I cannot… I will not… go through with it."

As Erenia watched, Fey Gherren's face went from smugness to anger.

"Mr. Ghat, the Regent for Urigor, is right when he says there is a danger here, and he is right when he says it is her." Mabb Youri had turned and pointed at Fey Gherren, who stared at him with dark malice. "But he does not know the true scope of the threat she brings like I do. This creature who calls herself Fey Gherren is a malignancy, a great evil that will do everything she can to bring down not only the Unification, but all of humanity as well. She had me under her thrall, and I was supposed to announce today my partnership with her, until I discovered the truth of what she really is. She has seduced the entire Territory of Ormnia, blinding them to her foul power. I call upon the Ormnian Council, and the Ormnian people, to wake up and shake off the shackles put upon them by this manipulator. Become the true Reformers you once were."

The entire Ormnian Council rose to their feet and shouted their outrage at the Shaeldori Regent. The Empress' Guards tightened their cordon around the dais.

Erenia looked at Mabb Youri in wonder, amazed at his words while at the same time hoping they didn't incite a riot.

#

In her seat with the Shaeldori Council, Thei Porrso seethed. The truth was out at last. Mabb Youri was a traitor.

There were many growls of disgust from other Shaeldori Councilors, but a surprising number murmured their approval. Thei Porrso was sickened. *Traitors all.*

She looked about the chamber and saw her father in his Empress' Guard uniform at one of the exits. He gave her a slight nod and walked out. The time was at hand. Porrso stood and excused herself, pretending she needed to use the bathroom.

Mabb Youri, and everybody else, deserved what was coming to them.

#

Fey Gherren stood and approached the Shaeldori Regent. Youri tensed but did not give way. Erenia knew it wasn't just her imagination when she saw a horrible emptiness reflected in the Gherren's dark eyes.

Gherren smirked and gave Mabb Youri a look of pure loathing. "You call yourself a Reformer. I call you a coward! How often did we discuss this, Mabb? We both know that great change does not come about peacefully. Before every cultural revolution, there is always a period of violence. It's unavoidable. Now that we have it, you want to disconnect yourself from it and deny that you are one of its prognosticators. Now that you have blood on your hands, you want to wash it off."

Fey Gherren turned her attention to the assemblage. "You are all cowards. None of you has the courage to do what is necessary. Only I, with the aid of my Council and the Ormnian people, have done what has needed to be done.

"Therefore I say to you all at this Seat that the Territory of Ormnia is of the Unification no longer. I declare Ormnia to be a sovereign nation, governed only by her own, and answerable to this Seat no longer."

For the space of two or three seconds, the silence was profound. The Ormnian Council then stood as one and thundered their approval of their Regent's words. The media went into a frenzy as the other three Councils found their voices and shouted their outrage. Nothing coherent could be heard as the noise rose to deafening proportions.

Erenia stared at the Ormnian Regent and held back the vomit that threatened to spew from her stomach. Fey Gherren had just, with a few sentences, destroyed the Unification. It was a catastrophe beyond words. She felt she should say something – anything – but she had no idea what. She had never felt so helpless and overwhelmed.

Then, as bad as it was, the situation got horribly worse.

Nevin Ghat stood, his face purple with fury. He pointed a finger at Fey Gherren. "How dare you call for Ormnian sovereignty? Do you actually believe you will be allowed to continue with your crimes and depredations on the other Territories?"

"Ormnia is free of the yoke of the so-called Unification," Gherren responded. "The Ormnian Council and the Ormnian people have spoken."

"Urigor will never acknowledge Ormnian sovereignty!"

"Urigor has no choice."

"Then damn you, and listen closely to what I say. If you go through with this foolish course of action, Urigor will not stand by idly while you continue to pollute this land. We will put a stop to your corruption and drug trafficking by any and all means necessary, including the use of military force!"

The Urigish Council erupted with approval.

Erenia's heart was a frozen lump. The Seat had spiraled out of control, and she didn't know what to do.

#

Nevin Ghat could not believe his luck.

Fey Gherren's declaration for Ormnian sovereignty had been a gift from Syrra himself. Ghat's outrage at the Ormnian harlot's audacity was real, but it had been quickened by sheer delight. The Unification was finally over, and history would show Fey Gherren as the perpetrator of its destruction. It was too perfect.

After a thousand years, Urigor would finally be free of insufferable Talgourgese ascendancy and the licentious, rampant libertarianism of Ormnia. Urigor would forge its own destiny, as it should have all along. This included the eradication of Vortex and other corruptions from the East.

Action was long overdue. It was time for the Urigish military to reclaim its pride and do what needed to be done.

Ghat saw Thei Porrso make her way from her seat and walk out of the chamber. That meant it was time. He left the dais as if in indignation and made a show of ordering his Councilors to leave the chamber in protest. He made sure he was at the front of the line.

CHAPTER 51

There were several broken bones and severe internal bleeding. Aest was seconds from death.

Kyu didn't allow himself to think; he dove into Aest's body and started to mend. He pushed aside his failures with Shair Marei and Ocelot. Aest was all he had left in the world.

With no sense of time, he fixed ruptured blood vessels and coaxed failing organs back to life. Aest's body began to produce more blood as Kyu mended the multiple bone fractures. He made sure Aest's lungs pumped in precious oxygen that reached every point of his body.

Aest started to breathe on his own, ragged at first then slowly stabilizing. The ravener's heartbeat, erratic and intermittent, strengthened.

Kyu weakened. Awareness drained from him. He finished what he could then pulled his consciousness out of Aest's body. Aest remained still.

Tears sprung from Kyu's eyes. *No, no…*

Aest coughed, and he slowly regained his feet. He turned to Kyu.

What happened?

Kyu wiped away his tears and embraced his friend. "Too much, Aest. Thank you for not dying on me."

Return!

The Empress' voice reverberated inside Kyu's head.

Events are reaching a critical juncture. You need to be here. Come quickly.

CHAPTER 52

Erenia raised her arms in desperation and tried to be heard over the din. "Please, let us all calm down and talk. Let us resolve our grievances now, while we are all still here."

Nobody paid the least attention. The Urigish Council, led by Nevin Ghat, filed out of the chamber, ignoring the taunts from the Ormnian Council and the pleas from the Talgourgese and Shaeldori Councils.

Media cameras swiveled everywhere and televised it all. Reporters were excitedly telling the shocked millions in each Territory their take of what was going on. A turning point in history was happening before them; they wanted to capture every second of it.

The Empress' Guards did their best to keep order. A few looked to Erenia for guidance. She had none to give.

Disaster had fallen over the Seat. The Unification was shattered. Inter-territorial warfare, nonexistent since the time of Harra Ardrassis, was once again threatening to ravage the land. The future was an open, festering wound. The cause of that wound, Fey Gherren, looked so satisfied at the devastating turn of events that Erenia felt an urge to grab a gun from an Empress' Guard and empty it into the malefic woman's body.

"Stop!"

The voice shook the entire chamber and stunned all into silence. Everyone, including the Urigish Council, stopped and turned to the main entrance.

The figure that entered the chamber was bathed in a multi-colored light. Her robe was purple, and as she walked down the center aisle everyone felt power radiate from her like heat from a bonfire.

The name was whispered by someone, and it was picked up by others and spread through the chamber on a gust of conviction.

"The Empress! The Empress is back! She's returned!"

The only one who looked neither surprised nor impressed was Fey Gherren.

Haena Ardrassis mounted the dais and stood before Erenia. Red, gold, blue, and orange light bathed her; Erenia could see nothing else.

"Erenia Sanna, do you know who I am?"

Erenia looked into the woman's stern, unsmiling face and swallowed. The proximity of the Empress made every cell in her body thrum as if plucked by invisible fingers. "Yes."

"Do you recognize my office and authority?"

Erenia bowed her head. "Yes."

"Look at me, Erenia."

Erenia looked up. The Empress' face was grim, but Erenia saw warmth and compassion in her eyes.

Haena Ardrassis mounted the steps to her throne. Still bathed in light, she sat upon it and faced the silent chamber. "A thousand years ago, my brother, Harra Ardrassis, created the Unification and brought together four diverse peoples while ending countless years of bitter warfare between the Territories." Her voice rang clear. "In the thousand years since, this continent has known peace and shared prosperity.

"My brother made many enemies, but only one succeeded in bringing him down, a creature from a world that feeds off hate, despair, and destruction, a world that has taken over most of this planet and has been steadily encroaching on our continent, the last sanctuary of the human race – a world hidden behind what we call the Disian Curtain. We have ignored this world, denied its existence, over the centuries as we pursued our inconsequential and petty games of power."

The Empress paused. The silence throughout the chamber was complete. No one so much as coughed.

Erenia looked at Fey Gherren. The Ormnian Regent's face was a mask of virulent hatred.

"I have come here today to warn you," the Empress continued. "The horror that lies beyond the Disian Curtain is coming, more quickly than you think. It has already touched the east coast of Xiaroc Isle, and has started to make that land mass its own. The entire island will be taken over within a year. Then it will focus on this continent. Once it reaches our shores, it's over. Every person will perish, but before they do, they will endure horror on a proportion that cannot be imagined by limited human minds. At first everyone will flee inland, but as the Curtain creeps closer on all sides there will be less room to run, and nowhere to hide. In time the Curtain will surround Empress Mountain, the nexus of the Territories. Once the mountain has been swallowed up, humanity will cease to exist."

The Empress paused again. The brilliant lights around her had dimmed considerably. Erenia realized that she could actually see right through the Empress in parts.

"Our world stands at the cusp of cataclysmic change. The Unification, as my brother had envisioned, is ending. Meaningless political ideologies are tearing it apart. Worst of all, the clergy of the temples of Syrra and Syssera have also taken partisan sides. Now, more than ever, the temples need to heal this spiritual schism caused by greed and power. They need to cast away the secular and embrace the ecumenical solidarity they once had, for only then is there a chance of turning away the evil beyond the Curtain. Syrra and Syssera are our Parents; they are much stronger together than apart, but their strength lies in their worshipers, and if their worshipers see each other as adversaries, as they do now, then they are made weak and ineffective. This unnatural separation has caused a spiritual malaise that weakens humanity while giving strength to those who wait beyond the Curtain."

The Empress looked out over the silent multitude. "I know each territory has its differences. I know my brother's methods of creating the Unification have resulted in resentment, especially from those who believe that Talgourge has always been the favored territory, but the result was an end to warfare for a thousand years. Now there are those who want the Unification to end, and for each territory to once again become sovereign countries. Well, maybe they're right."

Gasps ran like waves throughout the chamber at these words. The Ormnian Council smiled at this highest of endorsements for their goals.

Fey Gherren's face, however, darkened with what Erenia could only guess was mounting fury.

"Four independent territories who decide to work together willingly, instead of being coerced at the point of a sword, can do much to keep the Disian Curtain at bay, but it is essential everybody recognizes the real threat comes from the Diaboli Domini and the Infernals beyond the Curtain, and not from each other. It's imperative that the temples of Syrra and Syssera put aside their perceived political differences and rediscover their commitment to one another, and to the people as a whole, for only then will there be sufficient spiritual strength to resist the depredations that are coming. They are coming, make no mistake about it.

"In fact, it is already here." The Empress turned to Fey Gherren and pointed. "Asrath, I declare you for what you are, a Diaboli Domini, and I say to you your time in the human realm is over. I command you to leave at once and return beyond the Disian Curtain!"

Shock rippled through the chamber. Even the media was frozen in place.

Erenia's psyche had absorbed some major blows since this day began, but the Empress' pronouncement that Fey Gherren was a foul creature from beyond the Curtain, nearly blanked out her mind.

All eyes turned to Fey Gherren, who began to laugh.

#

Thei Porrso watched everything unfold from a hidden alcove in an upper part of the chamber. She turned to Argenta. "Could that really be the Empress? Is what she's saying true?"

Argenta's black raptor eyes locked on hers. "It doesn't matter."

"What do you mean, it doesn't matter? What if that's really the Empress?"

Argenta grabbed the front of her blouse and yanked her face up to his. "We will not back down from this now. You will not back down. Do you understand me?"

Fear gripped Thei Porrso. She knew Argenta would kill her if she showed signs of wavering now. The fact that he was her father would make no difference to him.

She closed her eyes. "Yes, we proceed as planned."

#

"What a weak and pitiful fool you are," Fey Gherren said to the Empress. "You have barely the power to appear before us. It is evident to all that you are slipping away."

The senior Ormnian Councilor, an elderly woman named Dier Lahte, stood. "Regent Gherren, please explain to us what is going on. Why has this person, who to my eyes is the Empress, spoken these words about you?"

Fey Gherren did not answer. Keeping her baleful gaze on the Empress, she shed her human form in front of all. Her olive skin expanded and turned a mottled, unnatural white. Her nails grew into black claws, and her dark brown eyes became terrible, desolate holes that none in the chamber could look at without fearing for their very souls.

The entire chamber, and all in the Territories watching on hundreds of millions of televisions, saw the Ormnian Regent cease to exist. In her place was a creature beyond their worst nightmares.

Someone grabbed Erenia's elbow, but she was transfixed by what was going on. It took several pulls for her to turn.

"Get away," Mabb Youri whispered in her ear. "Something very bad is about to happen. Get out of here now."

Erenia turned to the Shaeldori Regent. "I can't leave. I'm the Host."

"Don't be a fool!" Youri gave her arm a rough shake. "This is well beyond the Seat now. Go!"

Erenia looked into Mabb Youri's eyes. He had known the true nature of Fey Gherren all along.

"My soul is lost," he told Erenia. "My time is over, but the world will need you in the days to come. Now, go!"

Erenia stepped off the dais, where Norn waited. He put a protective arm around her and, surrounded by Empress' Guards, led her away. As Erenia walked she turned back to look. She couldn't stop watching.

Asrath smirked at the Empress. "You cannot banish me, and you know it. You never had the power, then or now."

The Empress bowed her head. "True."

Asrath laughed in triumph.

The Empress looked back up. "But somebody else does." She turned her attention to the main entrance. Everybody else, including Erenia, did the same.

Kyu Ardrassis, his claws gone and his face once again visible, strode into the chamber, followed by Aest. The red sword was in his hand, the crimson blade shining. His face was bleak as he marched down the aisle toward the dais. None of the Empress' Guards moved to stop him.

Erenia and Norn stopped and stared in disbelief. The sight of Kyu striding through the Seat chamber, bared sword in hand, at the behest of the Empress, was almost too much to comprehend.

Asrath radiated fury.

Kyu pointed the red sword at the creature that once was Fey Gherren and spoke in a voice that carried to all. "Mother, I banish you!"

Erenia turned to Norn in astonishment. *Mother*?

#

In the alcove above, Argenta handed Thei Porrso a small remote with a single red button. "Do it. Now."

Porrso took the device with a shaking hand. Her mind was locked in terror, both by what was happening below and by the threat of her own father.

She drew in a shuddering breath, closed her eyes, and pressed the button. Within a hollowed-out section of cross-brace in the Shaeldori Regent's seat on the dais, a detonator was triggered, igniting several pounds of plastic explosives.

Time seemed to freeze as Asrath's countenance changed from hate to triumph.

"I win," she said then disappeared in a blinding flash.

#

Mabb Youri knew death had come for him at last. He accepted it with dignity and relief, his burdened conscience finally freed as the blast tore him into pieces.

#

Erenia and Norn were halfway down the chamber, but the explosion was powerful enough to knock them off their feet. Erenia rolled into a protective ball and Norn covered her with his own body as deadly shards of debris flew overhead. They were bruised but not seriously harmed.

Dozens of others were not so lucky.

#

Kyu was thrown back several feet by the explosion. The concussion pounded his body and several flying splinters punctured his torso. He instantly healed the worst of the damage.

Aest had also been thrown back, but the ravener had been behind Kyu and had escaped serious harm.

It took Kyu a few minutes to clear his head and focus on what had happened. His ears rang, but he could still hear screams around him. There was blood and smoke everywhere. Empress' Guards, those still alive and able to move, ushered out Erenia and Norn, along with Councilors still in one piece. There were many who weren't.

Several torn and burned bodies lay twisted among the shattered wooden seats throughout the chamber. Severed arms, legs, and heads were strewn about.

The delegations from Talgourge, Shaeldor, and Ormnia had caught the worst of it. The delegation from Urigor, who had been on their way out until the Empress appeared, had escaped with few serious injuries.

Cries for help rang out. Some of the guards rushed to the infirmaries to bring back any doctors and nurses they could find.

Kyu looked to the dais where the Regents' seats and the Empress' throne had stood. The area was now a blackened, smoking hole. Several small fires triggered the sprinkler system; warm water sprayed over the chamber. Black, sooty streaks ran down the faces of survivors.

Two of the marble pillars had been blown apart. The thin, razor-sharp shards of marble had done considerable damage to flesh, but it looked as if the integrity of the ceiling had, thankfully, not been compromised. The media, in the upper level and mostly unscathed, were screaming into the microphones and cameras that were still operable. Asrath was nowhere to be seen.

The Empress appeared by his side. "You must go after her."

Kyu looked at his aunt. Large parts of her were wispy and insubstantial. She looked ready to fall apart in front of him. "You need to get back to your mountain."

Haena's eyes held a thousand years of fatigue. "My time in this world is over, Kyu." Kyu wanted to consider what this meant. The Empress wouldn't allow it. "Go. You are the only one who can banish her."

Kyu turned to Aest. "I'm sorry, but I can't take you with me. Help out here if you can."

Aest yelped in protest as Kyu disappeared.

#

Kyu followed his mother's trail. She awaited him in the timeless place, suspended in ethereal nothingness.

Her smile was cruel. "Even if you banish me back beyond the Curtain, I'll soon return, and you know it."

Kyu nodded. "I know, and when you do, I will banish you again."

"You little whelp! Do you believe I will allow that? Once I return with your brother, we will tear wide the Disian Curtain and our brethren will swarm over your world. None will be able to resist. Not even you."

"I'll stop you long before you have a chance to do that."

"You are such a fool. The key to my success is already in place. Your precious aunt has made sure of it."

Haena? "You're lying."

Asrath howled with laughter. "Yes, Kyu, I'm lying. Keep believing that. It will make my job that much easier."

Kyu turned away, fighting the doubts that circled his head like wasps.

Asrath approached. Kyu pushed his uncertainty aside and raised the red sword.

"Go ahead, Kyu. Draw in all the power you can so we can commence battle."

Kyu shook his head and allowed peace to settle over him. "No. You are not an enemy combatant. You are a malady, an infection, you and all your kind. Your presence in this world sickens it." The staca pulsed with a cleansing light. "To banish you, I can't be a fighter. I need to be a healer."

Asrath screamed and attacked. All hate, all fear, left Kyu. He stood his ground, a physician sworn to save a life – the life of his world. The sword struck Asrath. She screeched and backed away. The Infernal's body was dark and translucent where the blade had made contact.

Kyu advanced. Asrath turned to flee. The sword came down, slicing away more putrescence. Asrath howled in fury and pain. The sword came down again. Asrath's essence was reduced to shadow and implacable hate.

"This but puts off the inevitable." Her voice was distant and shrill. "You will be destroyed."

Kyu felt the life inside of her, waiting to be born, the life created with Eulos' seed. The sword came down a final time.

CHAPTER 53

The Seat was still in chaos when Kyu returned. Aest found him almost immediately, as did the Empress, who was transparent nearly to the point of invisibility.

"I healed whom I could," Haena sighed. "Aest performed a great service running written messages between physicians and guards."

Kyu looked around. "What happens now?"

"Asrath has been banished?"

Kyu nodded.

"Then you must lead. This world is on the brink of cataclysmic change. It will need you."

Kyu wasn't sure he had heard right. "What do you mean, 'lead'?"

"You must keep the Territories focused on the real threat to their existence. To do that, you must take on my mantle."

Kyu was aghast. "No, I cannot…"

"You must. I can no longer remain in this reality, Kyu. You are the only one who can replace me. The Disian Curtain is encroaching, and Asrath will return as soon as the creature she carries is born. You need to guard against her, and to do that, you must become an Odigos."

"What is an Odigos?"

The Empress was nearly gone. "It is my last service to this world. Come."

Aest barked in dismay as Kyu, along with the Empress, disappeared again.

#

Kyu and the Empress arrived at the top of Empress Mountain. They were not alone. Standing before them was what appeared to be a young girl, about ten years old. She wore a long, white dress, and her skin and long hair were jet black, but it was her eyes that captured Kyu's attention. They were silver, and as Kyu looked closer he noticed they were multi-faceted, like an insect's.

Immense power engulfed Kyu and permeated every bodily cell. It wrapped itself around his psyche.

May I?

The voice glided over Kyu's consciousness like a thin skein of cool water. Kyu found he understood what was being asked and gave his consent.

Every neuron in Kyu's brain was tapped and explored. The limbic system, and the hypothalamus in particular, went under intense scrutiny. This was awareness on a scale Kyu never dreamed existed. Alien thought sped through every synapsis and opened his psyche like a book. Intent, desire, motivation, emotional triggers, all was searched for duplicitousness and overt Infernal influences.

The girl's gift assimilated Kyu's own, and comprehension blossomed within him, transcending anything gleaned from physical senses. The duty of the Odigos was made clear to him. It was onerous.

The presence pulled away from Kyu's psyche, leaving him feeling curiously abandoned.

"Do you accept the office of Odigos, Kyu Ardrassis?" The girl's silver eyes reflected Kyu back to himself, and he understood his answer would not be given so much to her as to his own, binding word.

Kyu's chest caught as he stood on the precipice. The lives of millions depended on his answer. It was too much. He couldn't do it, yet he knew there was no other. He felt the collective consciousness of the world awaiting his decision.

The staca blazed and bathed him in light. All fear, all doubt, fell away.

"Yes," he said, and he meant it.

Kyu's reality shifted; a brief moment of helpless sliding was followed by a solid, permanent connection to his rebirth. His senses exploded and he watched the eternal, intricate dance of the universe, planets gliding around stars, stars swirling within galaxies that grouped into countless clusters that grew and expanded ever outward, into an unreachable infinity that even Kyu's considerable awareness could never comprehend nor contemplate.

Within this, lives on far-flung worlds, lives with consciousness and self-awareness continuously birthed, flourished, and died. Worlds without number, each with its own Odigos to keep the dance in proper time and rhythm, for it was all interconnected – a cosmic clockwork where even the smallest piece had an essential function in the intricacy of existence.

Kyu saw the differing flows of realities, not just the one his physical senses could perceive but an infinite array of others, all part of a massive river with differing levels of flow, some propelled forward by time, some running backward, some flowing from side to side, others still and constant. Some realities were anathema to others to the point of utter toxicity. Many were predatory.

Such as the one that had invaded his world and now threatened the sole land mass that contained human life… the reality his mother, Asrath, called home, and where Kyu had a connection in blood… the reality he had to somehow keep from invading the Territories and turning the living human lands into desolate landscapes of unspeakable horror. The responsibility staggered Kyu, but he bore it and remained unbent.

The timeless creature that wore the body of a young girl smiled and nodded. She turned to Haena, who by now was barely perceptible. "It is time for you to move on."

"Yes," Haena agreed. The Empress looked at Kyu. "This mountain is now your home. You have been shown, and willingly accepted, the responsibility I have borne for so long. Not everyone in this world will want you, but they will respond to you. You must give them what they need to resist that which encroaches."

"What happens to you now?"

"I will continue, Kyu. My time in this reality is over. Only my responsibility to the office of Odigos has kept me here for this long. Now you are Odigos, as was always intended."

"What do you mean, 'always intended'?"

"You are a being of two different realities, Kyu. This means you are especially well-suited for the tasks that await you. It also means you will struggle to keep the proper balance, both within you and this world, but this extra focus is exactly what is needed."

"What if Ocelot had lived? What if our daughter had been born and I decided that a simple family life was preferable to being the Odigos?"

"That was never meant to be, Kyu. Ocelot came into your life to bring out your human traits of love and compassion, counterbalancing your Infernal traits of violence and hate. You would not have achieved this otherwise." Haena Ardrassis sighed. "It's time you knew the truth. I needed you to come to Empress Mountain at that specific time not only for all the reasons I explained to you, but to meet someone I knew would be in Talmount, someone whose personality and essence were perfect for what was needed to make you complete."

Kyu's chest hollowed out. "Ocelot."

"Yes, Ocelot. I arranged for the two of you to meet. It was not by chance. I thought I failed when she ran from you, but when she sought you out again I knew the connection between you would be even stronger than I had hoped."

Kyu's fury stirred, thick and ugly. He looked from the dark girl to his fading aunt. "Everything in my life was manipulated; even Ocelot." Tears burned his eyes. "I've made no real choices. I was just along for the ride, along with my wife and my daughter, who never had a chance to live. Asrath was right. You've been using me all this time."

Kyu felt sadness and regret waft from Haena. "Yes, you deserved a happy life.You have no idea how sorry I am that it couldn't be. Yes, I manipulated you, but the fate of this world balanced upon me doing just that. Too much stood to be lost to do otherwise. The time for manipulation is over. I am nearly gone. From here, all of your decisions will truly be your own. Please think about what is at stake."

"Was Ocelot's death part of your plan as well?" Infernal rage, hot and bubbling, ran through Kyu's veins. "Did she need to die, along with my daughter, to get me here to take over your fucking job?"

Haena's shade wept in sorrow. "I cannot say, Kyu. Once everything was in motion, it was largely out of my hands. I could only trust in the process and hope for the best, for all of us. You have no idea how much I loved Ocelot. She was an absolute dear and she was family. Her death weighs on me, but I could not stop the process because of it. In the end, you needed to be here. You needed to be the Odigos."

Kyu wanted to scream, to lash out, but at what? At whom? The black fury drained away, leaving in its wake a corrosive, bitter residue. He turned to the dark girl. "What, exactly, is your office? Are you to be my boss?"

The compound silver eyes twinkled as the girl regarded him, giving her a level of humanity Kyu had not expected. "In part. My main function is that of Kidemur for the realms that lie beyond those you know. I am the… gatekeeper, I guess is as good a description as any, and, as you are new to this, I will be providing you with assistance and guidance."

"For what sort of realms are you a gatekeeper?"

"Realms well beyond your proficiency to comprehend; realms that are home to deities."

"You mean Syrra and Syssera?"

"Yes… among others."

Kyu wondered how much power this Kidemur was able to wield. He wasn't sure he wanted to find out. "What do I call you?"

The dark-skinned girl smiled. "In another life I was called Raelin. That will suffice." She turned to Haena. "Your time has come, my old friend."

At this point Haena was nothing more than an outline, barely visible. She had mere seconds left in this world. She turned to Kyu. "I am more sorry than I can say. I wish things could have been different for you, but they could not. The survival of this world has guided my every decision for the past thousand years, including the painful ones… especially the painful ones. I don't expect you to forgive me, Kyu, but you know what this world faces, and in spite of the pain you feel, you will not fail its people. That is all I can ask."

Kyu did not answer. His bitterness was a rot that ate away at his soul, but beyond that lay something stronger, a resolve that would heal but leave substantial scarring behind. He could no longer hold any anger toward his aunt. He looked at what was left of her and nodded. "Goodbye, Aunt Haena."

There was the slightest impression of a smile. "Goodbye, Kyu." The Empress, Haena Ardrassis, disappeared.

"I will go now," Raelin said. "You need time to adapt yourself to your new existence, but I'll return soon. There is much that needs to be done."

Raelin slipped away, leaving Kyu alone upon his mountain.

Kyu willed it, and Aest appeared.

The ravener looked at him. *What happens now?*

Kyu shook his head. "Good question."

CHAPTER 54

In her office, Erenia buried her head in her hands. "What now?"

Norn let his wife cry herself out. When she was done, he said, "You resume your duties as Regent."

Erenia looked up with a tear-streaked face. "What?"

"You heard me. Mabb Youri was right. The people need a strong, capable leader, now more than ever. That leader is you."

Erenia shook her head.

"Accept it, Erenia." Nia Kalla stood next to Norn. "There is no one else. Mabb Youri is dead. Fey Gherren, or whatever she really was, is gone, hopefully for good. The Urigish and Ormnians are on the brink of warfare. The Empress, if that's who that was, has disappeared. You're the only one left."

No. It's too much. I can't do it. But Norn and Nia were right. Unless someone stood and at least tried to establish order, the Territories would fall into anarchy and warfare. "Do you think the Empress was right about the Disian Curtain?"

"I don't know," Norn said. "But even by her admission the people need to be brought together first before we have any chance of defending ourselves against it. This needs to be our focus."

Erenia brushed away the last of her tears and stood. "Gather the surviving leaders of the four Councils," she told Nia. "Bring them here. Have the Empress' Guard escort them if they resist. Partisanship ends now. Then I want you to arrange a meeting between the Sysseran high priestess, the Syrran high priest, and myself. The political differences separating the two Temples must be discussed and dealt with. They need to be on the same side, and bring their adherents to the same side, if we are to have any chance of facing whatever is beyond the Curtain."

Nia Kalla nodded and left.

Erenia turned to Norn. "I don't think anybody will be getting much sleep over the next few days."

"You're probably right." Norn pointed at Erenia's swelling belly. "That child, and all the others, will be depending on us."

#

Thei Porrso allowed herself to be marched, along with the other surviving Councilors, to Erenia Sanna's office. Argenta had disappeared, taking all evidence with him. Porrso would probably never see her father again, and the thought brought relief.

The carnage the bombing had wrought was sickening, but necessary. Mabb Youri was dead, along with, presumably, Fey Gherren. The confrontation between the Ormnian Regent and the supposed Empress had been surreal almost to the point of hallucinatory. Gherren couldn't possibly have physically transformed into such a horrific creature, even if everyone else swore they saw the same thing happen. It didn't matter. Fey Gherren was gone. That was that.

As she was led to the office Porrso passed close to Nevin Ghat. His face was drained of blood and he refused to look at her.

He has no room to play the innocent. He knew exactly what was going to happen. He financed it. He's every bit as culpable as I am.

Thei Porrso wondered how close the inevitable investigation would lead to her then decided it made no difference.

CHAPTER 55

Kyu Ardrassis, upon his mountain, looked upon a patch of ground covered with yellow suncups. All destinies had a price, and this price he would be paying for the rest of his life. The time for grieving was over. Now it was time to heal.

Kyu Odigos Ardrassis turned from the grave and faced the world.

#

Raelin stood before gates of light. They flashed and parted; solid, brilliant lines that pulled away from one another.

The Kidemur stepped forward. A swirling energy filled her, infusing her with vibrancy and power. She shuddered with ecstasy, but resisted the desire to pull in more. Only the denizens of this world had the constitution to draw on the energy with impunity. Too much, and Raelin would burn out and be left a smoking husk.

A bright spark glided toward her, enlarging as it approached. Within was a feminine figure.

The light from the spark dimmed and the goddess, resplendent with an inner luminescence, stood before her. Raelin bowed her head in respect. "I bring you greeting, Daughter of the Dawn," Raelin said.

The brightness of the goddess' smile radiated warmth and ease through Raelin's body. "You know there's no need to stand on formality with me, Raelin. Let me see your face."

Raelin raised her head.

The Daughter of the Dawn nodded in approval. “That’s better.”

Raelin was not surprised to see the Daughter still wore the features of her physical incarnation. “You really came to love him, didn’t you?”

The luster of light in the Daughter’s face faded as her smile disappeared. “Yes. Being clothed in flesh was a revelation in many ways. Emotions are so much more stark and controlling. And love! So devious in its machinations, lingering, even after… I can feel his pain, his sense of loss. It hurts me, as well, but there is nothing to be done about it.” The Daughter’s lambent eyes darkened to a soft brown, and a glittering tear streaked down a cheek covered with a smattering of freckles.

Raelin remained silent and waited until Ocelot’s face assimilated into the Daughter’s own, which bore no discernible differences.

The goddess looked away. “My brother’s hold on his realm grows tenuous. The Diaboli Domini are impatient. They see a world for the taking, millions of souls on which to feast, and chafe at my brother’s restraining hand. They plot against him, and will move to dethrone him.”

Fear gnawed at Raelin. “Will we have time? She is but an infant. Will Kyu Odigos be able to hold back the Disian Curtain until she is of age? If the denizens of Dis take over this world and recognize her for what she is… surely Asrath knows, and if she takes possession of her, along with the one she already carries…”

The Daughter shook her head. “Nothing is certain, Raelin. We have done our part. Kyu is where he needs to be.” The Daughter’s face tightened and more tears spilled. “The child has been put in a safe place. For now, we can do no more.”

CHAPTER 56

The wet nurse in the orphanage in Cyphus hissed in pain and pulled the infant away from her breast. Her nipple was swollen and inflamed.

The baby was healthy now, but it had been uncertain when she first arrived. She had been born a month premature and had been delivered anonymously at the orphanage, wrapped in a blanket with a scrap of paper that had a name.

Yet the newborn had shown incredible resilience and strength, and had grown to full size without complications. The baby girl had a natural aggression for her own survival.

The wet nurse knew all about the aggression. The girl fed with a rage, chewing and pulling on the nipple with her gums, demanding more milk. The nurse was a firm believer in breast feeding, but this girl was going to be given a bottle.

The infant squalled, protesting the interruption. The nurse looked at the girl's soft brown eyes, which belied the baby's horrible temperament. The baby had a thatch of dark hair, and a smattering of freckles splashed across the bridge of her nose.

"I don't know whose child you are, Rhigh, but if you keep this temper into adulthood, you won't be anyone to mess with."

THE END

ABOUT THE AUTHOR

Paul Magnan has been writing stories that veer from the straight and narrow for a long time. He has a number of short stories published, most recently in Fantasy Scroll Magazine. He lives in Rhode Island with his family.

COMING SOON

Kyu, The Unknown, Book 2
The Oracle of Xiaroc Isle

72800833R00177

Made in the USA
Columbia, SC
27 June 2017